The Last of Ryn Dvarek:
A Journey Into Dreams

D.R. O'SHEA

Acknowledgements:

Writing is often a solitary act, but publishing, even self-publishing, takes more than just the author. Without the help and encouragement of family and friends this book would not be what it is today. I likely would not have written it at all. It would still just be an idea found in a dream.

Know that I appreciate you all more than a mere 'thank you' could ever show.

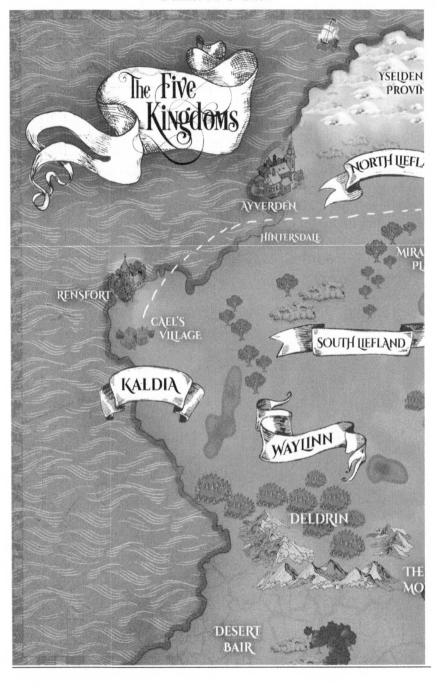

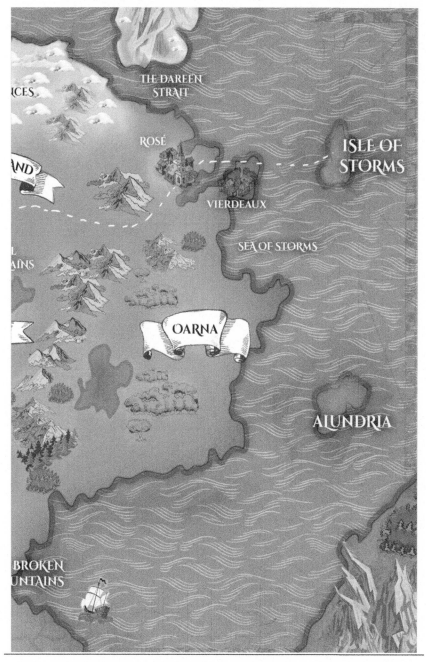

PART I:
CAEL

Chapter One

"We're running out of time! You need to remember me, Cael!"

"Remember you?" The words come slowly and I shake my head confused. My eyes are drawn over his shoulder down a grey stone path leading deeper into the forest. I can feel the moons shining bright but the trees are so thick that their light is barely reaching us. Such a beautiful night, but it feels strange... I reach out my hand and watch as the strange light rolls over my fingers.

The man grabs my head, directing my gaze back to his shadowed hood, "We've been here before, Cael." He sighs heavily, "I've tried this before. But tonight, I'm not the only one in this forest, I can feel them. They are coming for you and they will find you this time if you don't focus!"

Something pulls my eyes back to the stone path. It's dark all around us but the path is so clear, almost like a painting. He shakes me hard. "Listen to me! This isn't just a dream!"

"A dream?" As I say the words a shiver runs up my spine. I look around at the unfamiliar trees. This isn't my forest; this isn't my home. I don't know this man. Fear roots my feet to the ground like the trees all around us. I stare into the figure's hood, but no face can be seen. No eyes, no mouth. Just darkness.

The pounding of boots shatters the silence.

"We're too late! Follow the path, Cael. You need to run. NOW!"

His voice sends life back into my legs and I race down the path. Following the twists and turns, hurdling over fallen branches. As my feet fly over the stones I begin to remember; this is all so familiar. Even being chased... I have been here. This *has* happened before. I burst through the thick brush at the end of the stone path and into a clearing. I glance over my shoulder, checking the dark forest for anything still chasing me. They're gone. I take a deep breath and my nerves begin to settle. Nothing can reach me here.

A subtle golden hue highlights the tall trees that surround the grove. I move slowly towards a small pool of water in the center. Pushing aside the bright white and lavender flowers surrounding it, I stare into the blue water.

It's impossibly deep. Almost like it goes straight to the center of the world. So pure and clean. I hadn't realized how thirsty I was. Maybe just a little sip before I go.

I dip my hand in and as the cool water touches my skin the calm I felt entering the grove is shattered. I fall to the ground in a daze. The beautiful green forest a moment before is replaced by a familiar dull grey and brown one. My eyes dart upward to the sky and I sigh in relief recognizing the twin moons above. As my eyes fall back to my surroundings, I realize I'm still lost.

Where am I? What in Finra's name is going on with me? I was dreaming again but I've never gone this far before. When will these stupid dreams end?! If I'm lost, I'm going to get in so much trouble. Relax, just calm down and think. Search for familiar signs, just like Father taught me.

Alright, I know I couldn't have gone too far. There are just fields to the west so that can't be it. There's a small lake to the east. I could be in the forest over there. If I had gone north, I would've had to go through town. Someone probably would've seen me and hopefully woken me up but if not I'd be near the tannery and that smell certainly would've woken me. If I went south, there'd be a river that I'd need to cross. My feet aren't wet so . . .

The sound of moving water catches my ear. I must be near the river! I didn't cross it though so that's good. At least I'll have a direction to move in.

"Ow!" I mumble as I climb over a stone, opening thin cuts all over my arms. I touch the dried blood gently and a sharp pain shoots across my shoulder. This is just great. I'm beat like a lazy mule. These dreams... or nightmares, they're getting worse. If I end up like this every night there's no way Mother won't notice. They're definitely going to think I'm cracked now.

I need to hurry back. I spot the river and begin following it upstream. The forest begins to wake as I start walking home. The chatter of squirrels and birds is all around me. It's better that there are animals here; it's not so scary.

A heavier crunch in the fallen leaves breaks through the noise of the waking forest. I turn towards it and try to focus. Everything's still so dark. It's hard to see this early in the morning, everything's just a big hazy blend of dark blue. A darker shadow catches my eye.

What is that? It almost looks like there's something over there. It's probably just my eyes playing tricks on me. I'd never be able to see something that far away in this light. But what if it's....

The crack of twigs snapping underfoot comes from behind me and I sprint towards home. I don't want to know! I just want to get home! I throw myself over a large stone and land near a familiar small stream. I glance over the rock and find nothing following me. These dreams have me acting like I've lost my mind. I need to focus on getting home.

I remember this stream; it feeds the river. There should be a game trail that I've been down before. If I just follow this, it'll lead right home. I can relax. It was all just a silly dream. Probably just a deer or something making noise back there.

What are these dreams? And why is it always in the same place? What if they're real? I should tell them about it but if they think I'm cracked... No, if it gets worse maybe I'll tell them but not yet. I don't want to be taken away.

I break the tree line and let out a deep breath. Home, finally. I walk up the hill and get a sudden urge to water the old dead tree. I lean against it and yawn. I'm so tired, I just want to sleep. I finish and quietly creep inside, collapsing on my bed. What's happening to me? It's like I'm not even in control of my own self anymore. What if I go back into the woods again? It's almost morning, I'm too exhausted to work this out right now. I hope Father won't have too much wo...

Chapter Two

"Wake up, boy! I won't have any son o' mine sleepin' the day away!"

"Just a little longer." I mumble.

Father's hands roll me over and nearly off the bed.

"Ya can sleep after them chores are finished." he says, sitting me up.

"Why are you so tired, Little Cub? Have you been having bad dreams again?" Mother asks as she sits down next to me, laying her hand against my forehead. "You're not running a fever."

"No Mum, I'm not having nightmares again, just tired is all." I tell them, rubbing my eyes clear.

"Well hurry up and not be tired! Things ta do, boy!" Father says impatiently.

They walk out of the room, going about their morning routines. I stand up and my body aches with every move.

Moons above, I'm so beat down. I can barely raise my arm it's so sore. I could just tell them the truth; I had a nightmare, ran wildly through the forest, got lost while crashing into a few trees and all I need is a simple, quiet day of rest. Then we'd go on a lovely trip down to the city and I'd be taken away, strapped up and thrown with all the others who've gone cracked. Just like Kellen's parents after he died…. But at least I'd get to sleep.

"Boy! If you're still sittin' on your behind, I'm gonna make it so ya can't sit for a week!" Father shouts from outside.

He's probably already got the forge running. That man is always in a rush, doing things at the crack of dawn. When I'm on my own I'll do things the way I want and when I want. I hate living on his schedule.

The sound of Father's footsteps coming towards the house startles me out of bed.

"I'm coming! I just need to feed the goats and chickens." I call out, throwing on a sleeved shirt, rushing past Mother and towards the side room.

"Cael, it's getting warmer out, you should fix that fence and let the animals stay outside tonight," Mother says touching my arm as I fly past her. "And eat something. Don't work too hard on an empty stomach!" she calls after me.

I open the doors and shoo the animals outside. Clout races to the fields while the goats and chickens stay huddled in the corner. I manage to coax them out the warmth with a little trail of seeds and hay.

"Come here, Clout." I call over to him as he continues to run around in circles., "If you don't come you won't get brushed." I tease.

His ears shoot up and he trots over to our spot in front of the forge.

"That's a good boy. Look at you, such a handsome strong stallion!" I rub his sides before grabbing a brush and taking a seat on the stool. "What's got you all fired up today, boy? You want to go for a run?"

He starts huffing in excitement.

"Alright now, let's get you brushed first. Father and I have some work to do and then maybe we can go on an adventure. We could race down to the lake and maybe scout some hunting spots in the forest." I turn to Father, "How much work do we have today?"

Father rubs his head. "Not much, lad. I'd like ta finish work on these plow shares here for Marak, 'nd we've got another order in after that. We might be right on able ta start on it but we're gonna need Gahris to help with the scabbard."

"We've got a sword order in? Not many of those lately. Who's it for?" I ask.

Few can afford a sword right now. I suppose the Lieflands are nearly at war but they're so far away, don't think anyone would be ordering way out here. What would we do if a war came to Kaldia? I should ask Father to help me practice with the sword more, just in case.

"King Thain's advisor wanted ta get a new fancy sword. That cod won't be using our work for nothin' but a show piece." Father lets out a long weary sigh and moves the coals around in the growing fire. "I'd like ta get back on with the King, but I feel it's better fer us out of that city, too much trouble around all them people. Workin' on these farmin' pieces ain't too bad. Nice regular work, no ups n' downs." He goes quiet, eyes reflecting the flames from the forge, "But lad it sure would be fine to be makin' right strong works again. True masterpieces."

Clout impatiently nudges my hand. "You'd let me brush you all day wouldn't ya, you lazy horse." I smack him on the rump and he wanders back to the field while Father laughs.

"Boy! You're one ta talk. You been sleeping for half the day." He slaps me on the shoulder and I try to hide my pain.

Half the day?! The sun must have only just risen a few moments ago. Finra's beard... I've barely gotten any sleep at all! If he only knew what I went through last night he'd be letting me rest a lot longer. Or I'd be dragged to the city.

"Alright lad, time for work." He lifts the rough old plowshare onto the table. "This old'n is worn down and has a crack split straight through it. If you were fixin' ta do this alone what would ya do first?" he asks in his typical quizzing tone.

I pick the plow up and turn it over in my hands. This thing looks like it's been through the cursed desert and back. Does anyone ever take care of their tools? There's not a thing we can do, it's junk now. I really don't want to start from scratch. Plows are so boring. We've done them hundreds of times! Maybe if we weld some iron over the ... no that would just end up being more work.

"We can't use this, it's too worn," I say defeated. We might not be able to fix this piece, but maybe we could try something new. Maybe... yea maybe that would work. "We have to make a new landside. We should be able to make two from a larger piece of iron. Then we can move onto the share."

"Aye lad, that sounds good. Two you say? That would save us time later I suppose. How would ya do that?" Father asks.

"If we hammer a bit of iron down into a thinner wider slab, we can cut it diagonally so we have two and repeat for the shins." I motion the cuts with my hands while I explain. "Once it's shaped and welded we can repeat a third time and weld the final piece onto the inner side to cover the hole. We'll probably need to draw it down a bit, but it should work and we'll have enough for a second."

That makes sense, right? I think it does. Why would I even suggest it? We already know how to do this. We don't need to change anything. But this could work. It should work. Father is so confident he would never second guess himself. If I'm going to be on my own I need to be more like him.

I stare at Father as he plays with the bellows.

"Sounds about right, boy, sounds about right." He runs his hand through his beard as he turns away from the fire and says, "Well let's get to it then!"

He ruffles my hair, "We can make a new chisel while we're at it, I've got the old moldboard here ta put it all together once we're done."

I get to work on the bellows, grinning from ear to ear. I clamp the pieces together while Father works the hammer. Soon after we start, sweat begins pouring off my face. Father's face quickly starts to match my own. It's hotter than Vashir's fire this close to the forge. I wipe my brow and focus on pumping the bellows at an even pace. I watch Father closely. Drawing the iron out looks so simple when he does it. Everything looks easy when Father has the hammer. I would have missed that blow because it's so close to the edge. Why is it so hard to control my swings? Maybe I need more practice or maybe I need to get stronger. All his movements are so perfect. Every piece he makes comes out exactly how it should even before we sharpen or file. I need to pay attention if I want to be a master one day. I should start thinking about what I'll make for my masterpiece. Everyone always makes a sword. I'd rather do something unique and rare. But it would be fun to have my masterpiece be a sword.

"Alright, lad. We're workin' the share now. We need a bit more heat here," he calls over to me as he continues hammering away at the iron.

I push and pull the bellows faster, the heat exploding out around us each time I press down.

"Watch here, lad, focus on the angle of the hammer. Ya need it ta be just so. See how I press and pull with each strike? That's gonna help us out. We wanna make this here share even as the King's road. Work it from the point, lad. See here?"

I've already learned all of this. We always work from the point and ... Moons above, that's a first. He's not calling anyone who works the joint a fool?

"Never work from the joint, boy. Any man who does that is a fool," he calls out.

Right on cue. I wonder if it makes a difference? I've never seen another blacksmith working before. I guess I don't need to.

We continue our cycles of heating the metal in the fire and cooling it in the trough of water. My arms are too sore from last night and they're cramping. If I ask to rest now, he'll wonder what's wrong. I never tire this fast.

"Time ta burn them arms, lad, we're nearly done!" he calls as he begins putting the final touches on it. The heat gets so intense I can barely breathe. My arms are on fire from both the heat and the pain. I try and focus on the work as the edges of the iron get so hot it looks like they'll turn to liquid and drain away right in front of our eyes.

He pulls the metal out of the fire one last time and puts his hand on my shoulder. I sit down on my chair and watch him quench the iron and start hammering the final touches onto it. I drop my head on the table and catch my breath while the ring of the hammer continues to pulse in my ears.

"Here, lad," he says dropping a mug of water onto the work bench next to me.

"Thanks," I say before downing it all at once.

"Ya seem a bit off today, son. What's on yer mind?" he asks as he takes a swig from his mug.

"Just tired is all. Didn't sleep well." Don't ask about the nightmares. They always ask about the nightmares.

He sits quiet and ruffles my hair. "Alright, lad. I know I don't gotta say it but if somethin's on yer mind... Well, ya can tell me anything."

My stomach turns. "I know."

A cool wind blows past us and we stand up for a moment to take it in.

"This breeze, that's why we took those walls down, boy. The roof's all we need to have a good forge," Father says letting out a long breath.

I smile and close my eyes, inhaling the scent of spring flowers on the wind. "When I'd work alone in there it was hot but having both of us was like working in Vashir's fire."

He chuckles, "When you'd work alone? Boy I used ta have that whole forge to meself before you came along wantin' ta learn everything!"

We sit back down and enjoy the air for a moment. "Was a good idea, Cael. Two cuts, no waste, and preparin' for the next."

Father takes his time on a long stretch which spreads over to me as I yawn.

"Sometimes we get so used to doin' things one way, we never even consider another." He smacks me on the shoulder as he gets up. "Keep that in mind, lad. You've got a great way of thinkin'. Don't lose that."

I follow behind, cheeks hurting from smiling so wide.

"I'm gonna throw this together right quick. You go get us some jerky fer the trip. I'm starvin', boy!" Father says, throwing the moldboard onto the table and taking the old pieces off.

"Are we going to Marak's right now?" I ask excitedly.

It's been so long since we've been into town. I wonder what they've been doing? They've probably been back down to the city to sell everything. I wish we could go to the city more. There's always so much happening. Nothing ever happens out here in the middle of nowhere.

"Aye, lad. We'll be heading to see them soon, go and tell your mum to get ready. I think she's got somethin' fer Marak's girl." He waves me off. "Don't forget that jerky, lad!"

It must be new work clothes; I don't think Mother makes anything else for Laena besides those sturdy field clothes. Always working hard that one. Milly gets all manner of clothes though, mostly bright colored dresses. Oh I hope they have some good stories from the city! Always a few rumors floating around, they must have heard something.

"Hi, Little Cub, did I hear your father yelling about something?" Mother asks, quietly stitching by the table.

"Huh? Oh yea, we're heading up to the village to see Marak and them. He said you've got something for Laena? We're gonna grab some jerky for the trip," I say. Come to think of it, we might need more. Father's going to absolutely devour this. "We'll probably need some biscuits, too."

"Better to be safe with that one, he eats more than a bear." Mother chuckles.

"I was just thinking that!" I say with a grin.

"That's not too surprising, my beautiful boy. You get your brilliant mind from me!" She stands up to give me a hug and plants a warm kiss on my forehead. As she walks away to pack up a few things, she pokes me in the stomach and says, "Unfortunately for me, Orion gave you his appetite. The two of you keep me so busy cooking I can barely work!"

I scowl at her. "I don't eat that much." I say, rubbing my stomach.

She pats my head, "Alright, Little Cub, whatever you say. Tell your father that I'll just be a moment. I have clothes for Laena and Milly here. We might as well bring them both."

I grab the last handful of jerky in the jar and snatch a few biscuits from the mantle above the fire. Clout will want a treat, too. I sort through the vegetable basket and grab the last sad looking carrot.

"It's a good thing we're going to see Marak. Our veggie basket is looking awful skimpy," I call over to Mother as I rush out the door.

"You're right, it's almost like we need enough to feed two bears," she says with a smirk.

I stick my tongue out at her as I close the door.

Quickly tossing the food in the seat, I make my way over to Clout and give him a thorough scratch behind his ears. "I didn't forget you big guy."

I hand over the carrot and it's gone in a few bites.

"I bet you're ready to stretch those legs, aren't you? You're just like one of Vashir's demon wolves waiting for your chance to run as fast as you can, right buddy? You've even got a dark brown coat just like Vashir's alpha!" I say as I pat him on his side.

Clout rears up and whinnies.

"Looks like we have two boys who can speak to animals," Mother says as she walks outside with her bundles of clothes.

"That's just greeaaat, Malaena. Two boys 'nd a woman talking to animals while I'm over here slavin' away by the heat of the forge."

I pat Father on the back and smile at Mother.

"Oh now, t'ain't tha' bad, ya green lil' lad. There migh' be one dey now, when the great beasts o' the wild come over n' speak with ye. Dinnae dare give up hope boyo!" I mock him. Mother's bubbling with laughter and I follow suit.

"Hey now, I don't sound a bit like that!" Father takes a few swipes and lands one on the back of my head, but he can't help but laugh along with us. He grabs us both in a big hug, lifting us off our feet before putting us back down. "If ya want a true Wylaen accent, ya shoulda' heard your grandad. Even I could hardly understand him."

We set all our things on the cart and begin the long walk into town. I wish I could just flop in the back. I'm so tired, just a little bit of a break is all I need. Clout wouldn't mind, he's strong and well rested. But Father loves making us walk.

"When do you think we'll get down to the city again? I haven't seen Zaitah in half a year." Would be nice to see that big dumb brother of mine again, almost don't remember what he looks like.

Father's voice comes from the other side of the cart as we move along up the road. "Ehh, I dunno, lad. Been hoping to head down that way soon for new orders. Work seems ta be dryin' up and I'd like to see your brother, too."

Mother chimes in, "Don't bet on seeing him this time. He's got his end of season exams and he'll be studying hard to pass. If he is able to see us, it won't be for long." She tries to sound passive but I can see it hurts.

Zaitah is such a jerk, he should know Mom wants to see him. We all do. But she's more than likely right. He won't have time for us; he rarely does. Is it going to be like this forever? When he finishes at university, he'll start his apprenticeship and we probably won't see much of him once that happens. Then he'll get a family and he'll have even less time for us.

I wish I was as tall as him and Father. I hate when they pat me on the head. How tall were they when they were my age? I might grow to be as tall as them still. I have time. Fourteen is still young enough to grow, there's plenty of hope, but it's going so slow. I bet he's meeting tons of girls in the city, especially being a student studying medicines and … damn. What's the word for how the body works? Something -ology or –omy I bet. It's always one of those. I wonder if I'll ever be as smart as him. Or as good looking. All the girls are always scrambling to get his attention, but he's never got time for anything but his books. He could be so different now, we haven't seen him in such a long time.

The cart knocks into me and startles me awake. I look to Father and Mother and see they're off in their own thoughts, too. It's really nice just being with family on the road. There's something comfortable about it. I don't think I could leave them like Zaitah did. At least not so easily. It'd be pretty hard to move away. They want me to go to university, but I just want to be a blacksmith like Father. Do I really need to get a fancy education for that?

A rustling in the tall fields draws my eye. Maybe a rabbit or a fawn out for a stroll. As we walk I search the grass for animals and for a moment I see a deeper shadow but it disappears quickly. It almost had the shape of a cloak… It was probably nothing, someone wouldn't be able to hide in the grass that close to us. Even so, my heart begins pounding. I wouldn't be so on edge if it weren't for these ridiculous dreams! My education won't matter if these nightmares get any worse. Last night was different, it felt real. That man…. It's all in my head though. If I could stop sleepwalking, I'd almost be able to live with these nightmares. Almost.

A town too small even for a name… Why in the good green
grove did Father choose this of all places to settle. No one ever
comes here, it hasn't rained in weeks and still the tracks from the
last caravan are marked in the dirt. I suppose it is peaceful though
and the wildflowers are finally starting to bloom, even with winter
refusing to let go.

Father speaks up as we draw in closer to town, "Hey lad,
run off 'nd go see Gahris. Tell him we'll be needing a scabbard for
a –" He stops for a moment and measures his arm." One-and-a-half
arm three-finger short sword. No curves, beveled slightly. Won't
be much leather I imagine, but we'll make certain he's got it on
hand."

"This is for King Thain's advisor, right? Does he want
anything special? Like any gemstones or metals?" Father starts
rolling his eyes as soon as I ask.

"Aye, that's right." He stands up a bit straighter and fixes
his gaze ahead. "He'll be needing some *fluff* to patch on it. This
blowhard here truly requested, 'nd I ain't lyin', a 'mighty sword fit
for the gods!'" Father scoffs. "I don't know what god he's on
about but he won't be doin' much fighting and certainly won't be
handlin' anything bigger than two arm lengths. All the frills of the
court'll be needed to satisfy this twit."

He grabs the reigns hard and pulls Clout ahead.

"Why do I work fer these fools? He can barely call himself
a man," he mutters loudly.

At least he'll have something to gripe about when he gets
to Marak's.

"Alright then, I'm off to see Gahris and make sure he's not
too drunk to do work for us. It's good we have to see Milly
anyway, old Gahr probably won't have any gold leaf to work
with," I say.

Father throws his hands in the air. "Aye that damned drunk.
Swiggin' down all his ale rather'n workin on them hides!"

Mother looks to me and mouths 'help.' I grin and shrug
before jogging quickly towards town.

Chapter Three

It's so quiet around here, even in the middle of the day. It almost feels deserted. A dozen wooden buildings line the center of this town and hardly a soul to be seen. I wonder when we'll get a new healer. We don't really need one I suppose. Mother just handles everything but that old doctor's building has been dark and empty for so long. An abandoned building in the middle of this small, quiet, boring town. Sounds like the start of a fireside tale.

"Hi, Cael!" a voice calls out.

I spot Laena getting water from the well near the tavern and wave over to her. "Hey Laena!"

"It's so nice to see you. Where are you off to in such a hurry?" She brushes her knees clean and offers a beautiful smile.

Luther stands up on the other side of the well and puts his book and reading glasses in his satchel. "Don't bother the man, Laena. It's clear he's got business to take care of. Are you heading to see Milly or Gahris?" He gives a long stretch and before I can answer he continues, "It doesn't matter either way, I've got nothing better to do, mind if I join?"

Laena turns red and stares down at her hands. Why's he so rude to her? She was just being nice. I guess Zaitah would do the same to me. Older siblings are a pain on the best of days and to make it worse, Luther's probably still upset about school.

I take a deep breath. "That's fine with me. Laena we'll see you soon."

"So Gahris or Milly?" he asks. "Although I imagine you'd likely not be hurrying if it was just to the general store so the odds are leaning to Gahris's tannery just outside town?" He answers himself.

I nod and we set on towards the tannery in silence.

What a damn know-it-all. Why is he always trying to act like that? Does he even notice? Maybe that's just him being himself, not even trying to outshine anyone. That would be a nightmare to live with. Poor Laena.

Nightmares… I wonder if she has nightmares like I do? No, she seems normal. Nothing like me.

I shake my head free of thoughts of last night. It's awkward being with Luther and not talking. Not anything like with family. I can't help but get drawn back to those stupid dreams.

"What were you reading back at the well?" I ask. He'll talk for a while on that. At least it won't be quiet.

"Human anatomy and physiology by Marcus Alabas, a pioneer in the field. Did you know that he's mapped almost the entirety of the human body from the smallest bones through all the organs? He's not quite certain what everything's purpose is yet, but his theories are ingenious! Your brother lent me his copy after last semester. I'm sure he's learned much more since …" Luther rants excitedly before going quiet.

Still depressed about school, of course.

We continue through town in uncomfortable silence and as soon as we hit the fields the unbearable stench hits us.

"Whew, I can hardly stand the scent of Gahris's tannery. I wish he'd handle the tannings out near the forest and his leatherworking closer to town." I hold my nose for a moment.

Luther chimes in, "You, me, and the rest of the country wish for that same thing. Our collective prayers to Finra have gone unanswered and this beast continues to wage war on our olfactory senses!"

Olfactory? Why's he always doing that? He learned a new word and wants to parade around town with it?

"It's probably better that he's close. He's such a drunk that we can't trust him to be out in the woods alone," I say as we finish making our way through the field.

"There he is," I say pointing to Gahris lying on the ground in front of his workshop. "Probably passed out drunk from last night. Look there, still has a bottle in his hand and everything."

Luther walks up to him. "Bottles empty, must have been good?" he says, smiling. He nudges Gahris's still form with his boot. "Hey Gahris, are you awake?" He pushes him harder. "Come on then, Gahris, time to wake up. It's already late in the day, man!"

He shouts louder but there's no response. He could just be passed out cold from drinking too much. What if it's worse? What if he's hurt?

"Gahris, can you hear us?" I call to him. "Luther quick go grab some water!"

I run over to Gahris and lift his head up. What do I do? I need to check if he's breathing. I place my head near his chest and feel his shallow breath. "He's breathing, but he's not responding!" I call to Luther. "Gahris, wake up! This is Cael, Orion's son. Can you hear me? Move your fingers if you can hear me!"

Luther rushes over with the water and throws it on Gahris who promptly shoots up and begins flailing around.

"Agh!" He roars. "What in the name of the twin moons is 'appening?" His flailing hands grab Luther and his eyes begin to focus. "What're you kids doing here? What time's it? Damn, that sun's bright! Why'm I soaked to the bones?"

I reach over and grab Luther's arm pulling him away.

"Sir, you must calm yourself. We came to place an order and saw you unresponsive lying on the ground," Luther says brushing himself off.

"Oh undresponsiff alright, I was sleeping ya knobs." Gahris snaps back while patting himself dry with a dirty rag.

Luther continues, "Cael and I were startled into hasty action as we believed you may be at death's door... or more accurately, on death's floor." He smiles wide at his own joke.

What a walnut. I can't believe he's so calm and making jokes like that. My heart's still racing... I wish I could stay as relaxed as him; it's kind of impressive but moons above is he annoying.

"I suppose ya were in the right, kids. I'm sorry I grabbed at ya ... I fell 'sleep late in the night and well —No harm done . . . Anyway, what can I do for ya, Cael? I'm sure that old bear Orion's got something he needs, eh?" He walks inside the poorly built structure and we follow, plugging our noses.

"Why does it smell so awful in here?" I cringe first at the scent and then at myself. I close my eyes tight…I can't believe I blurted that out loud.

Gahris sits down at his desk, lights a small candle and begins ruffling through some paperwork. "Ah, yes, that smell. Well youngin', it's the process to tan hides. You need to soak the pelt in piss to get the hair and fat off so that'll make a ripe scent." He waves to the pools of foul liquid near the back of the room, "But the worst of it is when you put it in to soften. All these fools use scat, which is a length more disgusting than what I have here. I use a concoction of my own making, ale and barley! It's right genius it is. I buy up all this ale and what I don't drink, I dump in the pit!" He laughs hard which gets him started on a coughing fit.

I pat him on the back and he settles his breathing before continuing, "Well then, that sits for a right long time y'see, so it'll end up getting all manner of nastiness in there. Once that's done you get the brain grease and … Oh never mind, you kids are here for business. So let's do business. What is it that Orion needs, boyo?" He asks.

Gahris runs his fingers through his beard and picks out something and throws it in his mouth. My stomach turns. Please Finra let that have been food.

"Yea, Father, or. . . Orion, rather." It's so weird when I say his name. "He needs a scabbard some levels of fancy, fit for a king and what not. Do you have the materials here to make something like this?" I spot a piece of paper and ink near his desk and I write down the measurements. Gahris nods and scans over his inventory and back at the paper I handed him.

Damn it smells in here. I try to prod him into action. "We had guessed you would need some gold leaf and potentially some decorative stones so we'll be seeing Milly at her house soon."

Come on, man, speak! I can't stand this smell. I'm going to puke if we don't get out of here soon. "Do you have a design in mind… or should we just ask for the standard emerald and ruby combination?" I continue, barely able to breathe.

Gahris finally opens his mouth to answer. "Ahh, yes. I think I have an idea. Just have Milly come down here with a cart and I'll take what I need then. I can see you lads are getting queasy so you can run along now."

The stars have answered our prayers.

"It's a tough job being out here in this smell, but it's my lot in life. I don't like it neither but it's what I do," he says quietly.

I want to be sorry for Gahris but if I don't get out of here soon I'll die.

"Ready to go, Luther?" I ask out of habit, already moving toward the door.

"Yes, let's take our leave. Thank you, Gahris. Have a fine day." Luther says before he shakes Gahris' hand.

How can he stand to be in here any longer than he has to be? Mother would probably smack me for not having manners, but this smell! Maybe he doesn't smell it as much as I do? People are different like that, I think I smell more than Father does.

As soon as we're into the fields I turn to Luther. "Do you think he's ever not drinking?"

"If you had to deal with that smell all day, wouldn't you drink too? Think about it, alcohol numbs the senses so it is the most logical thing to do." He replies matter of factly.

I inhale the earthy and sweet scent of the tall grass fields. "I suppose you're right, I never really thought about it that way." Why can't I think like he does? Or Zaitah? They're always being considerate and proper and acting just the way they need to and not afraid to say things. I wish I had that confidence. "Well, let's pick up the pace and head over to Milly's. Mother brought some clothes for her and she needs to visit Gahris as well."

It'll be good to get Milly here for company, Luther is fun to be around for a while but there's rarely any laughing, it's all so serious. I wonder if he likes Milly? Now that I think of it, she's pretty cute and about the only girl around that's his age.

"What's that look for?" Luther catches my eye before I realize I'm staring right at him.

"What? Oh, I was just wondering if you liked Milly?"

He hesitates for a moment thinking far too long before responding, "Sure, she's excellent company and I suppose she's very polite too."

"Come on Luther, you know what I'm trying to say." I press.

"Well, I mean…" He blushes

"Haha, I knew you liked her!" I can't help bursting out.

He swats at me. "Of course I like her, you twit." He grabs my head and messes my hair, "Do you like Laena?"

"Well sure, I mean she's really nice." My face turns red and Luther chuckles.

"See, not so fun, is it?" He grabs my shoulder and we slow down. "Cael, we live in a small town. This place only has a few people our age that we could ever hope to marry. Orion and Malaena make a decent enough living for you and Zaitah, you are very blessed." His smile disappears slowly as he talks. "Laena and I really aren't that lucky. I can't go to the city to get a good education because we can't afford it. So, I'll likely have to spend my whole life here. Milly is truly my only option and if you stay here then Laena is really your only option." He pokes me in the chest, "You have a chance to learn at the university though. You could change your life, just like Zaitah is." He shrugs. "Anyway, me liking Milly isn't the problem. It's her father liking me that's causing trouble. He's wealthy, I'm poor. So it'll be hard to find a way to make that work. I might have to just get very lucky in Rensfort. Maybe I'll meet someone down there."

"But you can still go to school. You could bunk with Zaitah. He'd have to let you and we could help out, too!" I say.

He smiles sadly. "No, I can't do that, Cael."

I cut him off. "Sure you can! Zaitah probably has room and it'll be easier with you both there. You could share books and stuff."

Luther stands up straight and sighs. "You know, you're right. I'll ask him. We should get going though. Don't want to be late."

We leave the fields and emerge in the center of town. Turning down the main road we walk towards the general store. It's much bigger than the few other buildings around here, it's cleaner too. Do they have it washed? I wonder if Milly has to do that or if they pay someone. He's not wrong about their wealth.

Milly and her father must have money to spare because they definitely seem to live better than most of us. Being the only white smith and general store in the area clearly has its perks.

Luther opens the door while knocking on it and calls out, "Hello there, Miss Milly! How are you on this fine day?"

I follow in behind him and close the door. The temperature change is so sudden. It's so dark and cold in here away from the sun. A shiver streaks through my body. I shake my head and my eyes land on Milly. Luther could certainly do worse than her. She's healthy, maybe a little too healthy, which isn't bad looking. She's pretty and pale. Very much like royalty. Makes sense, I suppose, because around here I guess she is. Why doesn't royalty go outside? Outside is beautiful. Maybe they don't want sunburns? I'd always be outside if I could do whatever I wanted.

Milly shoots up seeing Luther and I and a wide, kind smile stretches across her face.

"Well, hello there, boys. What brings you to my lovely little shop this morning? Is there an order in the works or is it just my beauty that draws you to me?" she asks this last bit with a smirk at Luther, brushing her bright red hair out of her eyes.

He blushes slightly. "I do believe Cael could tell you better. I'm not really familiar with his work, but I do know it requires your *special* skills."

He's really bad at this. I hope I'm not that bad with Laena.

She turns her smile to me, "What can I get you, sunshine?"

She's so sweet to everyone, and she makes it seem so easy. She doesn't have a care in the world.

"To be honest, I actually don't really know what we need. I hope it's not too much trouble but Gahris just asked us to send you over with your cart so he can pick it over. Father and I are making a sword for a member of the king's court."

Milly's eyes go wide. "Well, well, look at you guys! I see you two are keeping quite busy over there at the forge. When was the last time you were in the city?"

"It's been a few months now. Certainly not since the summer. Luther and Laena usually go down every few weeks, don't you Luther?" I ask

"Yes, we usually make our way to the city market with some frequency." Luther gazes up at the ceiling for a moment. "I imagine we are due for another trip shortly. Oh, speaking of which I actually heard an interesting rumor when we were down there last. I know Cael wants to hear it." Luther smiles at me teasing. "This young scoundrel can't get enough of the gossip from the city. Come to think of it, Cael seems to have a strong desire to hear any story. Life must be much too boring up here for him."

He pets my head.

"You're damn right I want to hear it!" I swat his hand away. "But let's all get back to the farm so I can tell Father that Gahris has the leather. And I'm sure Laena would like to see Milly too."

"Alright, let me just tell my dad where I'm off to," Milly says as she jumps up over the counter and runs upstairs.

Luther and I poke around the shop until the sound of Milly's voice calls to us, "Let's go boys!"

I turn towards her and notice she changed her clothes. Her bright yellow dress flows behind her as she skips down the stairs. How'd she get changed so quickly? I bet she's trying to pretty herself up for Luther. I catch his eye and we laugh openly seeing each other with big dumb grins on our faces.

"I'll go check in with Father and grab Laena," I say running ahead to the farm.

Luther waves me on before turning back to Milly. They could use some time alone. He should spend more time over at the general store, maybe do some stuff for Milly's old man. Though Luther barely does any work for his own father so I suppose that'd be a hard ask.

I knock on the door and head inside. No matter how hard Laena tries to clean up in here, it still doesn't feel quite like a home. It's damp and poorly lit, they don't even have the hearth fire going. The boarded windows from last year's storm keep nearly all the light out. All except the few candles fighting to bring some warmth to this sad room.

Father and Mother wave to me as they sit close together at the dining table while Marak busies himself in the corner.

"Hello Marak, how are you?" I ask as I enter the room.

"Ah, I'm in good health, son. Did you bring that boy of mine back with you? He's been dodging his chores all day reading that silly book of his," he says pouring cups of cold tea.

He's not too upset that Luther's been avoiding his chores. Laena is probably doing everything for them, like usual.

"Yes sir. He's outside with Milly right now. I was hoping to grab Laena so that we could all visit for a bit, would that be alright with you?"

"Only for a short time, I need them both to help me before it gets too late. Go on now. She's by the stream washing clothes," Marak says as he sets biscuits and tea on the table.

I turn and walk toward my parents, "Oh, Father, we met with Gahris and he's got enough leather and supplies on hand to make the scabbard, but no stones or gold leaf. He sent us over to the general store to have Milly make her way over there with the whole cart, so I'm not sure what he plans on doing but it sounds like it'll be frilly enough."

Father's huffs, "He asked for the whole cart? Oh lad, yes… I imagine it'll be frilly enough, indeed." He rubs his head in frustration, "Alright, we'll be here for a short while yet so ya can visit with your friends until we leave."

Mother chimes in. "And don't forget to tell Milly that I have clothes for her!"

Putting her arm around Father, they both turn and shoo me outside.

I open the back door and find Laena wet from washing clothes and covered in dirt. Why isn't Luther out here helping? Or Marak? Why is she the only one on this farm doing any work? Luther is all clean and relaxing, reading books, and here Laena is washing their dirty clothes and probably plowing and planting and everything. I take a deep breath to calm myself.

"Hi Laena." I wave at her. "Can you visit for a bit? Milly is here."

I move over and help her to her feet.

"Hi Cael! It's so nice of you to come over but I have so many chores to do," Laena says as she begins kneeling back down.

"Don't worry about your chores." I say pulling her back up, "I spoke with your father and he said you and Luther can take a break while we're all here. I suppose Luther doesn't need the break though, does he?" I say jostling her with my shoulder.

Laena giggles, "He has been a bit lazier than usual, hasn't he? It's depressing just being around him these days, always going on about your brother and medicine. Are you sure my father said it was ok?" She asks, nervously.

"Truthfully! Besides he's inside talking to my parents so even if he hadn't said anything I doubt he'd notice." I take her by the hand and we begin walking towards the front of the house where Luther and Milly are. As we turn the corner I put my hand up to wave but Laena drags me behind the house again.

"I'd rather not spend more time with my brother. Do you think we could go for a walk instead? Just us?" she asks anxiously.

"Of course! Lead the way." I say with a bow.

She's acting a little odd. I guess I wouldn't want to spend any more time with Luther either. Moons above, I can't imagine what it's like for her every day. Marak not doing any work and just moping around. Luther not doing any work and complaining about school and the future.

Luther and Milly wave at us as we walk towards the wheat fields but I just shrug and wave back to them. They likely want to be let alone as well, they're getting all cozy under that old willow tree anyway. My arm is yanked towards the field as Laena leads us away. The wheat is already so full, even this early. If we duck down a little it's like the whole world disappears.

"I bet you can't find me!" Laena calls as she drops my hand and runs away.

I laugh. "Oh come on now. I can find you with my eyes closed!"

I race after her and we make a game of hiding and laughing when we find each other. Her smile is perfect.

She's like a whole different person when she isn't being forced to do an entire family's worth of work. I wish it could be like this for her all the time. It's so easy to have fun and laugh with her. Being around her makes everything better.

She catches up to me and grabs my hand. We begin to walk together as we catch our breath.

"Luther said that you all went to the city and gathered some interesting rumors, care to share?" I say, shoving her shoulder.

"You always want to hear about the world. I love that about you. Always so interested in everything!" She shoves me through the wheat and I almost fall over into a small area that's been harvested early. She sits down and grabs a handful of the wheat that's already growing back and begins to break it into pieces.

"Well, there's not much to say. It's just the same stories we've been hearing for months now. A whole family in Alkenridge apparently went cracked and got locked away. The Bensons over in the East Village lost their son, but of course they won't speak of it. We heard a disturbing rumor that a family was murdered a few leagues away in the town of Grimmond. The worst part of that rumor is they never found the body of the daughter. So they think the murderers may have kept her as a slave." She stops there for a moment before continuing. "Mercenaries are still making trouble as they travel towards the Lieflands. There was a weird story about a strange man leading some children. I only remember it because they said the children acted like they were under a spell. Like some sort of witch's spell."

"Sheesh, all this horrible news. I was hoping for some funny rumors! Like did the Oarnian prince really soil himself at the king's ball? Or did you ever find out if Madame Crazy Eyes murdered her husband and ran away with her lover? Or what about that one guy who could tell your future by eating your fingernails?" I ask.

"Nothing fun like that." She says, "Although, that fortune teller really got a reputation! They say he was actually called up to the King's Castle if you can believe that. I do also remember that Miss Amerind, or Madame Crazy Eyes as you love to call her, has a new rumor. Now they don't say she killed her husband; she just drove him crazy until he ran away."

"Well, that's not fun, but at least it's something. Do you have any other stories? I wish I could go down to the city to hear more," I say picking at the wheat and making a little straw fort.

She knocks it down and starts making a bigger one. "Nothing you haven't already heard before, but I can think of something for next time."

"Next time? That's so far away." I say.

She smirks. "Oh well. Looks like you'll have to come visit me more often then, doesn't it?"

After a short silence, Laena says, "Well sir, I believe it is time for us to get back to the farm, don't you?"

She stands up and dusts her dress off. She lends me her hand and I grasp it as she helps lift me to my feet. Her hands are just like mine, worked hard and rough. She's so strong. I bet Milly couldn't lift Luther up like this. He might complain about his life already being planned but if this is the path my life will lead me down, I don't think it's bad at all. I can't think of anyone else I'd want to spend it with.

"Hello, anyone in there?" Laena asks, bending down staring into my eyes.

"Huh? Oh yea. Sorry," I say embarrassed.

"You went all quiet on me there for a moment. What are you thinking about?" She tilts her head and smiles.

She smells wonderful.

"Nothing really, just something your brother was talking about earlier," I reply quickly. "Do you think he likes Milly?"

"I don't know, I suppose so." She replies standing up, brushing herself off. "If he has any eyes, I imagine he does. Who wouldn't like Milly?" she says flustered. "She's one of the wealthiest people for some distance. And if that didn't get all the boy's attention, she has pretty, pale soft skin and she's so nice … Everyone likes Milly." She turns and starts walking back to the farm, "I think it's getting late. We should probably get back anyway."

Oh great, I said something stupid. Why am I such an idiot? What did I say? She probably didn't want to talk about her brother. Of course I ruined it. I hope she's not too upset.

We slowly meander our way through the tall fields in silence. I stare at my feet, too embarrassed to find out why she's upset.

The silence is broken by the sound of someone charging through the fields right towards us. I look ahead but Laena is gone. The rustling of the wheat field grows closer. Before I can turn to run away, a strong breeze blows past me and the field goes quiet again.

I stare intently into the fields. I was sure it sounded like boots or something.

A hand grabs my shoulder and I jump before spotting Laena stumbling away. "Moons above! What has gotten into you?!" She gasps.

"I... thought I saw. Never mind, it was nothing." I mumble.

She stares at me and then into the fields before sighing, "Your imagination will be the end of us." She smiles before grabbing my hand, "Especially if we don't get back soon!"

As we make it back we meet Luther and Milly who are also just coming out of the wheat fields.

"Hey!" I call over. "What were you two doing in the fields?"

I start laughing and making a kissing face.

Luther kicks some dirt over and says, "Well, I haven't the foggiest idea of what you're insinuating. I'm a perfect gentlemen. I could ask you what you're doing with Laena out in these same fields!"

He mocks my kiss face. Immediately I feel my face flush red and Laena turns away.

"We were just talking about the city!" I spit out anxiously.

Milly runs and grabs Laena's hand and they begin whispering and giggling. Laena doesn't seem comfortable, though. She's acting like a scared animal. I hope she's not truly angry with me. She really is pretty. When they are next to each other, their differences are so clear. Laena is like the sun and Milly like the moons. Laena has such beautiful, tanned skin. She's strong and warm and has golden hair. I never noticed all the little cuts and scars on her hands before. Nothing like Milly. Finra probably didn't even create Veera with as perfectly smooth skin as Milly. Not a mark or blemish on her. So pale and perfect, like a doll or something. They're like the outside and inside. What a pair they make.

"Cael? Helloooooooo! Wake up man!" Luther is standing closer to me than I would've thought and waving in front of my face. "Just like your brother, always off in your own little world."

He claps me on the back and walks me towards the door with the girls. All of them are laughing and I smile along with them.

As we walk inside, our parents stand to greet Milly.

"Well, hello there little Miss Milly. I hope your pa is doing well," Father says.

"Did the boys tell you your dress is ready, Milly?" Mother says as she gets a bundle of cloth from the side of the table and hands it over to Milly. "You can have your father pay us or take it off the next order Orion makes."

"Thank you, Malaena. That's very kind." Milly unfolds the cloth bundle and a green silk dress flows down. She immediately holds it up to her chest with a gasp. The whole room begins complimenting Mother for making it and Milly for the way it flatters her figure.

"That's gorgeous on you Milly!"

"The sewing work is outstanding Malaena!"

"Where'd you get the cloth for…"

"Must have cost…"

"Can't put a price…"

"The green with the red!.."

"Thank you so much, Malaena. This is beautiful!" Milly cries out, "I'll bring this home right now so it doesn't get dirty," She says holding her new dress close.

"I'll walk you back and we can go see Gahris with your supplies." Luther puts his arm around her as they walk out the door whispering to each other.

"We should head out, too," I call to Father and Mother. They would just talk for days if I let them. How much can they have to talk about? What *do* they even talk about?

"The boy's right Marak. It's probably time for us to get goin'. We'll stop by again soon and next time we'll see about some of this new whiskey Gahris has been testin'." Father says holding a bottle up. Mother rolls her eyes as Marak kisses her on the cheek.

Marak stops midway through his goodbye and stands back, "New whiskey, eh?"

Great, now they'll talk about whiskey for half the day. Where'd Laena go? I hope she's still not mad. Maybe I should apologize. The house isn't too much bigger than ours so she can't be in here anywhere.

I move towards the open back door and spot her. Already back to washing clothes, the ever-dutiful daughter apparently.

They don't deserve her. As soon as I step outside I see her crying. She hasn't noticed me yet. Maybe I should leave. Is she crying about something I did? Maybe she's just sad about her chores? Finra's beard! I'm so useless. What do I do? I can't talk to her; it might make it worse.

I sneak back inside.

"Hey, are you ready to go yet?" I ask.

"Alright, alright. It's getting late; we should get back home before sundown," Mother says and they both give another round of quick goodbyes.

I glance back through the open door leading to the fields and Laena's waving back to us with a smile. But she still has tears on her face. Father says it all the time; men will just never understand women. But Mother says we should try to understand everything… I'll never figure this out.

We start our slow journey back home. I'm not in any rush and they clearly aren't either. They're talking quieter and laughing louder. They probably took a few tastes of that whiskey. I turn back and Father wraps his arm around Mother. I take the hint and push ahead with Clout.

I rummage through the back of the cart. Oh, this is definitely a new bag of goods from Marak. What did the two of you trade today? Ah ha, just what I was searching for! How did we manage to get these, they look so fresh. They can't be apples from last year, maybe they traded for some from down south? I didn't even think to go check out the Orchard while Laena and I were talking. How long were we talking? They loaded up pretty good. This is definitely more than we needed. Clout nudges my shoulder and I feed him the last bit of my apple. He nudges me harder after finishing.

"What do you want, boy? I already gave you my apple, you silly horse …. Hey!" I manage to cry out as I'm pushed forward by Clout's massive head. I try to regain my balance but stumble on a rock and fall on my hands and knees. "Ow!"

Clout gets startled by my outburst and stops short, knocking a few apples around in the back of the cart. A stray apple falls out of the open bag onto the ground and rolls between the wheels of the cart, right between Clout's legs, and rests square in front of his face. He quickly bends down and snatches the apple, gobbling it up in a few quick bites.

"Oh, that's a great! You shove me and then you get rewarded? Just for that I'm not brushing you when we get home. How do you like those apples now?" I walk up and shove his shoulder, but he barely notices.

"Hey lad, you okay? What's the holdup?" Father's voice comes from behind the cart.

"I'm fine. Just that stupid horse of yours getting all grabby with the apples," I mumble.

"Hey Little Cub, do me a favor and close that apple bag. It looks like they're rolling around in the back of the cart," Mother says.

Damn apple bag, they aren't my apples. Making me close these bags. I'm over here taking care of everything for you guys back there having a grand time, giggling like little kids. Don't even care that I just fell on my face. I grab Clout's reins and lead him back home angrily.

It really is getting late. It's almost dark. I wonder if I'll have dreams again tonight. I wish there was something I could do about them. They're changing. Dreams aren't meant to feel real like that and now it's like they're happening while I'm awake. I should just tell them what's going on. Mom might even know a way to help, she's really smart. But if I tell them and they can't help I'll just be locked up somewhere like all the other cracked fools, especially now that I'm running around in my sleep. So many stories of people getting locked up these days. I can't be one of them.

That man... he said it wasn't just a dream. What if he was right?

Our house is perfect. So warm with the fireplace going, casting light to the main room and both bedrooms. It's small, but we don't need anything bigger. It's happy and welcoming, and it smells like home.

We start work on dinner straight away. Father and I start cutting some vegetables on the table and we throw the venison we took out of our salt box into the stew pot over the fire. Mother begins dicing up apples for dessert.

"Oh dear, I can hardly wait fer some of that apple pie." Father says.

I agree. "It smells great, Mum."

I bet Clout's smelling this apple pie, too. And he'll get none of it.

She smiles. "Well, just finish up with those veggies so we can eat supper before we think about any dessert."

Father reaches around and sticks his finger in the pie.

"Hey! You rotten oaf!" Mom shouts.

I grab a scoop from around her other side and she swats me. "Not you too! You are both awful!" She covers the pie and kicks her feet out at us.

"We surrender! Don't hurt that pie, woman!" Father pleads.

"Just finish making supper and we'll see if either of you deserve any of this pie later." She scowls at us.

I barely let the stew cook through before taking it off the fire and serving it around. We all quickly finish eating and Father's eyes fall back on the pie.

"Please, dear?" He asks Mother with doe eyes and after a moment she cracks.

"Fine." she says with a chuckle and serves us the pie.

"This is perfect." I say as I devour it. Father agrees through mouthfuls. Big smiles on each of our faces, full bellies and all relaxed, we sit for a moment before cleaning up.

"I'll go feed the animals." I say to them. "I need to brush that beast too, even though he doesn't deserve it." I mumble.

They sit by the fire, eyes half open and snuggling happily.

I lead Clout outside by the forge, grab his brush and sit on the stool. It's a routine he's familiar with and he trots up in the worn space meant for him in front of me.

"Ahh look at the twin moons, buddy. I thought it was earlier, but it's already getting pretty late. Late at night, late in the season. Man, it's cold out. But I get to bring all you dirty beasts outside soon. Clean out Mother's sewing room and let her get back to work. I'd like to build a barn, maybe in between the well and the forge. That way all you guys will have some warmth from the fire, be close enough to easily carry water."

Wonder if I'd have to level the ground. It doesn't look uneven, but we've run into those issues before. I only have a few years until I'm on my own, start my life . . . . It's so hard to be sure of what I should do. Do I go to school? I really think I'd like to be a blacksmith like Father but I probably have to move somewhere else or I'd take business away from him. He'd probably let me work with him; he'd probably insist on it. I'd like that, but for how long? If I went to school, what would I do? Am I smart enough? I feel like I am, but what if I'm not? Zaitah would help, maybe we could do things together? I could be a doctor like he wants to be. He might not even want that anymore. What do *I* want? If I had a wish, I'd wish life didn't have to be so complicated. And I'd wish I wouldn't have any more damn nightmares.

"Cael! Are ya deaf boy? I've been calling you for days now." Father says as he walks toward me, "You need to learn how to think *and* listen, lad." He grabs my shoulder. "Witches britches boy, you're freezing! How long have ya been out here staring at nothing? Come on. Get inside, it's time for bed." He puts his arm around my shoulders and starts rubbing some warmth into me as we walk inside.

"Yeah, sometimes I just get lost in thought. Sorry."

Mother pats Father's arm with a sparkle in her eyes. "Don't worry, sweetie. Your father's just upset because he can't get lost in something he doesn't have."

Father gasps in shock and we begin laughing. He messes my hair and shoves me toward my bed.

"Oh, I have thoughts." He grabs Mother and closes my door.

I certainly wouldn't mind having my own house right about now. Well it won't matter anyway, I'm a fast sleeper.

Chapter Four

"They're going to find you! Get back here!" I whisper after her.

I peek out of the hollow tree trunk and watch as she disappears into the darkness.

"No! Come back!" I yell as loud as I dare. I can't believe her. She's going to get caught, I know it! Why'd she have to run? She could have stayed here; we're safe here.

The sound of footsteps charging down the path startles me. They're coming.... They must have heard us. I hope she can get away in time. Finra save us. Why is this happening?

"They're just trying to help you." A small voice comes from outside the safety of my tree. "You need to calm down. They aren't going to hurt you. I promise."

"What do you want?" I croak. "I'm not coming out, I'm safe here."

I can't trust them. This is all wrong. I wish Mother and Father were here. They'd be able to help me. Where are they anyway? They were supposed to be here by now.

"This is a dream. A dream you've had before," the voice settles near the tree's entrance.

No, this isn't a dream. I remember ... I was – We were walking in the forest. We? There was a girl. She was right here, I know she was. Right?

"Listen, Cael, you need to trust us. I promise everything will be alright if you just trust me. Take my hand, I'll help you out." A normal looking hand reaches out of the darkness and through the hole.

If this is a dream, nothing can hurt me, it's just a dream. If it was a dream, shouldn't I be waking up? But this is a dream because nothing makes sense. It *has to* be a dream.

I grab the hand and it pulls me from the safety of my hiding spot.

"So what now?" I ask, but the voice is gone.

"Hello?"

I try and search the forest but as soon as I focus it all twists into an inky blackness. Something else is coming from down the path. I turn to duck back into my hiding spot but it's gone too.

"Trust him," the voice echoes in my head as a hooded figure appears from the void, carrying a small lantern that pierces through the darkness. He reaches for me without a word and grabs my arm, taking me on his journey down the path.

"What do you want? Where are you taking me?"

The figure pulls me along silently, continuing through the forest. Suddenly, he stops and turns the light behind us just as something grips my waist and wrenches me backwards. Pain shoots up my arms as the hooded figure fights to hold on.

"This isn't real, this isn't real! This is just a dream, they aren't real. Help! Dad help me! Mom!" I scream as I'm ripped from the hooded figure and dragged through the woods.

I grab branches, grass, anything to try and fight back, but it's useless. Whatever has me is too strong. I can't fight back. I'm too weak. This was supposed to be just a dream. Why aren't I waking up! I don't want to be taken away!

"Help ... please," I mutter one last time before a clearing comes into view with a familiar small pool of water. The monster pulling me through the forest throws me into the glorious, frigid cold water.

"Cael! Wake up! Are you alright? Boy, speak to me!" Father's frantic voice startles me awake.

"Dad!" I cry as he lifts me up and hugs me.

"Cael... You're alright, everything's alright. It was just a dream," he says and Mother wraps her arms around me as well.

"My little boy! You're safe now!" She hugs tight and starts guiding us towards the house. "We need to get inside before you catch cold. It's freezing and you're soaked."

Father carries me inside and sets me down in front of the fireplace. They stir up the coals and wrap me in a blanket, barely taking their eyes off me. It felt so real, but it was just a dream. I'm home. I'm with my family. I'm safe, it was just a dream. Just like every night, these damned dreams. How far did I go this time? It couldn't have been that far if they found me. Maybe they followed me through the woods?

"Son, these dreams ..." Father begins and Mother cuts him off as her face turn from worry to anger.

"This isn't something we can just hope goes away anymore, Cael. I won't have my baby hurting himself! These dreams are making you crazy! We are going to see the doctors in the city!" she insists.

Father holds up his hand. "Malaena, dear, let the boy speak his side. We've already talked about this; it's got ta be his decision."

"No! It's not his decision any longer. I'm making it for us all. You saw what happened! He was in pain! Who knows what would've happened if we didn't wake up and stop him from running. He could've gotten hurt. I won't let him get hurt! At least let me take him to see the Draisek!" she yells at him.

Father lets her speak before standing up and hugging her.

"Love, ya know as well as I that it's got ta be his choice, whether he sees a doctor or them dream reading folk," he says as they sit back down next to me. "Lad, I think it'll help if ya tell us what these dreams is all about. Go on." He leans forward.

I take a deep breath. What are these dreams about? It doesn't matter. The only thing that matters is they're getting worse. Mother's right, I need help.

"I... don't know. They're dreams, but different. I'm in a forest somewhere, not anywhere we've been before. I follow a path and everything is calm and peaceful. Except this time. Well, sometimes it's not calm. When I see the man, it gets scary, but I don't always see the man. He's got a hood over his face, or some sort of cowl and his lantern always shines through the forest."

Father waves me on, "Alright, lad, keep going."

"This time I saw the man and he spoke to me. Someone spoke to me. He seemed different, he wanted me to trust them. He wanted me to follow them somewhere. I don't think it was the same man that I've seen before. Then the hooded man came out of the darkness and grabbed me. He started pulling me down the path. I got scared, but then I was grabbed by something else." I rub my waist. "It hurt. I can feel it now. It was real. I was pulled and I fought and fought but it was too strong. It pulled me through the forest but then, it wasn't a monster or a beast, maybe it was. But it was good because it took me to the water and the water saved me. It always saves me." I rub my head.

"Sometimes I move in my sleep, I walk or run …. Last night I woke up deep in the woods," I admit.

"Cael that's it!" Mother cries but Father puts a hand on her shoulder.

"Lad, we'd love ya no matter what. We'll always be there for ya, but you've got ta tell us these things. No more secrets," he says.

I nod and quickly drop my head. Father rubs my hair and Mother wraps her arms around me.

"We heard you tonight. You were talking in your sleep. Your father woke up and tried to shake you awake. We didn't think anything of it at first, but then you started screaming. It was so scary, Little Cub. Orion grabbed you and you started kicking and scratching. You were grabbing onto the chairs and the door and clawing at everything. If Orion hadn't thought to use the trough to wake you up, I don't know what we would have done. I don't want that to happen again, I just want you to be better," Mother says as she cries on my shoulder.

"I want to be better too. I just want this all to stop," I cry with her as Father hugs us tightly. "It's all getting worse, and I just want to be normal again. I wish everything would go back to the way it used to be. I don't want to be cracked but maybe if we go see the Draisek I won't be taken away?"

I try and catch my breath before pulling away. I wipe the tears from my eyes and see the worry written on their faces, clear as day. Why me? Why my family? What is happening! Finra, why?

"I'm scared to go see them, but if I don't do it now I might not get another chance. I don't know what'll happen tomorrow night if someone doesn't help me. It was just a dream before …. Just a damned dream."

Father and Mother both immediately wrap their arms around me again.

"Thank you, lad. It's not an easy thing… but it's the right thing. Thank you, thank you…" Father says before walking outside and collapsing to his knees. He buries his face in his hands and cries silently.

I never realized how much he'd been keeping everything inside. He must've been so scared and he never pressured me. He always helped keep Mom from forcing me to go to the doctors or those dream readers. He always wanted me to say it on my own. I could've saved them so much pain if I had just seen what they saw. That these weren't normal dreams, that these were something different.

I might be cracked, I could be locked away or they might give me medicine that changes me. Whatever happens is better than this. I can't keep worrying my family. I walk outside and Mother follows. We hug Father as he cries into his hands. It's so hard to see him like this. He's the strongest man I know and I hurt him. Moons above I'm so selfish, I hate myself. My throat goes dry and becomes sore. I want to cry but I can't. I don't deserve to.

Clout walks up to me. "I'm sorry bud, did we wake you up?"

He lays down next to us and puts his head over my shoulder. I rub his ears and neck and he snuggles in close. Everyone was worried, even Clout.

After a few more moments, Father stands up and he embraces us all once more. "We've got ta try and get a little sleep before we head into town. It's a long trip and we can't be feeling tired. We'll sleep in here with ya so don't worry about running off, lad. We won't let anything happen."

Mother nods and leads Clout over to her sewing room and then her and Father cram in on either side of my small bed, trapping me between them. It's not so bad, at least it's warm.

Tomorrow everything is going to change. But tonight, at least for now, I'm safe and snug between them.

<u>Chapter Five</u>

Ugh… every bone in my body hurts. At least I didn't have another nightmare. I wiggle out from in between my parents towards the edge of the bed and start picking at the straw through the hole in my sheet.

Well, we're finally going to the city just like I wanted. Not really *how* I wanted to go, but it's something. Maybe everything's fine and these are just some weird dreams. At least I'll be able to see my brother again, and we can get some pastries, and we can get some drinks at the tavern, maybe we can even watch a few fights! It's probably not even going to be a big deal. I bet there are loads of people who have weird dreams in the city. There's nothing to even be worried about. If someone can fix me, why should I wait to find out?

I have a good long yawn, stretching the soreness away. My cuts don't even hurt that bad anymore. Today feels like it's going to be a good day. A perfect day like in the stories. I head outside and go about my morning routine. While I'm doing my business right near the deadwood tree, I spot some frost on the ground, shining brightly as the sun begins to break the horizon. Even the morning sun is happy. I love a cold spring morning, maybe that's why I'm in a good mood? Winter is trying hard to hold on longer than it usually does. I grab some firewood on the way back in and stir up the coals from our hearth fire, bringing them back to life.

I wonder who we'll run into. It's been so long. We could get some orders in. We shouldn't waste a trip all the way to the city. Didn't Luther mention that they were going back down soon, maybe today? That would be fun to see them down there. We could all go see Zaitah together.

I let the goats and chickens out and give them some feed before I start unloading the cart from last night. I should do a bit of preparing for our trip to the city. We'll probably be buying herbs for Mother, some cloth, iron, maybe more coke and limestone? I should check our supplies. If Father gets his way he'll end up buying a dozen bags of pastries. He'll probably eat them all on the way home. Vashir couldn't stop me from getting my hands on at least a few. Fannie makes the best pastries!

As I search through our supplies, a rustling comes from the woods followed by a voice calling, "Helloo there young smith!"

A lean tall man in a dark cloak walks out of the woods waving over at me. My eyes dart to his bow and then a glint from his waist draws my gaze to a knife. I step back and place a hand on one of our forge hammers.

I plant my feet and call back, "What can I do for you master woodsman? It's rather early and we won't be working today, so let me know if there's anything else I can do to help you on your way."

The sun lights his hood enough to reveal a friendly smile as he makes his way over. "I won't be bothering you too much, lad. I was just hoping to warm my hands by the coals in your forge." He spots the hammer in my hand. "I won't be causing any trouble now, but you're a good man to be ready."

He pats my shoulder and opens his hood revealing a kind face that's much younger than I expected. I watch as he places his weapons on the table.

"Although with this bow, I could have easily marked you from beyond the tree line." He says smiling again. Something about him just feels trustworthy. His blue eyes, his clean face, even his few-days-old beard is friendly.

"You're right of course master woodsman. It was silly to think ill of you before we met. Let me stir these coals up for us and I can set some tea going."

The coals are still heated from the morning before so I turn them over and add some wood to get a nice fire going. As I set the tea pot on top of the forge, I glance over at the woodsman. He must be as tall as Zaitah and Father, but he's thinner by a length. I suppose it helps when you're in the woods to be thinner. I can't even imagine Father out there in the thick brush; he's so big! But moons above, that bow is incredible, the woodworking and carving is …. That must have been a masterpiece. What wood even is that? It's inlaid with metal too, this is a work of art if I've ever seen one. And Finra's beard, that knife! Shining as bright as silver. I hope it isn't though. That would be stupid. Silver is a soft metal. Maybe he was just some rich noble's son who wanted to be a huntsman? That bow must be brand new, no marks, and no worn places on the grip. I wonder if he's ever even used it?

"Oh, this bow is much older than both of us my young friend, used beyond counting."

I freeze still.

"What did you say?" My mouth hangs open and my eyes go wide. My mind isn't working right, I must be saying my thoughts out loud. Last night took more out of me than I guessed.

"What lad? I didn't say anything?" He asks, slightly confused.

Now I'm hearing things? That's great. Add one more issue to the growing list of things wrong with me.

He doesn't notice my confusion, "Well young master smith, let's pour some of that tea, eh? I certainly could use it to warm these bones. The air still holds a bit of winters frigid breath in it."

He stands up and grabs two cups from the rafters and pours our tea, hands me my cup and he takes the spare.

This woodsman … he' different than the people around here. There's something interesting about him. I did wake up happier, so maybe he's normal and I'm weird?

"Are you alright, master smith? You look a bit like you're unsure of the ground beneath your feet." He grabs my shoulder. "You know, you're right. I didn't even introduce myself, I apologize ten thousand times. My name is Landon. I'm a woodsman by trade but a traveler in my heart."

He reaches out for my hand and I grab it without hesitation, "I'm Cael, apprentice blacksmith by trade and … I, well, I suppose I don't know what's in my heart."

Landon pats me on the back and laughs. "An honest young man if I've ever met one. That's a good man there Cael. Don't lie for anyone's sake but your own!" He settles back down and we sip our tea.

"I've been all through these woods, day and night," Landon says as he stares into the fire. "I've gotten lucky on some days and been unlucky some others. It's a beautiful land and I'm grateful my travels led me here. But I've decided it's about time I move on. I'll be heading west, maybe a bit more southerly in the western direction."

I nod along as he continues, "Traveling suits me, I'm a wanderer. Perhaps that's a better word to suit my heart, a wanderer. Traveling tells of planning. Wandering? Well, wandering is something else. It speaks of no plans, no destination. An adventure just to adventure. A journey for journey's sake. It's truly a blessed life I lead. I hope you can find comfort in the path you choose as I have found comfort in mine." We both sit for a moment and enjoy the warmth on our faces and the chill on our backs.

It's almost like we're friends or family. To just sit and enjoy the silence between strangers? That's as rare a treat as I can think of. It's a shame Mother and Father aren't awake to enjoy his company. He seems so familiar.

He stands. "Excuse me for rambling there, my young friend. It's not often I get to see a new face. I should be on my way for now. I'll be in the area for a while longer, a few days most likely, but I imagine not long after."

"If you're back around this way you should stop in and share the fire again. I'd love to hear about your travels. Not many wanderers make their way to our corner." I say.

"A lover of tales!" He says with a grin, "Nothing's better than a warm fire, hot drink and a good story." He grasps my hand firmly, "I have the perfect story for you. But it'll have to wait until the next time we meet." He winks before walking away.

As he reaches the forest line, he calls back, "Happy hunting!"

I react without thinking. "You too!"

He turns to me for a moment staring blankly before smiling and waving a final farewell as he disappears in the darkness.

I sit back down and sip my tea as I watch the fire burn down again. What adventures could this day hold? Barely morning and it's shaping up to be an interesting one. Moons above am I hungry. Last night's dinner would be perfect right now. I can almost smell it .... I *can* smell it! It was left over the fire last night. It's probably bubbling hot by now. Oh, the stars are showing me favor today!

I walk inside and as I open the door both Father and Mother are stretching themselves awake and smiling wide at the smell of some hot breakfast. Father and I immediately set the table and Mother pours us some bowls. As we sit down to eat they stare at me.

"What is that big silly grin for?" Mother asks.

I hadn't even noticed, but I must have had a grin on my face straight through since Landon left.

"I just have a feeling that today is going to be good for all of us," I say.

After breakfast, I let them get ready for the day and finish preparing the cart.

"I've already checked our supplies," I say. "We could do with a bit more iron and coal. We should have enough lime. Mother needs a few antiseptics and herbs, but the herbs we can mostly get from town. We do need some cotton, and since Marak burnt his cotton fields for barley, we have to get some in the city."

Father's eyes search me over.

"Well you seem ta be in a right rush, aren't ya? What has got you all giddy this mornin'?" he asks a bit hesitantly, but I can tell he's happy too.

"I haven't a clue, I woke up feeling all rounds of awful, but only for a moment. I went outside and the cold spring air greeted me with a smile. Then a traveling woodsman, no – wandering woodsman, greeted me with a kind wave and a good conversation. It's been a good morning."

At mention of a stranger they immediately begin worrying.

"Who was this woodsman?" Mother asks quickly, "What did he want? Where is he now? Why was he here?"

She moves over to the door and starts searching the tree line.

"Mum, come back inside and settle down." I reach for her. "He was just a kind young woodsman. Barely older than me if I had to guess. He only wanted to warm his feet by the fire."

"Well what did he say? What did you speak about?" she continues, still flustered.

I turn to Father hoping for help but he's just as concerned . "Go on then, lad, answer your mother."

"We didn't really talk about anything. A few words about his travels and hunts around here. He said he'd be leaving in a few days. He was truly nice. Oh and Father, you would have tossed your anvil if you saw his bow!"

Father forgets himself and smiles. "Oh? What'd it look like boy? Was it – "

Mother cuts him off. "What was his name? Where is he now and where's he going?"

"His name is Landon, Mum. He only wanted to warm up a bit, it's pretty chilled out there. He disappeared back into the woods after a few moments by the fire. I can only guess where he is now, but he's leaving in a few days anyway. He's just a wanderer heading west. There's really nothing to worry about. Here today, gone tomorrow. Right?" I say.

Father puts his arm around her. "Like the boy says, dear, it doesn't sound like a thing to fret on. We've got enough ta keep our minds busy this day."

I change into some warmer clothes with Father and Mother and grab a bit of traveling food. Why do they keep looking at me like something's wrong? It's kind of funny. They think me happy is so out of the ordinary that I must be sick. But why am I so happy? I'm going to see the Draisek today, shouldn't I be worried?

Thank Finra I don't feel like that though. I'm glad that I feel so good. Today is the perfect day for it. I'd hate to be miserable and downtrodden on such a long journey. Especially as it's for such a silly thing like dreams.

I get Clout hitched to the wagon and corral the rest of the animals into our fenced in area. I hammer in a new fence post and repair the small break from earlier. Maybe I'll leave them out today. It's going to be a while 'til we get back. They could wander about and graze. I bet it'll be a nice day once the sun warms us up. No, we'll be gone all day and that's plenty of time for a fox or even wolf to get to them. Not that a fence will stop a wolf, maybe it'll even keep them enclosed for the wolf…

"Caaaaaeeel! Hello boyo?" Father's voice startles me from my thoughts, "By Finra's green grove, lad. I can't imagine what is goin' on in that head of yours. You are somethin' else, ya know that?"

I jog over to them and shrug. "Sorry, just in my head about things. We're all ready to get moving?"

Father picks me up in a big hug. "Yes, Son. We certainly are!"

Chapter Six

I'm actually excited to go to the city! Finally, something new to do. Being on the road is so energizing with all this fresh, crisp air. I can breathe deeply and not smell a forge or food or animals, just delicious open air. My legs are already getting tired. We absolutely needed this exercise. I bet Mom and Dad are hoping to get their traveling legs back soon, too. This weight, all that worry and fear, it's so much better away from home. Even they're smiling so they must've been carrying that weight along with me. I feel like I should be more worried but all I feel is happy!

"So, what else do you want to do in the city?" I ask them both as I race around the cart in circles.

"Little Cub, what are you doing? You're in such a funny mood!" Mother calls over to me as I rush past her.

"It's a good thing we're heading to the city, dear. Look at the man; he's gone off the tree!" Father laughs and tries to grab me as I speed by him.

I taunt, "Oh, you need to be faster than that old man. You're getting slow in your old age just like a grey old cat!"

He smacks me quickly as I get too close.

"Ow!" I cry out.

He smiles. "What, lad? Letting an old man like me get ya?"

I pick up a stick. "Oh, you want to sword fight!" I start swashing it around.

"Well, this isn't fair. I didn't pack my sword," he says, rubbing his beard.

I run into the tree line and find a weak looking branch and toss it over to him. "Unsheathe your weapon!"

He picks it up and starts swinging it, testing the weight.

"You sir! Did you just insult my dearest mother?" I accuse him and he flourishes his branch as if it were a true sword.

"Aye, that I did, ya miscreant! And just what're you gonna do about it ya little kit?" He gets into a dueling stance.

I can't stop smiling at how ridiculous he looks. What have I gone and started here?

I pretend to be shocked, "How dare you!" I call.

Father begins laughing harder but I catch him in the stomach with my wooden weapon. "I challenge ye to a duel! You foul oaf!"

He squares his shoulders and comes lunging towards me. I leap out of the way.

"Too slo..." I get caught mid-word on the rump with his sword.

He smirks. "Too what now, boy?"

I lunge at him and he quickly moves aside. I lunge again and again and he parries them all.

What in the Holy Tree am I seeing here? This man is the size of a bear and moves like a rabbit!

"That's it! Take this!" I scream out and charge wildly, ignoring his blows and start swinging my stick every which way catching him just enough to graze him. He picks me up and squeezes me tight.

"That's cheatin', ya walnut!" he says.

Mother's hysterical laughter spreads to me and Father. He drops me down catching his breath and I run to grab another twig.

I call to Mother, "You there, maiden! Help me with this demon. His speed was gifted by Vashir himself. Only a strike from a lady pure of heart can defeat him!"

We start swinging wildly together and Father tries to evade and block but quickly turns around and starts running, swinging his stick behind him.

"We've got him on the chase! Quick, strike him now!" I call to Mother and we both lunge out and poke him in the butt.

"Nooo!" He cries, "I've been struck by the maiden pure of heart!" He collapses on the ground.

"Oh, I'm not pure of heart," Mother says with a wry grin.

Father turns to mother confused. "I wasn't talking about you. The young delicate maiden over there!"

He points at me and I kick dirt at him with a scowl. A stone flies up in the dirt and it strikes his nether region. He crumples to the ground while Mother and I laugh harder.

"Look, sir knight! The strike of purity has brought this demon to his knees!" she says.

We pick Father up after a moment and brush him off. He shoots us both dirty looks and turns around angrily before smiling back at us. I take a deep breath and walk toward Clout as he's pacing around.

"It's alright boy, just a game, no need to worry," I say rubbing his head. I scratch his sides as we begin walking again.

A traveling group passes us by, having seen most of our show.

"I don't think they appreciated your acting, dear," Mother says to Father, shoving his arm slightly.

He puts his arm around her. "Was just taking it easy on ya both."

We set ourselves back on the road and pick up the pace slightly. It would be great to see Zaitah, he's always learning something new and fascinating. We could eat lunch and get pastries, and just relax like we used to. We can walk along the university gardens and talk about nothing. I bet he'll wonder what I'm going to do with my life. He never wanted to be a blacksmith. He probably won't like it when I tell him that's what I'm going to do. I suppose I could go to school too. Father says we have plenty of money and Mother would insist I get a 'proper' education. What would I even go to school for? Being smart was always Zaitah, not me. Well I suppose I'm smart, maybe just a different smart? Are there different smarts? Is smarts even a word?

The warm sun makes everything feel friendly. Even this old worn dirt road is welcoming, like home. The tall green fir trees that lined the road before are replaced by expansive wheat fields marking our progress.

It must be near midday already. We're definitely getting close. We should be ... There it is! The bridge to the city.

"We're here!" I yell out.

"Wow there, boy, we're not in the city yet. Loosen your pant strings," Father says without looking back. "Why don't ya use some of that energy and go see about findin' your brother? Where do ya think he'll be, Malaena, in that hall there or the room things?" He asks Mother.

"It's called a dormitory, dear." She says calmly. "But I doubt he'll have time to visit now, he's –"

I cut in, "I'll get him! We'll see you in the square. Let's meet by Fannie's?" I'm already past them and running to the city before I have an answer. I can't wait. It's been months since I've seen him. He's gonna get an earful for not making time for us.

Why am I so energized? I can't remember the last time I felt like this. Do older people have this much energy? Father was filled with pep earlier so they must.

It's so far, but I can't stop running until I'm out of their sight or they'll think I'm tired already. I am tired, but I can't show it. As soon as I cross over the bridge, the dirt road turns to cobblestone and branches out into a dozen different paths. I can never remember which is the right way, but the university is over there on the south cliff so I'll just head in that direction. The city is big, but the university is big too so it shouldn't be that hard to find.

I hurry through the fields outside the city walls. Those flowers – the smell reminds me of when Mother and I would go out and gather bouquets near town. The grass is growing well here, just like the fields in Umbledon. It feels like forever ago when we went over there to deliver a few orders, and those kids were so friendly. Everything smells so strong. I love that, all these memories. We always only ever smell the same thing at home. People who live here must really love all these smells. The lilies, lilacs, and magnolias are wonderful right now. The streams and grass smell so familiar, too, but what is it? It's something, or someone? Someone good ... Laena, of course! She always smells of grass and the fresh stream water because they work her so hard in the fields and washing clothes. She's such a good person. Too good. She should make them do more work. I'm glad I get to take her away from her family and chores sometimes.

I reach the university gates and bend over to catch my breath. I spot Zaitah walking through the gates right towards me, just as I stand back up. The days good fortune continues!

"Hey baby brother! What are you doing here looking like you just got your ass kicked?" He puts his arms around me and squeezes the little air that's in my lungs out.

"Unngh! Hey, lemme breathe. I CAN'T BREATHE!" I wheeze loudly and he puts me down but my legs are still weak and I drop to the ground hard on my backside.

"Dammit Zaitah, now I remember why I don't come and visit you more. Mom and Dad are down by Fannie's, and I told 'em I'd bring you down with me. Whether you want to or not!" I stand up and brush myself off.

"Alright Cael, I'm sorry. I didn't mean to squeeze you. Happy now? It's just been a while since I've seen my baby brother and I couldn't help it. You're just so adorable and tiny, like a wee baby lamb," he says as he picks me up and starts petting my head.

"Let me down, you turd! I'll thrash you ten ways! I'll break all your fingers!" I shout angrily, squirming to break free. After a moment, I give up and go limp in his arms.

"Are you all done now?" he asks calmly.

Moons above I hate him; he's so damned in control. I can't wait to be as strong as him so I can thrash him and make fun of him. I'll be stronger, too, because he's gonna be reading books and I'll be working hard at the forge.

"No … you're an illiterate ass. Now I'm all done," I say with a grin.

Zaitah shrugs and says, "Good." before dropping me. I land solidly on my face.

"Ow! What in the Holy Tree Zaitah! You could've broken my nose." I reach up to touch my nose and pull away seeing red on my fingers. "You complete moron you did break my nose!" I turn and stomp towards Fannie's bakery in the center of town.

"Cael, your nose isn't broken. You might not be a Marhyn but you're definitely not delicate enough to break a nose from a few hands off the ground. Cael, wait! Don't tell Mom! I'll beat you for real!" he calls after me as I hurry towards the center of town.

He chases me to the entrance of the inner city and starts to catch up.

"I'll get you! Don't tell Mom!" He yells again.

He reaches out to grab me and I collapse to the ground, laughing. "Alright, alright, you win. Listen, I won't tell Mom you tried to murder me, but you've got to spend the day with us and not be a complete ass about it." I stop to think if there's anything else I can make him do, "Oh! And you've got to bunk with Luther if he asks. Deal?" I reach out my hand and he grips solidly before pulling me up.

"Sure sure, whatever you say King Cael." He bows and quickly stands up confused. "Wait, what about Luther? He's coming down to study? How did he ever get the money? Marak definitely didn't give it to him. Did he swallow his pride and ask Dad for it?" he asks, staring at me.

"I have no idea about any of that. He sounded all woe-is-me yesterday, going on about his life being set in stone and not being able to change. You know the whole deal." I shrug and turn to the city, "Anyway, I told him that you'd absolutely bunk with him if he asked. And now you have to say yes, so I'm the hero. Luther, saved from a life of depressed, monotonous toiling about as a farmer. What valiant man could have done such a thing for such a poor soul?" I pretend to search around earnestly, "Yea, that's right, this gallant knight right here," I say, pointing at myself, "and his pitiful squire of course. We can't leave you out of this fireside story."

I turn back at Zaitah and stick my tongue out.

"Cael, you're an idiot wrapped in a moron and baked over some slow coals. Sprinkle on some extra arrogance and attitude too," he says, shaking his head and walking past me, "Luther isn't waiting on me, I've already said a dozen times we can bunk and I'll pay." He turns and grabs me by the shoulders. "But school isn't cheap. Tuition alone would be half of Marak's income." He starts counting on his fingers. "That doesn't cover books, supplies, food, or lodging." He says with a sigh. "Dad told Marak and Luther he'd pay for it all, but Marak won't have a debt like that over him, and he won't let Luther take money from Dad either. Not that Luther would do it anyway, he's more prideful than he is intelligent, and if nothing else he's got intelligence by the cart full."

He roughs my hair up and pulls me along towards the city.

"You're a good kid Cael, albeit naïve and a bit too self-involved, but certainly a caring person. This isn't your problem. It's a problem of pride and that can't be solved easily ... even if the solution is as easy as we all know it to be," he says letting my hand go.

I'm not naïve. What does self-involved even mean? Zaitah is more of a know-it-all than Luther is. I was just trying to help and he makes me feel like an idiot. Dammit, that's probably why Luther dropped everything, he knew I didn't understand the problem. I *am* an idiot.

"Wait Zaitah, I have to tell you something." I pull on his arm just before we enter the city walls, "We're not down here just to see you."

It's my brother. I can tell him anything even if he is a turd. But he's probably going to try and fix me or tell me how I'm insane and need to be put in the institution for observation, or that I'm cracked. Finra's beard I couldn't handle him lording that over me for the rest of our lives.

Zaitah stares at me waiting. "What in the Broken Mountains are you waiting for boy? Tell me!"

"I've been having dreams .... Well, I guess they're nightmares now. They've been happening for the past few months, but they got bad last night you see..." I rub my arm anxiously, "And well, they got real bad." I stop a moment and Zaitah wraps his arm over my shoulders.

"What happened, Cael?" he asks, obviously worried. He's got the same frightened face Mother and Father had.

He pulls us over to a bench just outside a tavern. "Are you down here to see a doctor at the university?"

I shake my head no and he shoots off the bench "No! I know people trust them, but I don't any more than I'd trust Vashir! You can't go see a Draisek. They aren't safe. They are evil; I feel it in my bones!" He starts shaking me by the shoulders.

I shove him off and stand up shouting, "We've already decided, Zaitah! You aren't even around anyway. You wouldn't know, you don't care! All you care about is your damn books and school!"

He cuts in. "That's not true, Cael, and you know it."

"It doesn't matter!" I say. "Dad and Mom are worried to death and so am I! I'm not afraid to say it. I'm scared! I want to be fixed. I want this to all just be over! This will make them happy and it's the right thing. I don't care if the dream readers can't be trusted, I don't even care if they are fake. All I want is for Mom and Dad to feel better again!"

I sit back down and take a deep breath. "Last night . . . it always seems real, but then it's not fully real. But something is happening. I don't know how to explain it. I sound cracked already. If Mom and Dad weren't home ... If I had woken up any later or... I honestly don't know what would have happened, Zaitah. They said I was trying to run into the woods. Something wants me to go into the woods. It's drawing me there when I'm asleep. I can't control myself. I think ... I think someone is trying to get me."

I drop my head. "The worst part is, I'm scaring Mom and Dad to the point where they're breaking. You didn't see them fall apart last night. My decision was made for me right then. If there were doctors that could help fix me at the university or at the clinics I would go; you have to know that. But this isn't a physical thing .... The best case right now is that I'm going insane and you know as well as I do that the doctors take all the cracked fools away. Worst case is there actually is something that's trying to attack me in my sleep. I don't know what to do, but something needs to be done, and these dream reading gypsy people, they're the only answer. There's not one other person out there I can think of that can help me. The Draisek, reading dreams is their whole thing. They know this stuff and right now ... they are my only option."

Zaitah puts his hand on me and I look up at him. He's scared. We all are. It's not fair for me to yell at him. Of course he cares; he's my big brother. I exploded for no reason. I can't even control my emotions anymore. I need help but If I see a doctor at the clinic, they would just do tests or keep me somewhere to watch me. It would be all very logical and by the book, but they wouldn't figure it out. And when they finally realize that they have no answers I'll just be sent away. Everyone gets sent away when they've cracked.

If I see the dream readers and they can't figure it out... Well, at least I can still go out in the world and try to live my life. They won't lock me up afterwards like an animal. We sit in silence for a few more moments.

He's still staring at the ground. It's useless to try anything else. Why can't he just accept it? What's so bad about these guys anyway? Sure, the doctors at the clinic think it's a bunch of un-researched smoke blowing, but that can't be worse than potentially being a prisoner for the rest of my life.

Zaitah stands up, "I have to go speak with someone, and you're coming with me. I'm not letting you out of my sight." He says nodding to himself.

"What?! We have to go to Fannie's! What about Mom and Dad?" I yank on his arm, trying to pull him backwards but he barely takes notice as he pushes ahead, dragging me with him.

I drop his arm and sigh, "Fine. We'll do this your way. But only for now!" I say defiantly.

I follow him to the university and as we enter the courtyard my mouth drops. "Wow." I say staring at the huge buildings and hundreds of people moving around the open fields.

"Yea, it's pretty big. Rensfort has one of the biggest universities in all the Five Kingdoms." Zaitah remarks without stopping. "Those two buildings on each end are the dorm rooms. And those two are the Halls. That larger one set directly in the middle of everything is Sleepless. That's what we all call it anyway. It's the library and also where we take pretty much all the written exams." He calls back to me pointing at all the buildings.

Manicured stone walkways connect in the center of the courtyard while small dirt paths cut through the expansive grass fields directly to the adjoining buildings.

"Hey, Alan! Have you seen Professor Gemble? I need to speak with him. It's urgent." Zaitah shouts over to a small plump student with buzzed short brown hair speeding through the field. Alan spins around and smiles as he sees us.

"Hey Zaitah! Aren't you taking this anat exam? It's happening pretty much right now in Lost Hall." Alan says anxiously.

Zaitah smacks his forehead, "Dammit I forgot! That doesn't matter, I'll do extra work in the infirm later to make up for it. We need to speak to Gemble. Have you seen him?"

"Oh yea, I just saw him with Beckett, they're in Sleepless pouring over some old books again." Alan answers with grin. "Beck never has time for any of us, I swear."

"Thanks, Alan." Zaitah grabs my arm and drags me toward the library.

"Gemble is a little odd but he's the man we need to talk to about all of this 'dream' stuff. Beckett being here is a gift, too. We roomed my first year but I haven't seen him much since he passed his finals. He travels so much he might even have more to say than Professor Gemble."

He leads us through the doors to the library. The warm air outside reaches into the building while the doors are open. The frigid stale air quickly forces itself back as the doors close and the sunlight leaves. I rub my eyes to adjust to the darkness. A few flickering candles cast moving shadows around the halls. Zaitah continues pushing along while I follow closely, keeping my eyes on his feet until I can see clearly.

He opens another door, "Professor Gemble! I have to speak with you. Cael go sit over there for a moment." Zaitah orders as soon we enter. Two men are hunched over scattered parchment and books.

"Oh now Zay, that's a little harsh isn't it? You didn't even introduce us." The younger man chastises Zaitah as he stands up straight and smiles. He's a full head taller than Zaitah and larger by a mark.

"Beck, it's great to see you again." They grab forearms and shake, "But I need to spe –"

"The dreams, is it?" Beck cuts in before Zaitah can finish.

Zaitah turns his head slightly, confused. "Yes." He says slowly letting their arms fall. "How'd you... It doesn't matter, but he's right, Professor. It's about those dreams." He continues in hushed tones, pulling the professor to the corner.

Beckett moves to the bench and sits next to me, laying his arm around my shoulders, "Don't mind your brother, he's in a little over his head here and he knows it. He always gets bossy when he doesn't know what to do." He winks at me.

I chuckle, "He's always bossy though."

Beck squeezes my shoulder, "Well then that must mean he's always in over his head." He touches his nose and grins.

We both laugh hard and Zaitah scowls, "I can hear you!"

"Wouldn't be fun if you couldn't hear us, now would it?" Beck wags his finger at him.

We sit in silence waiting for Zaitah and Gemble to finish arguing quietly in the corner. This is taking forever. What are they even talking about? Why are they hunched over keeping secrets anyway? I'm the one with the dreams, it's not like they need to keep that hidden from me...

Beck stretches out and sighs, "I can tell this is going to be a long discussion. I had planned on getting something to eat, mind if I take your little brother? He looks about ready to explode from boredom here."

Zaitah waves without looking, "Yes, yes." He turns to us, "Actually, how long have we been here? Cael, take him to Fannie's and grab Mom and Dad. Make sure you come back right away, no delays."

"Fine." I mumble.

"Trust me, it'll be better than staying here waiting for these two old owls to finish." Beck whispers as he opens the door, "Shall we?"

He leads us out of the many dark rooms and down the corridors. I hadn't realized how far we walked earlier. This place is a maze. Why do they keep it so dark in here? Shouldn't they need light for people to read?

Beckett opens the large heavy doors and the sunlight immediately rushes back into the building warming my face. The field is almost completely empty of any students. They must all be back in class.

"Tell me about yourself. I imagine you're tired of telling everyone about these dreams, so let's chat about you. Like, what do you want to do for work? Have you traveled much?" Beck asks as we enter the city.

"I love working with my dad at our forge. We build all types of things. I enjoy making things, it feels good when something comes out just right." I respond without hesitation.

"Creating and building is very rewarding work. But you know, smithing isn't the only type of creating you can do. There's a whole world of opportunities out there." Beck says, navigating the many alleys back into the city.

He slows down and turns, "You might even like to travel. It might be better if you did."

"Maybe, but I think I'd miss my parents too much. Zaitah is the traveler, not me." I say as I take the lead.

He puts his hand on my shoulder and stops me, "Everything is about to change, Cael. You're going to have to –"

"HELP!!" A scream comes echoing through the square.

We both shoot up. "You heard that?" He asks.

I nod, "What should we do?! We have to help, right?"

"Stay close." He orders as he charges down alley after alley, never second guessing his decisions.

"Wait up!" I yell, trying to match his pace. He's so fast. I trip over some loose ropes and slam into the ground.

"Blast it all." I mumble. Beck grabs my arm and pulls me to my feet before we start racing down the road again. A loud noise catches my ear from inside the house and I come to a halt before carefully opening the door. It falls from the hinge with a thud.

Beck turns, "Good ear, Cael." He pats me on the back, "Stay up here, please."

I watch him disappear down the steps into the broken-down building. I peer inside. Stay? I'm just meant to stay up here? What if he needs my help? Someone else is in trouble, what if he gets in trouble, too?

"Hello?" I say quietly under my breath, creeping inside. A crash comes up from the cellar. I sneak down the stairs and find a man covering the mouth of a girl in the corner while Beck holds a second man in a headlock.

"Let her go." He says calmly. He catches my eye and motions for me to stay back.

My heart beats through my chest. I blink and my eyes adjust to the light. Is that a knife? It's cutting into her side right now. I have to do something! But what? What can I do, I'm just a kid!

"Look out!" the girl cries just in time for me to watch as a third man charges from behind the door. I dodge to the side, tripping over my legs and barely avoiding his arms as they reach to grab me. I scramble to my feet and shoulder him into a table that splinters underneath our weight. Beck releases his headlock and the second man collapses to the floor unconscious. The man near me scrambles out of the debris but Beck grabs him and he stops moving, falling backward into the ruined table. The first man tosses the girl aside and lunges towards us, swinging his dagger.

I back away and trip over myself, falling into a small crate. Before I can move, the man is on top of me and he shoves the dagger down towards my chest. I grab his hands but he's too strong, the dagger starts to cut into me.

I shut my eyes tight, not wanting to watch the end. The blade stops suddenly and I hear a scream as the man attacking me rolls off. A pair of hands grasp my shirt and arm and I'm thrown to my feet. My eyes open wide and Beck is standing in front of me.

"We need to run!" the girl screams, shoving past Beck and grabbing my arm.

The man rolls around on the ground scratching at his face. He's crying? His face is burnt? What in the moons above is happening here!

She pulls me up the stairs and outside. She trips over the broken door. I help steady her and then we run. She's too fast. I'm losing my grip. I fall as we reach a church and try to scramble to my feet. She stops for a moment, but then continues running. I drop to my hands and knees breathless.

A hand touches my shoulder, "Thank you."

I try and reach out but she's already running away again. Beck charges after her, "Stay here!" He orders, "I'll be back for you." His voice echoes down the alleys as he disappears around a corner.

I crawl around the building to hide and catch my breath. That's it? Thank you and then gone? I barely even saw her face. I didn't get her name. Who were those guys? They must have been insane, and why were they trying to hurt her? Did she do something to deserve it? Maybe she didn't thank them properly. What if she did deserve it and those were guards? There's no way those were guards. What did Beck do to those men? They all just collapsed when he touched them. Maybe he's one of those Sfeln warriors from the south? I think they can do that type of stuff.

A hand grabs me under the arm and lifts me to my feet

"What the blazes happened to you?" Landon asks as he brushes me off and checks me over.

I sigh seeing him. "Thank Finra, it's you Landon. I have no clue what's just happened. There was a scream and, and an old building, and then there was a girl and some men with knives, and then we ran .… I have no idea."

A warmth trickles down my chest and I watch as blood drips onto my shirt.

"Are you hurt badly? Here, lean on me. We need to get moving. I don't know what's happened either, but it won't be good if we hang around here any longer," Landon says leading us away. He tosses more of my weight onto his shoulders. "Where are we heading?"

"I'm supposed to wait for Beck. We're going to get my family at Fannie's and head back up to the university to see my brother."

"Well, you're lucky twice then. I was heading that way myself. I don't know who Beck is but I don't think we should wait around for him." His head turns down at me. "Now, if you can, tell me what happened?"

"…and then Beck took care of all three of them just about by himself. He must have found a torch because the last guy was burnt real bad. I was certain I was going to die, actually certain of it. It's really weird."

I stop talking but Landon speaks, "So then you ran away?"

I nod. "We ran out as fast as we could, but I was already out of breath from running to find her. I couldn't keep up and I fell.

She kept on going though. Beck followed her and told me to wait and well, you know the rest."

Landon nods and we continue walking.

"I'm just glad to find you alive young master smith. I am a bit confused as to why the girl left you, though, but I'm sure she has her reasons. I will say you shouldn't be running off to save anyone in the city. It's very dangerous. Could you describe them? Did anything stand out? You said it was dark, but did you notice their eyes at all? Were the whites of their eyes tinged blue?" he asks

Of all the questions, were the whites of their eyes blue? Who even cares? They were cracked murderers trying kill me. Do their eyes matter? But the man with the knife, his eyes were blue. More crazy than blue, but definitely blue. Why would he ask that?

"Yes." I say slowly, "They were. What does that mean? Is it some secret cult?" Some group that kidnaps young girls and sacrifices them? I've heard of that in the stories but never in my wildest dreams believed someone would do that.

"What?" Landon says, chuckling, "No no, nothing like that."

Am I thinking out loud again? I hope it isn't getting worse.

"I think those men were droppers, just addicts. I shouldn't say just. They get very dangerous without their drug." I shrug confused and he continues, "You know, droppers? Sea fiends?"

I stare at him blankly and he sighs. "There is an urchin in the sea that has hallucinogenic properties in its mucous, that means it makes you see things that aren't there. It's also wildly addictive, which means the more you use it the more you feel like you *need* to use it. You usually find them around the docks because it's so close to the source. They end up dropping the gunk in their eyes because it works faster that way. After a while, the whites of their eyes to turn blue, then black because of the poison. At that point, you're completely blind and you usually die."

"Alright, but why kidnap a girl? She didn't have anything on her. She didn't have any discoloration in her eyes, at least I don't think. I mean her hair might have been a really light blue but I think that's because she was from way North Liefland," I say.

"When you take something like that you think differently. They might have thought she did have some slime. Or maybe they wanted to kill someone. They might have even thought they were saving the girl by killing her. The blue hair probably didn't help, slime is blue and they might have wanted her just for the color. It's not really possible for us to know exactly what they were thinking. Even if we asked, they'd likely not remember doing anything."

What? Why? How can you not have any recollection of something you just did? How can you take something that makes you so crazy? None of this makes sense. Why would they just kill people? Who was that girl? I'd guess she's about my age, about my height too. Her hair wasn't dirty, it was really beautiful. She's from far away so she must be a traveler. Where are her parents? She could be a merchant. Her shirt was a bit dirty, but nothing that would stand out. Could have just been from when she was taken by those men.

Landon's right, I shouldn't have risked my life like that. But I did and barely got a thank you? Those men could have killed us and not even thought twice! They probably wouldn't have even thought once if what Landon said is true. I hope the city watch comes to get them. I wonder if that guy is going to make it. Beck got them pretty good. Finra's beard that'd be rough. They probably can't even walk after collapsing like that. It won't be hard to find the other guy if he tries to run though. He's got a nice sized burn across his face. That would be so scary to wake up, not remember anything, and have a huge burn across your face. Even worse to take that drug and never wake up again I guess. Man, I'm hungry.

"Hello, sweet bakery! Do you smell that Landon? I'm starving, I wonder if she has those meat pies. I could eat anything right now. We must be really close!" I start running towards the smell.

"Alright. Alright. Slow down! I don't want your parents worrying too much about you so try and keep quiet for now about what happened, deal? Let's just get you cleaned up before we see them." He grabs me and leads me around a shop towards a well.

I suppose he's right. I have worried my parents a lot lately and telling them I was almost killed for doing something reckless of all reasons? It definitely won't sit well with them. At this point, they might think it's just my dreams pushing into my waking life .... No, that's not possible .... Is it? I would know. I always know it's a dream. Well not always, some dreams seem real. How can we know right now is real? We only know when those dreams are dreams when we wake up. That's about as far down that thought hole I'll go. I'm just going to assume everything's real until proven otherwise.

Landon sucks in too much air and starts coughing, startling me and he smiles at my confusion.

"Are you alright?" I ask.

He gazes down the road and still smiling says, "Ah nothing, I'll tell you later. It takes a bit of back story for you to understand." He pats me on the shoulder. "But you'll laugh when I tell you. Alright now master smith, let's clean you up a bit."

He takes off my shirt and washes it quickly with a cleaner from his pack and the blood stains almost disappear. Mother would love to get her hands on something like that. She's always complaining to us that blood is hard to get out.

"Dunk your head in and we'll dry you off. I imagine your parents are getting a bit concerned. They should be just around the corner, so we won't have far to go at all." He takes a jar out.

What is that? It looks wet and oily. He puts a measure on his finger and rubs it on my chest after wiping the blood away.

He moves me over to the water and dunks my head. He starts scrubbing the dirt from my hair. I could get used to this. It would be nice to be wealthy enough to have someone bathe you. It reminds me of when Mother and Father used to do this. He lifts me up and dries my head with a handkerchief.

"I can wash myself you know. It's not like I'm cracked yet." I say with my eyes closed.

He jostles my head a bit more and waves the handkerchief in my face. "Oh I wouldn't say that lad. You seem a bit more cracked than you let on."

I suppose I am a bit cracked aren't I? I hope it's not too bad. I could still be fixed.

Landon flicks my arm. "Come now master smith, I was joking. If you're cracked than I am too, and many others out there." He puts his handkerchief away, "That's enough chatting for now, Cael, we really need to get to your parents. I can almost hear them getting more and more concerned the longer we stick around here."

He speeds off down the road and I chase after. He stops just before the corner and puts his arm out.

I slam into it with a thud, "Oompf! Hey what's that about?"

"We don't want to look like we're up to no good," he says and motions for us to walk. "So tell me about your parents." He leads us out into the center of town.

"Orion, my father, is a blacksmith, one of the best! My mother is probably the only healer in our small – "

"Cael!" Mother calls out of the crowd as she sees us and runs over with Father close by. "We were starting to worry. Where is Zaitah? And who is this young man with you?"

She puts her arm around me and pulls me away from Landon.

"Mother, Father, this is Landon. Landon this is my mother Malaena and my father Orion. We were just talking about you guys," We all walk together to the side of Fannie's bakery.

"Landon is the woodsman who I met just this morning, lucky coincidence too as I got lost when Beck took off." I pat Landon on the shoulder. "A good day today. Thank you for helping me find my way, friend."

Mother chimes in. "Yes, thank you. I'm sorry but we really should be going. Cael, where is Zaitah? Did you meet with him? Who is 'Beck'?"

I tell them most of what happened, leaving out the girl and incident. "Then Beck had to go do something and left, which is when Landon found me." I lie and change the subject, "What brings you all the way here Landon?"

"Supplies for my journey, mostly anyway. I have some other business to tend to while here. What brings you all to the city this fine afternoon?" he asks quickly.

"We'll be heading ta see the Drais... Ow!" Father starts.

Mother grabs Father's ear and pulls down hard. "Orion it is not polite to discuss such matters in public with near strangers. Shame on you!" Mother scowls at Father and Landon.

"The Drais...?" Landon says confused before realization washes over him. "The Draisek? Is the boy having nightmares?" He whispers, looking around at us. "I've had dealings with them in the past. If you truly wish to see them, I imagine they await you even now. You should not delay further. Come, follow me." He turns and beckons us down an alley.

I follow Landon and can feel my parents following close behind. The mystery is so interesting. Why are we heading down these dark alleys? The Draisek set up shop near the docks, everyone knows that, it's where all the vagrants operate.

"There are two different types of dream readers," Landon begins. "The first type are the ones most are likely familiar with, the ones by the docks, the ones that will take your money and tell you what they believe you want to hear and send you happily on your way." He stops and looks to each of us. "The second type are the ones that I will show you. They study the mind and have true power over it, unbelievable power. Everyone knows of the Draisek, but few know there are fakes."

"Well, then where are we going?" I ask.

He waves his hand back, beckoning us down an alley. "True dream readers need silence. They need to be far from noise. Still, business is business, so they need to be in the cities. It's a real conundrum. Most have found that being underground suits their needs. The only buildings that still have basements, at least in this city of Rensfort, are in the run-down sections away from the university."

Mother grabs my arm.

"Can we trust him?" she whispers.

"I think so, he's helped me a lot," I say and shrug. "Besides, we're still going to see these people so it doesn't matter which one we go to, right?"

We continue following Landon down alleys and streets until we reach a building.

"What are these symbols carved in the doorframe?" I ask Landon.

He runs his finger across the symbols, "This set of symbols reads, 'Seeker Beyond The Storms.' And this set here reads, 'Ten - one hundred sixty.' I imagine these are updated every year or so, but that means they've been practicing for ten years and have treated one hundred and sixty people. Relatively new to the field but has seen quite a few patients."

"How do you know all of this? Why are you helping us?" Mother asks.

Father puts his hand on her shoulder and speaks up, "Now Malaena, this young man has helped our boy and we shouldn't look ta accuse him of nothing yet."

"It's no trouble at all, Master Orion, your wife has every right to be suspicious of travelers, especially these days. I've had dealings with these dream readers in other parts and my travels have granted me with some unusual knowledge. I'm simply happy to have it be of some use rather than to have it go unused." Landon says.

"That doesn't answer anything," She presses.

Landon takes a deep breath and sighs. "As a child I had nightmares. If Cael has nightmares anything like the ones I had … They are frightening and very dangerous. Towards the end, I would find myself in the woods, cut and bloodied, exhausted from running and lost. My family was filled with confusion and grief and I was scared every night. I understand more than most, and Cael seems like a friendly young man, and I'd like to make certain he's cured as I was."

He puts his hand on my shoulder and gives a sad smile.

He's had nightmares? Like mine? So I'm not alone? There are others, and these dream readers can help. He's so normal! He's all on his own adventuring and wandering. He can't be cracked, he's cured! There's a cure!

"Taking another one to your dogs?" Beck says coming around a corner. "Not satisfied with what your seekers are doing, Emir? Had to come down here yourself?" He continues viciously.

"Beck –" I start.

Landon holds his hand up. "I want no trouble. I'm only trying to help them."

Beck laughs furiously, "Help! You're helping them!? Helping them do what? Helping them by hiding the truth? Helping them by taking their memories? All of you are the same, you'll never understand what these dreams are meant to be. If you take him he'll be locked away, far from everything until your praetors say otherwise."

Beck shakes his head, "Do not hide behind your tricks. Speak loudly for them to hear. We will let him live freely! But you, you will take him and squander his gifts until you deem fit." He turns to face me, "Cael, you must come with me. I can protect you."

Landon is lifted off his feet and thrown to the side without ever being touched. His body slams into the wall and he crumples to the ground. Beck rushes towards us and extends his hand for me to grab it but his movement stops suddenly. Frozen in time. Landon struggles back to his feet as Beck's body begins twisting awkwardly. He turns to face Landon and Landon's legs are pulled beneath the cobblestone street. As the ground swirls, Landon's body is pulled further below. Beck frees himself and moves swiftly to Landon's side, gripping his head and neck.

Landon calls out, "Run!" before a flash of blinding light explodes through the alley.

I grab my parents and we run back into the city streets. We crash into the crowd and push our way through until we're out of breath. Mother finds a bench and sits us down.

"What is happening?" She collapses next to us and squishes me in between her and father.

"There you all are! I've been looking for you .... What happened?" Zaitah races up to us and Mother gives him a hug.

"Zaitah! Please tell me you know what's happening! What do these people want with, Cael?" She asks exhausted.

"Who? Did you go to the Draisek? I told you not to, Cael! Did they touch you? Did they do anything to you? Are you hurt?" He grabs my shoulders and touches my head.

"No, no one touched us. Landon was taking us to them but Beck... he was acting different, he said he wanted to take me? And then things started happening. Unexplainable things." I stare at my hands confused.

"I'd like to see any of those fools try and take you away!" Mother sneers.

"What unexplainable things?" He shakes his head, "No, never mind, we don't have time for that. I just finished speaking with Gemble at the University. He's had theories on these dreams for a while and thinks he might be able to help. We're leaving shortly and he's already making arrangements. Don't see the

Draisek and don't talk with Beck or this Landon guy until I come back. I know Beck might seem scary, but we can trust him. I have to leave now but I shouldn't be more than a few days." Zaitah says.

Days? These dreams have gone from nothing to everything in just two days. How much worse will they be by then? Finra save me from these dreams!

"What are we supposed to do for 'a few' days?" I blurt out.

"Go get your supplies. Go see Fannie. Once you're done here stay away from everyone and stay out of the city. As long as you don't come in contact with those freaks they shouldn't be able to affect your minds," he instructs.

"What do you mean affect our minds? How is that even possible?" Mother asks.

"I honestly don't know if it's true or not; it's all speculation and theories. But something is happening. I'd bet everything that these nightmares are connected to those disappearances we've been hearing about. You just need to stay safe and get out of the city." Zaitah hugs me tight, "I'll fix this, I promise."

Mother and Father wrap their arms around us, too.

Zaitah pulls away. "I have to go help professor Gemble and Suaryn prepare. We'll be traveling towards Waylinn. There's an inn on the southern road not far beyond our borders where we'll meet his friend."

"Alright, just hurry. His dreams have been getting worse, and tonight… well, I have a bad feeling," Mother says as they hug once more and Zaitah leaves.

Waylinn. That's so far away. What could an inn have on a traveling road that the city of Rensfort doesn't have? Why would he still trust Beck? If he had seen what we saw, there's no way he'd still trust him. Beck is the dangerous one. Landon saved us. He saved us and we just ran away. I hope he didn't get hurt badly.

How could my dreams be related to disappearances? Maybe the Draisek are related, but the disappearing people? If the Draisek are this powerful, what are they doing hiding that power in a basement?

Forcing our minds to change? Like real magic? This truly is starting to sound like a fireside tale.

Chapter Seven

I can only imagine what's going through my parents' heads right now. It all feels like a dream. Funny it feels like that now when dreams are what caused it all. Father's talking to Fannie but even his smile is tired. All of this sadness is like a contagious sickness. Everyone is so worried. I'm glad we're almost done with the city. I just want to get home and breathe. I'll give Clout a well-deserved brush to clean the dirty city out of his mane and then I'll sleep. But the nightmares will be back. I can't remember the last time I had a dreamless sleep.

"Come now, Orion. Let's get going now. I think we all want to get home and try and forget the day," Mother says with a sigh.

I guess I'm not the only one who just wants to leave.

Were they using … magic? It makes no sense! Maybe magic used to be real, but that's all stories now. It's not the world we live in anymore. Zaitah would say we live in a world of science, studies, and proof. There's no room for magic. I bet he's working on explaining what happened right this moment. But until then, I suppose magic is the best explanation we have.

The cold shadow of the city gates wakes me. I must have been following them without even noticing. Clout nudges my shoulder. "Hey bud, when did we pick you up?"

Mother and Father continue walking silently. They must be deep in thought, too. This is going to be a long and quiet walk home.

I take a deep breath as we start our journey and take in the cold fresh air. The city is convenient, but it's got every smell mashed together making a stew of stench. Heh, stench stew. That'd be awful. I like to visit here, but I don't think I would want to live here. It's so crowded and there's a lot of trouble hiding around every corner.

Life is so frustrating. We have no control over anything even if we think we do. I just wanted to live a normal life and be like Father. Then these nightmares happen and now everything I wanted to do is just a fantasy. I'll be taken away by the doctors or kidnapped by these people. Landon had these dreams and he's normal. Well, he seemed normal until Beck showed up.

There's the sticks that we used to do our great battle, just this morning. We went to the city for answers, hoping to have all our problems solved, and now we have more problems than we went in with. Before these were just dreams. At least they were to everyone else.

What do these dreams mean? Zaitah said they can affect minds; Wait! All those times I was with Landon and thought I was going crazy, he was in my head. There's no other explanation. They can hear my thoughts. Can they hear me now? It doesn't matter, I just have to figure this out.

What proof is there that I can hear their thoughts though? Well, I suppose there is no proof I can't hear their thoughts either. If I could, it would help explain why they want me. That has to be a pretty 'special' gift.

"Ah, home at last." Father sighs. "Hey lad, help me unload Clout."

He leads Clout over to the forge. We start unloading supplies and Mother comes over and kisses my forehead. "I'll put on some tea. That will help us get some rest, we all could use it."

She walks inside and we finish unloading.

"I'll let ye brush the horse, lad, but I want ya inside soon. We're gonna keep a close eye on ya tonight," Father says, patting me on the head and walking inside with Mother.

"Well bud, it's just me and you." I rub Clout's ears and we walk over to our brushing place and begin the routine. "Was a pretty crazy day, wasn't it? Not what I expected, that's for damn sure." I pat Clout on his side and dust plumes up, "Whew, you got all types of dirty in the stalls didn't you! Hmm, I wonder what your day was like. I bet it was about as you expected it to be, eh?"

Clout rubs his head against me and I scratch behind his ears.

To be a horse? It must be so easy. You just eat, get brushed, run around, and when your people need it, you pull a cart. No problems to complain of even if you could complain. That might be bad now that I think on it. If something was wrong you couldn't tell anyone. You could be having nightmares every night too and not a soul would know. A shiver shoots through my body. That's like being trapped inside yourself. Imagine if I couldn't tell anyone what was wrong with me...

Clout sways tiredly in front of me. I must have been lost in thought for a while there.

"Alright Clout, let's get you inside with the others." I lead him inside. "I think I'll stay up a bit longer." I mumble as I close the door.

Inside the house Mother is nearly asleep in her rocking chair. She's had her eyes on me this whole time. She touches my arm as I walk past. I head to the room and grab a quilt to throw over her and kiss her forehead. "Goodnight mum."

"Good night, Little Cub. I'll be up a while longer." She mumbles.

I pick up the cup of tea, already cold.

"Hey Dad, I'm just going to ..."

Father snores loudly. He's sleeping. Everyone's asleep already. That's good, I'd rather not get squished in the bed again. And they need the sleep just as much as anyone. I can't sleep yet, though. I should want to, but I'm not ready. I'm too awake. Probably just scared of the next nightmare. I'm certainly not looking forward to what tonight has in store. Last night was terrifying.

It's getting late in the spring season and still the winter air forces itself in. No clouds in the sky though, just a clear cold night. The moons are almost as bright as the sun, and those stars ... It's like a whole city in the sky. This would be a perfect night to go scouting. Mum and Dad would be furious, especially after today. But, if I sneak maybe Mom won't see me.

I grab my bow and creep past Mother. She rocks back and forth but I can tell she's on the steps of sleeping behind her eyes. With the moons this bright, it'll be easy to track anything. I quickly make it to the tree line. I should keep an eye on the markers I made. I reach the first one near the tree line and rub it. It's so worn down from the years, it's hard to believe how long ago it was when I would get lost as soon as the house was out of sight. These marks helped me a bit more than I'd admit to anyone, especially Zaitah. I catch myself marking the wood again on each tree. I should head to where I woke up a few days ago and mark all the way there. The way things have been going, I'll probably end up back again soon, maybe even tonight.

The forest is more awake for some reason. It's likely the light from the moons, they're full tonight. A night to stay awake and cause some mischief. It's almost like it was the middle of the day out here with all this noise. Squirrels, a few deer, owls and probably more than a few mice all awake and causing trouble.

Already here? Maybe it's not so far out as I thought. It is getting pretty late though. I'll need to start making my way back soon. I remove the water bag from my waistband and take a long sip while I sit down on a large rock. This rock is still so nice and warm, the sun must reach down here during the day. It's actually pretty comfortable out here alone…

Chapter Eight

Well that's enough resting for now. I should get back home before I fall asleep out here. Veera's eyes, the sky is so bright it makes the whole forest seem awake. I'll just follow this stone path back home. I'm so glad we made this path. It would be such a pain getting out here if we had to trip over tree roots and cut through brush.

"Hellooo, Cael!" Landon's voice calls out from the other side of some trees.

"Hey Landon! Over here." I wave my hand to motion him over. "What a surprise to see you out in these woods tonight. Have you had any luck hunting? The whole woods are awake. There's plenty to catch!"

"Tonight, I'm not out hunting young master smith. I'm out searching. I suppose seeking is a better word for my task tonight." He says cautiously reaching out his hand.

I go to grab it but stop short. "You were taking us somewhere. Zaitah doesn't trust you. That other man, Beck, he said things." I rub my head confused. "No, this isn't real. This is a just a dream. I can't be taken away by either of you. I'm staying with my family." I take a step back, "Only a dream." I repeat under my breath.

Landon's eyes match his sad smile. "Listen lad, this is more reality than it is dream. You are right and wrong at the same time. It's difficult to explain, but I suppose I owe you that much."

Landon puts his arm around my shoulders. The weight of it startles me. It feels real but dreams always feel real when you're in them. He leads us to a formation of old grey stones leaning against one another to create a solid bench.

"Cael, do you know what this forest is?" He asks after a moment.

I turn around in a daze, searching for anything recognizable. He grabs me calmly and nods.

"This forest here," he gestures around us, "is where it all began. It is where our minds are stirred to life. Our scholars have studied the dreams for as long as the academy has records. We have searched to all corners of the known world trying to find the true waking forest, yet some visit this sleeping one nightly in our dreams."

His gaze wanders to the stone path, "We start our journey all the same, Cael. We dream we are lost, searching the forest at night. Something within us wants to remain asleep, and so we run. We run to the water and its promise to keep us hidden. But while we journey, there are others who wish to help us. They are called seekers. I am not a seeker but I still wish to help you. What I said in Rensfort was true. I had nightmares the same as you have, we all do. The Draisek could have helped you. They would have ensured you rest easily until we finished your journey to the academy. But that can't happen now. Your mind is restless and confused."

"I don't understand what you're trying to say. I'm sleeping even when I'm awake? You're taking me to this academy? Is that where they fix us?" I ask.

"I don't think I'm explaining this right." Landon sighs. "I'm not good at this stuff. This isn't what I was trained for." He waves his hand. "I found you one night weeks ago. You were out here and for whatever reason, I've been keeping an eye on you ever since. These seekers don't want to hurt you, but because of who you are, what you're capable of, they will if they have to."

"But who am I? What am I capable of? Why me?" I burst out and jump to my feet. Landon motions to the forest around us and there are animals all through the clearing. Are they frightened of me?

"This forest is real, to a point. Our emotions have a real effect on these animals. You must calm yourself." He puts his hand on my shoulder and guides me back onto the bench.

"I think it might help if I told you a story. I know you're a lover of tales, and perhaps it's the best way for you to understand. This isn't some fireside tale about witches or demons or goblins that take your iron trinkets. It is a story about us." He points to me and back to himself.

"I don't want to hear a story right now, I need to know what's going on!" I shout becoming frustrated.

His arm rests on my shoulder again and I calm down. "I know it's hard, but just try and listen first. Besides, this is the perfect place to tell such a tale. The story takes place not far from here. Although it was long ago. So long ago that the truth of how long is lost to time. But the story has survived. Through countless wars and unimaginable pain and suffering. This story survived, just like we have.

I'm not great at any of this, but least of all am I a storyteller, so don't interrupt. It's going to sound crazy, all of it, but it's as true as anything. The instructors will tell you more than I ever could, but for right now this should do."

I nod my head and he begins.

"This is a story of magic, real magic."

The origins of magic start long ago when humans were hunted by everything. As small, weak and defenseless as humans seemed, they had one thing to rely on, and this was their intellect. It was a necessity to group together as there is great strength in numbers. The first chieftains were not the strongest or the most skilled with the primitive tools and weapons of the time. They were, however, genius strategists. This was a time when humans rarely fought amongst themselves. Why bother fighting each other when everything outside the fire's light is planning which of you to eat first? Caves were the safest place for man back then. They were cleared of any beasts and built to be the homes of the first tribes.

Our story begins during a hunt organized by the wisest of chieftains, Uukanil.

Chieftain Uukanil was leading the last hunt before the long winter with his son. Uukanil's son was overconfident and was ambushed and killed by the cunning beasts they were stalking. Distraught, Uukanil returned home with his son's body and told the tribe what had happened. Tahkalan, Uukanil's younger brother, had always been short tempered and he viewed the men who could not hunt as worthless. Tahkalan had always looked for ways to encourage those men to join with the other hunters and this was the perfect opportunity. He vowed to destroy every last beast to avenge his brother's son and asked for all able men to join him. His words stirred the anger within the men and women. They took up arms and began hunting all manner of beast. All, except Uukanil.

During the night, Uukanil took his son's body away from the anger and walked out of the cave into the wilderness alone. There are legends of walking trees that are said to be sages with knowledge of all things. Uukanil knew of these trees and planned to do the unthinkable. To find a way to bring his son back to life. As he walked through the wilderness, he never imagined actually finding one of these ancient trees. Yet not a few moments in, standing before him was the biggest beast he had ever laid eyes on. With a trunk of the most intense dark amber and leaves glowing pale green in the moonlight. He stood in awe at its beauty. The chieftain did not know why, but he moved without hesitation towards this massive tree and stepped calmly into its hand.

The tree placed Uukanil amongst its branches and began to move deeper into the woods. Moving through the forest with this giant tree as his guide on any other day would have been an experience to enjoy and revel in. However, the chief had much on his mind. Before long the chieftain began to speak to his son. At first, they were silent apologies for his mistakes and failed leadership, but soon he was having a conversation aloud about small things with no meaning at all. When the tree stopped walking, Uukanil realized the tree had been speaking to him, but no words sounded through the air, only Uukanil had heard them, and only in his mind.

Where the tree stopped was a beautiful grove, a small ground fed pool of water surrounded by trees with vibrant golden leaves. The animals in this grove seemed at peace with Uukanil and paid him no mind. There Uukanil decided to let his son rest. As the chieftain laid his son's body in the earth near one of the trees clad in golden leaf, he realized he was not ready to lead his people just yet. And so he asked to travel with the tree. For four days and four nights Uukanil stayed with the tree, observing the animals from his treetop sanctuary. The beasts he and his people feared seemed to be welcoming to the moving tree. Never noticing the chieftain amongst its branches. As Uukanil watched these beasts play and care for their young as he and his tribe played and cared for their young, he realized they were very much alike. He thought that if they could communicate, perhaps they could finally be at peace.

On the fifth day, the tree spoke to the chief again, "Every being has a place. Every being knows that place, save for man."

Uukanil asked, "What is our place? What place does man have in this world of beasts?"

The tree responded, "That is not for me or my kind to decide. It is up to men like you to lead others. In doing so you will surely find your purpose."

Uukanil thought long on what he heard before asking the tree to teach him to communicate with the animals. The tree informed Uukanil that every being can communicate, but they communicate in what he would call different tongues. To be able to communicate with all animals, he would need to learn to speak with his mind. And so the tree who had already taught him so much, opened the doors in his mind and granted him a gift to speak to all beings with thought.

After thanking the tree for all it had done, Uukanil took his leave. He began his journey out of the forest, back to his home without the burden he had carried in. As Uukanil arrived, he recounted his tale for all the tribe. With his new gift, he wished for no others to be harmed and proclaimed that he would usher in a peaceful age alongside the animals of the wild. Without doubt or hesitation, his tribe asked to help Uukanil and one by one he opened the doors in their minds allowing them to listen and speak to all living creatures.

When Tahkalan heard of this new peace, he became enraged and disgusted at the thought of all those inhuman beasts that murdered so many of his family and tribe, being given amnesty. He had only just urged the men to join his cause. Now he cursed his tribe and vowed to never allow peace between man and beast. Uukanil knew all too well how his young brother felt, and he was saddened to watch him leave the tribe alone so full of vengeance. But the chieftain had greater things on his mind. He had to spread word of this new gift and the opportunity for peace that they have all been given.

He gathered all the tribes in the area and spread word that they gather their neighbors as well. The largest gathering of humans ever to have taken place was not for war, but for peace. As the tribes entered Uukanil's forest, they noticed no beasts stood in their way. Uukanil had already tasked many of his tribe with brokering a truce with the animals nearest to their cave, and it had been extremely successful. As the chieftains of the other tribes saw how effective this peace was, they conceded it was a far better option and agreed that Uukanil's dream would be realized. The tribes began to make their journeys back to their own caves with the new gift Uukanil had endowed them with. Along the way, they began to assist in the peace talks with all the animals, and to their surprise, none objected. It seemed Uukanil's dream was wanted by all through the wild, except for one.

As busy as Uukanil had been in creating peace, Tahkalan had been busier destroying it. One vengeful man slaughtering every beast he laid eyes upon. The animals feared him and sent word as quickly as possible to Uukanil. The chieftain had to place all negotiations on hold to find his brother and stop his attack before he ruined the image of peace. At last, a wolf found its way to Uukanil and told him that his brother was climbing a mountain leaving dead animals in his wake. Uukanil left with the wolf immediately, though it would be days before he reached his brother. Tahkalan summited the top of the mountain and smiled a vicious smile, filled with hatred and spite as he saw the most massive and ancient of beasts, a kovukin.

A great winged creature with long solid feathers colored deep red. A sharp, boned mouth and a scaled tail that broke in three at the tip. Four legged with talons stronger than any metal.

But this creature was not just a behemoth in physical form, it also boasted a fearsome intellect, as did man. A foe like this would be impossible to overcome.

Without another moment's hesitation, he pounced and began attacking the kovukin with such ferocity that it was truly fearful, but only for a moment. The kovukin was enormous and had strength to spare, but Tahkalan was a strategist and knew speed was his friend. The kovukin spewed flame all around them and flew through the air, trapping Tahkalan in a ring of fire. Tahkalan threw the spears with deadly accuracy through the kovukin's wings and brought the beast down. Before it struck the ground, all of Tahkalan's weapons exploded in flame. Shocked, he dropped his axe and threw down his spears, confused but only for the space of a breath. Tahkalan began to fight with nothing but his hands. For a long time, they battled.

The second day saw the kovukin's wing broken and teeth bloodied, and his fiery breath could no longer reach past his mouth. Tahkalan had lost fingers and his shoulder was cut clean open. He had become stuck in the ground as if by quicksand many times that day, confusing him further, but still the battle raged on. By the third day, both Tahkalan and the kovukin had barely any fight left, broken bones, blood loss, fatigue, but still they fought knowing one of them would die soon. As the fourth day came and passed into night, they collapsed.

The kovukin acknowledged Tahkalan as an equal and as a reward for his strength he offered Tahkalan power over all things. Tahkalan was hesitant to accept a gift from a beast, but his confusion at his weapons bursting into flame and being tripped when nothing was around, or the frigid cold he felt on the mountain of flame, lent him a curiosity that he couldn't abate. He accepted this gift and the kovukin told him that everything was connected by an unseen force. You could feel the connection when the wind blew, or by the beat of the kovukin's wings, and the heat of fire, but the connections were more than just in the air. The kovukin went on; everything has three distinct forms, as a solid such as they were, as a liquid such as the water, or as part of the unseen world such as the air. By using this connection, you could walk on air, burn down a forest, or change solid stone into liquid rock. Tahkalan was amazed, but he did not intend to use this new power for impressing his tribe by walking on air. He would use it to place men at the top, to never live in fear, to command a peace brought by power.

Uukanil met his brother on the way down the mountain and he had heard the conversation the kovukin and his brother had. He knew what it would mean for the new peace he hoped to achieve with the animals of the wilderness. Uukanil pleaded with his brother to keep this power to himself, to find peace without bringing destruction. Tahkalan was too busy fantasizing about what his new gift could do to even listen to his brother. Food would be plentiful. Children could play without fear of animals. Everyone would be safe and happy. All would be well.

Uukanil heard his brother thinking these same things that he wished for, but the paths they would take could not be further from the same. As they walked back to the cave, Uukanil tried to speak calmly to his brother, asking that they continue with peace rather than killing all the animals. Days passed and Uukanil could not convince his brother. On the last night before they reached the cave, Uukanil thought of killing his brother. He had no other choice if he wanted peace. What else was there to do? His brother would ruin this new society of working with creatures in the wilderness, living side by side in peace. This was his only option, to kill Tahkalan .… But of course, Uukanil could not bring himself to do it. How could he usher in an age of peace by killing? The only way to work this through was by convincing the tribes that Tahkalan's vision of peace was war, and a long war that would cost many lives; the end of which not one of them then alive, would live to see.

So as they reached the valley of their people, they once again called the chieftains to listen to Tahkalan's path and leave the decision up to each one. As could be expected, many of the younger chieftains leapt at the possibility of power and controlling the beasts. The greatest defense is one you never have to use. By hunting the beasts down they could be granted the advantage. Only a handful of chieftains' respect for Uukanil outweighed their lust for power, and so a decision was made that, to keep the peace between humans, the groups would separate and only communicate on neutral grounds to avoid upsetting the balance.

Uukanil lead his followers to the forest, and Tahkalan headed to the sea, where men rarely ventured for fear of the water beasts. While Uukanil was filled with sadness, his brother was happier than ever, leading for the first time, newfound power, a new status among people who respected him more than any other.

Years passed with little contact between the two leaders. Uukanil had built a large farming community where they grew crops. His people were mindful of the animals and many worked as healers. Using the knowledge of all creatures, they were especially intelligent and made great leaps in the sciences in a very short time.

Tahkalan had built a city near the coast, his followers were great warriors who fought massive beasts in the ocean and across the land. The people of his city were beginning to understand the connection and becoming very adept at altering the natural state of objects. All were gaining new knowledge of their gift, yet each new bit of knowledge that gave them power also made them increasingly desperate for more. The corruption of that power was spreading. Men had rarely fought amongst themselves, but in Tahkalan's city, fights were all too common. It seemed that even the smallest argument could end with someone seriously injured or even killed. The men had a new strength, but it had taken control of them. When Tahkalan began to intervene in some fights, many started to see him as weak. Long gone was the mind of the strategist, and now all that was left was force.

Small towns on the outskirts began to break ties with the city, and some believed an uprising would happen. Tahkalan was no longer fit to lead the people. They wanted the strongest to lead. The people were anxious, not only because of this new power, but because their new diet of meat was harder and harder to come by. The area was overhunted. Everyone knew what they had to do, but Tahkalan was too weak to let them go. All wanted to hunt in Uukanil's forest. The abundance of food could not be ignored. Tahkalan finally agreed. He did not want to go against his brother's wishes, but even more he wished to continue leading his people. This was the only way. Tahkalan sent a runner to his brother, asking that they meet in the valley of caves where they used to live.

As they reached the valley, Tahkalan and Uukanil embraced for the first time in too long. Happy to see his brother, but not wanting to evade the subject, Tahkalan immediately asked permission to hunt in the forest. Uukanil was taken aback by the bluntness of the request especially considering it went against all that Uukanil and his people stood for. Uukanil refused, he told Tahkalan that he had much land to hunt, and the forest was a safe haven for all animals. Tahkalan pleaded with his brother, begging him, but Uukanil again refused, and he knew what his brother would say next. He saw it on his face before he heard it in his mind. Tahkalan told his brother that they would enter the forest without permission. They would kill the animals, and if his people tried to stop him, they would kill them as well. Uukanil looked at his brother and told him that he did not need to do this. If he entered the forest his hunters would die. The two brothers left without saying another word. When they reached their people, they told them there would be war.

No man or woman alive had ever heard of a war between humans, and now they would be forced to take part in the war? Fighting and death? Uukanil's people were scared. They did not know how to fight. They had no power like the people on the coast did. Uukanil reassured them that they all had more power than they knew, and they had something to protect. They were not alone. All the animals had something to protect as well, and Uukanil ventured through the forest gathering the support of all the creatures. Even the ancient trees could not stand silently. They too would fight.

At mention of war, Tahkalan's people were filled with the excitement of battle and began crafting weapons and training. They became unified with a common goal. All fighting amongst themselves ceased and Tahkalan saw everyone happy again. He realized he had given these people power without guidance and now all they wished for was destruction. How could he leave them? He had created these monsters and he would let their stories play out until the end.

And then it began. The battle was intense, each side underestimating the other, neither side budging. There were no days or weeks or even months. Only a continuous time of destruction. Many years passed before Uukanil's forces were finally weakened. Tahkalan made his way into the forest, fighting through towns. Uukanil saw everything he built being destroyed, all that he loved dying before him. He knew he needed to make a plan, he needed to do something, anything, to save his people.

The ancient trees spoke to Uukanil and told him of a place of power older than man or beast, a place said to be home of the seeds of life. Uukanil needed that power, and so he appointed his childhood friend as leader. He told his people not to give in, for when he returned he would bring the end of the war. One way or another, he knew it to be true. The trees and Uukanil made haste to the edge of the forest. After many days of running, they came to a clearing with a tree so small it should not have been called a tree. As they passed the threshold, Uukanil could not tell if the tree got larger or if they all got smaller, but in the space of a breath the tree was as big as a mountain with seeds of every color, some small, some large enough to fit a family. Standing before him were a dozen giant men appearing as small trees.

These were the Marhyn, the guardians of the tree of life, planted by Finra and betrayed by Vashir. These guardians were all that stood between life and death for all creatures.

The Marhyn had observed the peace Uukanil had brought, and the war that Tahkalan had so foolishly started. They would not allow the humans to destroy this forest, but they could not leave the tree. Uukanil offered himself as a conduit for their powers, and they saw in him a creature that only wished for peace.

They offered him the power he sought, but the consequence of this power would be an eternity of service. Uukanil knew that one man was not worth all the beings in the forest, and he pledged himself to the Marhyn's cause. The guardians brought a large seed to Uukanil. The colors were not outstanding, a deep leaf green cut with storm cloud grey. All along the center of this seed was an amber band. Uukanil could not stop staring at the contrast of this bright amber, and he walked towards the seed. As he came close, the Marhyn cracked it, and Uukanil felt himself pulled in.

For him, it could have all been a dream. In one moment, he had been Uukanil and in the next he was Marhyn. But for the world, it had been years, costly years. The people of the forest were beaten down. The creatures were exhausted. The more land that Tahkalan had taken, the stronger his people became. Uukanil sped through the forest, moving faster than anything before. It

seemed the forest was running for him. The day Uukanil emerged
from the seed, was the day he crashed through the front lines of
Tahkalan's forces. The Marhyn are massive in height and weight,
but the true power lies in their advanced mental powers. They are
not only gifted with speaking through the mind, but they can affect
how another moves and acts. With these abilities Uukanil forced
some of the enemy to fight one another, and while they were
fighting, he began to cut his way through the war.

As Uukanil's people saw the enormous creature charging
ahead, they knew it must be Uukanil. Fighting with renewed vigor,
the people of the forest pushed Tahkalan and his army back to the
city gates. Watching as his people fought and destroyed each other,
Tahkalan retreated up the mountain. He raced up to the kovukin
and begged for more power, for the secret to release his people and
defeat the Marhyn.

The kovukin looked at the pitiful man begging for power
before him and laughed vengefully. He spoke to Tahkalan as if he
were a child and said that nothing could defeat the Marhyn. The
Marhyn are the protectors of gods and life itself.

In a fit of despair and rage, Tahkalan attempted to kill the
kovukin on that mountain top. With no weapons and a clouded
head, he tried to use his new power to harm the beast, but the
kovukin had used those powers all its life and easily defeated
Tahkalan. Alone on the mountain, about to be devoured by a
monster, an idea was born out of hatred. An idea no sane man
would think, even in the depths of despair. Tahkalan focused all
his power on the kovukin and himself and began to converge both
beings into one. The kovukin at first was shocked by the insanity
of this plan, and quickly began to attack Tahkalan, slashing at his
throat and stomach. As the younger brother bled out on the top of
the mountain, he continued to focus on combining the forms of
himself with the powerful being. In the moments before his death,
the mountain top exploded and the kovukin's cry could be heard
clear through the battlefield below.

Before the dust settled, a winged demon flew with
amazing speed towards the center of the battle. No longer a man or
kovukin, this beast had the appearance of both but the memories of
neither, save for one, a burning hatred for the Marhyn. With no
regard for life on either side, the new beast, a Draahkin, soared

over the people spewing flame from his mouth and causing earth to churn by the beat of its wings.

The Marhyn and Draahkin fought for four days and four nights. Each so powerful that neither showed signs of exhaustion or pain. On the fifth day, the Marhyn saw the field of death that this battle had caused and Uukanil's soul inside was filled with such sorrow the Marhyn knelt down. Spotting a weakness, the Draahkin charged.

Seeing the destruction and death had caused Uukanil to question everything, right back to accepting the gift from the ancient trees. In one fluid movement, the Marhyn pushed the Draahkin aside and opened its mind to all creatures, ripping magic from every one. The humans, animals, and even the plants were parted from their gifts and left as shells of their former selves. In an effort to make certain this war was never repeated, the Marhyn closed all minds from ever re-learning these gifts.

With the end of the war, the Marhyn returned to the tree to take post as an eternal guardian. The Draahkin lost its power, but regained memory of a home, and it retreated, never to be heard or seen again. There are many who say that magic died that day. The world that once was, now lost forever.

But a seed once planted, will grow. No matter how long it lies dormant.

Chapter Nine

He finishes the story and reaches for me. "We were brought into this world with open minds. Minds free to hear and see things others can't. You already have the ability to listen, and soon you will speak. When we get you to the island, you may have potential for more than even that."

"I can alter the things around me, not to a great degree, but the gift is still within me." Landon puts his hand on the stone bench. I watch as it disappears beneath the surface and then reappears. I place my hand on the same spot and push on the unmoving stone underneath.

"So magic is real?" I say slowly. If magic is real, and the story is real ... am I magic? I can hear and speak to anything? I could cast spells like in the stories? Could I change the form of stone and air and fire? I could forge things without a forge. I could hear thoughts like Laena's. I could know why she was hurt. I could know when people wanted to hurt me or take me away. I could protect myself and my family... I could understand everything.

Landon chuckles. "Oh lad, I don't think we'll ever understand everything even if we can hear thoughts!" He steadies himself. "But it's true, magic is real. Well the instructors would smack me for saying that. We don't call it magic anymore. They've spent years studying how objects change and how we're able to use our gifts. Now that it can be explained they don't call it magic, but I still like the feeling of the word. It's still magical to me. One thing's certain though; don't say that word when you get to the island, my friend. You'll be running laps till you can't breathe."

"What is this island you keep mentioning?" I ask. "Is that where they teach us things? Is that where they take away the dreams?"

Landon stares down at his hands. "That's the thing isn't it? We're given a power that so few get to experience. So few are even aware of it, but we've got to pay some price. Nothing is freely given. We have to take you away. It's hard to accept it but I don't think you'll ever get to see your family or friends again. Some do, but most don't."

"Then no way! I'm not going to leave everything just to be able to hear thoughts." I say angrily. I can't leave my family. This gift can't be worth being taken away, a few magic tricks? This is nothing. I love my family. I just want my life back!

"Lad, in life you will always have choices, always. Even now you have a choice, but it's not going to make you happy." He sighs again and drops his shoulders. "You either come with me tomorrow … or they have to kill you." He stares at me with a blank face. "That's not all, " He gazes up at the stars, "Because of what your family has seen, they will have to die as well."

"Why me?" I ask as tears drip down my face. "What did my family ever do to anyone? They are good people. They don't deserve this!" I nock my bow and point it at Landon's face, "What if I just kill you instead? My family will be safe and so will I!"

Landon's eyes go wide tracking something behind me. I turn around and watch as the biggest wolf that ever lived charges us. Landon throws me to the side and grabs the wolf by the chest and neck and brings it down with a thud. It immediately calms itself and walks away as if nothing happened. I crawl to the edge of the clearing and Landon follows me.

"Cael, none of this needs to happen. If you choose to come with me tomorrow, we can persuade your parents to let you go. They will live. You will live. It's a simple decision. You either all die or you all live. I know it's not what you expected or what you want to hear, but that's how it has to go. We would just erase their memory of you, but the seeker here has advised against that. If the Sephalim hadn't tracked you here then it wouldn't even be an issue. We could just close your mind, you would be hidden forever. But this Beckett man has made a special case for you and the girl in the city. They aren't like us. They hurt more than they need to. Above all else, we can't let them take you."

What kind of choice is that? Who would choose to kill their parents? Even if it means I die, I still wouldn't kill them. Who in the great green grove are these Sephalim people? He's not any better than Beck. They all want to steal me and hurt my family. It's just like he wants, just like they all want. This is how they steal us in the night. They tell us our parents will die and then we have no choice. We have to leave with them.

Forced away from my family …

I wonder what my parents will do without me. Will they be happy? Poor Clout can't come I'm sure. I'm losing my whole life because of some stupid *gift*? What a great gift … lose your friends and family and you'll be able to … do this stupid useless thing. I won't even get to say goodbye to Laena or Milly or Luther.

"So this is how you take people?" My voice and hands are shaking.

"This is not normal. Typically the seeker would have reached you within the dream. In that dream they persuade you to go. They then either remove the memory of the child from the parents or give them a memory of the child dying. Sometimes though, we are forced to make decisions. Hard decisions. This rebel group is set on taking you. Our seeker from the academy thinks you could pose a threat if we simply leave you here for them." Landon says casually.

"How can you just kill families for no reason? What type of heartless bastards are you people?" I scream. The forest around me begins to change so I take a deep breath to steady myself.

Landon's expression changes to irritation. "We aren't killing these families without cause or reason. We do not influence minds just to suit or whims. We are not monsters! These are carefully calculated decisions. If the world knew there were people, children, with these abilities, they would hunt us down and kill us all. Just try and understand. Think about it for a moment. If history has taught us anything it's that differences are shunned not embraced. Different religions, different races, different languages, even different countries for some arbitrary border that was drawn on a piece of paper."

He breathes deeply and sits back on the bench. "Humans look for reasons to separate one another. If the masses knew that there were a few individuals with extraordinary powers, they would cut us down without a second thought. They would finally have a common hatred and work together to destroy us."

How do we know what the world would do if we don't ask? Why would everyone hate us? We can't be sure until we try. There has to be something, some other way. Anything but this. "It doesn't matter what I think or say right now, does it?" I say quietly.

"Well, I suppose it should, but I don't want to give you that option," he replies.

"What do you mean you won't give me the option?" I ask. The last choice I have and now he's taking it away? Why, what does it matter to him?

"You're right. You should have a choice, but I don't want to let you die tonight. I'm going to take you with me whether you decide to or not. I just hate this whole seeking business, which is why I stay out of it. You're different. I can't let you die or be taken by the Sephalim. Maybe you remind me of myself. Maybe you remind me of someone else. I don't know. But I can feel that you're a good person and I can't let you end your journey before it's begun." He puts his hand on my shoulder as he stands up.

"When I saw you running through the woods, I could hear you dreaming. It was different. You knew it was a dream, but you knew it was something more too. I heard the seeker's mind as well and it was so bizarre to see you both together. He was so linear, following one path without any other thoughts. You had branches of thoughts going all at once. Perhaps this is all my fault. I tried to reach you in that dream, I tried to explain. Then I wanted to meet you and your family to be sure that I was doing the right thing."

"You were the voice .... You spoke to me in the tree?" I ask, confused. Why would he do that? He's trying to take me away from my family, but he wanted to meet them? To meet me?

Landon runs his hand through his hair and smirks. "Yea, that was me alright. I figured if I tried to tell you that there was no threat you'd understand." He clears his throat and looks up at the sky, "I haven't been in this forest for so long. I can't remember the last time I just sat here ...."

I follow his gaze. The sky and the moons are so different than ours, but they're still familiar. They're almost like home. But it's not home, this isn't anywhere near my home. It doesn't matter.

"So what do we do now?" I ask.

"We take a plunge together in that pool. You'll wake up and go home to spend the morning with your parents. I'll come along before noon and then we leave." Landon pats my head and I look up at him, a few tears in his eyes. "I truly am sorry about this young master smith. If I can, I'll try and bring us around here again as soon as the opportunity arises. Deal?" He works a smile onto his face and wipes his tears quickly.

When we leave, I'll never see my parents again. He just wants me to agree, but why does he care? He could be pretending, but what if he isn't? I don't understand it. We just met, moons above, was it only yesterday? It feels like this day has been ten days. I hate him. I'll always hate him. Maybe not always. I don't know. But if even half of what he's saying is true, then he's really trying to help me.

I turn around, walk toward the pool and step in.

Chapter Ten

I wake up on the rock and grab my bow. I just want to see my parents. They were the best parents that I could have ever hoped for. I care about them more than anything, and I know they feel the same way. I could never just run and leave them. I might survive but they'd be hurt or killed. I can see them smiling even now. They smiled so much that I can hardly remember a time when they weren't. They are in love and that made everything so much better. I have to stop thinking of them as if they're gone already…

A gust of wind blows. My face is chilled where tears have fallen. They're always thinking of me and Zaitah, wanting the best for us. They worked so hard for us and we had more than we could have asked for. My parents would never leave me, but now I have to leave them.

Home …. I wish time could stand still. I open the door and find my parents sleeping right where I left them. I could wake them up, I could tell them everything and hold them and have them hold me. I want to cry with them, think of happy memories with them, spend our last morning just remembering our great life. But I shouldn't. I can't have them feel this way.

It's better if they spend the morning happy. Landon will come and we can tell them everything. Maybe he can make this a good thing, a happy memory. I want all their memories of me to be good ones. He can make it so they are happy forever, right?

I sit in the chair near them, quietly crying. I don't want to sleep. I have the rest of my life to sleep, but only this morning to spend with them. I rub my eyes and head outside. The rustling of the animals comes from the side room. I can do my chores early. When they wake up, we can spend the morning together without a care. I finish feeding the goats and grab Clout. I lead him over to our spot. This will probably be the last time that I brush you.

"Hey buddy, how'd you sleep?" I ask. My voice sounds so strange. My throat hurts so much. I grab the brush and sit down. Clout nuzzles my face and licks my cheek. "Yea, I didn't sleep so great …." I start shaking. "I think this is going to be the last time I get to brush you." I start crying and put my arms around Clout's neck. I don't want to lose you.

I jump on his back and he takes off. We race through the fields. The moons are still out, buddy. It's not even morning yet, but we've ridden these paths before haven't we? I know you'll take care of us, you always have. I hold onto him with both arms as we ride and I cry harder.

I'm never going to see you again…. You're my best friend. I should have taken better care of you. You deserved everything. I could always count on you to listen. You were always there ever since I was a kid. I remember when we first rode together, I fell off, and you came to help me up. When I was sad we'd always run. When everyone else was busy, I knew you'd be there. When I couldn't think, brushing you always cleared my mind. You never wanted anything and you gave me so much. I love you. I wish I could tell you. You understand me though. You've always been able to.

Clout starts running faster. I don't want you to be sad, buddy, I'm sorry. You always run faster when I'm upset. It's like you crying with me, like us crying together and I'll always love you for that. I wipe my eyes and pet his side. "Don't worry. I'll make sure Landon gives you the best memories."

My throat is so sore and my face is wet and sticky from the dried tears. "You must be spent. We rode hard there." He's sweating so I hop off and we start walking home. "It looks like you had already turned around, I can always count on you," I say petting him.

I don't want to let you go just yet, so I'm going to keep my hand right here.

We make it back home and head straight for the forge.

"You need a good brushing more than ever now, don't you, big guy?" I ask as I sit down. A stirring comes from inside the house. Well, they must be awake now. The sky begins to lighten. The sun will be dawning soon. "It's going to be a beautiful day.... I suppose we at least have that."

Father opens the door and calls out to me with a wide smile, "Good morning, lad!"

He yawns with a stretch. As he walks up to me he tosses my hair.

"What's planned for today, boyo? Should we work on that sword? Do a bit of hunting? Just take it easy?" he asks while he gets the forge fire started.

Soon I'll be gone. A few short moments is all I have left with my family. I have to stop thinking like that. I've just got to be happy for them. I catch Father staring at me.

"You alright lad? Yesterday was tough on all of us, but I think Zaitah is gonna fix it. He's going to make sure you get better." Father pulls a seat next to me and pats my back as his eyes move toward the woods.

The last thing I want is Mum and Dad thinking about yesterday. "I wasn't thinking of any of that. Zaitah has it all handled. This dream business will get fixed with no more worries. I was just thinking of how hungry I am."

I muster up a smile.

"Oh aye lad, me too. And I think your mother saved an apple pie from the other night! Go get that on the fire. It'll make a nice, tasty breakfast!" Father says rubbing his stomach.

Well, I suppose we deserve it and an apple pie does sound like one of the best breakfasts you could have. I stand up and start running inside but stop short and wrap my arms around him.

"What's all this then?" he asks with quiet laugh.

I hide my face and call out as I run inside, "I'm just excited about pie!"

I sneak through the door; Mother is still sleeping. I quietly get the fire going and set the pie on the hearth. It'll be a bit before it gets warmed through. I should grab a few biscuits for me and

Father. And a carrot for Clout, and an apple for him. Maybe two apples. I should give him the whole bag of apples.

"Sun and the moons, lad. I can smell that pie all the way out here! I'm hungry enough to eat Clout and not think twice!"

Clout's head raises at his name and he walks over to us. I toss a biscuit over to Father. "I grabbed us something to hold us over. I figured if you are half as hungry as I am, you'll be needing it."

"Thanks, lad." Clout pushes up against Father with his forehead. "Look at him, a brain the size of a chickens. I said I was gonna 'eat you,' ya stupid animal."

Father jostles Clout's middle. Clout turns to walk away and lets out a long burst of gas, kicking the dirt back with his hind legs before prancing into the field.

I erupt into laughter. "What in the world was that?" I drop my biscuit and grab my knees.

Father is trying to get away from the smell but trips over a hammer and loses his biscuit in the dirt. "Oompf! The stink is on me! Save yourself, lad, save yourself and the biscuits!"

We both laugh harder.

I catch my breath and help Father to his feet. "Well, I suppose you deserved that one for calling Clout a 'stupid animal,'" I say as I reach down and dust off our biscuits.

"No one deserves that, especially this early," Father mumbles as he cleans himself off. "Ah, we were a bit loud there. I hope we didn't wake your mother."

"Orion, what are you doing up this early?" Mother says as she stumbles drowsily through the doorway. "No good happens before the sun rises." Her eyes open wide as she sees me. "And my son, too? Cael, you should know better. I expect these things from that brute of a man, but not you."

"Oh Malaena, I'm sorry. Go back to bed, darling. We were just gettin' an early start. I'll make certain that son of yours keeps the noise down."

I snort but there's biscuit in my mouth and I start a coughing fit.

Father slaps my back. "Keep it down boy! Can't ya see your mother is trying to get back to sleep?"

A big grin spreads across his face and I slap the biscuit out of his hand. We both start laughing hysterically and Mother joins in.

As we catch our breath, I walk over and throw my arms around her. "I'm sorry we woke you, Mum!"

Father bumbles over and grabs us both in a big hug. "I'm not that sorry ta be honest."

"Is that my apple pie I smell?" Mother asks sternly. "You shouldn't be eating sweets first thing." She wags her finger at us.

"Oh, it's not that bad dear; we could all use a nice tasty, sweet, delicious, well-made apple pie!" Father says as he grabs her finger and her waist. "I can taste it already!"

He swings her around.

"Let me go, you bear! How are you always so full of energy? It's too early!" Mother brushes herself off with a quick smile. "We can have pie but only a bit! I'll make some porridge to go with it."

She turns to walk inside and Father and I kiss her cheeks and head toward the forge.

"Ah, that woman is good to us, boy. A bit too good," he says as he rubs his protruding stomach.

I mimic him and stick my gut out too and he jabs his solid finger right in my stomach. "Ow!" I yell out in protest.

He ruffs my hair and says, "Oh I didn't get you that hard, don't go chirping around like a little bird!"

I push his stomach in but he barely moves and says, "Careful lad, I might have a bit of gas myself. Don't go shaking things up or you'll be in for it."

"Alright, alright!" I plead. "You win this round, old man. But call me a little bird again and I'll get you."

He grabs my shoulder, "Deal…. Little bird!"

He shoves me to the side and jumps away in a half crouching stance.

I steady myself, "You're gonna get it now, fatty!"

He stands up straight. "Hey now boy that's not very nice." He looks at his stomach and rubs it again, "I'm not fat … ooof!"

I catch him off guard and charge his midsection. He stumbles back but before falling grabs my shoulders and pulls himself forward while swinging me around, regaining his balance while I'm thrown to the side.

"You've got to be more cunning than that to get this big bear down … little bird!" he says doing an impression of a bear.

"That's not fair. You're huge!" I pout and walk towards the east and he follows. As I crest the hill the sun's beams hit me.

I turn around and wave to Father. "I'm not done yet!"

He charges me. "Oh you will be!"

That's right old, man, just a bit closer; you're gonna get it! As he passes over the hill, the light blinds him for a moment and he covers his eyes. I close the distance and get behind him kicking his knees.

He falls over and laughs. "Cheater! You cheated ya dirty… cheater!"

I join along with him. "Nu uh, I didn't cheat. I used my abundance of cunning and speed to win!"

I bow. He starts to get to his feet but pulls me down with him.

"Ok lad, you win, you win." He rubs his knees. "I really am getting old. That tumble there did work on my knees."

I get up too and follow him towards the house.

"Mmm, smell that, boy? That pie must be nice and warm now!"

We grin at each other and hurry inside.

"Yes yes, the pie is ready and so is the porridge. Eat a bowl before you start on the sweets. Last thing I need is two children running around all crazy on sugar," Mother says sternly, but her eyes are laughing.

We quickly eat the porridge.

"Looks like we're not the only ones who are craving that pie," I say to Mother as she eats her porridge just as fast as we do. I look back and forth between Mother and Father as the pie is placed in front of us and smile. We devour our slices and go for seconds.

I could sleep right now. So full on sweet pie and warm from that fire, it's a perfect morning to be lazy.

"You're lucky, Cael. The first time I had apple pie it was just apples 'nd barley wheat crust. No cinnamon, no sugar. Nothing like the masterpieces that your mother makes," he says putting his hand on Mother's. The room goes quiet as we sit.

After a long moment, Father continues, "We weren't wealthy, but your grandparents did their best even though times were rough back then. We really are a lucky lot. If it weren't for your grandpappy I wouldn't be known around here at all. That fella came up from Waylinn with just a handful of ellings and a horse. Built a name for his own self and me while he was at it."

"I didn't ever get to meet either of your parents, tell me more about them," I ask with my eyes closed. It's so peaceful and warm, a story would be great.

"Oh well, your grandparents on my side met you when you were a babe, but they passed away 'fore you could walk. They were good folk, real good. Raised us right," Father says lazily.

Mother chimes in, "Orion's parents were very welcoming to me, such sweet people."

"What about your parents? Did I ever meet them when I was a baby?" I ask

"Hmm? Oh well, no they never did get to meet you. Actually, I don't remember my parents at all sweetheart. I was an orphan growing up," Mother says easily.

"Really? I never knew that. Does Zaitah know? What was it like?" I ask quickly.

"Haha, it's quite alright Little Cub. That was a world away, so long ago I can hardly remember. There were tough times, but I learned so much from a few friendly people and many more books. I got to work for a professor at one of the Universities in South Liefland. He was similar to a father I suppose, helped me get an education and taught me most of what I know about medicine."

"No Mother. Boy, that's why she can't cook!" He laughs and Mother swats at him.

"I cook just fine!" She retorts.

"It's true dear, the pie is wonderful." He kisses her forehead, "Everything else is a whole other story.... What was even in that porridge? I coulda sworn I ate a piece of actual wood!"

Mother gasps. "There was not!" She swats at him again, "You ungrateful beast." She pretends to be mad and turns her chair from him.

"I was joking, dear! Forgive me?" Father pleads as I throw another log on the fire.

We settle back down and I watch as Mother lays her head on Father's shoulder and he puts his arm around her.

"How did you two meet? I don't think I've ever heard that story." I rest my head on the chair and watch them lazily.

"Look at our wonderful son taking an interest in his parents, Orion. I think we might have done something right." She smiles at me. "You can tell the story dear. I'll listen while you spin stories of my beauty and perfection. How you were enamored with me from the moment you laid eyes on me."

Father chokes on a laugh. "Oh aye, that's exactly it. Beauty and perfection, swooning and enamoring or what not and ta da! In love!"

Mother jabs him in the ribs. "Oh go on tell the story then!"

Father looks pained for a moment but continues with a smirk, "Your mother had just made it to Rensfort and I was down with your grandpappy doing a bit of business, takin' orders, getting supplies, all the regular hubbub. Back then we worked almost exclusively fer the King 'nd his guard, and boy lemme tell ya, we had our hands full. Your old man wasn't always so perfect and confident with smithing, took a lot of work and practice. I was always a hit with the ladies though!" He lets out a hearty laugh and Mother glares up at him and gives another poke of her finger.

"Oh, come now, Malaena. You're the only woman for me." He leans over and kisses her head before continuing. "Well, after doing somethin, I can't recall, maybe haggling over supplies or an order, it don't matter." He waves his hand. "What matters is I look up, and even through a hundred people, I see this woman. She was following after an older man and barely able to keep up with books in her hands 'nd a big ol' bag on her shoulder. She was dirty, looked exhausted, really run through the woods."

Mother sits up with a shocked face and gasps. "You're horrid! I wasn't nearly that bad."

"Oh, it made no difference to me, Malaena." He continues seriously, "I saw her through the crowd and for a moment she saw me, but only a moment. It wasn't a faerie tale where the world stops and we get married right then and there. But something real hit me; my mind was on her for weeks until we came back down to the city. I snuck away from your grandad and went to the first bookstore, and lightning strike me if I wasn't the luckiest man alive to run right into her. Weeks of thinking about her and she was right in front of me." He turns to Mother who's smiling wide and they kiss.

"Well? What happened then?" I ask.

"What do ya mean? Your mother swooned and we fell in love of course!" He jokes and Mother smiles up at him.

"Well, it wasn't that easy, but a few months of him tracking me down and I did end up swooning. He was so annoyingly good at finding me, and he never missed a chance to tell me how it was the first place he looked every time."

"How well I knew you even then, eh?" He whispers to her. They snuggle close and talk quietly.

"I do believe I'll go for a walk," I say loud enough to wake them.

They giggle and Father says, "Oh none of that now, boy. We were just having a bit of fun."

Just then the animals start making noise followed by a knock at our door.

Chapter Eleven

It was the perfect morning; all I could have asked for and more. I open the door slowly, knowing it's Landon. My parents immediately rush in front of me as soon as they realize who it is. They force me behind them protectively.

"We don't want no trouble. We're grateful for yer help with that other fella, but we just want to be let alone. If it's money you're after, I can pay. Else I don't know what it is ya want with us, but we just want ta be let in peace." Father says putting his hand up near Landon's chest.

"Orion, Malaena, please sit down." He reaches out to touch them but Mother pulls Father away.

"No! I know what you're up to. You will not use your dark magic in my house! You're as evil as Vashir's wolves! Leave this instant or we'll do something everyone will regret." Mother is shaking and Father puts her behind him.

I step forward in-between Landon and my parents and reach out for them. "Please, listen to what he has to say."

"He's done something to you, hasn't he?" Mother cries and they pull me towards them.

"I have to leave with him!" I shout, unable to wait for Landon to explain. He rests his hand on my arm. "I have to go." I say again quietly. "There are people who are going to take me. If I don't go then they might do something bad. I don't want anyone to get hurt so... I just have to go with him."

"Well, that's what we decided, right?" Father says, confused, "This young woodsman should be able to teach you more'n those stuffy professors at the university. He seems a decent enough fellow. We can trust him, can't we, Malaena? What do you think?" He says turning to Mother with an odd look on his face.

"I think that sounds like a good plan if Cael thinks so. I just want what's best for you Little Cub. . . and – " She reaches for her head, unsteady on her feet. "I don't feel that well," Mother says quickly.

Landon's face is filled with confusion.

"What's happening? Did you do something to them?" I ask anxiously.

Landon walks past me and places hands on both Mother and Father.

"What are you doing now?" I ask stepping forward. Is he working his magic? Does he even have magic? Maybe Landon was lying about those men in the woods. Maybe no one is searching for me .... Maybe Landon is a slaver? Maybe he's trying to steal kids? I fell for it like an idiot!

"Calm down for the love of all that's good, boy! You don't know this yet but it's hard as iron to even connect to someone's thoughts through a conduit, much less alter them. I'd like to see you try it," he mumbles angrily and runs his hand through his hair. "It should be fine now, lad. I'm sorry I lost it for a moment. I'm not used to this stuff. It's not my job." He turns away almost embarrassed, "And ... I don't want you thinking this is all fake, or that I'm bad with this 'magic' stuff." He half smiles and shrugs. "Go ahead give it another go."

Just like that and it'll work? This is ridiculous.

"What do you both think of me leaving with Landon? Going on a trip from here to Oarna, maybe further?" I ask again.

"You don't need to ask, sweetheart. We already agreed! I think Landon has your best interests at heart. And I truly believe he can cure these dreams." Mother says happily.

Father chimes in, "That's right; he's a good young man and you need the education, especially for smithing! You butchered that last blade."

"What's wrong with the blade?" I ask indignantly. This magic ruined his memory or something. I'd never make a mistake on something simple like forging a blade.

"Well lad, for the past month or so, loads of the work you've let through's been a little shoddy. I'd fixed most of em, I guessed a lot of it was your dreams making you tired n' such."

Father goes outside and comes back with the last sword I worked on. "Take this blade and tell me what's wrong with it, lad."

I take the blade in my hand. "The edges are slightly round rather than beveled." I bend the blade slightly and frown. "It's been tempered at the wrong temperature, and this tang is too wide."

I know junk when I see it, and I can't believe I'm the one who made this. I hand the blade back and look away ashamed.

Father takes the blade and presses his thumb in the center while he itches his beard, "You're thorough. I hadn't noticed the softness of the blade. You just need to be a bit more thorough while working …. So that settles it then, right? You'll be heading off with Landon?" he asks.

"When will you be leaving?" Mother asks sadly.

"Actually Miss Malaena, we need to be leaving sooner than I'd like. We've got to make it down to the city so I can arrange for a ship to take us north. The earlier we get to the city the better luck we'll have getting passage out," Landon says.

"Wait, that's it? Everyone is fine with us just leaving right now?" This is all happening so different than I thought. What was I thinking? Maybe I wanted it to be short or easy. I definitely didn't want there to be any anger or confusion …. But, whatever this is … It's like they don't even care that I'm leaving…. I know it's Landon making them feel that way, but it's wrong, it's not what I wanted. No sadness at all?

"It's this or tears, Cael. It's much better this way for everyone, trust me. Besides we're about to go on an amazing adventure!" Landon says excitedly.

"Great adventures always start like this do they?" How can he think this will be fun for me? I don't even have a choice.

He grabs my shoulder

I immediately pull away. "Don't try and take this away from me too! They can't feel this but I can. This is my goodbye, and I won't have you screwing with my head now or ever!"

Father and Mother step in between us.

"What's wrong lad? You don't have to go with him; we just thought it was what you wanted," Father says concerned.

Landon waves his hands. "Please, Cael. You misunderstand, I wasn't going to … It doesn't matter. There's a philosophy I live my life by. When a decision is made, even a bad one, we just have to accept it and move on. There's no good that can come from dwelling on things that can't be changed. This is something that can't be changed, and it might end up being half decent. We just need to take that first step."

"This isn't something that should be rushed! I hate that they can't feel what I'm feeling! I need … something. Why is this all so hard?" I turn towards my parents seeing confusion on their faces.

"Why are you both talking like we aren't here right now? Why . . . am I so tired? I remember something … something about your dreams," Mother says and shakes her head.

"I'm getting dizzy. Malaena are you… alright?" Father asks as he sits down.

"I didn't think I wanted it to be like this … but I want you to always know the truth. I can't lie to you the last time we see each other," I say watching them come out of their daze. "Landon, give us a moment please …. I need this."

He hesitates before nodding and walking out the door. I sit down at the table and motion them to sit too. "These dreams … they weren't just dreams. Do you both remember yesterday?"

They rub their heads slowly and Mother says, "It's almost like yesterday was weeks ago, but I remember… vaguely." She puts her hand on her head. "What's happened to us, Cael?"

"I thought it would be easier to give you happy memories. To have you both want this. I was wrong and I'm sorry. The truth will be better for all of us." I take a deep breath, "These dreams are real and it means I was born with some 'gift.' At least that's what Landon calls it. I can be taught to hear thoughts, and I suppose change them at some point too." I recall the dream. "And maybe even change stone to water, but none of that is important."

Father scratches his head and Mother opens her mouth to speak but I stop her, "Please let me finish. I need you both to understand. People have been looking for me. These dreams… Maybe because of these dreams they found me or maybe they started searching and I had the dreams. They're called seekers. They find people with this gift. I don't know the whole story either but they found me, and because they found me they have to take me away."

"Take you away where?" Father asks. "When will you return?"

Tears start falling from my face. "I might never return. But I swear I'll try. I'll try and find any way to come back to see you again."

Mother starts to cry. "Why? Why do they have to take you? Just refuse to go!"

Father puts his arm around her. "Lad, is there anything we can do?"

I shake my head, dropping it in my hands. As I open my eyes, I notice the old floorboards . The same floor I walked on for my whole life. "No. If I don't go with Landon, the seekers will kill me. They might kill you, too. If they don't, they'd just find a way to alter your memories of me .... I guess they'd make a memory of me dying from something like a sickness."

"What if we kill them?" Father says, his voice shaking.

"I thought of that already. But they have to know where their seekers are. Even if they don't, I'm sure they'll find me again. I can't control my thoughts. I wouldn't even be able to use this thing to listen for them. We'd be like turkeys in roost. You saw what they could do. They did real magic. We can't fight against that."

"So that's it .... No way out?" Mother asks through her tears.

All of us crying isn't what I wanted, but it's better somehow. I put my arms around them and we hold each other.

After a time, I pull back. "Landon... as much as I hate him, seems to want to help me. It might all be some sick game, but for how much I shouldn't trust him I sort of still do. He's letting me do this my way, and I don't think many people get this chance." I wipe my mother's tears away and kiss them both.

"This isn't my decision, and I'm going to fight to come back to you. But I need to know you're both going to be alright. We can pretend I'm at University studying, just at a university far away." I finish and we sit silently for a moment.

"I don't suppose you can tell us where you'll be going, can you?" Mother asks.

"Honestly Mum, I don't know where I'm off to yet. I don't think Landon would tell me even if I asked," I reply.

"Why all this secrecy? Why can't ya just go study with these witches or wizards or what have you, and then come back home ta us? Or for Finra's sake at least let us visit you?" Father asks.

"Anything we can think of now I've already tried thinking of. I want to stay here more than I can say, you have to believe that." I sigh. "Landon says something about this magic needing to stay secret because of what people will do to us. We're different and stuff, which makes people hate us? It's all stupid to me, but he says that we're stronger than other people, which makes them fear us. The people who are taking me say they're worried that kids like me will get hurt if other people found out. I think that's the gist of it."

I shrug my shoulders and Mother and Father both nod.

"If it's true, lad, then it does make a bit of sense. It don't make it easier, but it makes sense. If ya have even half the power that ya said, even to hear thoughts … if someone found that out they'd surely want to use ya for themselves or kill ya for fear of it," Father says.

Mother adds, "Alright, Little Cub. What's written is done. Either we live with fear or we live with hope. Hope that we'll see you again, soon. If it makes it easier for you, we can do that. Your father and I can live with hope, can't we Orion?" Mother kisses Father on his wet cheek and they nod to each other.

"Aye, if it makes it easier for you lad, we can do that. We can't be happy with this, but we can hope to see ya soon. I'll just find my peace with it."

I tear up again. They'd do anything for me, and I swear I'll do anything to find a way back here someday. I won't stop trying to come home. I'll do everything these people want so that I can come home again.

They wrap their arms around me and we hug. After too short a time, Landon knocks on the door. I look around the room taking it all in one last time and finally back at my parents.

"I believe a suitor is at the door for you sweet princess," Father says with a sad smile.

I cough out a quick cry laugh as the tears roll down my cheeks.

This isn't how I wanted our goodbyes to go.

But it feels better this way.

Chapter Twelve

They squeeze me tightly again and hand me the travel sack that Mother packed. I'm sad. We're all sad, but there's something there with the sadness. Hope, I guess. I'll choose to believe it's hope or maybe … acceptance?

I step outside and Father and Mother hug me again.

"We will always love you, and we'll wait for you right here to come home." Mother says.

Father nods. "Try 'nd write if ya can, son. Anything ya can do, it'll help."

"I'll do everything I can; I promise," I say and turn to Landon. He's motioning for us to get moving. It's going to be a long journey.

My parent's reach their arms around me, squeezing again. And then, suddenly they aren't. I follow Landon down the road. I glance back and Mum is crying in Dad's arms as he holds tightly. The sound of pounding hooves catches my ear and I turn to see Clout chasing after us.

"I'm so sorry, bud! I never would have left without saying goodbye!" I wrestle with Clout for a moment and kiss his head before turning to Landon. "Can you … give him a good memory of today? I want him to be happy forever."

Landon face goes from confused to sad. "I … I'm sorry Cael, I can't do that with animals …. There are people who can but I'm not nearly skilled enough. I can't even communicate with them. I wish I could. I would give a hundred gold stater right now to help you say goodbye to Clout. I can feel how much he means to you. But I can't, and I'm sorry for that." He turns toward the road and waits.

I hug Clout close, "I don't want to cry again, buddy. I hate leaving you like this. I wish we could pretend that I'll be home real soon. We'll be riding through these woods again and never having to think about anything else. We've already had our sad goodbyes. We don't have to be sad now. We can be happy and look forward to seeing each other again. I'll be alright, and you will be too. You've always been stronger than I am. I'm counting on you to take care of Mum and Dad, and they'll take good care of you too. I think they need it more than we do right now, though." I hug him again. "I … have to go now, buddy. I'll miss you every day. I'll make sure to come home as soon as I can."

I wave goodbye to them all one last time and we continue down the road to Rensfort. We pass over the hill and I lose sight of them. That's the last time we'll be together for years, but it's not forever. I'll figure a way to get back to them as soon as possible. Landon is out in the world doing things, working for these people. I bet if I just get a job like him I can come home and visit. He's only a few years older. It really will be like university if I can just do what he does. What does he do anyway? Politician? Envoy for these 'magic' people? Assassin …?

"… city and we'll get something to eat. Are you hungry? Probably not, eh? You just had that pie. I could smell it all the way in the woods," Landon says.

"I don't want to talk right now, please," I say cutting him off.

An assassin would be an odd job. Could I even do that? Just get a piece of paper. 'Go kill this person,' I bet it says. And you just go kill him. Or her…? I wonder if assassins ever kill women. That would be hard to do. Harder than this though? Nothing could be harder than leaving your family behind.

"There's a few things that would be harder I imagine. Why are you thinking about assassins anyway?" Landon asks nonchalantly.

"Stop listening to my thoughts ….Wait, you can hear my thoughts now but not before?" I ask.

"What? When before?" He asks confused. "… Oh! It's very difficult to listen to thoughts and speak at the same time. I can't manage it at all actually. If you speak out loud, your mind automatically starts saying what your mouth is speaking. You'd need to be able to listen to yourself and to someone else with full understanding. It needs to be quiet in your mind to listen. Well, that's how it works for me at any rate."

I nod and we continue walking.

I wonder what my parents are doing right now. How are they going to deal with all this? Moons above! Zaitah! He's on the road south and won't be back for a few days .... I won't get to say goodbye to him. I might see him before I see Mum or Dad. He'll end up traveling a lot. If he keeps studying medicine he could go anywhere really. What does he even want to do with medicine though? I never asked him. I assumed he'd stay in the city or in one of the small villages like ours. He could travel all over. Will I study medicine? Landon said something like that. Will I study the same books or will I get secret books? Would be nice to rub it in Zaitah's face that I learned more about medicine than him. If I ever do see him again . . .

"…my thoughts before, telepathy is what we call it unofficially. The instructors will tell you all the scientific names they give these things."

I cut him off again. "For the love of Finra please shut your damn mouth, man! I don't care about any of this stuff right now. I'll probably never care about it. Just take me to this island place and leave me be," I say, shoving past him.

He's so frustrating. Why is he pretending like we're on a friendly little adventure together? My life isn't even my own. I hate that I don't have a choice, I hate everything about this!

"Don't you see, Cael? I'm talking so I can give you privacy. I can't turn this off. I can't stop listening to your thoughts. I don't have the time to teach you how to think silently right now. Maybe while we travel but right now we have to get to the city and get passage out of here. This situation is awful. I understand! I'm doing the best I can to make this easier for you. You still don't get it, do you? You're so lucky! Most kids with your gifts get dragged along kicking and screaming. Some have their whole families destroyed. Others don't even have a clue what's happening at all. You are acting so spoiled right now! Just suck it up!"

I glare at him and he turns away.

Try and listen on me? I'll just annoy the ever-loving tree out of you! Dirt! Trees! Birds! Ants! Dust! Grass! Rocks! Swords! Dumb idiots that steal kids from their families! Stupid face! Horrible clothes! Smelly butt! I'll just scream out everything I see in my head, forever!

Half the day passes before Landon speaks up. "You're something else. Do you want me to talk about things so you can think to yourself? I can't take another moment of listening to you scream out as if you've cracked."

I glare at him irritated. "Well, go on then. Start rambling!"

"Let me tell you, boy. I'm letting all this go for now because of what you're going through. But if you act like this all the way to the island, you might not even make it there," Landon says coldly.

Threats now?

I open my mouth but he cuts me off with a wave of his hand and says, "Enough. I'm not going to let a fight start here."

We glare at each other for a moment and he sighs. "Cael, do you understand why I wanted to help you?"

We stop walking and I yell, "Help me? I'm being torn from my life! Didn't you see my parents crying?"

I start shaking.

"I know you can't accept it now, but for as horrible as you think we are, there are others who would do much worse. I didn't think all this through, I had a fanciful vision of how this would go in my head. I thought I would come get you. You'd be like a fun little brother that I'd get to teach stuff to and we can go on this incredible journey and you'll see just how brilliant having these gifts can be." He reaches out and grabs my shoulder. "I didn't really get to spend too much time with my family even before I was taken. You think a lot like I do or a lot like I *did* before I was trained. We don't look too different, barring the fact that I'm much more handsome of course," he says jostling my shoulder.

I calm down. "Why, though? I just don't understand. Why do you want to help me? Why would you want to teach me things? Why would you want a brother? Zaitah and I fight all the time." I ask confused.

"Like I've said, you kinda remind me of me. I wish now that someone was there for me back then. I was angry like you. Maybe not just like you because my family wasn't as loving as yours. I resented everyone for a long time, my family, the seekers, the praetors, these dreams... myself." He gets quiet for a moment as he gazes off down the road.

"But one day at the academy during one of our courses, I looked around while the instructor was lecturing us. I saw a dozen kids all my age, all who had been ripped from families and loved ones, all who were in the exact same position as me. We had a unique experience and a unique gift that we shared. I realized that as horrible as being torn from your life is, I was given a new life with people who could understand me. A life where anything is possible. If you want to be a politician, an emissary to kings, a warrior, a scientist! Anything you can think of the academy helps you achieve those goals!" He grows excited and is nearly shouting at the end.

He settles himself and continues, "I envy you for your family. And what I said is true, I'll do whatever I can to get you back to them. But you have no idea how many opportunities will be given to you, how many doors will open simply by having the gifts you have!"

Maybe he's right? I'll absolutely work my ass off to get back to my parents, take any job this academy throws at me if it means I can see them. But does that mean I can't take advantage of this? Am I horrible for thinking that way? I can do whatever I want? I never really thought about anything besides smithing. It was the easiest thing and I love my father. I guess I really just wanted to always spend time with him. Other things . . . Would I have gone to school? I'd rarely see them if I had. Is this really so different? Could this actually not be awful? Education, training, knowledge, adventure ... family is a hard price to pay, but if it's only temporary...? Even Zaitah is paying that price at a standard university. He won't have gifts. We only see him once a year if that. Even if this isn't the way it'll be, I could pretend. I could accept it like Landon said and just pretend that it won't be the worst thing.

I spot Landon smiling. "Dammit man! You're in my head again, aren't you?" I say rebuking him.

He looks away.

"I suppose there's no harm in trying to make the best out of this whole thing. It's not like I have any choice really," I say.

"I knew it!" he says picking me up and swinging me around. "This won't be awful, I promise!"

I almost let myself smile. "Put me down man! Let's just get on with it then, shall we?"

"Isn't this exciting?" Landon blurts out. He must be younger than I imagined. Maybe he's closer to Zaitah's age than I thought?

"Alright, it's not that big a deal," I say calming him.

We turn towards the road and watch the city start to form on the horizon. Landon notices the sky and his eyes go wide. "Finra's beard! I have to go find us a ship north. Come on, Cael! We have to hurry, it's already past noon!"

We start running but I reach out and grab him. "Wait, where are we going? Where even is this island? How far is it?"

I wonder if it's somewhere warm, I've never really been somewhere that's warm all year round. I'd probably miss the snow and winter. Winter's already left us this year so it's not so bad.

"Our journey is a bit longer than it should be. I have to head north to North Liefland, stop in on the king there and then we travel to the east coast as fast as possible. We'll need to make good time crossing Liefland because then we'll have to hop another ship to the northwest tip of Oarna. We'll likely meet up with a few members of the academy, the fourth years are always in Oarna doing things. After that we're only a few days of sailing out from the island. It's going to take a few months. We're very far away. But you'll get to see almost the entire continent. We won't make it to Waylinn or South Liefland, but we'll be seeing kingdoms that you've only read about, some provinces that you likely haven't even heard about, too." As he finishes, we pick up the pace and hurry into town.

I hate myself. I'm actually getting excited for this; I shouldn't be like this. Is he making it so I'm happier? I don't think he'd do that after everything we've already gone through. Landon really is trying to make this easy for me. I can't believe I'll be going to Oarna! The coast is supposed to look like another world. A day ago I was living my life in a village too small to even name. Now I'm on a journey that will span the whole world, pretty much. I'll see things that no one in my family has ever seen, and I'll definitely have more opportunities to do things. I wonder if they teach smithing. If I could learn new tricks to teach Dad, he'd be over the moons with joy!

"Cael, I've got to head over to the docks real quick. Why don't you grab some traveling food fit for a long journey like hardy fruits, salted meats, cheeses and breads." He tosses me a bag of money filled with all types of currency.

I notice a few gold stater and silver marks as I dig through it. There must be enough money here to pay for a year's worth of smithing. I could buy a house and fill it halfway up with turkey and wine!

"Just the food is fine." Landon says with a grin.

I scowl at him. "You're going to teach me how to block my thoughts as soon as we get on that boat."

He grins. "Agreed. But you have to promise to be pleasant all the way through. I know it'll be difficult, but you have to promise to at least try. Deal?" He extends his hand.

I grasp it. "Deal!"

"Oh! Grab some ink, paper and reed or feather pens. I'll get you started on your lessons while we travel. Although the instructors will more than likely throw a fit if you show up knowing anything …. Ah well, I'll deal with that later. Maybe don't get the pens…" He scratches his face, thinking before shrugging. "Meet by Fannie's in an hour?" he calls as he walks towards the docks.

I take in the city streets. Back here again in the hustle and bustle of Rensfort's market square, I could certainly get everything we need for two solid weeks of traveling. We can resupply in North Liefland. What to do first? I'm on my own so I can do as I please. I could probably just head home right now, grab my family, and we could run away with all this money. But then I'd be found easily or at least I would be until I learn to block my thoughts. If only I could learn to block my thoughts before we left.... No, I have to stop thinking like that. This probably won't be so bad either way. The hardest part is over, the goodbyes. I just need to focus on what's happening now.

That smells like freshly roasted chicken. I'm sure Landon won't mind if I buy myself some lunch. The road down here is long and tiring; I'm already spent after everything this morning. I didn't even sleep last night really. I deserve a good meal, a good hot delicious chicken with some perfectly cooked sweet carrots. And potatoes! Oh, a whole bucket of potatoes with butter. I bet they covered everything in salt too!

I turn the corner and a plume of aromatic smoke is rising from the roof of an inn. This is definitely where the food is! As I reach the door a hand grips my wrist. I'm dragged nearly off my feet down alleys. Is that the girl from before? That hair can't belong to anyone else. Why would she come back now?

She skids to a halt by a church. Always a church near these fountains.

"Do you know who you're with? That man is dangerous. He plans to take you! Your family could be in danger, too." She says anxiously.

"Who? Landon? Wait ... How do you?" I lower my voice. "Can you hear thoughts too?" I ask in awe. I've only just learned about this gift and now there are people everywhere that have it.

"We have to keep moving. They'll be able to track you. You can't hide yet. I'll show you how later, but right now we need to get as far away from that man as possible." She grabs my arm again and starts to pull me away.

"You can teach me? I could be safe?" I stop short. "No, I can't run. My family could be hurt." I pull my hand away from hers. "I'll be found. I don't have a choice. Don't you see? Why do you even care? You don't owe me anything for helping you. It's like Landon said, my decision has already been made; I have to go."

She stares at me, stunned. She's a runaway. They must be after her too. But she found a way to hide her thoughts. This might be my only chance to run away and be with my family. But we'd always have to be moving.

"How did you get away? Is your family safe? How are you hiding? Is it just your thoughts? But where's your family then? Are they with you?" I ask her quickly. She continues staring at me but begins moving slowly backward. "Wait don't run! I need to know!" I reach for her.

She turns away and takes a step to run but stops. She checks for anyone else before pushing us into the church. It's empty so we find a pew and she sits us down.

"How do you know all of this? The men who came for me, I didn't believe them. He..." She turns away ashamed. "They killed my family." Her eyes begin watering.

"I'm sorry," I say touching her shoulder.

"I wanted to get away, but I didn't want them to die like that. They weren't good people but no one deserves to die like that ...." She cries into her hands.

I sit next to her in silence. It's almost like the first time she's actually said that out loud. Maybe she never really thought about it. What would I do if I was responsible for them killing my family?

I don't know what to feel. Landon was right; they would have killed my family. They killed this girl's family without even a thought? How could they do this? What in the moons is going on? I didn't think they were evil! What if everything he told me is a lie? Landon told me they sometimes have to hurt people, but killing a whole family? This actually happened to her? Her family was killed? My parents could be gone just like this girl's.

"I... I'm... I'm so sorry. Landon told me there were other people looking for me, a different group. He says he's different. I suppose he's even different than the normal seekers that are sent to find people with our... gifts."

She's still crying so I keep talking. "If Landon hadn't told me I would have done the same thing as you. I would have either ran away or fought them all off with my family. My father even asked if we could kill them. I wish I could tell you more, but I still don't really know anything. Except that I'm being taken away to some academy thing on an island far away. If I don't go, I'll be putting my life and my family in danger." I put my arm around her and she continues crying, wrapping her arms around my neck.

I start to cry. I feel your sadness.... I can feel your grief, your loss. I feel it all. It's like losing my family. We sit and cry together. It's better together. It's like she's taking some of my sadness and maybe I'm taking a bit of hers.

As the tears begin to dry, we let go of each other and she speaks, "Thank you for saving me before. I don't even know your name."

"You don't have to thank me." I say, sliding over on the bench. "I was probably just in the way before. I mean I should be thanking you! You came back to try and help me just now, even after all of the things you've been through." I reach out my arm, "I'm Cael."

She hesitates. "I... I really hate telling people my name. I've been running for a while, and I really was just trying to help you because you helped me." She thinks for a moment. "Wynn. It's been a while since I've told anyone that name but I suppose you deserve to know it." She grasps my arm and gives a half smile.

"Thank you. It's nice to meet you, Wynn," I say.

We sit quietly for a moment longer. It's so weird; Together, it's almost like my sadness is melting away. She's helping me so much. I thought I'd accepted it all.

"Who is Landon?" she asks. "And why did he tell you everything? About all these people and what they do?"

"I'm not sure. I think he wanted to keep me from making a mistake. He wanted to keep me from running away or being taken by Beck," I say cautiously.

She stands up and quickly says, "I wish everyone was told the truth of it! Those people are evil!" She paces back and forth "Killing whoever they want, taking any kid unlucky enough to have . . . to have . . . What did you call it? A gift? To have a gift of what? A gift that imprisons us to some life of servitude?"

I reach for her hand and grab it. I gently pull her down and we sit again. After a moment I ask, "What will you do? How do you stay safe?"

She breathes a heavy sigh. "I just keep running. I learned quickly that there are two thoughts, spoken thoughts and hidden thoughts. It's tough to explain, but they can't hear your hidden thoughts. So, I stay hidden like my thoughts. I can't really hear them, but it feels different when they're near. That helps if they are really close. They never expect us to be able to do anything. I guess I can hear them sometimes, but only if they're talking to each other. Or not talking but whatever it is."

"So what are you going to do?" I ask again.

She shrugs. "I have to get out of the city. If there are seekers here then I won't be safe. Will you come with me or go with this new friend of yours?" she asks, anger creeping into her voice.

"I have to go, Wynn. If I don't ..." I drop my head.

"I know." She says rigidly.

So this is it? The one person who can understand what I'm going through and we're just going to go our separate ways? I want to go with her. Maybe I could help her. She's definitely more skilled in this stuff than I am so she can help me, too.

No, I can't go. It's never going to be that simple.

Without turning to me, she says, "Goodbye, Cael. Good luck on your journey."

As she walks away, I call out, "Wait!" I follow her out the door. "I know it's not great, but I think Landon could help us both. He can take us to this island academy place and we can learn how to use these skills. You've already done more than I have and I bet it'll be real simple for you to pick up the rest."

She stares at me icily for a long breath before speaking. "You ... you expect me to go with you ... to the people who stole the only dirty scrap of a life I had? I thought I had nothing before, but I had no idea! I can't stay anywhere, I hardly get food most days! It's all because these people are trying to hunt me down like an animal! Have you lost your entire mind? I'm fine on my own and I don't need your help! Those people destroyed everything. For no reason my life changed in an instant! I might never have even used these 'gifts'. But because they thought they could use me, they killed everyone near me and they've been tracking me for months!"

"I'm sorry .... I just, I wanted to help you. I thought maybe –"

She cuts me off. "No you didn't think and I don't need your help. Go follow your friend to this island and become another puppet just like him! You think you'll stay innocent? You think they won't have you killing some family next? You're agreeing to be a murderer!"

No No … I won't be just like them. I don't have to be a seeker. I could do anything. Landon said I can choose. She's just mad because she killed her family. I'm not a murderer. She's a murderer!

I scowl at her and she scowls back. Just as she turns, a voice comes from the side of the fountain. "Calm yourself, Cael. She has been hurt more than we know." Landon stands up and walks to us. How long has he been waiting there? Did he hear us?

"Hello, Wynn. I suppose Cael's told you about me?" He extends his hand and Wynn prepares to run. "You don't need to be frightened," he says quickly, "I won't be forcing you to come along with us. You're free to make your own choices. In fact, I've heard about you. You've been running for a long while. I imagine if you wanted to that you could continue running and hiding for the rest of your life." He puts his hand back down and sits on the bench outside the church. "Let's sit for a moment, shall we? I'd like to say a few words to you before we leave, Wynn."

He pats the bench on either side of him and I walk over to take my place. Wynn refuses to move so Landon shrugs and mutters to himself, "I cannot believe how unlucky I am to find two An'aith, and two such as yourselves …." He sighs heavily. "We don't have much time, Wynn. Cael and I will be leaving soon and if I don't miss my mark, it appears he hasn't done any of our shopping." Landon looks over at me down his nose. I turn away.

He rubs my hair and lets out a laugh. "Oh, I'm joking, lad. No need for all the seriousness." He turns to Wynn who remains silent and still like a deer in the woods. "Listen carefully, Wynn. You may not believe they are gifts, but you are more skilled than any recruit I've seen. You are free to make your own decisions. I probably couldn't force you to come with us if I tried. But, you're missing a crucial piece of this puzzle. You represent a very large problem for people like us, and even more so for the Sephalim rebels. We wish to operate silently, some would say in the shadows, but that feels very dark and ominous. What we do, it's a necessity if we plan to survive. Our numbers are small compared to those who don't dream, and still the power we wield is unimaginable to most. We would easily be branded as witches or a cult of demon worshippers. Because of our differences, we would be hunted and killed openly. Our destruction would so fervently inhabit the minds of men that all other differences would be set aside, all other wars would cease. The sole focus of all men would be on our annihilation. A genocide the likes this world has never seen would occur. It is without a doubt that some dreamless, either sympathetic to our cause or just plain unlucky would die along with us, and of course we would fight back."

"You can't know that ...." she whispers. "There are different races and we get along well enough."

Landon stays quiet for a moment, thinking. "It's a dangerous secret that we carry with us, my young friend. Think to yourself what you would do if someone knew a secret about you. A secret that could cause harm to you or your family. You wouldn't want someone with that kind of power over you, would you? But now imagine you're a king, or even the church. A secret that could destroy your empire or reduce your religion to nothing. What would you do to keep that secret hidden?" He continues, "Now imagine your friends, people that have been with you for years, decades, all share that single powerful secret. One that could change the entire world. A secret that would threaten the throne of all kings and the legitimacy of most religions. A secret that would separate the dreamless from the dreamers and cause most people to hate you simply for being alive. Imagine what you would do to keep that secret safe. And imagine how far you would go to chase a little girl who could threaten your very existence."

Wynn stares into her hands as Landon continues on, "You're at a crossroad, apprentice wanderer. On one path, you have something similar to freedom, life to live it your own way. Freedom to hate what's happened to you and to continue running from it. But you must always be moving. You must always be wary. You must always be silent. On the other path, you have acceptance of what's happened to you, acceptance of your place in this world. You'll have the knowledge that comes with training your gifts and the backing of an establishment that can make your life easier. You'll have at least one friend, but hopefully two, that will be with you every step of this journey. You'll have the freedom to stay in a place longer than a day or a week. You may not get everything you want, but you'll have more than what you need. You'll have freedom to choose your place. I promise you, it's worth it."

"Worth it? Truly you believe what your praetors are doing is worth it?" Beckett sneers as he walks towards us. "Lying to children, Landon? Trying to make them believe in faery tales? Your praetors do nothing but play at politics while the world burns! They broker pretend peace treaties in the name of some false 'greater good'."

Wynn's eyes open wide seeing his face. "You…. You were there. You murdered my family!" She cries out in rage and rushes to attack him.

He puts his hands up defensively, "Calm down, child." He grabs her hands to stop the blows. "I've been—"

"No more lies!" Landon yells, slamming his foot hard onto the stone street. He moves his hands expelling an intense heat through the air towards Beck.

Beck throws Wynn to the side and lunges into the heated blast towards Landon. A mist of water forms around him and he grips Landon's wrist and neck, lifting him into the air and slamming him down. As he hits the ground it melts around him and traps Becks hands.

Landon swims through the stone as if it were water and thrusts a chunk of street up into Becks face. Beck recoils back but steadies himself quickly. He breathes in and the air all around stills. Landon freezes, half in the stone and half above.

Wynn charges Beck again swinging wildly. His focus shifts to her and Landon struggles free. Beck reaches his arm out for her. Just as he touches her a dagger slices through his arm leaving a wide gash.

"Cael, take Wynn and run!" Landon orders, breathing heavily. He throws another dagger but it's deflected in midair and Beckett charges him again.

I rush over to Wynn, "Are you hurt?" I ask, bringing her to her feet and half dragging her away. I turn to watch the battle behind just as Beckett throws Landon into a wall. Landon catches himself in the stone wall and disappears on the other side of it. Beckett charges after him.

We run down a long alley and around another corner before Wynn brushes me aside, "I'm fine…." She mumbles.

"So that was magic…" I say slowly, turning to face back down the alley. "Should we go back and try and help Landon?" I ask, concerned. Beck looked a lot stronger than Landon, I don't know if he can hold his own.

"What?" Wynn asks incredulously. "Of course not. Why should help? So one of them can end up taking us? Whatever happens over there it just means less people for us to hide from." She says simply, brushing herself off.

"Are you coming or not? We have to go before they come after us again." She says, waiting with her hand out.

I reach for her but stop short, hesitating. "I… don't know what to do." I admit.

Landon collapses around the corner, face bloodied. "Wait… Don't leave" He gasps.

I rush to his side, and he laughs for a breath before coughing, "He's a little better than I expected. I was too confident." He turns to Wynn, "I'm sorry he hurt you. I didn't expect to see him again." He faces the sky, "We're losing time." He coughs again trying to steady his breathing, "We have to go, Cael."

He struggles to stand. I throw his arm over my shoulder and lift him the rest of the way. "How did you do all of that?" I ask amazed.

"You'll learn soon enough." He winces, moving his wrist and neck before cracking his broken nose back in place. "He's got a solid punch." He mumbles under his breath.

I turn to Wynn, "I have no idea what it's been like for you. But I really think it would be better if you came. If Beckett followed you here, he'll keep tracking you. Maybe Landon can protect us?" I say.

Landon smirks, "I almost didn't protect you this time. But Cael's right, Wynn. We need to stick together. You'll be safer with us." He sighs watching her stare at the ground, "I know it's a tough decision to make. You've been alone for so long."

I wish I could help her decide. Having someone to trust on this journey would make it loads easier. We've already been through so much together and we hardly even know each other.

Landon stands straight and takes some of his weight off my shoulder. "It's a tough decision to make. Why don't you think about it for a bit. Cael and I will go finish getting supplies for our journey, and if you decide to come along you can meet us by the Broken Board Tavern at the northwest pier. Are you familiar with this area?" He asks patiently. Wynn doesn't move so he continues, "The northwest pier is just past the First Church of Finra. Do you see the large tree over there?" We follow the direction as he points towards a single wide sprawling tree peaking over the buildings. "Just west of that. Reach the tree and follow your nose to the sea. Heh, that rhymes." He motions to me. "Let's go. I need to get moving, my body is starting to ache already. Wynn, if we don't see you at the tavern, please stay safe. Whatever you do, don't trust that man."

He extends his arm and this time she reaches for it, still in a daze.

I reach out as well. "I'm sorry about before."

She opens her arms to hug. I awkwardly fumble Landon's weight around to allow a hug. He pushes himself up, standing on his own but she smiles and instead offers her hand to shake. As we separate, Landon pats my shoulder and guides me away. I follow him out of the tiny square and glance back to Wynn. She's already gone.

If she comes, everything will be easier, and it'll be less scary. I don't want to be at this island place alone. Sure, Landon is here now but he'll probably have to leave and go do other things. And I still don't know about him yet. He's part of this place, he's not like us. I'll be all by myself, far away from home and with no one to trust. The trip will be better, too. It might be alright with just Landon, but it might be really bad. It can't be really bad if Wynn comes. If she doesn't join us, I wonder if she'll end up with those other guys. She could fight back, but they'd probably just do some weird magic and take her. Will we have to fight other magic people a lot? That would be awesome. The stuff they did was actual real magic. But if they take Wynn, would I have to fight her? Would I have to fight lots of women? Would I really have to kill families?

What is he saying now? Did he ask if I needed clothes or if I liked oats? I check our surroundings to try and figure out what he said. Wow, it's getting dark already. Feeling weight on my arms I glance down to find that I'm carrying a bag of something heavy. Where has the day gone? How long have we been out?

"Not long. We were able to get everything we needed pretty quickly," Landon says. "I'm feeling much better now too by the way, thank you for asking. And it's a good thing that we were able to get all our shopping taken care of so quickly. It gives us a bit of extra time to head over to the Broken Board and see if your friend is going to join us."

"Do you think she'll really come?" I ask nervously.

"Truthfully, Cael, I can't even guess. She's been on her own for a long while, she's scared and definitely doesn't trust me. And after that incident with Beckett, she might be put off even more. But still, I can tell she's very smart. She can't keep running forever. It just doesn't make sense. And with that blue hair? Around here she sticks out like fire on water." He smiles knowingly. "Why do you ask? Are you excited for her to join us?"

"Excited? I wouldn't say I was excited about any part of this; it's all a shipwreck. But I do want her to come. I really just want her to be safe," I say. It would be nice to have someone I could trust, someone going through the same thing.

Landon sighs exhaustedly. "You are too young for your own good." He rubs his face and mutters, "What have I gotten myself into?" He stands up straight. "Let's just head over to the tavern, shall we?"

Chapter Thirteen

The marketgoers are already packing up their wares and heading home. These people have no idea who we are. What would they do if Landon just started doing magic? I bet they would think it was a show for a while until he did something completely unexplainable. But then what? Would they attack or would they run? Or would they just be amazed?

Landon guides us through the maze of buildings and herds of people as we make our way towards the tavern. "I heard that this city used to be on a cliff. There were no docks here, they were way south of the city. This was years ago of course, maybe a hundred or more. You see, after already building *this* town, they felt it would be easier to completely change the landscape rather than move. It took them decades, but they managed to achieve their goal. They must have been told by everyone on this continent that they were morons for going through with it. They started creating a hill from the cliff, moving boulders and building up land from the ocean floor. What they did was incredible, but pointless. Because not a days walk from here is a nearly *identical* landscape." He stares at me, waiting.

"Why didn't they just move the city?" I ask.

"Exactly my point! People are stubborn. They make a decision and they stick to it disregarding everything else. It only took a few men to make that decision for everyone in the town at the time. Before long, they were all defending the decision as if it were their own. A few men always make decisions for the masses because the masses are afraid to be held accountable. My point is this: it won't matter how many people look the other way if we do magic. It only takes a few, or in many cases a *single* person, to make a decision. The rest of the people will follow, fearing what would happen if they don't. It's difficult to understand now but before we reach the academy you'll see firsthand that what I'm saying is true," Landon says.

"Here we are." He points to the end of the road we're on towards a large broken board nailed above a doorway.

Is the name even the Broken Board or is it just Tavern? Because that sign just reads, 'Tavern.'

"Yes! But it's on a broken board." Landon smirks.

I sigh, "Stop being in my head."

We make our way to the entrance and a shutter falls off a window, leaving a hole in the wall behind it. Landon shrugs with a smirk and opens the door. He guides us to the bar.

"Barkeep." Landon calls out as he gives the bar a solid knock.

A few of the patrons glance at us.

"Two of whatever you've got cooking in that pot there," Landon says.

The barkeep grunts and tosses two bowls of some foul look stew in front of us.

"And some wine!" Landon calls out and puts coins on the counter while I try to choke down the barely warm mush.

"It's rude to keep a lady waiting you know." Wynn's voice comes from a corner behind us. "And you could have chosen a more reputable place to meet; I could catch disease here."

Landon and I turn around surprised while everyone else in the tavern begins glaring at us. Landon grabs us both by the wrists and pushes us out the door.

"Are you trying to start trouble?" Landon quietly yells as we make it to the street.

Wynn stomps her foot. "There's no need for us to stay around here, let's be on our way. Do you have supplies enough for three or were you expecting me to disappear?" She leads us down the streets quickly.

Before I speak, Landon laughs.

"Whew, I've never met a young lady with such a commanding presence. I can't help but feel like we're in over our heads here, Cael," he says as he jabs me in the side.

"What made you decide to join us?" I ask.

"It hasn't been easy. This seemed easier." She stops short and puts her hand out blocking Landon and points at me. "But you have to promise me that if these people turn out to be as bad as I think they are, we leave. Together. You have to stay with me. No, don't look at him," she says putting her hand on my face and forcing me to look at her. She pushes Landon back slightly. "We're in this together now, you and me. Not the three of us. Just you and me. Agreed?"

"Well doesn't that make me feel all types of important. There's probably a nicer way to do that," Landon says, pouting.

I laugh nervously. Father always said women should be in charge. I suppose there's no use fighting it.

"Agreed," I say as I pat Landon's shoulder. "Sorry, master woodsman. She makes a better leader than you do."

"That she does, lad. That she does." He laughs along with me.

Wynn smirks and leads us on.

"This one here." Landon points to a ship. "I have to speak with the captain, you both get our supplies on board." He directs us up the gangplank.

I've never been on a large boat like this. It feels old, the rough splintered planks certainly tell of age. I wonder where all these people are going; and how long are we on this boat? Wynn's legs seem steady, she must've sailed on the ocean before. She's got to be from the north, Mother said that's where you find hair like hers. I wonder if she's important. There are loads of royal families up that way. It's hard to imagine these seekers killing royalty just to get their hands on her.

Landon finishes speaking with the captain and waves over to us. "Alright, team. I was able to grab us a room, but it's just the one room. I hadn't planned for a third so I didn't make any arrangements beforehand. Honestly we're lucky enough to get a room last minute like this. Most of these passengers are stuck in the shared sleeping quarters. The good captain here only agreed because I've sailed with him a few times before. And more than

that, we have a young lady with us and he had concerns. So I
suppose you've already helped us Miss Wynn and we should be
grateful you came along. Unfortunately for you, that means we'll
all be sleeping together. Are you going to be alright with that?"

Wynn considers it for a moment before nodding. "That's
fine, I can think of worse things."

"Landon, how long is this journey?" I ask.

"The supplies everyone is bringing makes it seem like we'll
be here for a while," Wynn adds.

"Yes, this trip is about three weeks. Thirty full days of us
all getting to know each other. I suggest you prepare yourselves for
a long, boring and at times, tedious, journey." He scratches his
beard, "I suppose I could instruct you both on what I've learned to
help speed up the time, but we'll need to keep to ourselves mostly.
I can't be out on the deck teaching you or we'll be tossed
overboard before we could blink."

"So we're going to be learning in our cabin?" I ask.

"That's seems the best place for now, but it will probably
get a bit tight in there. What might help is if we could work at
night and that way we would be able to use the deck. I'll speak to
our captain and hint to him that with his light crew it might be
worthwhile to have an extra group awake during the night hours.
That actually makes more sense as I say it out loud. Storms pop up
without warning on this route north and we'll need people wide
awake to help batten down the hatches, make certain the sails are
secured, all the usual stuff. Karif should agree, I've worked his
ships enough times for him to trust me." he says happily.

"Sleep by day and learn by night? That's our plan? Won't
some people get suspicious of us? Three weeks is a long time for
rumors to start." Wynn points out.

"If the captain does agree, it won't matter what the other
folks think. Besides most of the men I've seen are mercenaries and
we don't want to spend any more time than we have to with them.
We're on this ship for a long while and like you said that's plenty
of time for things to happen. Plenty of time for hard-headed
morons like these guys to get an idea or two about a good fight or
... or well anything else." Landon says eyeing Wynn. "I'll go ask
the lieutenant where we'll be bunking."

The captain walks past. "Oy! This be a ship here, son, I expect more've ya. We don't have no fancy lieutenants. How many times it been, now, boy? Ya can't member a damned thing can ya? Call Brun by his name or call him me first," he says angrily but smiles at us. He pats Landon on his shoulder with a wink. "Brun, get yer ugly mug out here and tend to these folk." He calls out to the ship as he opens the door to his quarters.

A man emerges from below deck carrying a few sacks over his shoulders and drops them at our feet. We all stare up at him. This man is huge. He looks like he just finished carrying this whole blessed ship into port by himself!

"You all the folk need tending to?" he asks, obviously annoyed.

Wynn yells out, "Wow! How big are you? Could you lift a horse if you had to? Oh! Can you lift all three of us at the same time?"

Brun glares at us but stops when he sees Wynn and quickly offers a smile, brushing his greasy hair out of his eyes. "I reckon I could lift you all up if I had the right motivation. What's in it for me?"

Landon steps forward and slightly in front of Wynn as he speaks up. "I don't think that'll be necessary, Brun. We just need directions to whichever of the cabins we'll be taking."

Landon looks at Wynn angrily.

"I reckon the captain gave you all one of them private cabins? They all the same so you can choose. It's just right off the main sleeping quarters, same as they always are. But I'd be happy to show you," Brun says, bowing to Wynn.

We file past him down the stairs. Who are this man's parents? Even bowing, he's taller than me. Those shoulders are probably the same width as I am tall. Finra tend our trees! That man cannot be all human. I'd wager all the money I could find on it. He is huge, but he seems dumb as stone.

I move my head to follow and get a nose full of his odor. I can hardly stop myself from gagging. Wynn and Landon cover their mouths. What causes a smell like that? Has he ever bathed in his life? Moons above, it's like he's so big no one dare tell him that he stinks like fermented ass.

"Listen up folk. Ya got the galley one deck above ya. Food served standard times. No cryin' if you ain't get nothing 'cause it's first come and first serve. We got a caravan of mercs on this trip, so ya best move quick cause them folk can eat. Second deck down here is sleepin' quarters with the third deck right below ya for storage. Got anything ya need storin'? That's where it goes. You folk can choose either these three cabins here." He points in the general direction of everything as he says it. I stare at his arms as he moves them. Those muscles look alive.

He goes to head up to the main deck but stops and turns to Wynn. "My cabin is this one here if you need anything milady."

We watch him disappear to the decks above and Wynn giggles. "Not in his wildest dreams. That man is revolting! Men are so predictable. It's really sad if you think about it. Which now that I do think about it, I really don't want to. So let's find the cabin furthest from his. That smell is gonna waft; you can count on it."

Landon and I follow Wynn down the hall to the last cabin. Wynn takes the top bunk and Landon and I hop in bed feet to face.

I've never been on a sea boat before. It's not really what I expected. It kinda smells musty. Or maybe moldy. I figured it would smell more like the sea. It's cold and old. I bet there are splinters everywhere. Maybe it'll get better when we're on the open water.

Landon gets up. "I'll be right back; I need to speak with the captain about our nightly arrangements. I think we'll be off the hook tonight, so you guys try and get some rest. It's been a pretty weird and wild day." He walks out the door, each board creaking as he moves down the hall and up the stairs.

I should probably say something to Wynn. I wonder if she's thinking about Brun. He didn't seem dangerous, but he was huge. I bet he *is* pretty dangerous. Landon and I won't let anything happen. Maybe I should tell her that? What would I say? I don't want to irritate her.

"Hey, Wynn," I call up to her.

"Huh? What?" She pokes her head down and her hair reaches almost to our bottom bunk.

"Ehh, good night." I'm awful at this...

"Good night," she says, pulling herself back up.

I'm an idiot. Why am I so nervous? I'm horrible when it comes to women. If Laena were here she could help Wynn feel safer. Does she even need to feel safer? I wish I could be smooth like Father is. This is the last night we'll be this close to them. It would be so much easier if I knew we'd be together again, if we had some plan. I wonder what Clout is doing. He probably has no idea where I am. He probably thinks I'm out helping Marak and Luther and that I'll be back in a day or two. It'll be a while before Clout realizes I'm gone forever.

No ... Clout is smart. He knows. He has to.

If I do come back – I can't think like that. When I come back, will Laena be married? Who will she marry? Marak might send her away, trade her to the highest bidder. Dowries aren't really a thing around us but Mum's talked about them before. She always had answers to everything. Always talking about small things. Teaching us without us realizing. What a smart woman. Father says you can hardly ever appreciate what you have in the moment. It's only when you lose it that you recognize how important it was. I hope they know how important they are to me. I hope I showed them before I left.

I should just get to sleep. Maybe those dreams will stop now, or maybe they just keep going until you're one of those ... What do they call themselves? I'll have to remember to ask Landon. I hope I can finally get a good night's sleep. First good sleep in months, wouldn't that be something. Tomorrow the adventure begins and we'll be ...

Chapter Fourteen

Moons above, I have to pee! I try and open my eyes but can't. I reach for my eyelids and realize my eyes are open. My heart begins to race. My leg hits a solid body and I jolt back. What? What's happening? Where am I? Just calm down. I'm on a boat with Landon and Wynn. It's just dark, I'm not blind. It's just dark, it's just dark.

"Hey, Landon. Psst, Landon." I whisper to him. "Landon I have to pee so bad! Where's the head?"

I shake him hard, "Landon?" He lets out a fart and rolls over. Wynn begins to stir above me. If I wake her up, she'll be furious.

The sound of feet hitting the floor startles me. Please don't be mad!

"Cael?"

Her hand runs across the blanket until she finds mine.

"Is this your hand or Landon's?" she asks.

"Yea, that's me," I whisper back.

"Well do you have to go or not? I can sort of see and Landon showed me where it was after you fell asleep. Get ready to puke though, it's not a pretty sight. The mercenaries did a number on that thing when they got on board," she whispers.

I step out of bed. "Thank you. I have to go so bad I almost let loose all over Landon."

She chokes down a laugh and manages to snort a bit as she squeezes my hand. "Don't make me laugh, you ass! We'll wake up all the people. Just follow me and try and be quiet about it."

I follow her with one hand reaching the walls and being dragged forward by the other. Her hands are really warm, or mine are just really cold.

We reach a room behind the stairs and she pushes me in. She starts rustling around near the entrance for something before everything is lit up as she strikes a match and sets the lantern ablaze.

"Ok, make it quick. I have to pee too," she says as she stands back just around the corner.

Finra save me from this smell! What did those guys have to eat? It's disgusting in here. There's crap all over the head. Poor Wynn has to stand over this thing …. I'll try and clear off as much of this as I can with my stream.

I finish up and step around the corner. "It's close to a nightmare in there. I did my best to clean around the edges, but you'll still have to be careful not to get anything on you."

"What a gentlemen, cleaning up for me and everything. Don't worry, Cael. I'm sure I've seen worse." She says, her smile barely visible in the dim light of the lantern

She walks in and I take her place waiting.

"Yup, that's bad. I'll just hold it for the next three weeks," she says gagging as she walks out.

"Come now, Wynn. You can't hold it for that long. It's either this or you hang off the main deck and pee right into the ocean," I say as I shove her back in.

"I know. You're right …. I'm not used to ships, I'm used to at least having a seat. Unless I go outside, which I would much rather do." She sighs. "Fine."

"I wonder what it looks like out there. I've never been on the ocean before. Could we still see the land?" I ask without thinking.

Wynn walks out as she finishes. "Well let's go then. I've never seen the ocean from a ship either. We can see it together."

I stare at her. Did I say that out loud again or did she hear my thoughts?

"Speaking without thinking? I do that a lot. I can tell from your face. Don't worry I'm not reading your thoughts. I can't listen to thoughts, I can only listen to, I guess, conversations? I only hear if two people are talking. But yea I speak without thinking, alone mostly, just talking to myself," she says as she grabs my hand and leads us up the stairs with the lantern.

As we reach the hatch to the main deck she hangs the lantern and says, "Ready?"

I nod and we both smile, excited to see the ocean.

She opens the hatch and we step out, staring at the sky. I've never seen anything like this. The stars are so bright they almost block the moon. So many stars! I never thought there were this many. We gasp together.

"Look at the ocean; it's so calm that it reflects the sky perfectly," she says.

"It's like one big night sky, you can hardly see where they split," I add.

"So many moons," she whispers.

Wynn grabs my arm and we run over to the edge of the boat to stare into the water.

"Maybe this won't be so bad," she says. "If we get views like this even just a few times on this stupid journey, it might be worth it. Maybe. At least it's something new and different."

She's not wrong. This view is one of the most beautiful I've ever seen.

The sound of someone moving around up the stairs startles me into a panic. What if we get in trouble? Are we allowed out? Do they throw you overboard if you get in trouble? Could I swim back? What about sea monsters?

"That imagination, Cael. Reality's not going to come close to what you build it up to be." Landon's voice floats up from below deck and his face emerges with a grin. "What are you two doing up? I woke up and damn near lost it when I realized you were gone."

He walks over and grunts as his eyes gaze out over the ocean. "Sometimes you forget just how beautiful the world is. I'm always running around to all corners. I suppose I take these views for granted. When you're always traveling, beauty is measured by the last beautiful thing you saw. Rarely do you measure it by itself in the moment. It's a shame, too. Because this view is truly astounding." He stares quietly.

"Such a beautiful night, a quiet night. No wind, no noise from below deck. Only a few folks awake on watch. It would be a shame to let it go to waste." He smiles wickedly. "What say you two, are you up for your first lesson?"

Wynn and I look at each other for a moment. Our lives were ruined because of this. The least we can do is to let it play out, to see if it was close to worth it.

We both agree and Landon continues, "If I hesitate to teach you anything, trust that it's not because I'm hiding the lessons. It's because some things I cannot teach. I'm not an instructor. I will show you how *I* do these things, and maybe learning my way first and the 'correct' way later will be helpful. Maybe not. Probably not. But we're all going to be bored to tears if I don't try."

He puts his hand in the air and my vision goes dark, completely dark. Before I can fumble around he says, "Lesson One."

Chapter Fifteen

"Oh, come now! Spare us the theatrics and start teaching already!" Wynn hisses. Her hand grabs mine and squeezes.

"She's right, Landon. This isn't fair. We can't learn if we can't see you," I mumble. My heart pounds and my hands feel like pins are poking them as they begin to sweat.

Why isn't he giving our sight back? He's just trying to scare us; this must be his lesson. He's showing his power. "Stop acting like an ass and…"

My voice! It's gone! I can't speak…. I can't speak…. What's happening?!

My whole body is shaking and I squeeze Wynn's hand harder as the fear tears into me.

"Cael?! What's wrong? Are you hurt?! Cael?!! Answer—" Her voice cuts off suddenly. I can feel her start to panic. I can't help you. I'm sorry! I want to help. It's going to be fine! It's all just pretend! Everything will be fine! Please hear what I'm thinking. My voice is gone. My sight is gone. This is all just a lesson, it's not real.

The pressure in my hand disappears. I try and stand up, but the boat is gone, too. My legs, my feet, I can't feel them. Is this what death feels like? Emptiness? Darkness? No Feelings? This is it. He beat us. Whatever he wanted to do, he's done it. I just wanted to live a normal life. I didn't want any of this!

…Does death have sounds? It could just be my mind tricking me. It sounds like the creak of a board. Everything is getting louder. The boat creaking with every movement. Every splash of the waves against the hull is as loud as thunder. If I'm dead, would I still be hearing all this?

What's that noise?! There's footsteps pounding all around me. Who's there?! Help?! Someone! Help! I try and move my head to look around but it doesn't work, I can't move anything, I can't see anything.

The footsteps grow louder, they're getting closer. There's more footsteps further away, too! We're being surrounded. Wynn was right; we should never have trusted him! I'm sorry I didn't listen to you! I'm sorry!

The pounding of the footsteps is deafening. My chest tightens. I can hardly breathe. The air isn't going in anymore. Silence. No more steps. They must all be here. They're all staring at us. Moons above what's going to happen!?

Everything is still.

Am I dead now?

I can smell the ocean. I can smell something else that's closer? It smells like the woods, pine and dirt. Wynn, she's still next to me. We're fine, at least for now.

I begin to relax and can almost feel her hand in mine again, and all at once we're back in reality. Sitting on the ships deck, moons in the sky, stars all around. Wynn and I are covered in sweat and tears. Landon is staring at us blankly.

Wynn squeezes my hand in hers. I'm glad to feel anything. I turn to Landon filled with rage. "What was that?! Why are you torturing us? What type of lesson are you teaching us?! Are you trying to teach us what it's like to die? Or are you actually trying to kill us?!"

Landon waves his hand, motioning for me to sit back down. Wynn remains seated, staring at her hands. He's treating us like some experiment. How could he do that to us?

"It's the first lesson we all learn. It's an awful lesson, but it's necessary." I open my mouth to yell but he shoots me a look and continues, "Right now, I am your instructor and you are my charges. You will listen. You will not argue. All of your questions will be answered, I can guarantee that, but you must give me time to explain everything in order."

He hands us both an apple from a travel sack. When did he get that? How long were we dead, or asleep or, whatever we were?

He walks over to the edge of the boat and after a moment I reluctantly follow.

"Eat. I know it's scary. It was hard for me to do that to you both. I still remember what it was like... So eat, you need energy." Landon starts to eat his own apple and we all stare out at the ocean.

I wish I could tell Wynn thank you for just being there, for caring. She tried to yell at Landon for me.

She hasn't moved. She must be so scared. I throw my fully eaten apple into the ocean, shattering the perfect reflection of the stars. I didn't even realize I had been eating it. But it did make me feel a bit better.

"Wynn, try and eat. I think it helps." I lift her hand still holding the apple to her mouth and she bites.

We continue in silence until Wynn finishes eating. She looks better already. The fire is already coming back in her eyes and she looks ready to scream like I did. Landon cuts her off before she can say anything.

"That lesson, as horrible as it seems, is necessary. You are both going to be learning how to control your minds and the world around you in ways that most people cannot even fathom. Not even in their wildest nightmares would they imagine the things we'll do. Even your peers won't have the natural talents you both have. Most only have the ability to do one, which is either to alter minds or to alter the world." He sits up straighter and smirks. "Luckily for you, I am one such person who can do both. Although I'm not as trained on the alteration of physical objects as I am on navigating the mind." He shrugs. "But I'll still be able to provide some sort of structure, a framework, for you to build off of."

He shakes his head. "I'm rambling, I apologize. I'm already failing my first lesson. The point of that lesson was to show you how dangerous you both are and how much more dangerous you will become. And also how dangerous your peers will be. Some people will be trained at the academy but will leave for one reason or another. Others like Beckett and the Sephalim will be trained outside our academy. What you both just experienced was one of the tools you'll learn to use." He throws his core into the ocean and we sit back down.

"The first lesson serves two purposes. One to show you why you need to defend yourselves, and the second is to introduce you to what the instructors call sensory deprivation. That's a fancy term that means as you lose each sense, your other senses begin to compensate. In times of extreme stress, they compensate very quickly." He points to me. "Cael, you experienced something you couldn't explain. Most other things that happened you came to understand and accept fairly quickly. You heard footsteps. Do you know what those were?"

"I don't know! I thought you were going to kill us in some ritual!" I bark, feeling a quick heat in my face.

Landon smiles apologetically. "No, nothing so dark as that. What you were hearing was your own heartbeat. And towards the end, you began to hear Wynn's heartbeat alongside yours and then you even heard mine. I was impressed with your ability to accept the removal of your other senses so quickly. That's a good sign of your talent. If you still had your sense of feeling, you would have noticed your body vibrating with the pulsing of your heartbeat."

"Did you hear your heart beating too, Wynn?" I ask.

It's kind of amazing to hear your heart so incredibly loud. It blocked out pretty much everything else.

"No." She looks away.

Landon reaches out to her but sits back down, "Wynn's experience was similar to a lot of people's. Most of the students going through this for the first time have a reaction where their mind is overrun by fear. They lose their senses fully as soon as they reach a stage of panic. For you, Cael, I closed off your senses individually, as you very consciously felt. For you, Wynn, I only had to take away sight and your voice. When you began to fear for Cael's safety, the level of panic you experienced caused the rest of your mind to collapse into a full deprivation of senses. You were effectively trapped in your own head, only able to think and not feel."

I touch her shoulder as she wraps her arms around her knees and stares at the deck in front of us. "Why did we act differently? Is Cael stronger?"

There is no way I'm stronger. She's so confident and certain. I could hit something harder or lift a heavier weight, but she has to be a stronger person. She's gone through much more than I have. She already knows a lot of this magic stuff.

"Strength has nothing to do with it. It's a bit complicated to explain, but his mind appears to accept changes easier than yours. Or mine for that matter. I reacted quite the same as you when I was put through this. So you see, it has nothing to do with your strength or what you'll be able to learn. You just have to try a little harder, that's all." He gets to his feet and brushes off his bottom.

"It's never good to end a lesson with something so scary and traumatic as this. Some of the instructors would disagree but whenever I thought about teaching, I imagined my lessons would mean more if they ended with something really fun." Landon extends his hands. "If you are up for it."

I stand right away and look down to Wynn still staring at the deck.

"We're in this together, remember?" I reach down to her.

She looks up, still frightened and angry, but after a moment, she sighs and grabs my hand.

As I pull her up I say, "So you're ready to let Landon trick us again? Maybe he'll turn us into Brun this time."

She manages to smile and says, "One Brun is more than enough for the world! Let's just grab this fool's hand and get on with it."

We link hands in a small circle. I'm so nervous, my hands are getting hot and sweaty already. Are we supposed to close our eyes? Is this some religious thing? I hope this really is fun and not another terrifying lesson.

The sun begins dawning on the horizon. "Wow, we've been awake all night? I can't believe it's morning already."

Wynn turns to me. "Why are you making that weird voice?"

I shake my head confused. "What voice? I'm just talking regular, aren't I?"

The light from the sun gets brighter and we notice it rising fast. A moment passes and it begins setting as the darkness returns.

We turn to face Landon.

"You're doing this?" I ask.

He responds with a grin. "Just watch."

We stare in awe as the sun rises and falls more quickly. Suddenly we're hurtling towards a rocky coastline, the tide changes with every breath. We speed through an empty city, buildings flashing by us like streaks of lightning. A large manor flies into sight. We stand at the gates and watch as well-dressed men speak with guards in full metal armor. The crest on the guards' breastplate glows and they slowly fade to dust settling on the ground. Bright green grass explodes forth from the dirt that quickly expands into enormous trees. Thick brown leaves hang from the limbs, each filled with liquid. The large tree branches reach high and stretch over a narrow wooden path to each other before splitting into enormous sticky webs. The leaves drop heavily through the silvery webbing and thud onto the forest floor which starts to boil. The solid ground beneath our feet turns to liquid and we fall through it into an ocean. A warm blue ocean, so clear and bright. We watch as a beautiful colorful school of fish swim through plants and float above us. We reach out to touch their shining scales and within the space of a moment they turn back to stars. The same stars that started our short adventure.

Landon lets go of our hands and we are thrust back into our reality. My eyes feel so heavy. I look around to the familiar ship. Wynn is doing the same and as our eyes meet quickly, her face reflecting how I feel. Tired. Very tired.

"These gifts have two sides, and that's important to understand. They don't need to be treated like weapons. You can give memories or take them. You'll learn to show things or hide them. You'll learn to create just as you learn to destroy. I've found that sometimes it's better to use the lighter side, the happier side, of our abilities to achieve our goals. Some instructors will focus on the taking, the hiding, or even the destroying aspects because it is arguably more useful. I feel a proper education should include all sides. You should have more than one tool out in the field, because some situations don't need a sharp blade or pain. Some situations might just call for a fond memory, a peaceful vision. Sometimes a conversation can have a bigger impact than a threat." He rubs his chin in thought. "Maybe that can be lesson one."

Chapter Sixteen

"Cael... Cael, wake up."

"Let him rest if he wants. There might still be some food left when he wakes up."

Food? Oh man I'm hungry. "I'm... wait... waking up. Wait for me. I'm hungry. I'm hungry."

"You better hurry up then, because lunch just got placed and those mercs are going wild on it!" Wynn says.

I rub my eyes. Landon and Wynn round the corner as they leave our cabin and Wynn calls over to me. "Come on then, I'm not losing food waiting around on you."

I roll off my bunk and crash to the floor. I don't feel too good. I'm dizzy. I'm going to puke.

"Hey, I feel like I might be— I think I'm going to be sick," I call after them.

They walk back into the cabin. Wynn bends down to help me up, but Landon sighs in irritation.

"You're not sick. You're just not used to the boat yet. It happens to a lot of people especially if you've never sailed before. You just need to get some bland food like old bread and drink water. You'll be fine, I promise. Now get on your feet and let's get some food! Wynn is right, those mercs will eat everything." Landon says motioning to the door.

There's a very good chance that I'm going to puke before we make it to the galley. I hope Landon is right. I won't make it three weeks if it's like this the whole time.

As I stumble towards the door, my stomach churns. I charge towards the head and as soon as I reach the hole, the awful smell forces out everything in my stomach. I can't breathe. My whole body tenses up and I watch a stream of chunky liquid leaves my face. It doesn't even look real. It hits the wood before splashing into the ocean below. The sound is sickening. I puke again and again. Please let this be the last time.

I spit out what's left in my mouth and collapse to the floor. I've been awake for five minutes and I'm already exhausted. Just let this day be over.

"Are you feeling any better?" Wynn asks.

"I'll be fine. Don't waste your worrying on me," I say before coughing hard. The air in my lungs empties quickly and I can't breathe. My heart starts pounding and I cough every time I try to inhale. I can hardly keep the air in my lungs. Boots charge towards us and my body is lifted up.

"Cael, calm down. You need to relax. Breathe slowly, try and breathe only through your nose. Can you do that for me?" I can't see him but it's Landon. He carries me to a bed and lays me down.

"Wynn, go get some water. Cael, follow my lead alright? We breathe in together." He puts his hand on my chest and I open my eyes to watch him breathe. I slow down and only breathe through my nose and try to match his breathing, but I continue coughing.

Wynn runs in with a mug of water and a woman follows her.

"Please stand back. What are his symptoms?" she asks quickly. Please let her be a doctor or anyone that can help me. I don't care if it's some weird spell, just make me feel better. Landon stands back and she kneels by the bed.

Wynn speaks up. "He woke up not feeling well. He was nauseous and after vomiting he had a bad cough. He looks real bad."

"Right, well that could be any number of things. Most of them could be contagious so we need to isolate him as soon as possible. I have some medicinal herbs on board with me, but we're not going to be operating under ideal conditions here. Wynn, was it?" Wynn nods and the woman continues, "Can you go get my husband? His name is Rolin and he'll be in the galley with all those mercenaries getting his fill of gossip and food. Ask him to grab my herbs and lead him back to us." She points to Landon. "You. What's your name?"

"Landon." He responds curiously.

She smiles patiently. "Landon, can you go get the captain? We need to move him to an unoccupied cabin. Preferably somewhere close so we can oversee his recovery."

Landon nods back and both he and Wynn rush out of the room. It sounds like she knows what she's doing, but could she be a doctor at her age? She almost looks like Laena's mom. Probably close to her age when she died, too.

"How old..." I can barely get words out before I begin coughing again.

She immediately puts her head to my chest as I'm coughing. I recoil back, but she pulls me closer.

"Breathe slowly when you begin coughing, your lungs are sensitive right now." She pulls away and motions for me to lay down. "Yes I may be young but I have been studying medicine for a few years. You'll need to trust me because, if I don't miss my mark, I'm the only one with any training at all on this ship. Looks like you're stuck with me."

She puts her hand on my head and pulls my shirt up.

"What's your name?" she asks as she investigates my abdomen and chest.

"Cael," I whisper to not start another coughing fit. "What's yours?"

My voice is already rough and strained from coughing.

"My name is Rena. Where are you coming from, Cael? Have you been anywhere unusual, eaten anything different?" She pulls my shirt back down and waits for an answer.

"I'm . . . " I cough a bit and she rubs my back and helps me sit up. "I'm... from outside of Rensfort... I don't travel often... I'm probably just travel sick. I haven't eaten anything weird."

A group of people pound down the hallway. Wynn walks in followed by a young man, Landon and finally the captain.

"I've brought your supplies, love. Is there anything we can do to help?" the young man asks, smiling at Rena. He seems nice, I bet he's nice.

"Well then, pick this lad up 'nd follow me. If he's got anythin' dangerous we'll be turnin' round though so make sure he hasn't got anything dangerous, understood?" the captain calls over his shoulder

Everyone nods as Landon and Rolin pick me up. I can walk myself. I'm not even that sick. I try and move my arms but they're too heavy. Maybe I am sick. Could I be sick enough to die? I wonder how long death is. Forever is so long. It can't be forever. I hope it doesn't hurt.

The captain leads us to another cabin and they lower me onto the bed. Wynn brings in a bucket of water and Rena starts setting up a station with her supplies. What's in all these little glass jars? They don't look like medicine. They just look like powders, well that one is liquid, so powders and liquids. The captain pulls Landon outside and they start whispering before Landon comes back in and the captain walks away.

Rena speaks up, "Alright everyone, I think the best thing for Cael right now is for him to get rest. I'm not sure what we're dealing with yet, but we'll likely find out before nightfall, a day at most. The symptoms so far have been sudden and will possibly get worse. I'll start with a simple tea of chamomile and lavender. That will help you sleep so you don't feel the sickness as much. You'll want to sleep as long as possible. Sleep is one of the best medicines. I'll check-in every few hours and once we determine the cause, I'll set up a treatment and recovery schedule." She scans the faces around the room and we all nod. "Well? Time to leave. No need for you all to sit around staring. Wynn dear, can you go grab a biscuit from the galley? He'll need to eat something. I'll go get some heated water for his tea. I hope the galley has firebricks...."

I am kind of hungry, but I don't know if I should eat. It might just come right up. Maybe sleeping for a bit will help. Every time I've been sick before, a good night's rest always makes me feel bright as silver. This isn't anything like I expected. I just want to go home, sleep in my own bed. Mother would make some soup or stew, something hot, maybe some biscuits with honey, too.

When I'm better, I could ride Clout through the fields, maybe into town and see Laena. It's odd that I miss her. It's only been a few days since I've seen her. We've gone weeks without seeing each other before. Maybe it's because she was upset. I wish I knew why she was crying. Probably Marak, always treating her like some slave. I'd be mad about that. Maybe it's because I might never see her again, or if I do it won't be until we're fully grown. So much for my life being planned out. Luther would love this if he were in my place, anything to take him away from his path.

Bleh, I think I still have the taste of puke in my mouth. I'm glad Wynn brought in some water. And an extra bucket, must be for when I end up puking again. Moons above I hope I don't puke like that again.

I rinse my mouth out and spit into the bucket just as Rena walks back in with a steaming hot mug of tea.

"Here you are, Cael. Drink this up. Try and drink at least half before you fall asleep. It'll help you rest easier, trust me." She lifts my head up and puts the mug to my lips. She's pretty strong, but she's also gentle. She reminds me of mother. Mother was young once. Did she always act like she does now? Always motherly? Do all women act motherly?

"You are an unusual one, Cael. I feel like I can see your mind turning through your eyes. That's a good sign though. Maybe it isn't Rose Fever…. Well, no sense in worrying now, let's get you to sleep." She lays me back down and places the tea on a stool next to the bed.

"Try and think about a familiar story. You like stories, right? Concentrate on something and you'll be sleeping before you know it. I'll be back soon." She smiles as she closes the door and walks down the hall.

A story? I don't know many stories by heart. Mom used to tell stories when we were younger. She knew a bunch. Something I'm familiar with? That would definitely be smithing. Dad should be out by the forge right now, working on something for someone. Oh, that's right, that sword! Gahris should have finished with the scabbard. Father probably finished the sword. Gemstones, gold, a fancy sword. It wasn't going to be long. I wonder if Dad made it badly? He wouldn't need to make it strong. The counselor won't be using it at all. But no, Father doesn't take shortcuts. I would have been there with him. Maybe he needs help? He could pay someone, but there aren't many young men in our town. They would have to be from the city or a traveler. I suppose he could work by himself; he's done that before. What are they thinking about right now? Clout… What do horses think of when they go to sleep?

Damn, it's colder than a witch's nose in here. "Mum, did Father leave the door open again? It's still winter out there, we should have the fire lit." What would these two do without me? I stand up to close the door and light the fire, but my legs are so weak I fall backwards onto the bed. I can't believe I'm still sick. It's not supposed to last this long.

"Just relax, Little Cub, you need to regain your strength! I'll light the fire don't you worry a bit," Mother says as she gets me settled back in bed. This bearskin is a life saver right now; it's so heavy and warm.

"Remember when we got this bear, Mum? That was a pretty wild hunt!" I say smiling up at her.

Her eyes are a bit worried. I wonder if I'm sicker than she's telling me. Well, it won't matter. She's great with medicine. I bet I'll be strong as stones in another day or two.

Mother puts her hand on my head. "Shaira, feel his head and tell me what you think."

Shaira walks in. Can it really be her? I haven't seen her in ages! "Wow, it's been so long, Shaira! Where did you go? Does Marak know you're back? I bet Luther and Laena would be so excited to see you."

I could have sworn she died, didn't she? She was always sick, so there's probably no one who knows more about sickness than Shaira. Mum's bringing in all the doctors. I try and let out a laugh, but it starts a coughing fit again.

Mother reaches out and lifts my head up as she tilts a mug of tea in my mouth. Chamomile and lavender, just like before.

Father is in the corner pacing, but he smiles quickly when he sees me staring. "What's got you looking so worried, Father?

Why are you all so anxious, I feel fine! I actually feel pretty good except for this cough. A bit hot now that I think of it. Maybe congested, but I feel good."

Father grabs my shoulder. "Cael, snap out of this!" he says, shaking me hard.

What in the world has gotten into him? His eyes don't look right. Mother and Shaira shoot him dirty looks and he stomps out of the room. Serves him right, yelling at me for no reason. He might just be worried. He gets mad when he's worried.

"Hey Mum, where's Clout? Can he come in for a bit? I'll go sit in the sewing room with him. Just want to brush him before his mane gets out of control," I ask, trying to stand up again.

"Settle down, we'll bring Clout in later. You need to rest a bit more. Shaira is going to check you over before you go back to sleep, is that alright?" she asks as she steps out of the way letting Shaira take her place.

I nod and get up on my elbows.

"So how do I look, Doc?" I say beaming at her.

"You look horrible, but I doubt it has anything to do with you being sick!" She says with a goofy smile.

I laugh for a moment before I begin coughing. It's not as bad as it was though. Shaira lifts my shirt up and I follow her gaze down to my chest and stomach.

I told them I'm fine. What are we looking for anyway? Their eyes go wild as Shaira pulls my shirt back down. "Well, what's got you two looking like you've seen a ghost?" I ask.

Shaira starts hastily mixing some ingredients together out of her glass bottles and puts them in my mug of tea. "Go ahead and drink this down, all the way to the bottom. I'll be making these cups of tea four times a day, and you need to drink all of them. When you need to go to the bathroom ask me, your mother or father. One of us will always be close by. Don't walk anywhere by yourself, deal?" she says extending her hand.

I reach out and shake it. "Deal." She hands me the mug and I drink half of it. "Gross! What have you done to this tea? It was so smooth before, now it's all chunky... reminds me of puke," I say putting the mug back down.

She snatches it off the table and puts it to my lips. "You need to drink this right now, Cael. All of it! Please listen, you need to listen to me and do as I ask if you want to get better. No questions."

Why are all the women around me so bossy!? This tea is disgusting, but I suppose Shaira does know her sicknesses so I should trust her. She's a good woman.

"I'll drink this mud water, but you've got to tell me why Laena was so upset the other day. I think I saw her crying, but I don't know why," I ask her as I down the rest of the tea.

She turns to Mother and says, "Oh she wasn't upset. She was just annoyed at her brother." She almost forms it as a question and Mother chimes in, "Yes, Luther, her brother, he was picking on her earlier. Don't you remember?"

I nod my head as I lay back down. That's right, Luther was picking on her. Was it about chores? I can't remember. I'll ask her tomorrow when I'm better.

The water is so warm! Those girls would love this. "Hey ladies! The water is divine! Come on in, don't be scared!" I call out to them. They stand up and run down the white sandy beach and into the cerulean waves. I splash at them and we all laugh as we play fight in the ocean.

Everything here is beautiful. It's so easy to relax. I watch as they swim back to shore and get back to weaving their fishing nets. What are they drinking? It looks delicious. I'll try one when I'm finished swimming. Take a look at those trees! I can't remember the last time I saw those colors. They're so tall, and those leaves are pure emerald green, the longest leaves I've ever seen. I'm so lucky to be here.

The water is perfectly clear, I wonder how deep I can dive. A school of fish swims by being chased by larger fish. There's so much life down there. I wish I could breathe under water, then I could swim forever.

I move further out and notice the ocean turning dark then suddenly it's pitch black. I can't see past my chest as I float. Things live in the ocean, big things, dangerous things. I turn back to the beach but it's gone. I must have swam too far out!

Something slimy grabs my leg and pulls me under. I gasp for breath as the last bit of light from the surface disappears.

I shoot up sucking in air. I can breathe! It was only a dream. Stupid dreams... Will I ever have a dream that's not terrifying? I open my eyes, but my vision is blurred. Why are my eyes so sensitive? Did I poke myself while I was sleeping? They feel like they're on fire or something. They quickly water up and I pick at the gunk in the corner of my eyes. I rub them hard but still my vision is blurry. It smells different. I reach to the hole in my bed to pull at the straw but it's not there.

Right, I'm on a boat. I was sick. I'm with ... a young man and a young girl. The man and girl, man and girl... why can't I remember their names?! We're traveling away from home. Why would I do that? Wynn! And Landon!

It all comes rushing back. I cry remembering that I'll never see my family, Clout, or Laena again. I wipe my eyes shake my head. I will be with them someday. I can't let them down. They're waiting for me. I'll do whatever it takes to get back. Wynn is counting on me, too. I have to make sure we both get out together. She's a good person. I can trust her.

I rub my face and nose quickly. I've already cried about this. I've already gone through it all. The path I'm on is set, I just have to make the best of it.

My stomach rumbles and an aching pain grips my insides. By all the stars in the sky, I could eat a whole deer! I try and stand up but fall back on the bed. How long have I been sleeping? Where is everyone? This place looks well and truly lived in. They could have at least cleaned up a bit, those rags in the corner are disgusting. Ah, a mug. That woman wanted me to drink this. I reach for one and notice all the mugs on top of the small dresser are empty and dried out. Someone has to be here, the lantern is still lit.

"Hello?" My voice is so coarse it barely sounds human. I rub my throat and sit up all the way. A full bucket of water rests on the floor next to the bed. I reach out and smell it. It smells clean enough.

A thumping comes from down the hallway and sets my heart racing. What's happening?!

"Cael!?" Wynn's voice reaches me before she comes bursting in the doorway. She throws her arms around me. "We were so worried! Rena was so sure you'd be fine, but after five days even she started getting scared. But you're awake! How do you feel? I bet you're hungry. Do you want some food?"

She pulls away and my heart is racing. I rub my eyes again to see better. Her eyes are wet with tears and her hair starts sticking to her face.

"I'm fine, Wynn. Wait! Did you say five days? How long have I been sleeping!?" I ask

Landon busts in the door. He looks around and when he sees me he sighs. "Finra save us, boy, I thought you were gonna die!"

Rena pushes him aside and walks over.

"Let me take a look at him," she says as she guides Wynn up and takes her place. Everyone stands still as she lifts my shirt. "Well, your rash is almost gone."

I reach down and feel the raised red skin across my chest.

She pokes me in the stomach, "Does that hurt?"

I shake my head, "Open your mouth and say 'Ahhh.'" I follow her command and she sticks her finger on my tongue and moves it around as she searches around my mouth. "Your throat and tongue look better as well." She forces me to the side and puts her head on my back. "Breathe."

I do as she says. Bossy, just like I remember. She turns to everyone in the room and nods.

"You're better! You're really better! You survived!" Wynn jumps on the bed and hugs me. Landon joins in as well and my head is smothered by them both.

Out for more than five days and so sick they thought I was going to die? What in the world happened? How did I get so sick? I'm too hungry to even think. I start to wiggle out.

"Alright!" I say struggling to get them off. "I'm glad I'm alive too, but can someone explain what in Finra's name happened to me?" Rena opens her mouth, but I hold up my hand, "Before that though, can I get something to eat? I'm starving."

They smile relieved as Wynn helps me to my feet. She puts my arm over her shoulder then starts leading us out of the room. She carries almost my full weight while my legs struggle to walk. I feel helpless. Rena and Landon follow us down the hallway and Landon helps Wynn and I when we reach the stairs to the galley. I'm like a baby. I can't even get up these steps. It's impossible to even lift my legs right now. The weight of my body is too much. I feel like my face is sagging, too. I must look a sight.

As we reach the galley deck, Wynn continues leading me to the table and sets me down on a chair. Landon and Wynn sit next to me and Rena sits across from us. She waves down Rolin and he plops next to her. The captain follows shortly after.

"Ah, the lad lives! Glad to see ya up, boy. The ship was fearin' for ya somethin' awful these past days," he says as he sits beside Rolin. The captain calls out to the side room, "Trep! Grab a few plates, will ya!?"

"Trep?" I ask.

"He's the cook. I almost forgot you haven't met anyone. You scared the sense out of all of us you were out so long!" Wynn says as she jostles my shoulder.

"How long?" I ask feeling uncomfortable at how close everyone is to me.

Rena, Wynn and Landon all speak together, "Ten days."

Ten days? A whole week? How? I don't remember anything except a dream. It felt like a few moments, a day at most.

"It's almost lunch anyway. You'll get to meet everyone soon. A lot has happened!" Wynn says with a huge smile on her face.

"What happened to me?" I ask

Everyone starts talking at once, but Rena lifts her hand and speaks, "You had Rose Fever. It could have been very serious, but we got lucky when we caught it early and we had adequate supplies. I wasn't sure at first. It could have been anything during the first few days. But after the delirium I saw and the rash growing from your chest, I knew it had to be Rose."

"How though? I don't understand, I felt fine. How much more serious could it have been? I was unconscious for ten days!

How did you treat me?" I ask quickly before falling into a coughing fit.

"You need to relax, Cael. You won't be fully right for another few days yet. I'm not sure how you contracted the illness, it's not contagious so far as we can tell. The seriousness varies, but people die regularly if left untreated. Marcus Alabas has a theory about it being from contaminated food or drink, where the contamination is some sort of fecal matter, whether animal or human he isn't certain," Rena says.

Wynn stares at me very seriously, "That means poop." She starts laughing, "You ate someone's poop!"

"Ha ha, very funny," I say rolling my eyes. "But I don't think I ate anything different. It doesn't make a difference. What's done is done," I say with a sigh. "I do feel better though, and I'm starving. How did you end up treating me if this is a deadly sickness? We're on a boat. Mother would say that these were less than ideal conditions to treat any illness, let alone a serious one."

"Luckily for you, I am training to be a doctor. I actually was granted apprenticeship to Doctor Alabas. I'll be studying under the brightest mind of our time. That's where we're headed now! He practices in North Liefland, but he travels all over. That's how my father met him." She finishes and starts blushing as she sees everyone staring. "I'm sorry! I didn't mean to ramble."

Rolin walks up. "No need to apologize, Love. You should be proud. Finra knows I am. I'm more proud than I can put to words." He kisses her forehead.

I shake my head. "But how did you treat me?"

Why do I need to know so badly? Maybe it's because Zaitah will ask if I ever see him again. Maybe I do like medicine? Maybe I'll end up being a doctor, too?

"Rose Fever is an illness that's been around for as long as we have records. The earliest medicines used were simple, and they are still the best we have. I had a powder of echinacea and some goldenseal leaves. I was able to make a tea out of those and some honey, we gave that to you as much as we could. Right near depleted all my supplies, too. The galley had some garlic, which we steamed with water to help your cough and congestion. You slept pretty calmly throughout, which is lucky for you. If we had night lily, you would have been better in a day or two, but we made do with what we had," Rena finishes as a man comes in with plates of food.

"This him then?" he growls as he dumps bread and some type of soup on the table.

Finra's beard, he's so old! Father would be impressed. He's pretty fit for being so old. He must be a hundred. His wild white hair makes him look like he's just seen a ghost.

He looks me right in the eyes and I stare back. His eyes are so clear for being so old. Gahris isn't even that old, but his eyes are getting fogged up already. Those eyes almost take a few decades off him. Will I get as wrinkled as him? His face is like folded leather that's finally been stretched out after a year in the sun.

"What you starin' at boy?! Ain't you never seen a beautiful man afore?!" he asks as he chokes down a laugh and a few giggles make their way around the room.

"Huh? No, it's not that. Sorry. Just so hungry I can hardly think. What's in the soup anyway?"

He stops short, eyeing me intently and my face goes red under his gaze.

"That's a seacrut boy. Cooks don't tell nobody what's in the soup," he says seriously.

"Why?" I reply.

The captain speaks up, "Cause then nobody would eat it!"

He and Trep laugh hard. Well, now I'm definitely not eating the soup.

"Don't worry," Wynn says. "It's just potatoes and corn. It's less of a soup than a porridge. Looks really thick." She ladles us out some of the slop. "But it's way better than what we have been eating."

As soon as it splatters into my bowl, sharp hunger pangs streak through my body. I've never felt hunger like this before.

I take a bite as soon as Wynn pushes the bowl in front of me. "Wow this is pretty good!"

There's definitely some fat in here too. This is delicious! Is that duck fat? Moons above this is amazing! The bread is so soft! He must have just made it. Butter too!?

Trep speaks up, "Enjoyin' that food, lad?"

Mouth full, I shake my head in agreement.

"We're all just glad to see you up and about, boy," the captain says. "I had Trep make up somethin' nice for all of us to celebrate your resurrection. Don't get too used to this now, though. This is a one-off type of deal here, understood?" He looks around at everyone and we all nod.

Oh man, I want more. Maybe I should wait until everyone finishes? No, why should I? I've been out for ten whole days! Everyone has eaten way more than me. I'm too hungry to even be thinking about being polite.

"So, tell me what's been going on while I've been descending the tree of death." I ask. Maybe they won't notice me getting more food if I can get them all talking.

"Most of the excitement has come from you, Cael. Everyone just asks when you're going to wake up, if it's contagious, if you can hear us," Rena says.

"Yea, loads of talk about death, too, and if we could eat you if you died. Rena said it wasn't contagious, but we would have to cook you through just to be safe." Landon cuts in with a grin.

"Sure, very funny." I mumble through mouthfuls of food.

Wynn pats my back. "Oh, don't let Landon fool you. We wouldn't have eaten you. You looked far too sickly for any of us to stomach you. Even the thought of it made Trep's cooking taste like food fit for royalty!"

Trep shrugs his shoulders. "I ain't seein any of ya complainin' right now. I can't turn a stick into a steak, but ya bet your asses I can cook the best steak any of ya ever ate!"

"Hear, hear!" the captain shouts.

Everyone raises their mugs and I follow. "Hear, hear!" we shout.

"Hear, hear!" echoes down the galley from the stairs and a dozen mercs come through and sit down at the tables around us.

"What are we agreeing with?" a smaller roundish merc asks as he starts ladling a few of them some soup.

Landon smiles, "Trep's cookin, we got—"

"Who's the kid? Damn place is feeling like a nursery," A larger mercenary cuts in.

Brun comes down and sits next to the captain. "The kid's the reason we're eating well, so shut your damn mouth." Brun nods over at me with a smile. "Glad to see ya up, boy."

"Oh, fancy food for these babes? What's wrong kids? Can't eat the trash they feed us?" the large merc says and some of the others grunt in agreement.

The roundish one keeps quiet. He looks nice enough. Those other guys are probably just waiting to bash their heads against something. The two groups sit separately and appear to be keeping to themselves.

Lord, that big guy is the same size as Brun. If those two ever fought it'd be like a mountain fighting a mountain. Why are they all still in their hard leathers? That's gotta be so uncomfortable. If they didn't bring traveling clothes for a three-week voyage, then that's got to be one of the stupidest things I've ever heard.

The big merc looks over at me and scowls. That face is scarier than Vashir's wolves. He's definitely seen a few fights with all those scars.

"Hey, boy! Din't ya hear me?! Did that fever boil your brains? Look at his face, just starin' around at everyone. Can't even speak!" he says.

"You better fill your mouth with that food, Derik, and quit all your belly achin over this lad. He just woke up from a week under," the round merc says from across the galley.

"Oh ya, Gav? What're ya gonna do if I don't?" Derik says as he stands up.

Brun stands up as well. "Sit your ass down unless ya feel like swimmin back!" He pounds the table and sends his soup flying. The captain catches the bowl and most of the contents easily.

Everyone sits down and focuses on their food. The captain hands Brun his bowl and pats his shoulder.

"Is it always like this?" I ask Wynn.

"Huh? Oh these guys?" She says barely taking notice. "Yea, unfortunately the mercs are getting worse by the day. We all try and keep to ourselves. It's almost like they're looking for a reason to fight. Just ignore em and they'll focus elsewhere pretty quickly."

Landon nods. "It's true. They've already ended up fighting amongst themselves. A week into a three-week trip. That big oaf, Derik, clobbered one of his own crew just yesterday. That fella sitting alone with his back to us."

Landon subtly motions with a nod to a man about the same size as me. That definitely wasn't a fair fight, that poor guy looks beat ten feet down. Derik who's deep in his soup doesn't have a mark on him.

Landon speaks up. "That poor kid got knocked on his ass and Derik kept on him until Brun threw him off. Looked almost like those two bulls were gonna go at it, but Derik stomped away."

I catch Rena eyeing me. "That's enough about all those brainless fools. How are you feeling? Try not to eat too much. Here." She stands and pours a bit of the soup in another bowl and puts it to the side of her. "We'll save a bit because it'll be gone before we can blink twice. I imagine you're very hungry, but your stomach has shrunken to half its size. You need to portion your meals for a few days. Agreed?"

"Agreed," I say. "Why are there so many mercs on this ship anyway?"

I catch a few confused glances from our group.

"Ah, the life of a blacksmith outside the city," Landon says and they all nod to themselves.

"There's a war brewing, Cael. I'm sure you're aware of it, but we're heading to North Liefland right now. They're nearly at war with South Liefland over land dispute or some such," Landon says.

Rena and Rolin shake their heads and Rolin says, "I don't believe it's the land, I'm almost certain Hector had an affair with King Thokrin's wife, Esnir. They would meet during Queen Esnir's travels to her family estate on the border of South Liefland. When King Thokrin found out, it was the last straw that broke the recent armistice signed between the North and South."

One of the closer mercs barks out, "Who gives a damn what this wars about? War is war and it pays good. Thokrin pays more and that's all there is to it. Nothing else needs saying."

"Oh stop your pissin, Kell. Not all of us are keen on putting our lives out there for a few coins," a young man says. He's definitely not a mercenary like these guys. He's too well dressed, and thin. Way too thin.

He looks over at us. "He's not wrong about Thokrin though. Man pays a hefty sum for seeds as well as souls. I'm not lookin to sell my soul, but I've got plenty of seeds. Word is he's got trading stations posted all along the border. Most well defended places outside the city, too. Besides, I heard it's all about Thokrin having a claim to the South Liefland throne. The way I hear it, he's first in line, Hector is second. Not the land or the women, just more power. If he's fightin' for a unified Liefland, I don't see the harm in that."

The captain waves his hand. "No no no! Shut your traps. Don't be believing that nonsense. Those all be just easy rumors and what them royal bastards want ya to think. The real reason is the uprisings." He leans in close and almost whispers, "You all heard, right? These young folk that be goin missing? Mostly just the young, but sometimes whole families just up and disappear into thin air. Sometimes they're found, all dead. Murdered in the woods. Don't let these stories fool ya, kids. The real reason be the uprisings. Folk're scared. They want answers and they be getting silence on all sides. That silence causes more fear, and fore ya know it, everyone's got their pitchforks and clubs and they blame the crown for that fear."

"But that doesn't make sense. Why would a war stop all the questions?" Wynn asks confused.

"Ah lass, you're so young yet." He smiles gently. "The poor folk don't really want answers y'see; they just be wantin to blame someone. The kings are right smart. They can't take the blame on themselves or folk'll want a new king so a war gives everyone something real to focus on."

"What happen'd to them good folk down the way?! Where'd they go?" He elbows Brun in the side.

Brun looks confused, but realization slowly spreads across his face. "Ah, those cowards down in South Liefland! They're after our land, probably stole those poor folk from the town over, too!"

The captain pats Brun on the back and grins. Brun basks in his praise with a big dumb smile. Everyone else sits quiet for a moment.

The disappearances are causing a war? But... *we're* those kids. My family has to answer those questions. Wynn, her family is gone. Her family is who everyone would be talking about. Did we cause this war? Not us, the people who took us. Landon? He's just doing what he has to like we all are. Aren't we supposed to be stopping the war?

Landon pats my shoulder and breaks the silence. "To each his own, right? So Rena, how did you manage to get an apprenticeship under the good Doctor Alabas? He must be turning people down day in and day out."

Rena looks at Rolin and he nods. "Well it's actually a difficult story. But, I'm proud of my decision and I have nothing to hide." Rolin puts his arm around her as she continues, "Rolin and I met while I was studying medicine in Rensfort. He is an amazing poet and I fell for his words and his lovely face right away. We knew we wanted to get married, to spend our lives together. I was so excited I didn't even think. When Rollie asked me, I said yes before he could get the words out." She looks at him with adoration. "I told my mother and she was so happy, too. But when I told Father, he was, well, he didn't really care about our love. He wanted details about who Rolin was, what his family did, how much money they had. You see, my father is Baron Lasaks."

We all gasp.

"Well I'll be damned, lass, your pa is right near famous. He's got to be third or fourth in line for Kaldia now," the captain says.

Rena nods. "Yes. He never misses a chance to say that to people either. With the King not having any heirs yet, my father is quite close in line. I'm not sure it's fourth but it's close enough for him to dream. Well, that's why he was so angry when I told him I was marrying Rolin. Sweet Rolin is every bit as important as my father, at least to me. He's not a noble and Father told me if I married him I had to leave and never come back."

She begins tearing up. Rolin kisses her cheek and wipes her tears.

"So now I have no family other than Rolin, and he has no family other than me. Whether pity or guilt, or my mother, Father sent word to Doctor Alabas that he needed a favor and that's how I was granted apprenticeship." She sniffs in.

Landon shakes his head, "Forgive me for saying this, but a favor like that, even from and for a Lasaks, would be an expensive favor. I think your father cares for you deeply, and this must have been the clearest solution. He can't have his daughter marry a nameless poet, apologies Rolin, but instead of saying no and locking you up, he gave you a life, a chance to be happy, and still make a name for yourself. I think your father, in his own mind, made the best decision he could for a daughter he loved," Landon says.

Rena sits silently for a moment as tears fall.

"Thank you, Landon. I don't think we would have ever thought of it like that. Even if that's not the true way of things, it is easier to believe," Rolin says, rubbing Rena's back.

Wynn wipes her eyes. "Way to go, Landon. First, we're all concerned about war now we're all sad. I think I'm done for now, we should get rest anyway. Come on, Cael."

She picks up our empty bowls and walks to the kitchen area to put them away. On her way back she grabs the bowl that Rena had filled for me.

"Thank you for caring for him," she says to Rena.

Landon stands up and follows her.

"Til tomorrow!" He waves at the group.

Rena and Rolin wave back, still teary eyed. The captain sits near them hiding his face. Brun stares at them all, still confused.

Chapter Seventeen

"So what else has happened? I still can't believe that I've been sleeping for ten days…" I say as we enter the room. I collapse on the bed while Wynn closes the door behind us.

"I can't imagine what that's like. To lose so much time, it's got to be surreal, almost like a dream. But for us, those ten days were filled with a lot of worry and a lot of waiting. We tried to take our minds off of everything, but…" Landon scratches his head and takes a bite of his bread roll. "I wanted to wait for ya, I truly did, but ten days is a long time. I started Wynn on some basic lessons. With us on nights it was getting really boring. The crew keeps to themselves mostly and, well we only got around to learning a few things."

I could have guessed. They shouldn't have to wait, I can't blame them for learning without me. It wasn't my fault I got sick though. I bet ten days won't matter too much. I can catch up. I hope I can catch up. How long are we at this school? Zaitah's been at the university for years.

Wynn starts shuffling her feet and rubbing her arm.

"What's wrong?" I ask.

"I just feel bad that we started without you. I didn't want you to be left out and now I feel guilty. We didn't do too much, though!" She blurts out.

"Don't worry, Wynn. Truthfully, we should have begun sooner." Landon looks at her with a smile before facing me. "To answer Cael's questions, this whole training process is pretty structured, but it comes down to your aptitude and how hard you work. They like to keep it at five years but I've seen recruits move quickly through the ranks and finish their training in four years, sometimes less. I'm sure it seems like a long time, but it's necessary to cover all the basics and to get a thorough grasp of whichever field you'll be placed in. Every student, or recruit, or whatever you want to call what we are to the academy, has to learn a little bit of everything before specializing. I, being so wonderfully spectacular, finished my education in a mere three and one half years." He waves to us and bows slightly. "Yes, I'm impressive, oh so fantastic! The best of the best, truly!"

Wynn slaps him on the head and sits next to me with a thud. "Forget him; he's nothing special. But what we're learning is really.... Well it's amazing. There's no other word for it. It feels like something out of a story book with witches. I can't wait until tonight when we can teach you, too! Landon can change things. He can turn the air into water, and he can turn that water into ice! He can change wood into dust and even light it ablaze with nothing more than his mind! It's the most breathtaking thing to see, real magic... and we can do it!"

I remember Landon in our dream sticking his hand through a stone bench. Can he do that in reality, too? True magic! The possibilities. We could do anything we wanted. I've never thought about being a king before, but with that power? We could have any kingdom we wanted, maybe even the whole world!

I turn to Landon with a wide smile.

"Calm down, lad, we aren't going to be ruling the world." He flicks a piece of bread at my head. "At least you won't. Maybe I will, I haven't decided yet." He looks at the ceiling, rubbing his chin.

That's definitely not going to happen. He can't even control us. But what if he is serious? I don't know what he's capable of yet. Maybe he does have the power to rule the world.

Landon laughs and throws the rest of his roll at me. "I'm joking you daft twit!"

I rub my head and stick my tongue out at him. "What have you learned so far?" I ask before grabbing his roll and eating it.

"Um, we first tried to learn about... what did you call it, Landon?" Wynn asks, tilting her head.

"Well, the fancy title is maruleth but in practice we just refer to it as telepathy. The topic we focused more on in our lessons was dakileth which we call alteration or manipulation."

"Why do you have so many names for it?" I ask.

"The end part of the word there means to force change upon, apparently. The beginnings are which sense we're focusing on. Maru being the waves emanating from the mind and daki meaning the waves coming from the physical objects around us. That might be right and it might not, I can't really remember." He shrugs

"Alright, so what did you learn? Can you teach me now?" I ask. I want to learn but I'm so exhausted. If I sleep I'll be eleven days behind. I don't want to miss any more lessons.

"I think we should try and relax. You've been damn near dead for a week and Wynn and I have been up nights for our shift on deck and up most of the days worrying about your sorry behind," Landon says as he swats my hair.

Wynn nods her head and yawns. "Even thinking about it I'm getting sleepy. It's not easy worrying. It's tough work. Now that you're better I think I'll hit the hay." She climbs to the top bunk and collapses with a heavy thud on her bed.

I'm such an idiot, these guys have been worrying so much, and they're probably just as tired as I am. Probably more because I've been sleeping this whole time. Does it count as sleeping if you're sick? I did almost die though; that's got to be exhausting. Sleep is probably for the best, but I want to learn!

"Alright, Cael. Stop thinking so loud. I think we all should try and get some rest. Tonight's your first watch. Nothing crazy ever happens but it'll be a big change for you staying awake all night." Landon shoves me to the corner and plunks down on the bed next to me.

"See you on the other side," he says as he closes his eyes.

I lay down on the bed and stretch. Not really sleepy yet, but I suppose I could try.

Chapter Eighteen

A dreamless night. It feels weird not having them but I'm glad I can finally get some rest. I guess it really was the seekers searching for me that caused the dreams. Or maybe Landon just stopped them somehow.

I take my time on a nice long stretch. The sun must be out still, doesn't sound like anyone is setting up in their cabins for the night just yet.

I sneak over Landon's body to put my boots on, carefully avoiding Wynn's arm as it hangs down from the top bunk. She's still sound asleep too. I'd rather not wait for them to wake up. I shouldn't get in too much trouble if I just look around the ship. Not like there's anything else to do here. I hadn't thought of that, there is really next to nothing for us to do on this boat for our weeks long voyage… Well, we have night watch at least. I should see the captain and ask about my job.

I creep out of the cabin and close the door before heading up the stairs. I pass Rena and Rolin as they head to their room.

"How are you feeling?" Rena asks, stopping next to me.

"Much better. I was hoping to see you so I could tell you how grateful I am for your help. I don't want to imagine what would have happened if you weren't here. I wish there was some way I could repay you properly," I say.

She touches my arm, "There's no need for any of that, Cael. I couldn't sit by and let such a sweet face be sick without helping now could I! Don't worry another moment, and don't exert yourself too much tonight. You're still recovering!"

She touches my forehead instinctively and nods.

Rolin pats my shoulder with a grin. "Doctor's orders, lad. You'd best listen." He waves before they disappear around the corner.

I pass the galley and see Trep setting aside some food. He calls out, "Hey boy! C'mere!"

I wave. "Hey there, Trep. What can I do for ya?"

He waves back at me irritated. "Hush a moment boy! I set this food out here, y'see?" He points to the plates. "Every night for the night crew and that group o' yours. This bein' your first time out I figure ya don't know much about how'n it goes. Don't go snoopin or scroungin through me stuff. I give ya 'nuff food and some ta spare even. If I bust in here and see some of my stuff messed round with, I'll be givin ya a whoopin ya won't soon forget. Sound good, boy?"

He looks up at me with wide eyes.

"That sounds... fair? I suppose?" I say dumbly.

He's small now but I wonder if he was bigger when he was younger. He's so old and wrinkled; I can hardly imagine him young, but he had to be. I wonder if he really could lay a beating on me.

"Well what then? Ya need sumthin?" he asks impatiently.

I shake my head. "Oh it's nothing. What's on the menu for tonight?"

"Same thing ya get most nights, boy. It's a ship after'n all. Ya get a biscuit, salted pork and bowl of rice tonight. Some ale and wine if'n it please ya." He nods to himself with a smile. "Some nights we get fish instead've pork if these useless twits can catch anythin. I gots some raisins 'nd cheese, too. And I always plan ta make a few right decent meals fer the crew when it goes and gets real tense 'round here. Like'n it did this afternoon, right near boiled over. But that food sure calms them fools down quick!" He smacks me on the shoulder. "Now go on, get up ta the cappin. He'll tell ya what for," Trep says as he shoos me out of the galley and up the stairs.

I follow his instructions. It can't be too much work at night. Do we have to steer? How do you steer a whole ship? If it just floats along, then what do we actually need to do?

"Hey, Cael!" Gavin calls. He starts towards me as I step on the deck.

"Oh, hi Gavin. How's the mood up here?" I ask.

Gavin shrugs. "About the same as usual, which isn't to say it's good, mind you." He pats my shoulders, "Walk with me." He leads us to the ships bow.

We stand silently for a while before he speaks.

"We've got a long trip still ahead of us. Have you ever traveled before?" he asks, staring out at the ocean.

"Not far, just to the towns and cities close to our home. Never on a ship before," I reply

He nods., "Well for whatever reason Derik has got a hunger to put a beatin on you. Might be cause Brun told him off in front of everyone, might be cause he just wants to thrash someone. Traveling weighs heavy on some folk. They just can't handle it in their minds. Stuck in one place for weeks, sometimes longer. It gets to you. You feel trapped, and you've got nothing to do but think." He drops his shoulders. "What I'm trying to say is, try and keep your head down around Derik and his boys. There's a lot of folk on this ship who've grown used to caring on you these past days and Derik has a lot of guys just itching for a reason to fight. I'd hate to see the ship torn in two. There's no need to cause a rumble."

I stare at him. Why would that guy want to hurt me? I didn't even do anything! I've been sick, I haven't said two words! Derik would probably love it if half the ship defended me, more faces to pummel. I definitely don't want anyone getting hurt because of me. What is it with these mercenaries? They're so stupid!

"If I apologize would that help? I don't even know what I did, but I don't want anything bad to happen," I say.

Gavin shakes his head quickly and waves his hands. "No no no! That'll just heat em up more. All you need to do is keep quiet and don't make any trouble. It'll be easy because you have nights and won't run into anyone too often. Thought I should just tell you the situation on the ship. It's not fair and you didn't ask for none of it, but that don't matter much. Derik is fixing to hurt someone and if you can just keep out of sight, I'd bet he'll forget about it in a week or so."

"Alright." I sigh.

I wish I could understand why these mercenaries like fighting so much. It can't be for the challenge of it if they want to fight me. I'm half the size of those guys. There's no point; there's nothing to gain from beating me. Even if I were close to their size, I've been sick. I can hardly move around yet, let alone fight. They must just be after the weakest guy. Like a wolf after a wounded deer.

"Come on, Cael. Let's go see the captain. I'm sure he's gonna want to run through the night watch do's and don'ts. Not a tough job, but each captain likes to hear themselves talk so we might as well appease him." Gavin guides us to the captain at the helm. "Don't worry overmuch about Derik and his boys. Just mind yourself and stay out of their way."

Gavin squeezes my shoulder as we walk up the stairs.

"Ho, lad!" the captain calls us over. "I tell you, boy. It's good ta have you alive and well! Bad business having a dead body aboard, specially a youngin!" He smiles wide and I count his few remaining teeth. Twelve.

"Yea, I'm happy to be alive, too. Sorry for all the worry though," I say. "Gavin and Trep said you wanted to see me?

"Aye, lad, you'll be up nights with Landon and that little lass there. Now I know Landon well enough, a good man, smart. But you've got your land legs. Never been on a ship so you'll have to learn how to batten the hatches, when to heave to, when ta go leeward or windward and when ta be laying ahull. I only got a few proper sailors up nights with ya, so you best mind their orders!" The captain steps away from the helm and Brun's huge form take his place. Those two are such an odd pair.

He sits us down on some crates and Gavin joins too.

"Listen Captain, this ain't my ship and these ain't my charges, but I'm a fair sailor when I'm being paid for it and I've seen what laying ahull can do. It's mighty tricky and we can't walk a first timer through the once in a lifetime scenario when it'll actually work. I'm not trying to wake up drowning," Gavin says pointedly. He continues with a shrug. "No offense meant, son. It's a smart thing to do but only if the winds are sustained and predictable. If you lay ahull in the wrong storm, this ship will kick broadside and flip before any of us know what's happening."

The captain scowls at Gavin. "Now you listen here, Gavin. I'm the captain and you're my passenger. I don't need you tellin' me or anyone else how to sail proper. Understood?" The captain's face is red with anger.

"Aye aye, Captain. Apologies for overstepping." Gavin puts his hand out and the captain shakes it after a few moments.

"No harm done then. You were just doing what ya thought right, and there's some truth ta what you say."

"Well then, Cael, let's get your lessons started. With some luck, you won't set us too far off course or kill us," Captain says as he settles in.

Wait, why am I responsible for everyone? There's a chance I could kill everyone by making a mistake? How can these people be fine with putting their lives in my hands? I have no idea what I'm doing!

"Calm yourself, lad! Your eyes are going wild. The nights are quiet this time of year. I rise just before dawn and that's the most dangerous time to sail around these parts. Trust me boy, nothing to fear out here. You'll do fine. Just trust that scrawny friend of yours, he's had watch before. Sides, I'd never leave land folk like yerselves up alone. Lian will be watchin' with ya." the captain says as he and Gavin chuckle to themselves.

"The main thing you'll be doing is tacking. Just adjusting the tiller between two points. If I don't miss the mark we'll be heading into the wind over the next few days and we need to make a little to and fro pattern up the coast."

"How are we sailing against the wind?" I ask.

"Ah, the age old question! I've told it a thousand times and still don't quite understand it meself, but it does work. Some time ago a few right smart folk discovered that setting up sails along the keel rather than crossing it allowed the wind to suck the boat to the side. The keel stops the boat from movin' straight sideways 'nd the wind blowing towards the boat, along with proper sail trimmin' and tiller positions, pull the ship forward at an angle. That angle is why we got to be alert and continue tackin' so long as we sail into the wind," the captain finishes and Gavin nods along.

"That doesn't make sense. How can wind that pushes you, end up pulling you?" I ask, still confused.

Gavin shakes his head. "You don't need to understand the how or the why; you just have to trust that it works."

This time the captain nods along. "I can't show you that now as we're sailing with the wind." He rubs his beard and scratches his head. "Lad, I truly don't know what I can show ya right now as we're sailing smooth today."

Gavin sits up and clears his throat, "We could show Cael how to jib the sails, batten the hatches, down the sails or—"

The captain waves his hand. "No no, the young lass there wanted to show him the basic stuff she learned. I been given strict orders."

We sit for a moment and I watch them look around, thinking.

"So what now?" I ask, breaking the silence.

"To be right straight with ya, lad, I don't know!" the captain says, grinning.

"Well what about you? I bet you've got loads of stories to tell. If it's smooth sailing right now, care to share a tale?" I ask with a smirk.

The captain laughs. "Oh, aye, I've got a few tales to tell. You're not wrong. It's smooth today, easy sailing. Getting a little later, too. Good time for stories." He stands up and stretches, "What'll it be then, boy? You want some witch's tale or something that rings true all the way through? Or perhaps a bit of both?" He gazes off the stern and we follow his eyes to the wake of the ship. "I think... a bit of both is a right good place to start."

We've traveled all corners of the Five Lands. Taking cargo, whether people or supplies, from ports here in Kaldia to the Lieflands. From down in Waylinn through them icy seas to the north and on to Oarna. I been on this ship in sun so hot ya can't breathe, wind so strong ya can't stand and snow and ice so thick ya can't move. I got tales by the cartful about people we've seen, thieves we've fought off and creatures that've tried to sink us. But this tale here is something different. This story is about a place. A place we've only seen once, so many years ago.

We were hauling trade goods from Oarna to North Liefland. This was during a rare time of true peace between the North and South. King Herald, the ruler of the day, made plans to have a celebration with all the five rulers. He commissioned a hundred trade ships to bring goods from every port. A thousand caravans to gather supplies from every land. This was set to be the most extravagant celebration ever. King Herald was smart, he knew the world would see this celebration take place in his own Kingdom of North Liefland. And he knew the people would love and revere him above all other rulers. It weren't a bad plan at all, and Herald was as deserving as any ruler before or since. He was just and fair, well-traveled and well spoken, a brave warrior in his youth, and he'd proven himself in battle time again.

The stories of Herald are so many that it's hard to speak of that time without mentioning them. But we're not spinning stories of Herald now. This is a story far from our shores. On the sea route from Oarna to the King's Port in North Liefland, a ship has got to travel north through the icy waters of the Dareen Straight. The storms can pick up and throw blocks of ice so big that they rival castles. Lifted right out of the ocean and tossed aside like a small rock. A boat like ours had no chance if we got caught in a storm like that. We were lucky nine times making that route. Nine times we navigated through that ice so narrow in some spots the men had to get out and chip away at it for us to fit through. Nine times Finra watched us. It was the tenth that paid for all others. A storm formed so fast off to the west that by the time we saw it, it was already upon us.

The sea rose and fell with such force that all the ice around us shattered. We were being thrown along with it, the keel completely out of the water at times. The wind was straight and it was sending us far from our route, but I knew I had to make a decision. I ordered the crew to lay ahull and have the hatches battened down. The only choice we had was to let the wind take us. I posted on the helm for a whole day and night, holding that wheel steady. The slightest rudder movement would spin us broadside, but we held true. Like a stone I was, I had become a fixture of the boat. Clenching all my muscles to not let that wheel move. The darkness was pure, and only when lightning struck did we see the endless seas still churning around us. From within the storm I started to see that we were being drawn towards land. A long lone dock stretched out into the waves. We found ourselves ashore the most stunning and eerie place I'd ever laid eyes on. The trees were the truest green you'd ever seen. The land appeared to be well and truly lived in. The field perfectly trimmed like a royal estate, and yet not a house or person as far as we could see. Just an open clearing of green grass surrounded by those tall, beautiful trees. Beyond the trees were cliffs of ice as tall as any mountain where the storm still raged on, strong as ever.

The waves were calm near us, but out in the distance we could still see the nightmare from whence we came. All around us the storm continued, but not there. Not in that clearing. The men and I set anchor and walked down the path laid before us. The only thing we found was a still burning fire. When we set eyes upon the fire, we stared into it. The fire captivated us for not a single sound came from within, not a crackle. We stared into the flames deeper and saw no wood, no fuel to keep it burning, yet still it burned. The fire sprang from the ground itself. But it wasn't just the fire that made no noise. No sound came from our boots either. We walked along the land and no sound could be heard at all. The breaths we took were as silent as the air around us. A completely still world. We set camp around that fire and no man nor I could muster the courage to break the silence. It was the purest most peaceful quiet. We had no fear then, but as I remember the silence now it sends shivers up my spine.

We laid down without eating and exhaustion quickly stole us from the world. During the night, I awoke feeling something moving near me. The fire still burned and in its light, I saw a woman kneeling beside the men. I watched her over and over as she knelt beside the men, reaching into them. She took something from each, and when she arrived next to me our eyes met. The deepest amber eyes shining brighter than the fire behind her. She bent over my body and I was still as stone. I couldn't move even though I tried. I saw her hand reach into my body and lift out my soul. I screamed, but no noise came, silence all around. As I lay there imprisoned by my own body, I saw the men all staring at me eyes wide trying to scream, trying to move. But none could.

The woman left as silently as she came. She disappeared beyond the trees and sleep stole us again. When I woke up I found myself freed and able to move. I went to wake up the rest of the crew but stopped. Something about me was different. I felt alive. I felt rejuvenated. I felt young again. The woman didn't take our souls; she took our pain. She healed us more than any healer could. At least ten years younger I was, Harry had a broken leg from the storm and it was fully healed, no sign of even a limp. All the crew who had grey hair or any blemish were youthful again. We stared at each other, but none spoke of the woman. We broke camp in silence, just as we had set it up.

As soon as the last of us boarded the ship, we could see the storm start to break. It was like the island itself was telling us that if we didn't leave then, we never would. I knew we all thought the same thing in that moment. We could stay forever. But just as the storm broke, our chance was gone. The sea swept us away, expelling us from the holy glade. We made port in North Liefland the next day, a full week ahead of schedule.

I tell you lads that was some forty years ago and I was about forty then. I'm older than any captain I know and I'd bet everything I have it's because of that woman. Not a day passes that I don't pray to see her again, hoping beyond reason to regain my youth. But I know I could never whether that storm at my age. So not a day passes that I don't pray that Finra keeps me away from her.

Chapter Nineteen

The captain looks up noticing the crowd and his face is as surprised as mine. He gives a bow and shoos everyone away as they compliment his story telling. The sun already dipping below the horizon and making room for stars that begin shining brightly. Stories always seem to make time go by so much faster.

The captain calls out to the crowd and crew. "Thank you, thank you!" He gives another bow. "I've got plenty more stories to tell if ya enjoyed that one! But tonight, I'd rather drink some fine Oarnian wine 'nd enjoy the silence of me cabin."

He makes his way through the group, all patting him on the back and continuing to gush about treasure as he pushes on right into his quarters.

"That was some tale!" Rena says. "Do you think it's true? A fire that cures ailments and bestows youth?! Think of what Doctor Alabas could do with that power!"

"I think it was the woman who cured them, wasn't it?" Rolin asks

"Forget some old doctor, that fire would sell for this ships weight in gold." A young trader pushes to the front and half the ship agrees.

"No ya dumb twit, it was the woman! The woman cured them all, not some damn fire!" another trader says smacking the young one on his head.

I bet everyone will be dreaming of adventure and riches tonight. That's some story though. A woman who took something from them... but what *did* she take? What if she took more than just their pain? What if she took something from them? What does your soul look like?

"Come on, Rena dear." Rolin grabs her out of the throng of treasure seekers. "It's time for bed. Goodnight all. I'll pray for a quiet night for you, Landon." Rolin says as he shakes Landon's hand and he and Rena head below deck.

The crowd realizes the time at Rolin and Rena's departure and they too make their way below deck, still talking about the riches that the fire or woman could bring. They all wish us a calm night before disappearing down the stairs.

I wouldn't get too much use of some cure all like that. I don't have anything really wrong with me, but I guess I'm still pretty young. But to go on an adventure and that be the prize would be an amazing journey! If it's true, of course. The captain doesn't seem like a liar but ... a woman taking away all your pain and giving back your youth? It feels a little wild.

But magic is real, so everything I thought I knew is wrong and that means that fire could be real. That woman could be real. What a journey that would be!

"Landon, have you ever— "

He cuts me off. "What we're calling magic doesn't really work that way, Cael. But to be honest, the storm is familiar, and I have seen ancient objects that are unexplainable by our researchers. The fire could be one such object, but the woman? Well, the woman doesn't fit with anything I've learned. That doesn't mean she's not real, though."

"What do you mean the storm is familiar?" Wynn asks as she plops down on the crate beside me.

Landon joins us. "The academy is found in the sea of storms, which is where we're heading now. Those storms never cease unless the praetors command it."

"What?" Wynn and I say together.

"There's a stone at the top of a tower on the island and the storms center on it. There is a barrier or some reason why the storm doesn't affect us on the island." He says.

"But how?" Wynn and I say together again. We look at each other and laugh.

Landon sighs, obviously growing impatient. "I don't know. No one does. That's the whole point! But, the praetors have a way of causing the storms to stop or calm down. They just subside for a moment. It's kind of like our own impenetrable fortress built by nature itself."

He shakes his head, "Enough about things that cannot be explained. It's time for things that can be. Let's get to our lessons."

Landon checks the sails and the wheel, nodding to the few crew who remain on deck. When he's satisfied, he guides us to the edge of the ship, just out of sight. "Where were we, Wynn? Altering stones?"

"Maybe we could start with heating things?" Wynn suggests.

"No, no, I don't think we should start with that. Maybe we should try something like blocking thoughts?" Landon replies, scratching his head. "I think that's where he wanted to start and you need to learn the correct way as well."

"Let's start over with everything. I don't want Cael to feel left behind." Wynn decides.

"Altering stones? Heating things? Blocking thoughts? I think I'm already left behind." I reply in irritation.

Useless again. I've been dead weight since this whole thing started. She's already learned so much. Why did I have to get sick? Everyone else was fine. Wynn is so far ahead now that I'll just slow her down.

"I'm sorry, Cael! You were sick for so long. We waited for a few days but we needed something to take our mind off your sickness. Rena suggested that we play a game or tell stories but lessons seemed like the best way to spend our time. I really haven't learned much, I'm having a lot of trouble already." Wynn says apologetically.

"Listen Cael, we're a team and you shouldn't feel upset that Wynn is trying to learn. You're not going to slow us down so don't be so sensitive. We would have done the same thing had Wynn been in your position," Landon says simply.

"I'm not being sensitive about it. It's not like I'm some child." I say angrily.

"Then stop worrying like a child would and let's just get started already!" Landon says becoming flustered.

"It's not my fault that you can hear my thoughts! I didn't say anything out loud! Now you say I'm a child because you can hear me thinking? I wouldn't have said a thing if you just left it alone! You two are up here pretending to be witches out of fireside tale and I'm the one acting like a child?" I burst out.

"Quiet!" Landon sneers. He leans around the mast and checks the crew before turning back to me. "Sit down and calm yourself. Wynn and I were worried the whole time you were sick. She was by your side damn near every waking moment. Rena saw she wasn't sleeping and asked me to do something. Yeah, you were sick, but we had to live this past week constantly worried that just days into our travel you would die. To you it must have felt like a single night, but it was ten days! So quit crying and grow up fast. I'm teaching you because I choose to and for no other reason. This isn't some right that you have; it's not something I have to do!" Landon growls back.

"Well, then why even teach us anything? You got what you wanted. You stole us from our families. You win! Why are you pretending to be our friend!" I explode.

"You're right! Maybe I should tie you two up and drop you off on the next caravan to Oarna, let the seekers or the Sephalim deal with you when they find you! You have no idea what I've saved you from, but if you want to see firsthand, I can show you! Why do I even feel guilty about taking you? You're the luckiest damn kid I've ever met! You get these gifts and your parents are unharmed. You're crying about not learning with Wynn. She's not crying and her parents are dead!" Landon hisses in my face. He's nose to nose with me and shaking with anger.

"For the love of the moons, stop all this ridiculous fighting!" Wynn cries out. "What has gotten into you two? You're both acting like children." She stands up in between us. "Maybe we don't need to do lessons tonight. We can just take a break and relax."

"Fine." Landon walks over to the railing and stares out at the ocean.

"No," I say. "I just want to learn, at least what you already know. Do you think you can teach me without our jackass captor?" I say jokingly.

Wynn sighs. "He's not been a jackass until you woke up. And I won't disagree with him. But yes, I'll try. I said we were in this together and I meant it whether you did or not." She grabs my hand and sits us down by the base of the foremast.

"Hmm, where to start," she says, settling down. "Well I can't teach any memory or thought stuff. Landon says the professors will have to show me. I've learned the wrong way or something. I don't do it right. He says I can hear a little, but I'm doing it wrong, and he even said I could speak a little but again, it's not the right voice or something? He says I'm using the wrong thoughts? I block my thoughts, but it's not really blocking them." She shrugs.

"Can you teach me how to do that?" I ask. "I just want to be able to block everyone from my thoughts. That would be a good place to start." If I can just do that then Landon will finally be blocked from my thoughts. I hate not being able to think without being heard. I bet he's listening even now.

I look over at him and he says, "Of course I can hear you. You think so loudly that it's like you're screaming."

Damn you! You damn ass!

"Cael, are you listening?" Wynn asks, folding her arms.

"No, he's not!" Landon laughs.

"He won't stop listening to my thoughts! I can't work like this!" I go to stand, but Wynn pulls me down.

"Just ignore everything. You said you wanted to learn so let's learn. I can't show you how to block thoughts. I don't even understand how I do it; it's like a reflex. But I can sort of show you how to alter temperature. That was the first lesson that Landon showed me after he showed off for a half the night like an ass!" She jokes.

We laugh and Landon makes a rude gesture our way. We laugh harder.

"Alright, enough being petty. Let's start learning." She grabs my hand and within moments she's ice cold, then so hot that I have to pull away before she burns my skin.

My mouth drops open. "How?" I ask dumfounded.

"I wish you'd let Landon help explain, but I'll do my best." She scoots closer and starts waving around and blowing at me.

"What are you doing?" I ask before I start blowing back at her.

"Yuck! Our breath stinks!" she says, blocking her nose. The smell hits me a moment later. Our breath is disgusting! How long has it been since we've cleaned our mouths out?

"Well, why would you do that!" I mumble through my hands.

"I was trying to show you something," she says, plugging her nose.

"Just tell me first, then you can try and explain it."

She nods slowly and huffs, "Fine but you have to listen and not try to talk, deal?" She looks at me, waiting.

"Deal," I say.

"Everything is connected. The whole world is made up of these little, tiny things like grains of sand but even smaller. So small you can't even see them." She yells over to Landon, "What did you call them?"

He waves back still irritated. "Particles."

Wynn continues with a smile. "Right, particles. These particle things are so tiny that even the grain of sand has too many to count. And we can't see them individually, but they're all connected. They move around, some move fast like in the air and some move slow like the stones, but they all move. You can feel it when the wind blows. You can't see anything, but you can feel the wind. You can feel the force of it. I can push air around with my hand or breathe it in. The wind that's blowing now is so strong that we can sail this huge ship through the water."

Confused I cut in. "But what's that have to do with temperature?"

She scowls at me and I bow my head embarrassed, "Sorry. I'll be quiet."

She pats my head. "Good boy. Temperature is really important to all of this, and it's the simplest explanation. All these particles have a strong relationship with temperature. To heat them up, we make them move faster, and to cool them off, we slow them down. It's sort of like all living things. When I'm really cold it's hard to move, but when it's hot I can move around easily."

"But if you're too hot, you just want to sit in the shade." I immediately put my head down. "Sorry."

Wynn sighs again. "You're right. I'm not good at explaining any of this. I told you!"

I can see Wynn thinking about what to say next. After a few moments, a large wave crashes against the side of the boat and water splashes up. I gasp from the cold and Wynn lets out a scream through her teeth.

As we're wringing our clothes out Wynn shoots up with a smile. "I've got it! Water is perfect! When water is warm, it flows freely. All the water particles are moving around fast and when water gets real cold and slow, it turns to ice. All particles are like that. We can heat them up and cool them off by making them change speed. When you realize everything is a bunch of little particles, you can start to feel them and make them move. It takes concentration, but when you feel them you just focus on something like my hand and try to use your energy to change the particles speed. So with the temperature thing, I just close my eyes and concentrate on my hand until I feel the air particles."

She acts out her instructions and puts her hand in the air.

"When I feel them, I can tell how fast they are moving. To get them to move the way I want, I focus on my hand and try and move them. It kind of feels like my hand is vibrating. I make my hand match the speed I want and the particles follow my lead, I think."

She puts her hands one me, one burning hot and one ice cold.

"Your muscles get really tired but it's really cool!" she says, sweating slightly. "Here, you try in this bucket of water." She stands up and brings over a small bucket. "Put your hand in and focus on the water. Think of the water as hundreds and thousands of little bits all coming together. It's water now so it'll be moving quickly, but not fast like the air. You should be able to feel them bounce off your hand, kind of like little bubbles in the water."

I nod along in agreement. This all sounds easy enough. I dunk my hand in the bucket and wait. I just have to focus, not really my biggest strength, but it shouldn't be too difficult. I focus on the water and... wait? I just wait for the bubbly feeling. Alright, think bubbles in the water, particles and bubbles and water? Are bubbles particles too?

....Wynn speaks up. "Do you feel anything yet? It took a bit for me, too. It hasn't been that long yet, you just have to keep trying."

"No," I mumble, hand still in the bucket. My hands been under so long it's going numb. There's no way I'll be able to feel anything now.

Maybe I'm not magic; maybe they got it wrong. I could go back home, see my family and Clout and Laena. Would the dreams start again? The seekers make those dreams. With no magic, they'd have to stop. I could be a blacksmith like Father. A blacksmith doesn't sound that good now. Magic is real. Being a blacksmith, it feels so boring now that the world has magic. I'd probably miss these guys. Wynn is so nice and caring. She really is holding us together. What would she do if I left or wasn't special like she is? She'd probably continue with Landon. She probably has to now.

"Come to join us?" Wynn says as I notice Landon walking over.

"I figured I might as well. Cael doesn't appear to be taking your lessons seriously. He's off in his own thoughts again. Not even thinking about the wind or water." Landon grabs my hand and pulls me to my feet and does the same for Wynn. "Let's stretch out a bit and take a breather."

He reaches out his hand. "I'm sorry for exploding earlier."

"Me too." I return the gesture. "I guess I just felt left out or something. I'm sorry." I say shuffling my feet embarrassed.

"Wynn was right. I didn't mean what I said. We're a team and we're on this adventure together," he says.

I nod my head and look down. Wynn was right. I shouldn't have acted that way. It's not fair to them, especially after they cared after me for so long. It's kind of weird that they've known me for longer than I've known them.

Landon pats me on the back. "It's water under the bridge, Cael. No need to think any longer on it."

I should still apologize to Wynn. She shouldn't feel bad about learning. Besides, if we're in this together, anything we learn on our own we can just teach each other. We walk over to the ships railing and I stand next to her. "I'm sorry about earlier. I was a jackass and you were still kind enough to try and teach me." I smile and jostle her shoulder. "Even if I'm too dense to learn anything."

She laughs a bit. "It was nothing really, I'm sure you'd do the same."

I shake my head. "Not just tonight, I'm sorry for not thanking you for everything you've done. You, Rena, Rolin, Landon, the Captain, Brun, even Trep and Gavin have all been kinder to me than I deserved. And I've just been a twit this whole time. I've been selfish and, and well I'm sorry for all of that."

My dream? When I was sick, was that her? Maybe it wasn't a dream. She was there, and so was Rena. She really has been taking care of me this whole time.

"I think you were in my dream, Wynn. You called me Little Cub, just like my mother does. Landon, you were there too. I think you worried just like Father would have been. You all worried just like my family...."

I stare at the ground realizing how lucky I've been. I miss my family so much. But I am grateful for Wynn and Landon. My throat starts to hurt as I try and hide my emotion.

"You've both been so kind and caring and forgiving. I've been such an ass. It's hard to understand how I can still be so angry with you for what's happening, and all that time see you actually trying to help. I hate this; everything about it. I hate being taken away but you've both done so much to make it better, to make it easier for us all. I've only made it harder for you and still you try and help me. Thank you. I'm sorry."

I cover my face, hiding my eyes. Wynn's arms wrap around me from behind and then Landon pick us both up in his arms before setting us down. Just like Father did all the time. How can I be so unlucky and lucky at the same time? Taken away from my family but given amazing friends.

I turn around and Landon clears his throat and scratches at his eye. "That's enough blabbering for one night." He looks to the horizon. "We've got time to return to lessons if you'd like to give it another go?"

"Definitely," I say.

Wynn and I sit back down in our spot. Landon motions for me to put my hand in the water.

"Wynn did an excellent job explaining, but I think the problem is your impressive lack of concentration. Manipulating these particles is reliant on your ability to focus enough to feel the tiniest movement."

He thinks for a moment before lifting my hand out of the water. "I think you both might be opposites."

"What do you mean?" Wynn asks.

"Wynn, your ability for altering particles is truly remarkable. I've never seen someone understand it so quickly. It takes months to realize what you've explained to Cael tonight and years to be able to teach it so well. I think Cael might have that same ability for thoughts. I've seen it before. I've heard him speak. I can feel that you're both gifted in telepathy and alteration, but the extent seems to be polar opposites. We normally start with the mental side first as it has more immediate use for people in our field. But you, Wynn, were so quick to grasp alteration that we skipped telepathy altogether."

Wynn beams with pride and as Landon sees her, he chuckles. "Oh relax, just because you're talented doesn't mean anything yet."

"So we're learning something else now?" I ask.

Landon nods. "Yes, I should have recognized sooner. This whole time we've been communicating at points with just thoughts. You've already been doing it. We just need to direct your natural ability. Something I imagine will be difficult as you can't focus to save your life."

"Hey!" I shout defensively. Well, he's probably not far from the truth. "But Wynn already can do a lot with her thoughts. She can make it so you can't hear them and more than that, right?"

Landon shakes his head. "Yes but she's using her unconscious voice. She isn't in control of what she thinks and that's why it's so difficult for her to learn right now."

"What?"

Landon shrugs. "We'll talk about that later. Let's just move on to your lessons. Don't worry, I have the perfect one for you. Wynn, you follow along too. It might help you have a breakthrough."

"Close your eyes…. Concentrate on the darkness…. Picture yourself sitting alone in your mind, surrounded by nothing at all. Maybe picture a little beam of light with you in the center. All around that circle of light is complete and utter nothing. Now begin thinking of anything, nothing in particular, just focus on a thought. Let's try focusing on this ship, the wood, the smell of it, the feel of it. Imagine you're hearing your thoughts coming from the you that you've created in your mind. The thoughts are coming from the person you're seeing in the center of that circle of light surrounded by nothing. Keep thinking of the ship, the salty sea air, the cool breeze at night, the stars and moons in the sky. Now picture that circle of light expanding to me. You can see me standing in the circle, just you and I. The words you're hearing aren't spoken now. They are my thoughts. Picture my thoughts entering your circle of light. Good, excellent! Now expand the circle to Wynn. You can see her, sitting in the circle next to us. You can see her mouth moving, now listen to what she's saying."

"The straw beds are so uncomfortable and there's no way to wash your clothes. The foods not bad though, and everyone's so nice. Rena and Rolin are my favorite so far, they're so sweet. They are the perfect couple. I wonder if I'll ever meet someone."

"Wynn, quit talking. I can't hear anything else," I call over to her.

Wynn and Landon jump up. Landon smacks his leg, laughing. Wynn's cheeks flush.

"You did it, lad! I knew you had the gift. That day we first met, you heard my thoughts, I knew it!" Landon exclaims with a pat on the back.

"Great, now two people can hear my thoughts. I'm going to have to block them forever." Wynn pouts and kicks her feet.

She turns her face up, excited, "But it is great news that we are both blessed with genius!"

I heard thoughts? I really do have magic? What else can I do? Landon took us on that journey into his memories, that would be amazing! Real power…

"Wow," I say slowly.

"Yes, wow indeed. Well this makes lessons a little bit tougher. Hmm." Landon stares up at the sky.

It's already almost dawn, the sky is purple and soon the captain will be up. He said he gets up earlier than everyone else. He would crack right in front of us if he caught us doing magic!

"Alright kids, give me a moment to think of tomorrow's lesson. Off to bed with you. I imagine Cael is quite exhausted."

"I'm starving, not exhausted," I say and Wynn grins before darting down below deck.

She calls back through giggles, "Me too!"

I chase her down and we grab the food Trep left on the tables. We devour the cheese and rice and start chewing mouthfuls of pork and raisins. It's not as good as the stew he made, but Trep must really try to make everything decent and at least a little bit different.

After a few mugs of wine, everything begins tasting much better. A lot better. Wine should be a seasoning! Why don't we drink more wine at home?

"What stirring conversation we've just had. We haven't even said a word or nothing," I say as I try and stand up. "Man, I'm a little dizzy. We should try and go to bed."

Wynn laughs. "Dizzy already!? You are such a walnut!" She stands up. "Wow, I'm dizzy. We should try and go to bed."

I laugh as we stumble down the hallway. "I just said that you drunkard!"

We support each other until we get to the doorway to our room and get stuck trying to fit through at the same time.

"Ladies first, you scoundrel!" She shoves me aside and we both fall over losing our support.

Footsteps come from down the hall. "Oh no! We're in trouble, quick hide!" I whisper to her.

We scramble inside, collapse onto the floor and pretend to sleep. Landon's exhausted voice floats into the room, "What have I gotten myself into...."

Chapter Twenty

"I'm dying…. Someone get me some water." Wynn moans.
"Me too." I croak.

My mouth is so dry it's hard to speak. I can barely open my
eyes I'm so dehydrated. I roll out of bed and collapse on the floor.
I sit up and get hit by Wynn's swinging foot as she slides off the
top bunk. "Ow! Watch where you're going!"

"Oh shut it. Don't be so loud I've got a splitting headache."
She slides down and looks around our room, rubbing her eyes.
"Where's Landon? Did we oversleep?"

I don't know! Why is she asking me? I just woke up. I
don't want to think about anything right now; it all hurts. My
heartbeat is pounding so loud in my head it sounds like someone
working a forge. I'm still so exhausted from being sick. I'm just
too weak and tired for this day to start…

"No questions please," I say rubbing my face.

"I have to pee really bad. Let's go." She grabs my hand.

"Can it wait? I'm so thirsty I just want a little water first."

"Just come on!" She pulls me along.

"This whole ship is so dirty." Wynn calls from the toilet.

I really don't want to go in there. It's a turd covered hole in
the boat. I'm getting sick just thinking about it. I wonder if there
are other holes we can pee through or if this is the only one.

She walks out. "Alright I'm a little better. Let's go get
some water."

"Well, now I have to pee. I'll meet you up in the galley." I walk in and pee out a brown stream. I really need to get some water. I've never seen pee that color before. It can't be good.

I walk out, Wynn already standing by the stairs waiting for me. We make our way to the galley. It must be just after noon. Still a few people grabbing something to eat.

Landon waves us over to a table where he's sitting with Rolin and Rena.

"Look who finally woke up! You two really need to learn how to handle your wine." He looks at Rena and Rolin. "I had to pick these fools up off the floor and put them to bed last night."

Rolin chuckles with Landon but Rena gets serious.

"Cael you need to be drinking water with your wine, or at least some beer, especially during recovery. You can't afford to get dehydrated. Our water rations are limited, but don't be afraid to use yours and ask one of us for ours. Your body needs to be fully hydrated to properly recover," Rena says, rebuking me. "And you Wynn, you're supposed to be looking after him until he's well again."

"Sorry," we say as we sit down.

Landon pushes mugs of water in front of us and we drink them down quickly. Landon points to a barrel and flicks his head. "It's over there."

We follow his direction and dip our mugs in the water before returning to the table.

"Ahh the ignorance of youth," Rolin says with a shrug. "The worst part is that they'll be perfectly fine in a few breaths whereas we'd be recovering all day long."

The three of them nod in agreement before Wynn speaks. "Is it long past midday?"

"Not too far past, still a while yet before we break for supper and hand the helm over to you," Rolin says.

"What have you all been doing to pass the time?" I ask.

All of them think for a moment before Landon says, "Sit here and wait. Sit in our cabins and wait. Sit on the deck and wait. Just sitting somewhere and waiting mostly. Making nice with everyone, trying not to give Derik and his goons a reason to start a brawl."

Rolin chimes in. "We've got a few fishing rods and nets that we use when we get overly bored. Plenty of food on the ship, but a fresh catch is always nice. Although the sun can be a bit intense around this time of day."

"So, we just do nothing most of the time?" I ask.

Father and Mother would beat me for being lazy if I didn't work just one day without reason and here we are on a three-week voyage doing nothing? How do they deal with being confined like this? It's like we're animals or something. No, it's even worse because animals get to wander around. I wonder if this is what being locked in a dungeon feels like.

"Well, you could always swab the deck or clean the head," Wynn says getting a smile out of the group.

"That 'toilet' is more disgusting than week old dead bodies," Rena says and Wynn shakes her head quickly in agreement.

"Hey youngins, get over here and eat some of this porridge. Made it up nice with a hint of cinnamon. Mackey, one of them merchant folk gave it over yesterday," Trep calls out to us.

He hands us big bowls with the sweetest smell.

"Make sure ya thank that nice fella, was mighty kind to part with his spices. Good folk on this boat by n' large I'd say, good folk," Trep says walking away.

"Trep come and join us? You're always back there working, take a load off, and stay a while." I call out to him with a wave.

Trep hesitates before smiling with a shrug. "I can spare a few moments to get off these old feet."

He seems like such a kind old man. I wonder if he has any family? How long has he been on this ship?

"Were you with the captain thirty years ago when he found that fire?" I ask.

"Aye, lad. The most prettiful place we'd ever seen it was," he says as his eyes wander to the ceiling.

"You've been with the captain since the beginning then? What made you decide to join him?" I ask.

"That'd be a right long story, folks," he says waving his hands.

I gesture to everyone sitting down, "We've got nothing but time here, Trep. I'm sure we'd all like a nice long story, the longer the better!" I press him.

"Oh, no. Ya won't get nuttin outta me boy!" He retorts

"Why not?" I say deflating.

"On account of me story being like a perfectly cooked stew. It can't be rushed none, and I ain't got the time ta do it proper." He smirks, "But boy, do I have one to tell!"

"You can't leave it like that!" Wynn cries out and the room agrees.

"Oh but I will." He says standing up and leaving the group in disappointment.

I huff, "Well what're we supposed to do now?"

"Oh, I forgot! I wanted to show you all about how to sail." Wynn grabs my arm and drags me up the stairs.

"But the food!" I call out, watching the galley fade away.

We emerge onto the deck as the sun begins to set, casting an orange hue on everything it touches.

"Alright, ready?" Wynn asks excitedly. "So these are called masts! They are where the sails are. Obviously. And there's a front one and one over there called the fore and aft, or after and fore? I think it's fore and aft. Well anyway...."

It's so odd to think that everyone has a story. They've all lived their lives and made decisions and I've never met any of them. The whole world is full of people that I'll never see or know anything about. So many people living and dying and I won't even meet most of them. So many people that could be making choices right now that could affect me or the people that I do know. Just like these magic people, they've made a decision to steal us all, and those other people made a decision to kill Wynn's family. But Landon made a decision to try and help us. It's all too much to even think about. So many decisions. Crazy to think that just a few days ago magic wasn't real and now it is. Journey's like this were just in stories and now I'm living it. Sometimes it's not so bad. The view sure is gorgeous.

"Hey! Are you even listening!" Wynn shoves me.

"By now you should know the answer to that." Landon says smiling.

"It's so easy to get lost in thought, staring at the sea, even for us regular folk. Can't imagine how hard the pull is for you, Cael," Landon says catching my eye.

He turns around and leans on the taffrail. "I figure we can split the night between practicing our alteration skills and our telepathy."

He checks the sails and the wheel before we sit down by the foremast again. The moons are already high and bright. How long was I staring?

"Being as our good friend Cael appears to have some issues focusing, we'll start with thoughts again," Landon says.

"We can begin where we left off. See if you can find your way back to my thoughts. Wynn, I'll direct you silently so Cael can concentrate."

They sit cross-legged facing each other and Wynn closes her eyes.

Alright this should be easy, I close my eyes and pretend I can see myself. Something about a light on me for some reason. Then I imagine the light expanding and picture Landon and Wynn. Why do my eyes need to be closed? I could see them right now if they were open. How does any of this work? I guess it did work last time… I'll focus on Landon and see what this walnut has to say.

"Now try and picture yourself first." Landon instructs. "Finra's beard, that was fast Cael!" Landon nearly shouts.

"This is stupid! I can't even get past the first step. Isn't there another way to teach me?" Wynn complains.

"Yes of course, at least I think so, but we'll figure that out in a moment. Let me see how far I can go with Cael. Practice your alteration for a few moments. See if you can heat a splinter enough to have it catch fire." Landon faces me but quickly swings around. "But don't light the whole boat on fire!"

He turns towards me. "Close your eyes again. It's easier this way, trust me. Picture yourself and picture me. Hearing thoughts is basic, everyone is always thinking and constantly projecting those thoughts outward. The louder they think to themselves the easier it is to hear. Speaking directly into the mind is the next step. In your mind, imagine us talking. Imagine my mouth moving as you hear my voice. Now picture yourself talking to me, but only in this clearing in your mind. Try it now."

Can you hear me?

"Yes!" Landon explodes, but he quickly deflates, "Hm."

What is it?

"You think so loudly that I'm not certain if you're actually speaking to me or if I'm simply hearing your normal thoughts," he says out loud.

"Why don't I try on Wynn?" I ask.

"Excellent idea! Wynn, Cael is going to attempt to communicate with you directly. Tell us when you can hear him." Landon says as he sits back down.

"Works for me," she replies.

I picture Wynn in my imagination. This is all so surreal. I need to know how this works. Why does this work? Focus dammit! Alright, Wynn, the light, thoughts.

Wynn, can you say something? I need to imagine you're talking to me.

"He asked me to say something. What do you want me to say?" she asks

I think that's fine. It doesn't matter what you say I only needed to be able to imagine your mouth moving. I guess, anyway. I have no idea how this works.

"Oh, alright," Wynn says.

So now I just speak? Uh, Wynn can you hear me now?

"Yup! I can still hear you!" she says.

What were we supposed to do again? He wanted me to speak to you, but I don't remember how I was supposed to do that.

Landon bursts out laughing. I open my eyes and he's on his side clutching his stomach.

"What?" Wynn and I ask together.

"You!.... You!..." He rolls over, laughing harder.

"Moons above man! Pull yourself together! What in the world is so funny? I was just doing what you told me to do!" I scold him.

He sits up and wipes his eyes, "You were talking to her that whole time with your thoughts! From the very beginning of, 'Can you say something,' it was all in your head!"

Wynn starts chuckling now as well. I suppose it *is* kind of funny.

"This is good! So we can speak and we can hear." He settles down and starts thinking. "There are so many things to teach you but they will begin to get advanced now."

"Like what kinds of things?" Wynn asks.

"At the academy, once a student shows an aptitude for telepathy, we usually begin teaching them to focus on guiding the subject's thoughts. Normally in an attempt to get information. But we can also plant our own memories or fabricate new ones, control senses, some can even take over the motor functions of another. These skills could even extend to animals, but I've never mastered that. Basically, you can know everything about a person, make them believe anything and eventually make them do anything."

"Wow… that seems so dangerous," I say. Someone who is practiced enough could do so much damage. That's a scary amount of power for one person to have.

"Yes. It is dangerous and it should seem very scary," Landon says. "Luckily, we've found ways to recognize when someone is trying to get in our minds, and also ways to defend against it. It might not work if the attacker is skilled enough, but it will at least deter them."

"I think I'd like to learn how to defend my brain first," I say. I'm a loud thinker so anyone could get in my brain I bet. Defense first, Father always says.

"True, very true. I suppose we can start with the basics of how to block your thoughts. You have to understand that a good defense comes from understanding the attack, though." Landon finishes.

"But I can block my thoughts!" Wynn says excited.

"Yea! She's been hiding for months by blocking her thoughts. How could she do that?" I chime in.

Landon shakes his head. "No, no, no, you aren't blocking your thoughts. I've already told you, it's different. You're simply thinking in a different way. You're thinking quietly. You're using a stream of undirected thoughts, living in the moment, trying not to focus on anything. Now don't get me wrong, that's impressive in its own right. It takes a long while before recruits tend to understand that, but it's not the same thing. Having no directed thoughts and protecting your thoughts, those are completely different things."

"This is all so confusing." Wynn complains.

"And it's only the beginning." Landon smiles. "I'm sure there are a few recruits whose skill stops here, but most will learn enough to be dangerous."

He settles us down again by taking a deep breath and we follow his direction.

I wonder if Wynn will ever be able to actually block thoughts. It shouldn't matter too much, I mean she can already hide. If I never understand the alteration thing, will I be able to defend myself? I'm lucky to have her here; she can do the other magic thing and I'll do the mind magic stuff. Although, Landon says we're both gifted, so I bet with enough practice we'll both be really good at it all!

"Alright, we can do a basic exercise to practice shielding your thoughts and then we'll move on to alteration," Landon instructs.

"Finally!" Wynn sighs.

"I'm honestly not quite sure how to begin...." Landon continues as he scratches his nail against the foremast.

After a moment he speaks up, "I'm not really an instructor and I don't think they'll be appreciative of my lessons. They're always going on about needing the freshest minds because it's easier to mold them or shape them or whatever they say."

"Then why are you teaching us?" Wynn asks again. "We're grateful and everything, but if you could get into trouble, or worse, we get into trouble, why do it anyway?"

Landon sits thinking for a moment before shrugging. "I don't know! It probably seems a bit odd, but I think it mainly is the fact that we're on a long trip and we'd all be bored to death without something to do. There could be something else I suppose, but I can't think of it." He shrugs and Wynn shrugs along with him, accepting his explanation.

"Alright, if we're satisfied let's see about the next lesson for Cael," Landon says as he stands up.

Landon gets a bucket filled with seawater and places it in front of us. He reaches into his pockets and a few loose pebbles scatter across the deck. He looks crazy chasing the small stones around. They're barely visible as they roll away from him. He manages to capture some and returns to our spot at the base of the foremast.

"Where'd you get those pebbles?" Wynn asks.

Landon waves her off, "It doesn't matter, just listen. Our minds are constantly sending out these waves. It's kind of like sound, but not really. No, no, forget that, it's not like sound. Well, we speak, the sound gets quieter the further away we are, right?" he asks, looking at us and waiting for us to agree. We nod and he continues, "So maybe sound does work. But this bucket is like our mind. And every time we think something it's like dropping a pebble in." He drops the smallest rock in the bucket.

"Now if I have an aptitude for hearing thoughts, it's almost the same as hearing any other sound. It's easier the closer you are. And we can hear pieces of a thought, like these small waves that come after, from much further away. Anyone who *can* hear your thoughts, *will* hear your thoughts if they are close enough. Or in our friend Cael's case," He drops the largest rock in and it splashes out. "I'm guessing they could hear from a bit further away."

Wynn chuckles and Landon smirks at me.

"Yes, yes, I think too loud, I get it. That's what we're trying to stop from happening so just get on with it then," I grumble.

Landon points to me. "You do think too loud! But that's beside our current lesson." He motions to the edges of the bucket. "If these edges weren't here, the ripples would spread very far. But this is a bucket, not the ocean or a lake, so it's these walls we're focusing on. The walls contain the ripples and right now your minds are uncontained. They send waves out constantly and those waves are far reaching. This is how our seekers could find you, and also how the Sephalim found Wynn."

"So how do you contain the thoughts?" I ask impatiently.

Will my thoughts bounce off the walls I build like the waves in a bucket? If my thoughts are louder, will I be able to think at all or will it drive me insane just echoing in my head?

Landon continues, "You need to confine your thoughts to a specific place. We're so used to thinking freely and letting our minds wander that it's difficult to change. At first it is very hard to constantly be aware of your own thoughts, but it gets easier with practice. The best way I can explain how to do it is to think of yourself in that circle in your mind and picture a house there. You can only speak inside that house. It's a wild concept, but that's how I do it,"

"Can we just whisper instead?" I ask. That would make about as much sense as building a house in my head and pretending to live there.

"Trying to lower the volume of your thoughts is a good idea in theory, but that's not what we're trying to accomplish here. It's a muscle movement, that house thing. It's an actual muscle in your brain that is engaging. Like when you have an eye twitch or some random bit of muscle twitches on your leg or hand. A small muscle that we need to find and then learn to use at will."

He puts his head in his hands and then shoots up.

"Have you ever seen someone who could wiggle their ears?" he asks

We both shake our heads no.

Landon sighs but continues, "Well people can do that and it's a weird muscle. Not many people can do it, but I bet there are many more people who *can* do it but don't know they can. Do you understand what I'm trying to say? Learning how to hide or conceal your thoughts is like that. You have to try thinking odd things until you finally move that muscle. Once you isolate that muscle movement you'll be able to contain your thoughts. Everything we do takes energy and being able to use the energy correctly is the key. And no, Cael, containing your thoughts doesn't make them echo in your head. Although you can absolutely hear the difference, oddly enough it sounds like you're in a place with no walls and no echoes. It gets exhausting, causes severe headaches, some people can even have strokes or bleed from the eyes or ears. But all this stuff has side effects. We risk a lot to be able to use these gifts which is why it's that much more important that we train all the time and practice with caution."

Great, bleeding from the eyes sounds like a real treat. What's next, death?

"So what exactly are you asking Cael to do right now?" Wynn pushes on.

Landon looks over slightly confused. "He has to find a way to block his thoughts."

"Just like that?" I ask. "Oh yea, just block your thoughts. Build a pretend house in a pretend circle in your imagination, works every time!"

"Well, the house works for me, but everyone has different tricks they use. It's up to the individual to learn what works best for them. You have to try new things until you find it. I told you I'm not a damn professor." Landon stands up annoyed.

"There aren't any other instructions?" Wynn asks, frustrated. "Surely there must be something else?"

"Well, Cael is so good at this already maybe he can explain it better when he finally figures it out. But right now you can't, so you have to try it my way. It's like an intense concentration, but you need to focus on the goal, and your mind will figure it out. Just trust your mind and body. These things are already in you. You're just trying to uncover them," Landon says.

"What do you guys do while I'm over here trying to 'figure it out?'" I ask.

"I guess I could move on to Wynn's lessons and just leave you to it. That was my plan at any rate," he says.

"How will you know if Cael does learn to block his thoughts?" Wynn asks. "Won't you need to be concentrating with him to see if he's getting closer?"

"Oh trust me, I'll know! That kids' thoughts are as loud as mine to me. Maybe even louder. It's sort of weird to be able to hear thoughts. It's easy to separate them, but once you figure it out, it's rarely ever quiet again." Landon sits down and gazes into the sky.

I follow and see that it's already getting late, probably just before midnight. These lessons really do help pass the time.

"They do and I hope you guys continue learning," Landon says as he smiles my way.

Wynn looks confused but just for a moment. She must be getting used to Landon responding to my thoughts by now.

"What's it like being able to hear everyone's thoughts?" she asks.

Landon breathes deeply and lets out a long, heavy sigh. "It's overwhelming really. No one ever expects anyone to be listening to their thoughts. What they think is personal, it's all very private to them. Sometimes it's easier to block out everything, especially in cities. Every step in a city brings new thoughts. You wouldn't believe if I told you the thoughts that some people have. Some people even have multiple voices in their heads! It's hard to understand them at first, just like real voices, I suppose. There's almost a privacy being in the crowd because there's so much noise it's hard to focus on a specific stream of thoughts. But with practice you can focus and hear individual thoughts as clearly as your own even in a crowded city square."

He stops a moment and stands up. "It's not easy." He walks to the railing and stares out at the water, "We hear all their thoughts, and we can feel emotions. The happiness, the fear, the anger... the sadness. Let me tell you there is more sadness in this world than either of you could ever imagine."

"Why don't you just block it all out all the time?" I ask.

He shrugs and turns to face us. "It's useful. And we're trained to be useful. We could block it out, and sometimes we do. But what *you* need to do is learn to stop other people from hearing your thoughts. So get to it, lad! Come on Wynn; let's move away from Cael so he can attempt to concentrate. It would be a miracle if he does." He smirks and Wynn waves to me as they walk towards the helm of the boat. Landon motions to the two crew who've been mulling around the wheel and they shake his hand before heading below deck. He's probably giving them the night. I'm sure they're dying of boredom with nothing to do. I wonder if Landon is in charge at nights?

Lessons. Alright. Where do I even start? This is so unnatural. It's a muscle, but I don't know I have it? It's almost like a puzzle. The instructions have to be able to be explained better than this. Mother always says that a good teacher is able to explain anything that they truly understand. Maybe Landon doesn't grasp how this all works yet. It'll be like a blind man trying to hunt. I'm sure he'll teach us stuff, but it's not quite with purpose, mostly luck.

It doesn't matter. He's all we have for now. He is trying and this is definitely better than nothing. I guess he is a pretty decent guy. Maybe I'm too hard on him. He did say he finished at the academy early. Maybe he does know what he's talking about. Maybe this house thing will work for me.

Focus, deep breaths. There's the imaginary me in my brain clearing. Moons above, I hope there's better words for this stuff at the academy. It's crazy that I can hear thoughts just by doing this. It doesn't even make sense! Stay focused! Just need to picture a random house in the clearing in my mind. My house would be perfect. It's small but just the right size for our family. There's Mom and Dad. I wonder if I could hear their thoughts? How could I tell if it's really them and not my imagination? When I heard Wynn, it sounded like her real voice, so I suppose I could tell that way. It's hard to get voices just right when you're imagining them in your head. But Landon said it gets quieter the further away you are. We're so far away now, I don't even know how far away we really are, halfway to North Liefland maybe? There's no way I could hear them this far. How far can the seekers hear?

Clout's probably bored out of his mind without me. I wonder if they're still sad. What did they tell the town? What did they tell Marak and Laena? I can barely picture her anymore. I wonder who she'll marry? It's odd to think of us getting married but I guess it was as set in stone as anything. Luther was convinced of his future and was so upset about it. I bet if he knew people could steal you away and kill your whole family he'd be fine with being a farmer and marrying Milly.

At least Mother had us save everything we earned so they could be fine without working at all for a long while. They could move, become traders. Father likes to be settled but Mother always wanted to travel. With me and Zaitah gone, they could do just about anything they wanted. Clout would like traveling, he'd get to stretch his long legs and enjoy the days.

Dammit! I need to focus!

Clearing, me, house, alone. Got it. I can sit on my bed and … What now? He never said anything else. Just be in the house in your mind. I'm just meant to know when it works? Nothing seems different.

Oh man, I'm hungry. I stand up and stretch my sore legs. Landon and Wynn are still learning all the fun stuff. What?! They made a little fire?! This mind stuff is so boring! I want to learn how to make fires and cast spells like a real witch in a fireside tale!

They don't even see me. I'll just go eat by myself.

I walk below deck and down the stairs to the galley. Trep left us some jerky and cheese. Oh and a bit of rice. That man loves his rice.

I sit at the table and dig in. Have to make sure to drink a bit of water with the ale tonight. Waking up was awful this morning. Definitely no rum or wine, but ale never tasted good to me. Father doesn't like it much either, but Mother loves herself a good mug of ale. It's just too damn bitter for me, makes my mouth all dried out. This rice really is good, salty from the sea water. Trep has a gift.

They still probably don't even notice I'm gone yet. Up there in their own pretend world doing magic stuff. The fun stuff too, none of this boring stuff. I'm just going to bed. It's late enough. I'm still so run down, I hardly have any energy at all. I wonder when I'll feel better again.

I finish eating and clean up my space before heading down to the cabins. It's so loud down here, all the mercs snoring echoes down this tight space. I could probably run right past them with iron greaves on and they wouldn't come close to waking up. At least we have decent quarters, somewhat private from those guys. It would be like the White Days of Winter for Derik if I was sleeping out with them. He'd murder me.

I fall onto the bottom bunk and kick my shoes off. Will I ever learn to do the stuff they're doing right now? None of it makes any sense. If Landon just said it was magic and left it at that, maybe it would be easier. It's so much more difficult trying to have some sort of explanation behind it. Maybe if I had to do it all again, I'd pretend there was no reasoning. But small things that are a part of everything? Controlling those things controls everything else? It's all nonsense! The air has these little bits of floating junk? But so does the water? If everything has these particles, people and animals must too, right? I mean it makes sense. Well none of this makes sense, but if we pretend it did then that would make sense, too. The air, the wood of the ship, the water. Yea, so if all that stuff is little particles than people are too. Are thoughts particles? We can control them, so is everything that we can control particles? Why is it so much easier for me to hear thoughts but Wynn gets to make fire like a real witch from a faery story? If I could do that stuff smithing would be a breeze! Everything would come out perfectly. I bet Father would get so jealous! No, he'd probably just be proud.

Damn, I could do so many things with those gifts. I wonder, if magic is real... are all those fireside tales about witches real?

I can't wait to learn everything!

Chapter Twenty-One

"It's not real anyway." Mother says nonchalantly. "Just some silly story your father told, don't believe a word of it!" She kisses my forehead before heading towards the kitchen.

"But it seemed so real," I say. It was real, too real. People chasing me. They... they wanted something. They wanted me.

"I told you they weren't real!" Mother yells. She suddenly turns red with rage as she clenches her fists.

"I'm sorry, Mum. Take a breath!" I plead. Did she hear my thoughts?

Mother disappears and is replaced by a cloaked figure. Face hidden in the shadows of its hood. Reaching towards me with a monstrous claw and screaming in pain.

"Wake up, Cael!" Wynn yells as she shakes me out of bed.

"What!? Where are we!?" I cry out as I roll off the bed and slam onto the floor. A sharp pain streaks through my throat and I reach for my neck.

"Everything is alright. You just had a bad dream," She says as she falls back onto the bed. "You scared me half to death with those screams. You sounded like a dying animal or something." She drops her arm over her face, covering her eyes.

"I'm sorry," I say climbing back onto the bed. "It was so weird. I don't remember most of it, just the end. Mother was saying something about not believing any of it, but then she turned into something. Almost looked like... never mind." It couldn't have been. It's just a dream anyway. I can't wait to get off this boat.

"Well, that's enough excitement before breakfast, wouldn't you say?" I ask Wynn and she nods her head underneath her arms.

"Where's Landon?" I ask.

"Dunno, must've gotten up before us. I only just woke up, thank you for that by the way. I think I peed a little," she says.

I laugh. "Sounds like a problem. You should get that checked out." She throws her arms off her face and scowls at me. I hold my hands up and back away. "Sorry! I was joking! ....So do you feel like eating?"

"Of course I do, you nitwit. Just let me finish peeing first, preferably in that sad excuse for a privy. Although now that I think about it, I don't really prefer using it. Maybe I'll pee on your bed instead," she threatens as she stands up on the bed, "It'd probably make it smell better anyway, I swear you two have created some demonic odor around you. Why do boys smell so bad?"

"Well, you're no autumn apple yourself! We haven't cleaned ourselves in weeks. It's bound to happen. It doesn't help that we're locked down here so we just fester like a dead fish." I shake my head. "Enough, enough, let's go use the head and go get food."

She jumps off the bed and nods in agreement. "That sounds lovely."

It's almost a normal routine now. Almost normal. That's a funny thought. Norma was such a faraway idea, I never even considered life could be anything but miserable after leaving home. We forget everything and move on so quickly. I have to make sure I don't ever forget my family or my village.

"Go on then, I'm starving." Wynn yawns as she shoves me into the head.

I relax a bit as I relieve myself. Someone must have cleaned up in here. There's definitely not as much poop all over the place. Finra save who had that job.

"Did you clean up in there?" I ask her as I walk out.

"No way! I just told you I'd rather pee in our room than come back here. You couldn't pay me enough to clean that thing," she says. "But, I'm glad someone did. I could almost breathe in there. To the food!"

She grabs my arm and we walk up the stairs. As soon as we emerge from the lower deck, we spot Landon sitting with the usual group and they wave us over.

"Well, look who it is, folks. These children would sleep all day I tell you," Gavin says with a smile. "Though I suppose it *was* getting a bit boring without the young folk to liven it up."

Rena and Rolin nod along with Gavin.

"Time does seem to go by faster when you're both awake," Rena adds as Rolin cleans their plates.

I wave my hands. "Hey now, don't put all that on us. It's just the stories that everyone's been telling. We're strangers floating on a ship in the middle of the ocean. The only thing that could make time move at all is a good story."

I scan the crowd. We've already heard from the Captain. Trep sounds like he's got something special to tell us but he's holding that story tight. Rena has given us a little bit of hers. Those mercs probably can't tell a story to save a life. Rolin is a poet! He must know a hundred stories! I bet he could entertain everyone for the next two weeks by himself and still have stories to spare!

"Oh no, I see the way you're looking at me, lad. These stories aren't my own and I only tell 'em for coin!" Rolin says swatting my hand as I grab his shoulder. But I notice a smile forming and Rena gives him a nudge.

"Oh, everyone just wants someone to listen to, dear. Just one story and Cael will move along to the next victim, right Cael?" Rena says and I nod slowly.

It'll be hard to get anyone else to talk especially after a real story. But maybe if I just ask him questions about his stories right after he finishes he'd lead into another?

"'Tis true, on my honor, I'll wollop Cael if he asks for more," Gavin says with his hand raised and his eyes closed.

"What!? I didn't even say anything!" I protest as we all laugh.

"Even all these folks can hear you thinking, Cael." Landon says smirking.

I anxiously search the group for a confused face but everyone is too busy laughing along to take notice. I shoot him a dirty look and he shrugs.

"So what do ya say, Rolin?" the captain asks.

"Well I'm not sure which tale to tell. I've got some big shoes to fill here. You've told an impeccable tale." He pauses for a moment.

"My life is not filled with adventure, or dramatic choices. I had a typical childhood in the city near a university. I loved books. The story books were my favorite. They didn't need to be real. I just had a fondness for the words," Rolin says.

"So what story, man!?" Gavin pushes.

Rolin smiles. "I'm not a bard or travelling storyteller, just a poet."

Gavin slumps down.

But!" Rolin says, catching our ears, "I do know an interesting story that might relate to the captain's..." He pauses.

Everyone perks up. This definitely sounds like a good one! Wynn and I rush to fill our mugs and plates before he begins.

"This is a story of magic, and faraway places."

All have heard tales of the Broken Mountains and the strange things that are said to happen around them. People tell of witches and faeries and of other beings that have no place in our waking world. Few stories, though, reach far enough back to see the why of it all. To try and make sense of the mystery.

I've heard of one such tale, a tale older than any other I know. It's said that those mountains served as a barrier between realms. A realm of our reality and a realm of something different... Something magical.

All that lie beyond the mountains now is a vast and unforgiving desert. Seeing that expansive nothingness, many stop their journey right there and turn around. But if we choose to believe the stories then our realm stops at those mountains. If you possessed the strength to cross the Desert of Bair, perhaps you would be granted leave of our world and entrance to another. This tale is a tale of what lies beyond.

Long ago, before books, even before history, there were two kingdoms. One was a kingdom of man, as we are today. The other was a kingdom of something older than man, something so ancient that even time has forgotten. It was a kingdom of beings that defy reason, a kingdom of monstrous creatures that were part beast and part man---

Derik slams his fists down, "Damn all! When are we gonna hear about some wenches!? Where's the war, love and drinking!?" He bursts out.

The other mercs shout in agreement and Derik continues. "We're sick of these faery tales for the kids! Give us some damn action, something real that we can listen to!" He roars.

Rolin starts to speak but the captain stands up first.

"You best shut yer trap! There'll be no disrespecting these folk here! If you want some rotten story 'cause yer brain's too small to understand these then ya can go find it elsewhere!" the captain shouts.

"You think I won't teach you a lesson to mind your betters just because you're old?" Derik whispers calmly behind a dark grin. "I'll set you right, and then we do things my way!" Derik leaps over the table and swaggers up to the captain. Before he gets too close, Brun stands up and matches Derik's pace so they meet right in front of us.

"If you want to get thrashed in front of everyone here, be my guest. If ya don't move and let me smack that fool of a captain for disrespectin' me, I'll lay a hurting on you like you ain't never seen," Derik says, staring Brun dead in the eyes.

Brun moves slightly and Derik's body goes flying. He lands with a crash on a table that cracks in two. Three of Derik's mercs jump in and start brawling with Brun. A mess of hands flies towards him and he absorbs them all. Landon and Gavin throw their bodies in and it becomes a blur of fists and feet. Gavin gets knocked out quickly by a stray punch and collapses to the floor. Derik leaps on top of Brun, throwing a storm of blows down while another pair of mercs hold Brun's hands back. Brun's face is hammered blow after blow as he struggles to break free.

My feet start running towards the tangle of people. I grab one of the mercs in a tight headlock and squeeze as hard as I can. Wynn charges in and starts kicking wildly. Hitting any part of him she can reach. He falls to his knees, scratching at my arms and struggling to breathe. His body goes limp as she lands a hard kick right to his face.

I drop his head and jump to my feet. Brun manages to break free of the other merc, throwing him and Derik clear across the galley with one arm. He angrily rushes towards Derik as he scrambles to his feet. They swing their fists like hammers as they fight. Neither avoiding the other, they let their faces take the full weight of each strike. I look over the fighting for Landon who's moving almost too fast to see. He's fighting two large men at once. The rest of the mercs begin to pile in and the room explodes into chaos. Wynn drags me to where Rolin is fighting a larger man. I jump on his back, reach my arm around his neck, choking him. He grabs my hair and arm, trying to pull me off but Wynn lands kick after kick to his groin. The merc falls over and starts vomiting as I let go of his throat.

Two more mercs charge us.

Chapter Twenty-Two

"Ow...." I groan.

Other moans echo around the galley as the injured are treated.

"I tell you; you two are some team!" Landon says happily. "But your chin is too soft for a fight like that, Cael." He adds.

"Oh shut it. That man was ten stone more than Cael, and he had at least ten years on us, too!" Wynn scolds Landon.

"What in Finra's name happened?" I say, feeling a lump on my head and working my jaw back and forth.

"You did good until one of Derik's goons caught you off guard. One hit to the face and you were dropped like a rock. Wynn tried to help you up but you were out cold. She looked about ready to fight those guys but luckily they didn't have the heart to hit a young girl and turned back towards the melee. Was a brave stand, but reckless." Landon chastises her.

Wynn smiles and grabs my shoulder. "We're in it together, Little Cub."

I return her smile. Saved again I suppose.

"So how'd it end?" I ask.

"Rena saw Derik charge the captain and lay him out. She lost it. Yelling at everyone, breaking people up and telling everyone how dangerous it was to be fighting. We all looked proper ashamed at that. She timed it right. Most of the fighting was done, seemed all the desire to fight left the mercs once Derik crossed the line of laying hands on the captain. His men knew it was over at that and Rena's words made doubly sure of it," Landon says.

Landon pats Rolin's shoulder as he nurses a fat lip and black eye. "Some woman you got there, Rolin my friend. She told us what for like it was a command from the sky!"

Rolin tries to smile but winces at the pain. We sit quietly as the room settles and watch Rena make her rounds.

"How's your head, Cael?" she asks as she reaches us. "You took such a strong hit to the lower jaw. We're lucky you don't have any serious injuries. Especially as you're still recovering from your sickness." She scolds.

"I'm fine," I mumble. "How's the captain and Brun doing?"

"Brun is in good spirits. I think he wanted that fight as much as Derik. He's covered in bruises along with a broken nose and, somehow, a broken foot. Finra only knows how that one happened. Derik lost a few teeth, fractured his hand and dislocated his shoulder." She smirks while listing Derik's wounds.

"What of the captain?" Landon asks.

Rena drops her head down. "Well he looks pretty bad. I can feel a broken arm, but there's certainly more that we can't see. I'm worried about internal bleeding and trauma. It's difficult to be sure until we see the outward signs. He still hasn't woken up yet, which is worrying, but as he's so old, it's not cause for serious concern. It may be a day or two yet. I can say that he's alive right now and I am hopeful that he'll make a full recovery."

"Is there anything we can do for him?" I ask.

Wynn follows. "Or anything we can do to help you?"

Rena shakes her head. "I'm sorry, dears. This is just part of the process. We need to be patient and wait for the captain to recover on his own. I've set his arm and patched him up. He only needs a bit of rest now. If his condition changes, I'll let you know, but right now there's nothing else any of us can do."

Rena looks around the room. "Alright then, I think I'll do another round and wash my hands of this evening." She gives Wynn and I quick hugs. "You did a good thing trying to help out today, but you're young yet, you need to be more cautious. These are trained mercenaries, this could have ended much worse for you. Both of you." She eyes Wynn.

Rena smells of antiseptic and herbs, but also of something sweet. She's so eager to help. She'll be a wonderful doctor. Her mentor is lucky to have her. Zaitah might even read a book Rena writes about medicine. They might even meet if Doctor Alabas takes more students.

"Cael, come on lad. Let's clean up the galley," Landon says, putting his hand on my shoulder.

"Sheesh, this place looks like a storm rolled through," Wynn says.

"More like a brawl happened," I say, rubbing my jaw.

"True enough," Landon agrees. "Let's get to it then. Shouldn't take long with the three of us. Put all the broken furniture in the corner, all the broken dishes in this crate," he says, sliding a crate to the center of the room. "Food in this bucket. We'll toss anything we can't salvage over."

The room doesn't look too bad; most of the tables and chairs survived. The bowls and mugs took a beating. I wonder if Derik will have to pay for all this?

...As we finish cleaning, Landon drops in a chair. "Truth be told, I'm not up for lessons tonight. I'm exhausted."

"Well that's no problem. Cael and I can join the crew on watch tonight. We're learning our own stuff now anyway, right?" Wynn says.

He didn't get hurt, did he? I got hit and I'm not even that tired. Maybe he's older than he looks?

"Alright, that sounds good. Like Cael is thinking, maybe I'm a bit older than we all thought. I could use a nice long rest. Without Cael kicking and squirming all night, I might actually manage to get a decent night's sleep," he says with a grin.

"Rena was right, you two did a good thing, but you need to think about your own safety first. I wasn't even paying attention to you in there so if something worse happened... well let's just be more careful," Landon says, patting us on the back as he walks past us. "Have a safe watch."

He calls back up after he's disappeared down the stairs, "Oh! Try and teach each other. Maybe you'll have a breakthrough or something."

Wynn grabs my arm. "Come on, I'm so bored and it's too stuffy down here. I need some fresh air."

We race up the stairs to the deck, open the hatch and are hit with a nice cool refreshing sea breeze.

"Who was the genius that closed the hatch? It's getting real gross below deck without fresh air," I ask Wynn.

Derik comes walking out of the darkness and into the light coming from below deck. "Well if it isn't the two brats. Where's your keeper? Too weak from getting thrashed?" He sneers.

"Oh, go beat your chest somewhere else, you oaf. Look at you limping out of the shadows. I bet you can barely raise a first after the beating Brun laid on you. Needed two of your buddies to make it close to a fair fight." Wynn scoffs at him as she pushes past.

"You little trit, I've got more than enough left in me to stomp both of you!" He screams.

"Just get out of here. It's our watch. There's no need to fight," I say.

Derik laughs sharply. "Your dog here has more bite than you! Too bad, I was looking forward to making you cry. But you couldn't even stay on your feet long enough to cry, could you?" He waves as he walks below deck, "...Maybe next time."

I start shaking with rage. I hate him so much, I bet we could have taken him. He's already hurting.

Wynn's hand lands on my shoulder. "I'm sorry for getting him all riled up, I just can't stand him. Picking on people half his size, and twice his age like the captain."

I'm still shaking. "I think the captain is more like a quarter his size. But it's fine. We didn't get in another fight so we can just forget about it," I say through clenched teeth. Deep breaths. He's gone now and soon I'll never have to worry about him again. He'll probably die shortly after we get ashore. He's so dumb. I'm surprised he's lived this long as a mercenary.

"So, it's just us tonight. Should we do our own lessons, or would you like to try and teach each other like Landon suggested?" Wynn asks.

"Maybe we should do our own thing?" I say. I don't know… I wish I could do the stuff you can but I can't. It's stupid to even try, especially without Landon.

"That works," Wynn agrees, making her way over beneath the foremast.

I follow her but stop short. I'll need quiet to work and so will she. Better for us to separate for now at least.

I move toward the tip of the stern and stare out at the ocean. I sit and take another deep breath. This whole mind reading thing is useless. I want to be able to show people things, or see their memories, or make them do things. If I could use magic, I would be able to really hurt Derik, or make him hurt himself. I wish Landon would teach me useful stuff. Maybe he used magic before and that's why he's so tired? Or maybe he really did just get hit. I got knocked clean out. I can't even remember getting hit, just seeing those two goons coming towards us. Holy forest, that's so embarrassing. One hit, just one hit is all it takes? I bet Wynn thinks I'm some weak child, Landon too probably. It doesn't matter! I can't do anything about the past. I just need to focus on the now.

I shake my head and close my eyes.

I really wish someone could explain this stuff to me, really explain it to me. Not this whole fake explanation. I'm meant to simply imagine myself in this clearing and … who's with me today? I guess Wynn again. She has to be. She's the only one here. It's so eerie that all it takes is me picturing her in my mind. How many people could have read my thoughts over the years. Concentrate! Me, check. Her, check.

"This is so frustrating! I'm done heating my hands. I want to learn how to do amazing things! Why is Landon taking a break anyway? He didn't even get hit. Cael got hit and he's up here on watch."

What?! It's working, I can hear her thoughts. Wait! Can she hear mine?

"I wish I could do more with telepathy. Cael and Landon can talk and probably show stuff to each other. I hate how hard this is. It's not fair that he can do that and I can't."

This is wrong, I shouldn't be listening to this. It's like eavesdropping but way worse. What if she thinks of something personal? What if she thinks about Landon, or me?! Those are private and this is wrong.

"If Cael is working hard, I have to, too. He's over there doing his lessons and I'm just wasting time. I'm horrid. I have a gift and I'm not even training. What I would have given to have powers back then. But I can only change temperatures! Landon, you ass! I need to learn something new. This is such a waste! I wish Cael and I could talk. Why doesn't he want to learn together? We're supposed to be a team. Maybe he doesn't want to be a team."

Enough, I can't keep listening.

I walk over to her and she perks up. "Hi, Cael! Are you bored too?"

I flush red. "Uh well actually." Just tell her, you're a team after all. "I was focusing on my lessons and I heard you getting a little frustrated. I thought maybe we could learn together."

She stiffens up. "You were listening to my thoughts?"

"Yes, but only for a moment!" I blurt out quickly and heat rises from my chest as my face turns red, "I'm sorry but I couldn't think of anyone else to focus on. It was wrong, I'm sorry." I stammer.

Wynn huffs, her face glowing red before she turns away from me. She whips around and her face immediately lights back up.

"I've got an idea!" She reaches for my hand and pulls me down so we're both sitting.

"Well what is it?" I say, still nervous.

"If you can hear my thoughts, maybe you can guide them?" she says, smiling and hopping on her butt in excitement.

"I mean it might work, but I'm new at all of this. I have no idea what I'm doing, and I can't even begin to understand how or why it works. It seems so simple, but I really truly need to know *how* it works," I say.

"You just have to think to me how you would think if you were doing it alone." She says, still bouncing, "Please try! Please, please!?"

I chuckle a bit. "I don't even understand what you're saying! How do I think to you? It's nonsense!"

She deflates and drops my hands.

"But that doesn't mean we can't try," I say.

She grabs my hands again and smiles wide.

We settle in by the foremast and Wynn says, "Alright, so what do we do first?"

I try and think of something but can't so I shrug. "I have no idea where to start."

Wynn grins and says, "I suppose we should have seen this coming."

She rubs her hands together and stares at the ground.

I wish I knew how this worked. I can barely speak to her by thought. Think! Well, we've already decided to do this so we need to start somewhere.

"I could try and connect with you and… and then recall the lessons with Landon? That might work… I guess? Maybe. Yea, now that I think about it, that really actually might work!" I say, excitement growing.

She nods "I'm sure it'll work! It's better than nothing, so take us on our journey, Master Cael!"

We sit facing each other and I close my eyes.

"Can you hear me?"

"Yup!" She says.

"Good, good. Alright… Try and imagine something in your mind. Like imagine me or Landon."

"Done. What next?" She asks.

"Uh, try and picture a house or something bigger." I instruct.

"Alright, I'm imagining a house." She says eagerly, "Now what?"

"Now, I think you have to picture me and then try talking."

She sits quietly for a moment before opening her eyes, "Did you hear any of that?"

"No…" I shake my head.

She shrugs, "So what's next?"

I sigh, "I don't think this is going to work. I thought that maybe I'd be able to see something or… I don't know. This whole mind thing is so ridiculous. All I can do is imagine you and sometimes hear you. I thought that if I could actually see what you saw, like be inside your mind, then maybe I could help sort of guide you." I drop my head, defeated.

She puts her hand on my shoulder, "It's alright. We just need to think of another way, that's all."

"But what other way? There isn't another way. Landon only taught us this one path, this one route." I slow my words.

It's been a while since I've had those dreams. That stone path, it was with me almost every night for such a long time. I dreaded those nightmares but now that they're gone I sort of miss them. Landon was right, that place was special.

"Don't go all quiet on me now." Wynn says smacking my foot. "What's on your mind?"

"The dreams we had. That stone path just popped in my head." I say, lost in thought.

Wynn shivers, "Those dreams were awful. Some nights they were just bad, other times they were terrifying." She looks at the sky, "I haven't had those dreams since I've been with you two…. Maybe Landon is protecting us?"

"He could be." I stare up to the stars as well, "He was with me in my dreams. Twice actually. We stayed in the grove for a while. He told me a story about magic."

"Like, he was really with you in your dreams? He remembers it too?" She asks incredulously.

"Yea, he was trying to get me to go with him. Telling me all about the seekers and stuff." I pause, "I think… you were in one of my dreams? I saw someone running away. I was safe inside a tree. We were safe."

She stares at me, eyes wide and mouth dropped, "That *was* you! I knew it!"

"Wait, you remember? You knew this whole time?" I ask.

She shrugs, "Well, no. I didn't *know*, but I sort of did? I do remember that dream, though. It was the first time someone besides those seekers was with me. I remember all of those dreams… You seemed so familiar when we met."

"Yea, I thought the same thing." I say quietly. "If we had that dream because we were close to each other, that means we're pretty much the only ones in that whole area that has magic."

She grins, "Of course. It's not like everyone has these abilities."

"But what if we can join each other in dreams again? What if we could find a way into each other's head and then really see what the other is seeing? I bet I could help you that way!" I get excited.

"Yea..." She says slowly, "Yea! That sounds like it could work!"

She stands and pulls me to my feet. "We're gonna head in early. Cael's not feeling well." Wynn calls to the two old crewmen on deck. They nod in understanding, "No worries, kids. Was a good fight, lad." The smaller one replies.

"Do you know their names?" I ask, as we walk down the stairs and towards the galley.

"Those guys? I don't think so. They haven't said much to us at all. Probably used to it being quiet at night." She responds plainly.

We eat the dried fish Trep left out along with some hardtack. I was never a fan of this stuff, it sits like a stone in my stomach. I wish we had some of that delicious bread from Rensfort. Oh, the pastries! That would be perfect. I wonder if I'll ever eat Fannie's pastries again?

Wynn snatches the plate from in front of me, "Hey, I wasn't finished!" I protest.

"Oh come on, you were moving around that last bit of fish for half the night! Let's go, I really want to try this dream thing!" She says impatiently.

We enter our cabin, light a candle and climb up to the top bunk and stare at each other.

"So, what now?" I whisper to not wake Landon.

"Don't look at me, I wasn't the one with the idea." She shrugs, "But for us to be dreaming we kind of need to be sleeping." She says sarcastically.

"Yea, I figured that much out you nitwit. But *how* do we make sure we dream *together*?" I ask seriously.

..."Exactly." I continue after a moment of silence. "We don't know."

"Well we have to try something!" She whines loudly.

I swat at her and whisper, "Landon's still sleeping you walnut!"

She leans over the bunk and pops back up. "We're fine, he's still as stone. Now back to the question at hand: How do we dream together?" She asks.

"Let's just start with the first thing we think of and if that doesn't work we can try something else tomorrow night." I suggest.

"Well?" She presses, "What's your idea?"

"I don't know…. Maybe I can talk to you in your mind until we go to sleep? If I'm there when we start dreaming, maybe something could happen?" I say, working the plan out as I speak.

She plops her head down on the bed, "Works for me." She yawns. "How about a story, until we fall asleep?"

I yawn along with her, "A story could work." I stretch out, leaning against the wall thinking for a moment. "Landon told me a story about magic…."

Chapter Twenty-Three

"Hurry up, I'm freezing to death over here!" I yell to Wynn over the harsh wind.

She huffs, "Do you think I enjoy being out in this cold? I'm hurrying as fast as my frozen feet can take me!" She shouts back.

I grab her arm and we rush through the deep snow, down the mountain and straight into the tree line.

"The weather here is so sudden." I say through chattering teeth as we shake the ice off our traveling cloaks. "I didn't even see that storm come in."

Wynn stands up straighter, "Do you feel that?" She whispers, "It's... warm?"

I take a deep breath to steady my shivering body. A few steps into the forest and the snow disappears, revealing a sunny springlike forest.

"What is this place?" I ask.

She shrugs, "I don't know. It looks like a trail over here. Let's follow it?" She suggests, setting down the path.

"This is too worn down to be a game trail. It feels more like someone lives here." I say as we walk.

"It's beautiful, look at all the flowers. How is it so warm and colorful here but so cold a few steps away?" She asks, bundling up her deep blue cloak and shoving it into her travel sack.

Something doesn't feel right here. Where are we going? Why are we here? How....?

The dreams.

"Exactly right, Cael." A soothing voice comes from the forest.

We scan the trees; the sound of a fast-moving stream guides our sight to a clearing just off the trail. A beautiful woman stands up near the water's edge. She greets us with a friendly, oddly familiar smile.

"I'm so glad you two finally found each other. You've been lost for so long already." She says, waving us over before bending back down to dip a pail in the water.

"Do we know you?" I ask, confused.

"Where are we?" Wynn's tone matches my own.

The woman's long white hair swoops around her as she pulls herself up to her full height. The snow colored locks perfectly fall around her smooth tanned face, highlighting her piercing green eyes.

"Would you care for some tea?" She asks, not waiting for an answer, before leading us further into the forest.

We follow her through the tall trees. The bright colorful flowers that surround the path almost seem to reach for us as her flowing deep green dress greets them all with a light touch. Her bare feet make no sound as she walks through the woods.

The path opens to a field of plants all blooming different shades. She moves purposefully to a spot filled with sunlight and whispers to the world in a foreign language. The ground moves up, pushing our knees forward softly as we ease onto our newly made chairs. A fire crackles to life and begins boiling the pail of water she rests on the air above it.

She waves aside the trees revealing a large lake, the high mountains we came off clearly visible in the distance. This place is amazing.

"In our dreams, everything is as simple as a thought. You only need to know what you want, and it is yours." She says with a wide smile as she gazes at the view.

"Where are we?" Wynn asks, barely able to form words as her eyes stare at the beauty around us.

"Is this real?" I whisper.

"I am Arimel, and we are in your dreams." She says easily. "Dreaming is powerful, and to dream as we do is truly special."

"But why are we here? Are you a seeker?" I ask still confused.

She frowns, "No, I am not what you call a seeker, nor am I one of the Sephalim. I am from... another time. Ryn Dvarek was our home." She turns away, "Even after all this time that name is still painful to me." She pauses, her gaze lost in the pristine water for a moment.

When she turns back to us her frown is gone, replaced again with her beautiful smile. "For why you are here, well I suppose the easiest answer, at least for tonight, is that you have come to learn." She claps her hands together and sits up straight, "And so, before we leave, I will teach you."

She reaches out and grasps our hands in hers, "Listening to one another is as easy for you as it is for water to flow through this stream. Speaking is as simple as the wind blows. You only need to believe here."

Wynn stares, still unsure of the ground beneath our feet. "We are dreaming together." I place my free hand on hers.

Her expression changes as she recalls the night before. "It worked..." She faces Arimel in amazement, "So I just think what I want, and it happens? No mind clearing or little lights?" She asks.

Arimel grins, "No little lights. No tricks. It is as simple as breathing. At least here it is."

"Can you hear me?" Wynn asks, her thoughts as loud as her voice.

"Yes!" I reply.

I press my hand into the dirt and it sinks deeply with no effort. The ground embracing my fingers before I easily draw it back. Wynn matches my movements, and our eyes light up. We open our hands together and the air above them begins shimmering from the heat.

Arimel laughs at our excitement, "You two can do so much more than speak or make the little fires in your hands."

She leans forward, whispering something in our ears and we're lifted upward, weightless as the world falls away. We gaze out at the stars and watch as countless lights flash passed our eyes. We plunge back down towards a city floating high above the ground. A man stands alone, pulling enormous mountains from the earth, shaping the world around him. His eyes turn to us and he offers a knowing smile before we fly back to our forest. Landing lightly on our seats.

Arimel smiles again before placing her hands in our palms. "For us, it is as simple as breathing." She repeats. "The first step is simply having the confidence to truly try, and now it will all become easier for you." Her head tilts and her hair falls easily to the side, "It seems our lesson must be cut short, I'm afraid."

The world starts to shake hard and Arimel drops our hands. We're tossed into the air and she calmly calls out, "Did you want honey with your tea?"

...."Wake up, Cael!"

Chapter Twenty-Four

"Get up now!"

"Hm?" I groan as I rub my eyes.

"Wynn, wake up! Hurry!" Landon shouts again.

I roll out of bed and I'm thrown into the air. My eyes open just in time to see the floor before I slam down. "Oof!" I croak as Wynn falls on top of me.

Landon grabs both of us. "There's a storm. We need all hands! Follow me!" He drags us up the stairs to the main deck.

"What do we do?! I'm not a sailor!" I shout loudly but my voice barely overcomes the sound of the storm.

Wynn grabs my shoulder, turning me around. I watch her mouth move but I only hear the crashing of waves and pounding of rain.

"I can't hear anything!" I shout back and she throws her hands in the air giving up.

"Follow me," Landon thinks to us.

Wynn and I grab onto him and stumble our way across the deck. The captain's voice calls out over the storm, shouting barely audible orders while he mans the helm.

"Crew hurry up and take down those damn main sails before we're tossed over! Brun, get that sea anchor tied off and throw it in when the sails are down! Trep, get all those mercs and help tie down anything that isn't already!" The captain's eyes fall on us, "Landon, Gavin, tie off those oil bags! Kids, help Trep!"

Landon shouts to us, "Stay close to each other!" And disappears into the mess of bodies all running frantically trying to follow orders.

Wynn grabs my hand and we race across the deck where Trep is calling for people. "You seen all that stuff flyin 'round now go get it tied up!" He calls over the sound of thunder.

Rolin and Rena hand us some rope and Rena shouts, "Stay close to us!"

A wave hits and we're all thrown to the side. We scramble out of the water as it rolls across the deck. Rena steadies me and we help tie the sails as the crew finishes taking them down. The ocean spray pounds into us. The sky is almost too dark to even see. During a strike of lighting I check for Wynn and relax seeing her next to me.

There's no end to it. The water crashes across the deck again, scattering the crew. My whole body is in pain as a never-ending barrage of water pelts us and I struggle to keep my feet beneath me.

A chorus of shouting and then I'm up into the air again. Everyone floats around me, suspended for a moment before we slam back down into the deck. I grab for Wynn and we get right back to tying the sails as quickly as they take them down. One of the sails is ripped from our hands and flies out into the storm.

A hand grabs me and Landon joins our line. Where in the stars has he been?!

I check for Wynn again and see she's bleeding. Just past her a wave the size of a mountain is coming at us broadside. This is it! Finra save us!

An arm reaches around my waist and I grab for Wynn as the wave slams into us.

The ship rolls to the side and everyone is falling. The railing rushes past me. I reach, but it slips out of my hands before I crash into the ocean.

Every part of me is stinging from the impact, but the water is freezing cold. I can't make out which way is up, I just start swimming as fast as I can. My arms start to burn as I struggle to the surface. I break through and suck in a lungful of air.

"Wynn! Landon!" I scream. Where are they? I watch as the ship rights itself. Finra's beard! I thought it was the end, but if we still have a ship we can survive this!

"Wynn! Landon!" I shout again. A hand grabs my shirt and we shoot across the water. Landon tosses me towards the ladder. "Stay here!"

And he sets out again, moving faster than a fish through the water. I climb up to the deck and search for Wynn. She's not here yet, she must still be out there!

Rolin dives into the ocean right past me and Gavin follows. Flailing hands are all through the surface of the water as the lightning flashes across the sky. Heads bobbing up and down. I can't just sit here. One of those people has got to be Wynn!

I run and dive over the railing, slam face first into the water and immediately my face lights on fire with pain.

There! Someone in the water! Please, Finra let this be Wynn. I frantically swim over to a flailing person and pull Trep from under the waves. Damn! Damn! I can't leave him. Wynn hold on just a little longer.

I grab Trep and try and drag him back. "Swim, man, swim!" I shout at him. He continues swinging his arms wildly even after I reach him. Why are you fighting me! Just swim! What in Finra's name are you doing man? I need to get back out there to save Wynn!

We finally reach the ladder. I shove Trep towards it and immediately turn around to find Wynn. I'm not stopping for anyone else. I have to find her.

I search the sea one last time but there's no sign of anyone left.

"Cael, please hear me!" Wynn cries out. "Wynn!" I frantically look around the ocean but don't see her. I try and concentrate but I can't. I won't leave you! Just hold on! I swim out further.

"Help! Somebody! Anyone please hear me." Wynn calls out again.

I start desperately swimming away from the ship into the darkness.

"Wynn!" I yell. I still can't see anyone. Veera! Finra! Vashir! Anyone! Please help me find her!

I swim further and further out. Hands, I see hands waving! It's her. It must be her!

I swim as fast as I can to reach her. "Wynn!" I shout as I see her face and hug her tight.

"Cael! Thank you! Thank you, thank you." She cries.

The ship is barely visible on the horizon. "Come on, Wynn. We have to swim for it!"

I'm so exhausted. My arms are burning. My lungs can barely suck in air. We can't give up, but I can't keep going, I'm just so tired.

"Thank you, thank you." Wynn repeats over and over again as we swim.

We're moving too slow. The storm is going to push the ship too far out of reach. I found her and now we're going to be left behind. Why! Dammit! Just keep going. We can't give up, I refuse to give up. I'm not going to let it end like this. We're not going to stop trying. But I'm so tired. These waves make it too damn hard to move. I need to breathe, just for a moment.

I can't move. My arms aren't working. I roll to my back, "Wynn I need to take a break. I can't go on. I'm just too tired." I try and shout but I can't.

"We can take a break, Cael. I'm tired too." Wynn says.

She rolls onto her back next to me. *"Arimel was right. It's a little easier now."*

We lock arms so we don't drift too far. *"Arimel... She seems like a world away already."*

"She was always a world away." Wynn replies as a wave rolls over us.

We can't make it to the ship. That's not an option. Land is our only chance now, but where is land? Maybe when the storm calms down, we'll be near land. It's hard to breathe on your back, but it's easier to float like this. The waves keep rolling over my face. I have to close my eyes. The saltwater stings so much.

"I think this is it for us," I say.

"I'm sorry I called out for you. You were probably safe and now we're both going to die. I was just so scared I didn't think," Wynn apologizes.

"I was already out looking for you even before I heard you. I wasn't going to give up on you, I never would have gone back until I found you," I say as I squeeze her hand.

"Thank you, Cael," she says, relieved. Then, excitedly she starts shaking me. "Cael! Why are we giving up!? You can talk to Landon!" She shouts.

"He's so far away, I don't think we can reach him." I say hopelessly.

"It's as easy as breathing!" She reminds me.

"But even if we could, we're in the ocean, Wynn. There's no sign pointing to us or a landmark he can use. We could be anywhere. That's probably why he hasn't found us," I say. I'm too exhausted. I'll just close my eyes, just for a moment.

She shakes me again. "We're not just anywhere. We're off the starboard side, far behind the ship! We can see it and Landon can use that to find us!"

She's right! By all that's good in the world, she's right! Focus, focus!

"Landon, we need help! We're to the rear of the ship off the starboard side, maybe a thousand meters out. Please help!"

I keep repeating the words over and over until Wynn grabs my shoulder. "Did you do it?" She asks as the water stirs around us.

"I did it, I think. If he could hear us then he did." I say.

"What if he's hurt, or what if he's dead?!"

"I'm not dead yet!" Landon's voice calls to us.

"Landon! You came!" I shout back. "Where are you?" Wynn and I scan the surface but can't find him.

He bursts out of the ocean and grabs us. "Damn you both! You had me breaking down. I was certain you were goners! I searched everywhere. I couldn't hear either of you!" He scolds us and then squeezes us.

"Sorry," we apologize together.

We're safe now... we're really truly going to make it. By the holy forest, he did it. Landon did it!

"Oh, you'll be sorry, Cael! I already saved you and you jump back in?!" he scolds.

"I had to find Wynn!" I shout back.

"Enough! Let's just get to the ship!" Wynn yells.

"You're right, I'm sorry. You two must be exhausted and freezing," Landon says as he pulls us under.

"What are you doing!" Wynn and I yell as we are dragged below the surface.

"How are we talking underwater?" Wynn asks.

"It's all dark and forbidden magic! You'll learn soon enough," Landon says jokingly.

I open my eyes but can't see anything. It's darker than a cave on a winter night down here. I can't even see Landon. He grabs my arm and pulls me forward.

We surface by the ladder and Landon helps us grab the rungs. Rolin's hands reaches out to lift us the last bit. My hands almost slip from his. Everything is so greasy.

"Moons above, Landon, you found them!" Rena screams and runs over hugging us all.

"Any sign of Brun or the others?" Landon asks.

"None yet. We'll need to wait for the storm to clear and then search the area. We can't risk anyone else going back out again," Rena says.

"We're through the worst of it, but don't rest yet!" Gavin shouts.

My arms can't take anymore. I can barely hold on to this rail. Just a little longer, though. Only a little while longer. Finra save us from this storm!

....It's calming down, I can see the stars! The clouds are clearing, the rain is finally letting up! We made it, we survived!

"We did it, everyone!" Gavin says over cheers from the crew, "But we're still missing folk, we've got to turn this ship around and begin the search."

"Who are we missing?" Landon asks.

"Yes, that's good, that's smart. Everyone take count of your groups. We need to track how many are missing and who we're looking for." Rena calls out.

I throw my arms around Landon and Wynn. "Our group all accounted for!"

Rena nods quickly and looks over to the next group.

"Francis is missing!" one of the merchants say.

One of Derik's mercs calls out, "Adam and Jones are gone!"

Gavin speaks up, "Marcus is gone as well."

"Brun is gone," Trep says quietly.

The captain calls out from the helm, "Brun is fine! That lad knows his way around the water, just you wait and see! We'll find him. Don't ya go sayin' he's missing. You just wait; he's gonna turn up all fine, you'll see."

"I can't see anyone," I say to Landon and Wynn.

"Me neither and I can't hear anyone out there, which really concerns me," Landon says.

"I see something!" Derik calls out.

We rush to him and see something floating. This is really bad. If they were alive, they'd be calling out to us. Maybe it's just cargo or anything else.

"Body!" Gavin calls out. He throws a rope out to pull the body in. When they finally rope it and reel it in, it's the trader, Francis.

They pull him up quickly and start pressing on his chest.

"Don't die on me yet!" Rena says, continuing to push down hard on his chest, over and over.

He coughs up water and sucks in air, struggling to breathe.

"He's alive!" Rena shouts as she lifts his head.

"Another one here!" the Captain calls out over the noise.

We reel in the body of Gavin's comrade Marcus, already blue from the cold. There's no saving this one. Rena still rushes over and tries to help him. She drops her head after a few moments. Gavin and his friend take the body with silent tears.

"Two more!" Landon shouts. Two bodies just beneath the surface. Adam and Jones, their leathers probably weighed them down too much. Derik and his crew gather their bodies and retreat below deck without a word.

Brun is still missing. This isn't good. If the trader survived though, maybe Brun did too? But he had a broken foot. That couldn't have been easy. At least he wasn't wearing leathers, just some linens. If anyone could survive this it would be Brun. He's a good man, Finra wouldn't allow this. Brun is....

"I see him," I croak.

Brun, face down, floating in the water. He's dead. Landon throws the rope and he and Rolin start pulling him in. They start to struggle. I move next to them and help pull his body up.

Brun is gone? He was so strong. How did he die? What are we all going to do? Brun was the strongest of us. He protected us all from those mercenaries.

"No…. no no no this isn't real. That's not my Brun! This is a nightmare! I just have to wake up, it'll all be better when I wake up…" the captain cries.

Trep puts his arm around the Captain. "I'm sorry, Karif, I really am. I don't know what ta say."

"Every one of us knew the risks, Captain. None of this is your fault. It's no one's fault," Gavin says. "I'm sorry for all of our losses. Brun was a good man. No one deserved this but we have to move on. We have to finish this journey." He goes back to Marcus's body.

"We'll let everyone grieve today. Tomorrow we'll have a funeral, send them all off together," Landon suggests.

Silent nods but everyone is done talking. We survived; they didn't. But why? Who decides who lives and who dies? Is it Finra? Vashir? Is my life so easily taken? All of our lives? One storm, four dead. Just our ship. What of other ships that were on this route? We're lucky we had Landon, more could have died. More would have died. I suppose we're even now. He took me from my life and then saved me from death.

"Thank you, Landon. Thank you for everything. I'm sorry I've been an ass. I was just… Thank you," I say when everyone disappears below deck.

Landon pats my shoulder. "It's all forgiven, lad."

"Wynn, are you alright?" he asks.

Wynn is silently staring at her feet.

"I'm fine," she mumbles. We stand next to her and stare at the churning ocean.

I can't imagine what it was like for her out there. I was struggling to search for her but she was lost and alone. If I hadn't heard her… I'm just glad I finally found her. I'm glad she wasn't alone the whole time.

We stay above deck for a long while before I turn toward the stairs hearing footsteps.

Trep and Gavin wave as they stagger up from below deck, both carrying rum.

"Landon, let thems kiddies sleep, man. We's been storm defendin' all day. It's darkness out right now but we watch fer you," Gavin slurs

"Alright, friends," Landon says. "Thank you."

He grabs an offered bottle and says, "To the ones we lost."

"Cheers!" Gavin and Trep cry out.

"To the survivors," Landon says.

"Cheers!" they respond.

Landon hands the bottle back and guides us down the stairs. A shawl of soft crying and hushed talking surrounds the ship. "Let's grab some food and bring it to our room. No need to bother the grieving."

Food. It doesn't feel fair to eat it. They'll never get to eat again. I could've died. We all could have. They'll never smell or see or taste anything. It doesn't feel fair to lay down on this bed. Death. Nothing is fair about death.

What happens when we die? Can the dead think?

Can they dream?

Chapter Twenty-Five

Ugh, my body aches all over. It must still be early, I can't see a thing. I roll out of bed to go pee and jump seeing Wynn standing silently in the corner of the room.

"Moons above, Wynn!" I quietly screech. "You scared me half to death!"

She turns to me and grabs my hand. "Come with me."

She leads us top side and the sound of Gavin and Trep snoring floats over from their place near the helm. We move to the front of the ship and Wynn stands silently for a moment, tightly holding the railing.

"I was so scared... I never want to be that scared ever again. It was like I knew I was going to die. That's all I kept thinking about, about how long it would be and what it would be like. I was certain it was going to happen."

"I know." I touch her shoulder. "I'm sorry you were out there alone."

"It was empty. I was empty. This stupid journey, all because of these stupid *gifts*. It's only just started and we've almost died!" She wipes her eyes. "You almost died twice." She sniffs.

The tears on her face reflect a small bit of the light from the stars and moons above. The sky is so clear right now. Not a cloud in sight. Everyone forgets quickly, even the sky. Not even a full night ago it was filled with anger and now it's like it doesn't even remember.

"These abilities, they've caused us so much trouble. Really nothing but trouble," Wynn says. "I've been trying to think of something, a way that we could use this curse to help us. To at least help us survive this stupid journey." Wynn stares back over the ocean before turning to me. "I think… I may have thought of something. Maybe."

Her eyes are wild and she's shaking. I move next to her and watch the waves. "We're in this together, you've said it yourself. What's the plan?" I say.

"When I was floating alone in the water, I wanted there to be a way for us to be connected. Not just speak to each other using our gifts. We have to close our eyes and it doesn't work far away, it barely works when we're close. But what if there's a way for us to always be in contact no matter how far? Constantly speaking and thinking. Like, I guess like we're in the others head? Landon said he's heard people with more than one voice in their head. If we could do that, then you would have known where I was right away. We could protect each other. We could be safe. I'm just tired of feeling weak and alone…" She drops her head.

"Wynn, you're not going to be alone. We're partners now so you're stuck with me until this is through." I turn around and lean against the railing. "So, how do we do this mind connection thing you want?"

"I don't know." She shrugs then slowly grins, "But I know who might."

"Arimel." We say together.

"Wynn, how do we know she's even real? She could just be a dream that we had. And if she is real, why is she in our heads? Who is she? What does she want? Why is she helping?" I rattle off questions.

She sighs, "Maybe she's real, maybe she's not. Maybe she's only in our imagination. But she *did* help us before, and she seems… familiar?"

"Why are you so trusting of her? She didn't even really help us, it's not like she was teaching us like Landon does. She just told us to believe in ourselves." I continue.

"I know… I just don't want to feel helpless anymore. With a connection we could be stronger. We might actually be able to defend ourselves. If Arimel can't help us then we lose nothing. But if she can… then this whole thing might get a lot easier." Wynn says.

She's right, we could be stronger. It might get easier. This may even help get me back to my family. But who is she? Why us? Why is it always us?

Though, I suppose there's no harm in trying… What's the worst that could happen?

"Alright." I agree.

We sit down on the deck. The worn wood still damp from the storm. We rest next to the mast and I recall the stories again. "It worked last time." I say.

Our eyes close and a heartbeat later, the warm sun shines down on our faces. It doesn't feel like a dream. I remember everything. There's no confusion this time.

"Back so soon?" Arimel calls to us as she brushes aside the hanging vines that act as a door to her small home.

"We need to ask you something!" Wynn rushes over.

"You don't need to be in such a hurry, child. Time rests now." She pats our seats, still raised from the night before and encourages us to sit. "Come, sit."

She takes the tea off the fire, just now boiling. She hands us intricately crafted cups and pours the tea into them. The color of the liquid changing for each. Wynn's cup is filled with a blue tea while my cup is filled with green. As Arimel pours the last of the tea into her own mug, it flows out a pure white.

"Drink." She encourages, putting her own cup to her mouth and sipping.

Wynn matches her movement. "It's so sweet!" She gasps.

I stare at the liquid in my cup and watch as the steam rises steadily. "Are you real?" I ask.

Arimel sighs, "Real… is difficult to describe." she replies slowly. She closes her eyes as she rests her head on the earthen chair. "What you truly wish to know is if I am an illusion, some figment of your imagining." Her eyes open and she smirks, "For how powerful your mind is, Cael, it is remarkable that you have not truly awakened." She leans forward, "I *am* real, Cael. And with my help, you will finally be real too."

She presses her solid hand against my chest and I feel the warmth of it spread through my body. She leans back and I nod to myself. It all seems real but if it isn't, well then it's all just a dream anyway.

I swallow the hot, bitter tea, "Mine's... different." I say, disappointed before choking the rest down.

Arimel grins, "It will be easier this way." She says and quickly stands, "You have come to ask something of me. Something unusual for two so young. Unusual and dangerous." She paces back and forth, uncertainty written on her face. "I have expected this day, counted the time until this very moment... but still it is strange. The others have done this so often but this is unfamiliar to me..." She mumbles to herself.

Her emerald eyes stare at us intently for a long while before she sighs and faces Wynn. "What you wish for is what I wish for as well. The two of you fit so perfectly, but the decision we make here will forever change your lives."

I shake my head confused, "What do you mean it's what you want? Why are you helping us?"

"Because it has been long enough..." She smirks, "I would like to watch what you can become. What we *all* could become."

She takes our cups and they turn to dust. She wipes her hands together before extending them, "Are you willing?" She asks ceremoniously.

"Yes!" Wynn replies quickly.

I turn to her and she nods enthusiastically, encouraging me to agree. I sigh, "Yes..."

"Cael, this is not a journey solely for Wynn. It is one for you as well. Her mind accepted this choice even before you came to me. You, though, are still uncertain. In every life you are thoughtful but in this one you must become decisive. You must trust each other. If we continue, we will be bound to one another. Is this truly what you wish?" She asks.

I notice Wynn's eager face out of the corner of my eye. No hesitation. We don't even know what this is. Bound together? Arimel says this is serious, but we don't have any clue who she is. Why is she helping? How is any of this real?

"It feels like there is so much that you haven't told us yet." I press.

"I know you wish for more but all will be known once we are joined. I cannot say more, your minds must be unaltered for this to succeed. For all to remain and still yet be joined, this decision must be made free of temptation." Arimel says, an unspoken apology in her eyes.

I take a deep breath, inhaling the intoxicating scent of this imaginary forest. ...I wonder what it would be like if it actually worked.

"Yes, I'm willing." I decide.

Arimel's face matches Wynn's excitement. "I find myself rather curious. A feeling I have not felt in quite some time." She closes her eyes, "For the binding to begin you must be granted access to the others mind. Their memories must be as your own. The freedom to search, the freedom to live. Cael, let us share in your memories first. I will act as your guide and host your memories within myself. When you wake you *must* return to us here. Remember, this is very important, you must return." She breathes in long and slow, "As easy as breathing." She reminds us with a wide smile.

We match her breathing and I feel memories being thrust forward in my mind. Wynn's voice echoing in my head as she begins sorting through images like pages in a book. The world around us changes quickly.

This must be your home. It's smaller than I imagined, but it looks warm, friendly. You're alone here? No, Clout is with you. He's so beautiful with that dark brown coloring and bright amber eyes, I've never seen that before; those eyes seem to know something. He's like you, always thinking. I could almost reach out and touch him. Oh, he's sturdy, but smaller than the others. I feel like I know him so well. We love him so much it's hard to put to words.

There's Landon. This is the day you first met. He looks like a villain with that dark cloak on, skulking near the tree line like a creep. It was meant to be a different type of day, a better day.

Your family loves you. I can see it. Orion... That's his name. His blue eyes are smiling and inviting. He's always laughing. He's not old, but his reddish hair is turning grey around the edges, isn't it? How'd he lose that tooth? It's no wonder your mother calls him a bear though. He's not just the size of one, he's got hands like paws! And the cutest little bear nose.

Ah, your mother. She really is a sight. She smiles less and worries more. But her face is so beautiful. It still looks so young. Her green eyes are yours. They look like they could light the dark. Her hair is kept short? Just below her shoulders. Of course, she works as a healer. She's smaller than you all, but her hands are just as strong. She has a commanding presence. I feel like she's looking at me now. The story of how they met is wonderful. Was it all always so perfect?

A brother, Zaitah? He's taller and stronger. You were always jealous. Smarter? We'll see, he has a few years on you, plenty of time to grow. He looks just like your father, only less around the middle and younger. Long red hair, no time to cut it? You fought and he would always win. It's hard when they're older, it's not fair.

Getting yelled at for not listening? Your father looks upset. If only they knew how hard it is to control our thoughts. Your mother was much more patient, but even she would yell at us. When Mother hit you that was the worst. Everyone hit you, but they loved you. It's easier when you know you're loved. When Gahris yelled at you, Father protected you. When Luther fought with us, Zaitah would fight him back. There was pain, of course, but there was so much more love.

Laena, she's different than Milly. So different. Her scars are bright on her tanned skin. They treat her horribly. Her blonde hair turns brown with mud. Her blue eyes turn dark with exhaustion. She does all the work and still they yell. She's taller than you? For a moment in time. Women grow first. Your hands are the same. We were going to marry her. Maybe we still will?

I remember that day. Our first kill. It was only a little bird, but I still cried. I couldn't help it. It was an accident. I never thought we would actually hit it. Father was proud, proud that I could hunt. No, not that. He was proud that I took it seriously. Death isn't a game.

Hunting trips were frequent, but we only went a few times. Zaitah and Father went more. We loved learning with Mother. She knows so much; her stories were my favorite.

Hunting is necessary. We loved going alone. It proved I was brave enough. Our first deer, we had no idea what we were doing. I just sat in the brush in a field and waited. I wanted a story to tell, I wanted to be braver than I was. As quiet as the mist, a deer walked right in front of us. She saw me but didn't know what I was. I had a hand on my bow, but I couldn't shoot. She was beautiful. Perfectly quiet, perfectly at peace with the forest. She was a ghost in those woods, no noise at all. How could we shoot something so beautiful?

The winter festival in Rensfort was the best time of the year. That was my first kiss. We all celebrated and would play games and have a huge ceremony. Laena took my hand and we went near the church fountain. It was frozen and reflected the moons above. She looked at me and my heart was beating so hard and fast I kept looking around, certain someone would catch us. She kissed me. I didn't know what to do. I tried to kiss back, but I was like a statue. Then she was gone. I always knew we'd get married, but that was real, not just a story in my imagination.

They called me Little Cub. I was a baby and would cry like a baby bear. It stayed because Father was a big bear and I followed him around. I don't remember anyone getting angry when I was little. Always smiles and laughter. Babies are good for that.

I didn't want to leave. I don't think I ever would have, but Landon didn't give me a choice.

Chapter Twenty-Six

I'm burning up. It's too hot. My eyes are blurry, I can't see anything. The world is spinning…. I think I'm going to puke. I rush to the railing and throw everything in my stomach overboard.

"Wynn, I feel sick. I really hope we got what we needed, because I never want to do that again," I say crumpling back down next to her.

I look over and Wynn's eyes are still eyes closed. I shake her. "Hey, Wynn! Are you still digging around my memories with Arimel? That's not fair!" I shake her a bit harder, "Come on, enough is enough. Let's go to bed, I really don't feel well."

As I stand up, Wynn falls over. It almost looks like she's unconscious…. or dead.

"Wynn!? Wynn, are you there?! Wake up, please Wynn, wake up!"

What's happening!? Oh no, I'm supposed to go back! But how do I get back to Arimel without you?

I check her pulse. She's still alive, but I need help. I don't know any of this. I have to find a way back in. I need Landon. He has to be able to help!

I pick Wynn up and rush below deck. As I run, I trip down the stairs and we tumble. I turn to protect her and my back slams into the floor as her body crushes me.

"Oof! Dammit, I'm sorry for that Wynn. Don't get too mad when you wake up, alright?" I say as I continue rushing to our room.

"Landon! Landon, wake up!" I whisper yell as I enter the room and put Wynn on the bunk. I close the door and start shaking Landon frantically.

"What in the burning sun are you doing, man!?" he says groggily. "Have you no respect for the sleeping?"

"Wynn is –" I say before he cuts me off.

"What did you two do!?" he shouts as he lights the lantern and examines her body.

"I knew it was too dangerous, I tried to tell you both, but you thought you knew better. You thought it was all a game! I thought you'd appreciate how dangerous it was after our first lesson, but no. You had to play at it like children and now look at her! She's gone! There's nothing of her left! You tell me what happened right now!" He screams through clenched teeth.

"Nothing left? How is she gone? This can't be real. You have to be able to fix her, right?" I say as tears start streaming. "I didn't know this could happen. I never would have agreed to be connected if Arimel had told us! You have to believe me! Please, please, we need to fix her. There has to be something we can do! I'll go get Rena, she can help!" I say rushing for the door.

Landon grabs me. "Sit down. Rena cannot help us. You don't get it, do you? This isn't a normal sickness, this is different. No normal doctor, no matter how skilled, can help us now. We're on our own here." He sighs and puts his head down. "What do you mean 'connected'? And what is wrong with your head. I can't understand anything. It's just a mess in your mind right now."

"I don't know, probably because I'm scared to death!? Wynn wanted—No, we both wanted to have a connection that was always there, you know? It's hard to have to close your eyes and imagine stuff before you speak and it doesn't work that far away so she had an—"

"All of this because you wanted to skip a step?" Landon cuts in. "That's just there to help you learn! None of us use it past year one! It's just to help you!"

"We didn't know that, how could we! You didn't tell us!" I cry out.

Landon puts his hand up. "Enough, what happened next?"

"I can't think straight," I say rubbing my head. "I've got a sharp pain in my head… it sounds like a constant buzzing or something."

"You have to try and remember, please." Landon urges.

"We went to see Arimel again and… They found a way into my head. I felt her there and it felt real. Then she started thinking for us. Maybe she started thinking of my life? We saw it all clear as water," I say grabbing my head. "That's it. I woke up and I checked on her and she was like this. I picked her up and ran to you. I tripped but I made sure she didn't hit her head, honest!"

"Who is Arimel? Where is she?" He asks confused.

"I don't know. She's someone we found in our dreams. She was helping us learn. I have to go back. Arimel said I had to. You have to help me get back to them…" I say squeezing my head between my hands.

Landon stares blankly, his mouth is wide open in shock.

"You two are unbelievable…. You have no idea what you've done." He stands up and starts pacing, mumbling to himself. "It all makes sense now. Why she's empty and you're overflowing. You two have just fallen down a hole you will never come out of, you'll never be the same. But we can save her. We can save you both. At least I think we can. I don't know who Arimel is but we have to help you before we try and figure out that puzzle. You both might end up empty, but we've got to try or else you both will die. You did make it this far after all. But how? It takes an immense amount of concentration, ability far behind you both. Perhaps too much strain individually but together? The strain would break most minds. I wish I knew more about your dreams with this Arimel. I can't see anything in your head right now."

I shake him. "What are you on about, man!? Can we help or not? We can't just let her be like this while we run around in circles!"

"You just performed a bit of that story book magic, lad. You've been linked. Well only half right now. You have to do it again. I don't know much about this kind of stuff. It's very dangerous even when done right. I think her mind is trapped inside yours. She lived your life just then and now she's confused. There's two of you in your head right now. It's an echo of you.

You have to get in her mind and go through her memories together. She needs to see herself and go back. I might be able to guide you, but we should do it now. Are you ready?" He finishes suddenly.

I can't think straight. I don't remember how Wynn did it. I don't think I can do this without Arimel. I need to be in her dream. But if I do nothing she's trapped forever? I have to do what Landon says. It's the only option. As easy as breathing…

"I'm ready."

"Close your eyes. Picture yourself right here with Wynn. She's sleeping now but see her awake. She's walking around. You can hear her thoughts. What do you hear?"

What do I hear? Nothing, I hear nothing. Wynn are you here? Hello? Dammit my head hurts.

"That's not working. Perhaps trying to recall a memory you both share?" Landon suggests.

"What are you saying? You don't know what to do?" The pain is almost too much to bear.

"We're in uncharted waters here, kid. Not many people have our gifts; fewer still are idiotic enough to do what you two did. And I imagine you're the only pair who stopped halfway. So yes, I have no idea. Just do as I say," he instructs.

This is too much! We weren't ready for any of this! Breathe. The pain is burning. Think, think, a memory we both share? Damn, it's so hot in here! Focus, focus… When we first met should work. But Landon might need to help. When we decided to travel together at the tavern.

That's right, we were talking about the city. I remember…

"Exactly my point! People are stubborn. They make a decision and they stick to it disregarding everything else. It only took a few men to make that decision for everyone in the town at the time. Before long, they were all defending the decision as if it were their own. A few men always make decisions for the masses because the masses are afraid to be held accountable for their own decisions. My point is this: it won't matter how many people look the other way if we do magic. It only takes a few, or in many cases a single person, to make a decision. The rest of the people will follow, fearing what would happen if they don't follow. It's difficult to understand now but before we reach the academy you'll see firsthand what I'm saying is true," Landon says.

"Here we are." He points to the end of the road we're on towards a large broken board nailed above a doorway.

This is a trash bin of a building. Is the name even the Broken Board or is it just Tavern? Because that sign just reads, 'Tavern.'

"Yes! But it's on a broken board." Landon smirks.

I sigh and we make our way to the door and a shutter falls off a window, leaving a hole in the wall behind it. Landon shrugs with a smirk and opens the door. He guides us to the bar.

Are they coming? Maybe they left already. Probably for the best. What am I even doing here? I can't trust them. That man works for those monsters and the kid is a sheep being herded by a wolf. I'll be fine on my own, I've always been fine on my own. Anyway, there's got to be somewhere I can go. There's always another option.

No. I need to learn more before I can run. I need to use them if I want to survive. The boy didn't seem so bad. He helped me, and I can probably trust him. He was taken.

"I think it's working. I can hear Wynn's memory!" I say to Landon.

"Focus on her. She's thinking of this memory as you are, hear her thoughts, and guide her memories. You need to repeat what she did," Landon instructs.

"How?! You need to tell me what to do. I'm like a fish in the sky. I have no right to be here. I have no idea what I'm doing!"

"Focus on a piece of her life. Something that you have strong ties to in your own life will make it easier. Picture your parents. Everyone has parents; it's the perfect gateway. Picture your mother, and she'll begin to imagine hers. You're tied now. You just need to guide her mind and you'll watch it play out. Once you know what to do you'll be able to sort through her memories." Landon says.

Alright, alright easy, like reading a book. My mother, just imagine my mother. And imagine her mother....

Your mother is striking. Her hair is white, no it's a pale blue, like ice. Her eyes are the same. She's warm though, like a frozen flame. Friendly, and tall, taller than your father? Perfect snow white skin, just like true royalty.

Your father is thin, too thin. He's dirty, and missing teeth. His eyes are dark, they look dead. Why was your mother with him? Your home is so big! But everything is broken. It's dark and damp.

He's hitting her. He's hitting all of you. She's changing. Your mother isn't kind anymore; she hurts you too. Her eyes are dark now. You're scared when you see her.

You have brothers? Four brothers; they're not like you. They're like him, like your father. They all hurt you. But why? You're alone; no one loves you. They all love the mepin. They're droppers.

It was better when you were little. A normal family, your father was a courier back then. Your mother was a seamstress.

Jacob was nice. Tall and strong. He helped your father. Tanned from the road, you liked him. He sees your family frequently. He smiles, always smiling.

It all stopped. Everything changed. Your father is manic. He's flailing and screaming. He's laughing, but he's not happy. He forces your mother to do it. Your brothers join. You hide, always hiding. They have no money. They spend everything on it. They sell everything. They find you and try to sell you.

Jacob bought you. You hide alone in your mind. You ran after. They found you. Jacob hurt your family. They hurt you for running. No one wanted you then.

The dream came. You weren't scared? Why should you be. Anything was better than life. Your dream was different. The woods and the clearing were the same, but you sat by the water. Never touching it. You knew it would wake you. You just wanted the shadows to take you, to kill you.

The figure comes, but he doesn't chase. He speaks to you. He tells you that you must go with him. You are given a choice, join them or your family will die. You cling to those words. They warm your blood, your bones. You feel alive. You tell him you won't go willingly. He laughs and throws you in the water.

As you wake, he drags you through the forest to your family. Another man comes. They argue. While fighting they light your house ablaze. You watch as he burns them all. He uses magic. You've never seen anything like it. He chases and cuts the ones that run. You watch as the fire boils the spilled blood on the ground.

You're scared, stunned silent. You didn't believe it, but now it's right in front of you. Your family is gone. You run while he chases your brother through the flames.

You keep running. Thoughts are gone. Only feelings. The cold stones of city streets. Pain. Numbness. Hunger. The noise of life. You steal food to live. You keep running. Woods, nothing to steal. Hidden in the silence. You try to hunt and forage. The only thing left on your mind is survival. Needs. Your memories are empty.

A new city. Familiar pains. Someone who cares, someone who helps. A new choice.

"You should come with us!" I say and reach out to her and Wynn reaches back.

PART II:
ARIMEL

Chapter Twenty-Seven

The creaking of the dry, old boards is almost familiar. The still air of the cabin echoing the subtle sounds around the room. A steady beating that comes from just outside the door acts as a guard standing vigil against the eerie silence that suffocates the rest of the ship. The hushed tones of grief continue to grip the passengers tightly. Cael and Wynn, ignorant of the worries all around them, remain in the depths of sleep. Their rest is calm and relaxed, dreaming of a new past, one shared between them. The soothing rhythm of Landon's footsteps draws them ever deeper, holding them ever longer.

It's slowly becoming easier to separate the two of them, yet their thoughts still wish to rush together like a wave crashing against the rocks. Awake their thoughts are unbridled and chaotic, flowing between their minds rather than within. Sleep is easy; dreams are easy. They dream as one without care for being more, sharing single thoughts rather than overflowing with many.

They dream of things that were, but were not theirs together. Desperate for the family that Cael had, Wynn leads their dreams to his life. Moments that she relived with him. Moments she wishes were her own. She breathes the air that is brimming with life. Deep in the forest, they stalk their prey. They move silently. Excitement fills her chest, determined to get her first kill this day. They spot a deer in the distance. Orion places a hand on her shoulder, signaling a full stop. He's waiting for the right moment, the perfect position. The deer looks up as it becomes aware of a new scent on the wind. Orion lets go and Wynn releases the arrow perfectly. He marks her forehead with blood.

"You're a real hunter now, son," he says, beaming.

Cael smiles at Wynn and they embrace as brothers.

The waking world has changed so much. It's freeing to return here, like a well deserved stretch after time untold spent sleeping.

The lullaby of footsteps suddenly comes to an end as Landon hears someone walking towards their cabin. He quickly composes himself, wiping the concern from his face and replacing it with a forced smile as he sees Rena lean around the corner.

"How are they?" she whispers.

"I honestly don't know. Do you have any guess as to when they'll wake up? Are they sick?" Landon whispers back, letting a hint of concern creep into his voice, playing the perfect part.

Rena steps closer and offers a gentle squeeze. "Stop worrying so much. This is normal." She pushes him at arm's length and gives him a once over. "You need to rest, Landon. You're no good to us like this. If you stay up much longer you'll be in worse shape than they are."

Landon shrugs and steps away. "I just want them to be well again." He keeps his true emotion out of his voice.

He wishes he could tell her more, to find out if maybe she had some bit of arcane knowledge that would help them, to search her memories for something, anything. But he knows that it's hopeless, any knowledge she has, no matter how foreign, could never have information on what they've done.

"It hasn't even been two days and what they survived was incredible. What we all survived... I'm not going to be too worried just yet. Exhaustion is powerful and their condition is completely within normal boundaries. So get some rest, doctor's orders!" she says as she pats him on the back.

Cael and Wynn begin to stir fitfully as they are pulled from their peaceful slumber and thrust back into a new uncontrolled reality. As soon as consciousness flows through their minds, a pounding pain hammers in their heads. They fight to control their thoughts, but they are fighting against each other.

They groan as they open their eyes.

Rena rushes to them. "Are you in pain? Where does it hurt?"

"Heads, our heads..." they call out in chorus.

Landon glances at Rena to see her reaction.

"Water. They might be dehydrated." Rena directs Landon as he fills their wooden mugs. He hands her the cups, relieved they are finally awake but still frustrated he can't do more to help.

Cael and Wynn sigh, rubbing their heads.

"Thank you," they mumble, sipping the water.

Rena quickly and efficiently assesses their condition. Taking note of their skin color and elasticity, eye color and pupil dilation. She measures their temperatures with her hand. Seeing no reaction or swelling when applying firm pressure to their abdomens she moves to their heads, ignoring the wincing and cries of pain that echo around her as she prods their skulls for fractures or any sign of injury. Soon her gaze begins to wander as she focuses on potential illnesses and solutions. After a few moments she stands up, face wrinkled with irritation and disappointment.

"Anything?" Landon asks, already knowing the answer.

"I'm just in training right now..." she replies helplessly. "This is so frustrating. I should know what's wrong with them! If a real doctor were here, they'd probably be fine, but I have no experience. I need to study more. I'm sorry, I just need more time to think. Keep fluids in them please." Rena huffs as she stomps away, annoyed and embarrassed by her lack of knowledge.

"It's not her. You both know what's wrong," Landon says, taking their mugs and refilling them. "You did something very rash and stupid, and now everyone's worried. But at least you're both still alive."

"Just make it stop. It hurts," they moan.

"Clearly, it doesn't hurt as badly as before or else you'd be descending the tree of death." Landon scolds them. "I still cannot believe you were both so foolish. I should never have taught you anything." He hands them their mugs. "Drink."

"We... I can't. Focus... We're not well."

Landon whips around to yell at them, to tell them 'of course they aren't well.' But he quickly sees how weak they are. They're like wounded animals, helpless and completely lost. He sits down and lets his anger wash away. Anger is fair; anger is warranted. But anger will have to wait until they are themselves again. Though, hearing them speak even as broken as they are, lends him hope that they might still return to the ones they were.

"Well, we're getting somewhere. You can talk a little." He rubs his temples, "I wish I knew more about this, you two truly have no idea how little I know about joinings." He closes his eyes and tries to think, blocking out the sound of their constant moaning.

"We need to think this through slowly," Landon says more to himself but Cael and Wynn groan in agreement. "You can understand me, but you can't think straight enough to give me any real answers. I can try and help, but without either of you able to speak or think clear enough for me to hear, I can't really do anything. Rena has no clues, but we can expect that. There's no one else on this ship who could even attempt to help. You were fine enough when you were sleeping, or at least you seemed fine, but we can't keep you asleep forever." He puts his face in his hands and closes his eyes.

He excitedly shoots out of his chair. "We don't need to keep you asleep forever! When we make it to Ayverden, there should be someone who can help! They work with the king. They have to be able to help. We just need to keep you asleep until then!" He runs out the door. A moment of silence before his heavy boots pound down the hallway boards followed by a much lighter tapping.

"You're sure? It might not be helpful.... We could hurt them more since we don't even know what's wrong," Rena protests.

"Trust me, we just need to keep them asleep. I'll talk with the captain and see how much further we have to go," Landon says, rushing out of the room.

Rena sigh. "Just put them to sleep... sure Landon, even I can't mess that up." She grumbles as she sorts through her herbs and tonics. She chooses carefully and begins brewing an aromatic liquid.

"Drink this and try to sleep. Landon's right, once we get to the city there'll be a real doctor who can help." She says handing them their tea.

As they sit up to grab the mugs from her, she seems to notice something off. She watches them closely. Analyzing their movements. A light in her eyes begins to flicker as her mind turns with questions.

Chapter Twenty-Eight

Landon rushes to the main deck, knocking into a few of the crew who barely take notice. They all move slowly, still lost in their grief. As he reaches sunlight, he searches for the captain but is stopped short by the sight of those around him. It hits him then that only a few short days have passed since the storm. The captain, while physically on the main deck, drinks bottle after bottle of rum. Still hoping to find some cure for his sadness. Some way to forget about his dear friend Brun. Trep, no longer caring to make meals, is at the captain's side, ensuring he does not forget himself alone.

Those who were not still trapped in thoughts of that stormy night carry the hopes of all by attempting to maintain course and safely reach Ayverden. Gavin mans the helm with a determined focus on salvaging the voyage. Rolin and Francis take charge of the galley and preparing meals to fill bellies while sweet Rena stops at every bedside to hold the hands of all who need her.

Landon moves with purpose to the captain who stares numbly at his broken arm hanging in a sling. "How long till landfall?" He asks promptly. Karif remains still so Landon continues, "Cael and Wynn are sick and we need to get them to a doctor as soon as possible."

The captain doesn't even turn away from his bottle as he responds, "Wouldn't have ah mattered anyways…. Let em die now. Peaceful." He hiccups. "We all die.. Better in a bed than…

than… at the bottom of the sea!" He begins sobbing and hiccupping uncontrollably. Trep manages to focus his eyes on Landon just long enough to shoot a nasty look in his direction before his head falls back to his own rapidly emptying bottle.

Frustrated but sympathetic, Landon searches around for anyone else who might have an idea. As he faces the helm, he hears Gavin call out, "Land Ho!"

"Already?" Landon shouts with confused excitement. There on the horizon, a sprawling city comes into view. The crowd gathers around to the front of the ship and begins cheering.

"One heck of a tailwind I'd say!" Rolin chirps from the middle of the group.

"I'd reckon it was the storm," Gavin says dumbly, gazing at the ocean behind him. "We were tossed around for a long while. It must've thrown us a damn sight further than we'd imagined."

At mention of the storm, the crowd's elation of the journeys end falls away and their thoughts turn back toward those they lost.

Derik shoves his way to the front. "A few lives to shave a week off our journey? I'll take that deal every time! Quit all your crying, what's done is done," he shouts as he heads below deck to begin packing.

Gavin gazes over the passengers all on deck, still saddened from their losses. He calls out above the murmurs, "It's true. There's no worth in dwelling on what's past. We may not find joy in this day, but we can accept that we've survived…. We must accept it. We went through the depths of darkness and lived to see the light on the other side. Soon we'll walk off this ship going our separate ways. We might never see one another again, but we'll all remember this journey and you can find comfort in that. Your family, your friends… the ones who were lost, they won't be forgotten by any of us. Adam, Jones, Marcus and Brun, they'll live on in our memories. Be free to mourn, but don't punish yourselves or anyone else, and don't carry their regrets. They died by the sea, and there is no shame in that. Live good lives to honor them and remember them whenever you can. They deserve to be remembered. We all do."

The passengers, moved by his words, silently shake their new captain's hand before disappearing beneath the deck to prepare for landfall.

Landon walks toward Gavin as the last of the crew disappear to gather their belongings. He takes Gavin's hand in both of his. "It was well said. You'll make a damn fine captain," he says as he pats him on the back.

The atmosphere of the ship is a mixture of grief, guilt and strangely, excitement as they make port in the North Liefland capital city of Ayverden. In spite of the clinging sadness, they're all anxious to move on and continue their journeys.

Landon returns below deck to check on his charges, brushing by Rena as she makes her way out of their cabin. "They appear to be sleeping well. It's a strange sickness, isn't it? Have you ever seen this before?" she says to Landon with a hint of suspicion in her voice.

He eyes her curiously as he instinctively searches her thoughts for unspoken words. He's interested in how quickly she determined that the illness may not be natural. But his curiosity cannot be indulged right now. He must play his part at the courts to ensure they are cared for properly.

"I don't have much training in the medical field. But I don't think I've ever seen anything quite like it. I hope you'll excuse me. I really should hurry to find help for them. If I don't see you again, I wish you and Rolin a safe journey," Landon says with a farewell wave as he quickly changes focus to Cael and Wynn.

"You as well," Rena says slowly.

They enter the port and dock with an easy thud as the plank is dropped on the long wooden pier. Landon takes one final look at Cael and Wynn sleeping soundly before making his way off the ship. In his haste he passes a few stragglers saying their goodbyes and making halfhearted attempts at future meetings. He spots the captain stumbling his way into his quarters with Gavin helping steady both him and Trep. Gavin sends a quick wave his way before continuing to navigate his drunk shipmates to their beds.

The mood on the ship could not have been more different than that of the city. The moment his boots touch the cobblestone off the pier, everyone he passes has a smile and a friendly greeting.

The streets are clean. The shops are in order. The residents and vendors are all happy, almost delighted. Landon moves with purpose passed all of this, barely taking notice. He's already aware that there is no other city in this, or any other country, that operates quite like this one.

Before long a runner catches up to Landon, a young messenger boy from the king. 'Scuse me woodsman sir... Are you called Lampton?" The young boy wipes sweat from his brow.

Landon nods impatiently. "Close enough for me. Where can I meet the king, boy?"

The messenger lifts his chin. "I'm ten years old, sir. I'm no boy no longer. Name's Harry!" He chirps as he extends his hand.

Landon shakes it firmly. "The king boy—Harry. Where's the king? It's urgent."

Harry shrugs. "He's off wandering the streets by the gates, told me to tell ya to meet him in the gardens afore noon." He stretches out his open hand waiting for payment.

Landon pushes it down. "Come now, boy. You're a king's messenger. I know you're paid. Don't be getting greedy." He scolds Harry before speeding off towards the gardens.

There are the public gardens and the king's gardens. Despite being a very personable king, Thokrin could only mean his personal gardens. Landon heads towards the center of town where the new royal residence is and informs the guards of his appointment with the king before he's hastily led into the guest wing to freshen up.

"No one should see royalty smelling like a fisherman lost at sea," they say to him as they hand him off to workers ready to scrub his body raw while clipping his hair and shaving his face clean.

As he steps out of the tub a long while later, he's given a new overly perfumed set of clothes. He reluctantly parts with his knife as his weapons are confiscated before being ushered into the gardens.

Irritated with the delays but knowing courtly procedures must be followed he sighs a heavy breath to compose himself before stepping out into the manicured lawns of the lush colorful king's garden.

Shortly after stepping on the grounds, he sees Thokrin towering over half a dozen elderly advisors. Landon hears rather than sees the ones he's searching for. They are a bit younger and having a separate conversation unheard by the rest. The king notices Landon and nods lightly to him with a smile, signaling Landon's audience. Landon bows politely before walking calmly over.

"Master Woodsman, my dear chap, it's been ages hasn't it? You look like you've just been forced to endure one of those pesky wash downs, haven't you? The perfume is always so much. I really have asked them to refrain from such things." The king says, placing an arm around Landon as he gracefully joins the retinue. The weight of his arm surprises Landon for a moment.

"Alas, the courtly life, it's difficult to get used to but impossible to change." He continues.

"It's no trouble at all your majesty. Truthfully it's quite nice to have such a refreshing bath so soon off the ship," Landon says easily, forcing himself to obey protocol or risk delaying his conversation with the advisors further.

The king continues, "Oh, of course, you only just arrived. Quite earlier than expected if I do recall. I hope your voyage wasn't too dull?"

Landon senses an opportunity and decides to break the rules rather than waste it. "Quite exciting. Actually a little too exciting. I do apologize but the journey has had an unexpected impact on a few charges of mine and I was very much hoping that you could perhaps lend me your advisors to assess their condition? If it's not an inconvenience of course." Landon stops and bows as he makes the request.

"A favor so soon, Landon? You are losing your sense of the royal dance, my boy!" King Thokrin pats him on the back but doesn't seem upset by the request. He waves his followers away. "Give us a moment, won't you? Alek and Julia, you both may stay."

Landon nods to Alek and Julia who he recognizes as members of the academy. Anxious to hurry this along, he lets the façade fall as soon as the other advisors leave them.

"King Thokrin, I have two young charges with me. They've done something very rash and very stupid and we need

Alek and Julia to help in any way they can. I have them sleeping on a ship at the docks. I can go get them right now." Landon spits out

Alek and Julia give Landon a questioning look of disapproval. This was still the court after all. You could not simply demand anything of royalty. No matter how pressing, you must maintain reverence towards the king. Yet King Thokrin is not typical royalty and, against his advisors' wishes, he too often slips back into the commoner's way of life.

"Of course, Landon, I can see this is very important. We'll have a few of my own guard bring them and your belongings to our guest rooms at once," Thokrin responds kindly waving to a few men in the corner.

"Thank you, your grace." Landon bows.

The king guides Landon back up and replies, "However, there is something I would ask of you in return. Something that also cannot wait."

Chapter Twenty-Nine

The guards carry the still sleeping children into their new royal quarters. Before Landon can explain what happened, both Alek and Julia begin searching their minds. They promptly let out a shocked gasp and turn their focus to Landon.

"How could you begin teaching them?! Who gave you the authority to even seek these two out? You could have killed these children!" Julia yells.

"Calm yourself, Julia. Landon clearly acknowledges his responsibility in this. It's also evident that he believes he is doing the correct thing by delivering them personally. We mustn't let our feelings fog our vision," Alek gently rebukes.

"That doesn't excuse his actions... although I suppose it does explain them," Julia says. "Please forgive my outburst."

Landon takes her hands. "It's already forgiven. Please, help them."

The two advisors stand over Landon's resting charges and for a moment not a thought is heard between them as they let their minds wander alongside Cael and Wynn's. Landon watches closely, impressed by their advanced abilities and how easily they manipulate their thoughts.

After a short mental stroll, the advisors come to a definitive conclusion. "If you had continued your studies rather than leaving early simply to be able to call yourself the youngest Emir, you would have easily deduced their condition," Alek says disapprovingly to Landon.

"The voice you hear in their minds is their combined selves at a point during the joining when they as individuals should have ceased. However, the pain they felt has apparently caused this new consciousness to begin a separation, being the only identifiable solution. The joining was prematurely stopped and they were separated, but this new consciousness continues and it binds them." Julia states simply. "Though there is an unusual echo present."

Alek continues matter-of-factly, "This third consciousness is causing them pain when they attempt to think as they always have, but that way of thinking is no longer possible. It is also the most likely cause of this echo. They will be able to retain their identities, but they must be trained on how to utilize this new 'self'. Once they are educated they should in theory be able to separate the flow of thoughts from their own and live relatively similar lives to what they had."

Landon cuts in. "But they cannot learn anything right now. They can't even think. How will you train them in this state? They are sleeping now, but when they wake up they'll be in constant pain, you'll see it soon enough."

Julia and Alek sigh impatiently together.

"We of course will compartmentalize their joined consciousnesses while we train them and slowly filter the flow of thoughts back as they progress," Julia says in irritation.

Landon is surprised for a moment. "Are you two… joined as well?"

Taken aback by his question, they laugh wholeheartedly.

"No of course not!" Alek says as he regains his composure.

"The risks far outweigh the potential rewards." Julia says condescendingly.

Alek turns to Landon who is still confused, "Then how are we so close? It's obvious, we have worked together for near our entire lives. I know we must seem severely aged to a youth such as you, but this connection is no different than anyone, gifted or otherwise, could attain."

Julia finishes. "All it takes is time, you'll understand one day." They smile at each other before looking back to Landon.

"Off with you now, the king has business you'll need to attend to. We'll handle this from here. Shoo, shoo!" they say as they wave him out the door.

"This will be interesting," Alek says after Landon leaves.

"It certainly will be." Julia agrees as they turn back to Cael and Wynn. "The solution is sound, but the execution must be perfect or else we'll risk causing a full joining."

"Or worse, our forceful separation of the alternative consciousness could cause an immediate and permanent break, and eventual death," Alek says with a shrug.

"Should we simply guide them to a full joining? It would solve the ethical issue of their survivability." Julia suggests.

"Ah, true, true. However, how many have officiated a partial joining? The information we could gain would be far more valuable. To both us and the academy. I daresay it would be an injustice to science if we let this opportunity go to waste," Alek says decidedly.

"Indeed, I suppose you're right," Julia concedes.

Chapter Thirty

Alek and Julia slowly draw them out of their sleep, separating their minds and allowing them to think freely. It's difficult to recall exact details when they are separated, senses become unreliable and the cacophony of thoughts impossible to navigate. With no touchstone for reality, all there can be is interpretations. Conversations and thoughts are like whispers in the corner while colors dull and blur. Time moves differently when they are away. The freedom of the waking world is taken as the separation isolates them.

As they progress, Alek and Julia slowly release the barriers blocking our thoughts. Senses begin to filter back through.

"It doesn't hurt as bad, at least as bad as it did before," Cael says, rubbing his head.

"I don't have much pain. Maybe you're still fighting it?" Wynn suggests.

"Regardless, you're both doing quite well given only a few days of lessons. I imagine you'll both excel quite nicely at the academy. Perhaps we even have a few aspiring scientists here, Alek!" Julia says proudly.

"Quite quite, they are an impressive pair for certain," Alek agrees. "But we're not finished here so soon. We have made astounding progress giving some control back to you both. However, reasoning and logic must prevail. You should be aware of the full extent of your gifts and the consequences that your joining could have."

Alek and Julia nod together to their patients.

Julia walks to the front of their makeshift classroom in the guest wing and brushes her long blonde hair from her eyes. She begins quickly instructing Cael and Wynn while they take notes at their table.

"The list of consequences is more important, so we will begin there," she says waving her hands.

"One. You cannot be separated for any length of time. The distance at which your ability to communicate telepathically will directly correlate to the distance at which you can safely reside from one another. If you stay outside this range for any period of time, you will begin to have serious symptoms. Likely a forgetfulness of who you are as individuals, general confusion and malaise, mixed or altered memories, hallucinations, bleeding from the skull due to brain hemorrhages and if you survive that, death will come as your minds fully break and your internal respiratory systems fail."

Cael and Wynn look at each other as a shiver runs through them both. The realization of their actions hits them like a stone.

Julia continues, "That is not all, just the most relevant to your predicament. I'll go on; Two. You will feel pain as the other feels pain, up to and including death. Three. The more closed off you allow yourselves to become you'll likely notice things like queasiness, vertigo, inability to regulate body temperature among other minor symptoms. Four. You can no longer dream alone. You will likely sleep at the same times and dream as one. This could be viewed as a positive. Although being together both awake and asleep for all eternity does certainly seem daunting. Five. You will of course have no secrets. You must be completely open for this partial pairing to maintain its delicate balance. Six and finally, you may still fall into a full joining where your individualities will cease to exist. There is potential for the stronger of you to retain some of yourself as you essentially assimilate the other's self-control with yours. The weaker will be as a prisoner, forever bound to the will of the host."

Cael pats Wynn on the shoulder sarcastically, "Well great idea, Wynn! Death by brain bleeding is top on my list right above being a prisoner for life with no control over myself!"

Wynn shrugs. "We haven't even heard the positive things yet. Maybe it's worth it?"

Alek shakes his head earnestly while fixing his shirt collar. "Almost certainly not, but we'll let you determine the value of your actions. The positive side effects of your partial joining would be…" He steps up alongside Julia and reads off a piece of paper in front of him.

"One and most importantly, you both maintain your own identities, but still are able to utilize the others senses at will. Likely difficult to achieve now, however given practice you'll be able to see what the other sees, hear what the other hears, etcetera."

Wynn smiles. "Sounds good so far, right!?" As she elbows Cael in the arm, wagging her eyebrows up and down.

Alek sighs, looking down his nose and over his large glasses. "May I finish?"

Wynn nods apologetically

"Two. You'll both have access to a combination of knowledge and memories to allow for more efficient comprehension of difficult topics or situations. Three. The act of joining essentially eliminates the risk that your minds will be infiltrated, unless the individual knows or suspects you're joined of course. It also reduces the waves that communication between one another will create, as such reducing the likelihood that your thoughts will be heard."

They all sit in silence for a moment before Cael speaks up, "That's it? Just those three things? Julia went on about how we'll probably die or be prisoner and can't be ourselves anymore and all we get is, 'Oh hey you're a bit smarter?'"

"Alek and I are of the thought that a joining, even partial should it be possible, is not a sufficient reward to outweigh the stated risks. A full joining erases self-identity and is viewed as a last resort for most. A partial joining, and again I state if possible as it is only very rarely so, while allowing for self-identity to remain, removes the smooth and fluid capability of the fully joined and in doing so removes any benefit therein. So yes, we agree with you, Cael. What you and Wynn have so ignorantly accomplished, with our help, is no great boon. It may prove to be more of a hindrance," Julia says kindly as she recognizes the anxiety they both have.

Alek chimes in, "Although, as you are both the youngest to my knowledge who have ever attempted this, it could prove to be such a boon." Their eyes light up with surprise at this idea and Alek continues, "Surprising as it is, you both have entered into this covenant very young and will grow with this connection being part of you. Very unlike most who sign their lives over with full knowledge at an advanced age. If you utilize your abilities, practice with them, and open the doors to each other frequently, you might become something greater than Julia or I can imagine right now. I look forward to watching you grow and of course taking notes for our research."

"Remember now, your connection is still tethered. It's not fully free yet. Only your ability to think separately has been unchained. But, you have all the tools to allow your connection to expand into senses and deep thought, subconscious thought," Julia says.

With that Alek and Julia gather their paperwork and shuffle out the door. Leaving without even a goodbye to the children they spent so much of their time helping over the past few days. Cael and Wynn sit alone in the guest room staring at the door their recent experts just exited, silently, at a loss for what to do next.

Wynn speaks first. "I'm sorry for this. But maybe it won't be so bad? It sounds pretty great to me!"

Cael smiles at her. "Of course you'd feel great about it." He takes in a long deep breath and lets it out slowly. "Well, honestly it's not much different than what we wanted to happen, besides the whole death and dying things."

He stands up and stretches. Realizing for the first time that he's wearing clean cotton clothes, dyed white and green. He turns to Wynn who also is noticing her clothes, a blue and yellow dress.

"We look pretty good!" Wynn says, matching his smile. "Want to go walk around the city?"

Cael, hesitant at first, simply shrugs his shoulders. "Well, we can't let these clothes go to waste in a dry old room like this. Alright, lead the way, captain." He feels something in his pocket and pulls out a small purse, heavy with a few gold stater and silver marks.

"Spending money!" They shout together.

They link arms and make their way through the royal grounds. Not large enough to be a castle, more a large manor with a garden in the center and small gated entry way. The beautifully maintained building and busy servants are the only details that reveal a hint of royalty.

As they exit the grounds, the guards stand at attention. It's almost as if Cael and Wynn were truly royal guests, which draws a smile out of them before they begin leisurely walking in their brand-new clothes out of the king's manor. A murmuring hits their ears. They listen to the rumors starting to form of who the new guests are and where they are from. Appreciating the attention, but not wanting to cause trouble for Landon or the king, they pick up the pace and enter one of the markets.

"It's such a beautiful city," Wynn mentions while they pass another friendly vendor, this one giving out free samples of his candied pecans. They eagerly take him up on his offer and devour their sweets.

"I could get used to a city like this," Cael says in awe of all around him.

"You and me both!" Wynn agrees.

They slowly wind their way through the stunning city and are greeted with a quick smile and kind words from everyone that crosses their path. Coming to a silent agreement, they decide to make their way back to the docks and have a look around. Hoping to meet with Rena, Rolin, Gavin or any of the other friends they made on their journey.

They enter dockside, marked by the fresh sea air and vendors selling the daily catch. As they near Karif's ship they spot a thief stealing a young woman's purse. Not an unusual sight for a large city, especially near the docks. Though it strikes them as the first scene of anything but peaceful serenity they've encountered throughout the city.

They watch the events unfold with focused curiosity. The thief steals the purse and is almost immediately hit gently upside the head by a guard who appears from nowhere. Shocked more than anything, the thief speeds away down an alley, and the guard returns the purse to the relatively calm victim. Everyone continues on as if nothing happened. The guard doesn't give chase. It's as if the thief didn't matter to anyone.

"Did you see that?" Wynn asks incredulously.

Cael laughs. "Of course I did, you walnut. I'm right here! And I'm pretty sure we see everything the other does now, right?"

Wynn brushes his comments aside. "Who knows, but what do you think that was all about? Why didn't that guard arrest the thief? Why is everyone so weird around here? Everyone is way too... way too smiley? And friendly."

Cael shakes his head in disbelief. "You're joking, right? I mean, look at this place. It's beautiful. The king doesn't live in a grand castle looking down on everyone. He lives right in the center of the city. Everyone lives well so no one has a reason to be upset. I bet that woman wouldn't have even cared if that thief did steal her purse because everyone looks to be taken well care of here. We haven't seen a single poor person. Think on it, the king here must be one of the most generous rulers of all time and that's why everyone is so happy."

Wynn nods her head slowly in agreement but continues to have her doubts.

It would be easy for anyone else to miss the vessel that they called home for so much of their journey. Despite its inexplicable sameness and lack of any descriptive characteristics, Karif's ship stands out like a thumb to both of them. They meander their way to the boarding plank wondering who they'll see, if they see anyone at all. Not long after their feet hit the ship, they hear a familiar voice, "You're both looking well!"

Rena scoops them up in a quick hug. "I was really beginning to worry about you two!" she says as she begins analyzing their condition.

"We're fine, Mother!" Cael says with an easy laugh.

Wynn smiles uncomfortably at the affectionate greeting but pushes through her awkwardness. "We're glad to see you here, we weren't sure if anyone would still be here honestly."

Rena continues investigating their health, "We had already secured passage from Ayverden to Dr. Alabas's estate months ago so unfortunately our being ahead of schedule didn't impact our 'end of adventure' timing. Rolin and I figured we'd stay aboard to watch over Trep and Karif, not to mention we're quite short of funds until my apprenticeship is concluded."

Rena looks them both over once more before smiling her suspicions away. "Before you left this ship, I could have sworn something very odd was happening to you two. What was the cause? Did your doctors say? Who were your doctors?"

They are taken aback by the bluntness of Rena's questions, but as they reach into her mind they sense only caring thoughts and quickly put aside their unease.

"Landon actually knows the king!" Cael says excitedly. "Some guards brought us to stay with him!"

Wynn becomes wrapped in Cael's excitement. "And he has a beautiful garden with so many flowers and fruit trees! It smells amazing! And look!" She cries out as she spins in her dress and Cael follows along, "New clothes!"

Rena smiles wide listening to them. "It all sounds amazing! Do you remember who your doctors were though? I'd love to learn more. I was very frustrated when I couldn't solve your case. Understanding would help me rest easy."

Cael and Wynn look at each other for a moment, trying to figure out what to say and how much to tell.

"We really just talked for a few days and then felt much better. I don't even think we were given any medicine. King Thokrin's advisors are amazing, but we wouldn't even have made it this far without you so we wanted to thank you again," Cael says as he gives Rena another big bear hug and lifts her off her feet.

As Cael plops her back down, she changes the subject away from themselves. "Karif and Trep still aren't doing well.... It would be wonderful if you both could stay and maybe get them to talk about anything other than Brun and that storm. If anyone could do it, it would have to be you two."

"Of course!" Wynn says. It seems like ages to her and Cael, but those stories helped the journey move along so much faster.

The trio follow the sound of slurred sea shanties and upon opening the captain's quarters lay eyes on a depressing scene. Karif and Trep surrounded by empty rum bottles, in naught but their sleepwear, singing about losing the love of the sea.

"They changed songs at least, but they aren't much better. I managed to get them to start drinking some water, so progress?" Rolin says greeting them after the song had finished. "It's so good to see you up and moving again. Rena here was worried sick about you two, lucky for us we had new patients to tend to." He nods towards the drunkards behind him.

"My my, that's quite the situation you have there. Are we sure that they're going to be alright?" Wynn asks, looking at them with a mix of pity and disgust.

"Karif is mourning Brun and Trep is very empathetic and refuses to let Karif mourn alone. I'm certain it makes Karif *feel* better, but I think it may actually be feeding his grief. That's where you two come in, just get them talking, about anything really. We need to stop the cycle and Rolin and I can't think of anything to get them talking," Rena says, concern seeping into her voice.

Cael rubs his hands together. "Alright, time to get to work! Let's fix this mess, Wynn."

Wynn nods and they approach the drunks. As they begin another song, she cuts in. "Captain! Trep! It's so wonderful to see you both. Cael and I were just talking about how much we missed you!"

"It's true. A moment scarcely passes that we're not thinking of the great food Trep would cook for us or the stories that the captain would tell us," Cael says as they sit on the captain's bed looking down at Karif and Trep sprawled on the floor.

Trep comes alive first. "Look Rif; it's them jolly kids! Oh, we missed ya well and proper. Look how ya've grown!"

Karif eyes them up and down with distaste. "Ya look to be doin' just fine fer yerselves in the city, all dollied up. What brings you royal twits down here, eh?"

Rena and Rolin both look shamefully at Karif, but Trep quickly agrees with him, "Comin in ta this ship dressed like that! No respect in them youngins, bunch a city pricks they are!"

Trep and Karif laugh as they repeat the phrase 'city pricks' over and over.

They let the hubbub die down before Wynn continues as if nothing was said. "We were roaming around out there and we got to wondering about the city. Something feels off. Do you guys know anything about Ayverden or King Thokrin? Why is everyone so happy?"

Cael elbows her in the side but he notices Karif actually thinking of some stories.

Karif stands up and stumbles to his desk chair. "We be in Ayverden? Oh aye, I know a bit about her, little lady. This city's an old city. King Richard the third, brute of a man, ruled here back in the day. Nothing like his old man." He says peering over his maps.

"The South and North've been at war for many long times. A bit less of a long time ago, King Richard, the ass, wanted nothing but a war, and the South wanted nothing but *not* a war. He thought nothin' for his people, and King Richard putted all his things and all his food to the big war fighting. Lots of inoncensed people starved to death, froze in the streets, killed by meanderers parties or forced to enlist. The people hated him."

'You getting any of this?' Cael thinks to Wynn.

'Not really, but we can puzzle it together.' She responds.

"So, after a long time, the North had nothing left and the South was like rats in a corner. They had nothing neither, but they had to defend to survive, feeding on justice! So the South won a short peace and King Richard's bastard son from some trollop comes to the city saying he'll make everything better or some such rubbish. All them people were looking for change, so the armied people and regular people people stood behind Thokrin as rightful hairs and first thing he did was put his pappy to the axe man. That won a lot of people over, meself included!" Karif says as he slowly begins to close his eyes. He rifles through his maps, knocking a bottle off the desk.

"So what about the city then? Why's it different now?" Wynn presses, while Cael catches the bottle and stands it back up neatly.

Karif's eyes shoot open. "Aye the city... There'd be poor folk wandering the streets, murderers in daylight with the city guard not even putting in the effort to look about whilst it happened, lets alone lookin' ta punish nobody. So Thokrin, he be king now remember, sprouted about equalness and everything being fair and deserved. No one had belief in him ... at first. But he walked the city, helping people, caring on people. But change is slow, too slow. All the peoples weren't just gonna trust him on his word, and even the little he did weren't good enough. His old man ruled with a unjustly face for decades. His dreams was just dreams. Nobody wanted to be happy, almost like they felt they deserved to be sad and angry. Then it all changed, we took a trip down south and came back a few months later and the city were a paradise. Friendly faces, no fighting, no killing, no yelling, no nothing bad."

"But *how* did it happen?" Rena asks, becoming just as interested as Wynn.

"Oh I dunno. Maybe it's got ta do with all the fighting early on? Ripe like a plum, the city was wanting change. Rich folk, poor folk, all em witnessed bad things, real bad things. Nightmarish things. Ya get a bastard king in there, something they all feel they deserved, they was owed a bastard king. But this king be nice and kind, more than they deserved. He did the impossible, but maybe it all was timed rightly, juuust rightly? Was only a few years ago." Karif shrugs and coddles his nearly empty rum bottle before quickly falling asleep.

They turn to Trep for more questions, but he's already passed out on the floor, snoring peacefully.

"Well, that was a productive exercise, well done!" Rolin says with a chuckle.

Rena nods in agreement. "Thank you both. It took their minds off everything long enough for them to get some much needed rest."

"Anything for our friends," Cael says, suddenly feeling ill.

Wynn begins feeling sick soon after and they excuse themselves for fresh air.

Rena and Rolin follow them out.

"Are you both feeling well?" Rena asks with an analytical eye.

"Just sea sickness most likely." Cael says as he steps off the ship with Wynn not far behind.

"We don't really get seasick. It's weird. Maybe it was the fumes in that room?" Wynn suggests.

Cael nods in agreement as he breathes in the fresh sea air.

"So, what are your plans in the city? Where's Landon?" Rena asks.

"Landon went to meet with King Thokrin, but I'm not sure where he is now. We'll likely catch up with him before leaving for Oarna," Cael says proud of his friend's station.

Rolin appears sufficiently impressed. "Conference with the king? Travelling to Oarna? You two certainly have an interesting life for ones so young."

Wynn smiles uneasily, trying to change the subject. "What will you both do until your wagon arrives?"

"Oh, I imagine stay here helping these fools quit the bottle." Rolin motions to the ship. "We only have a few days left in the city. We'll soon be off to bigger and better things, just like you two!" He gazes adoringly at Rena who blushes and plays with her hair.

"Do you two have time for a quick meal?" Rolin suggests.

Cael and Wynn nod quickly, "Lead the way!" They reply in unison.

They walk the docks to the first tavern they see. A smoothly sanded and freshly stained sign. No broken boards or doors, no fighting or yelling. An apparently idyllic dockside tavern.

The inside has a soothing sandalwood scent wafting through that intermingles with the smells of good food and drink. The group begin to salivate at the smells and let themselves relax as they sit down at their table. A shorter, thin man approaches their table offering the daily special, a hearty stew, of which all at the table greedily accept. He returns swiftly with aromatic fruity wine, soft warm bread, and bowls of steaming, perfectly cooked lamb stew.

As the man leaves, they begin ravenously devouring their stew. Once they've all finished, they sit back and mop up the remnants with pieces of bread and relax while sipping wine. After a few glasses, their faces flush and they smile wide at each other.

They overhear a small group of road worn travelers talking in the corner of the tavern. "…seen him in weeks. I swear he ain't like this. He ain't one to run off without us. I reckon something happened. This city, it ain't right Sam. It ain't right at all."

The one called Sam speaks. "Ya think he was taken? Like all them missing folk down in Kaldia?"

"It ain't just Kaldia. It's all over. Even Oarna and Waylinn. It's worse here in the Lieflands," a bigger man says.

Rolin sighs wearily. "Folks disappearing even here? This city seems so perfect; you'd think we were a world away from stories like that."

"They aren't really what I pictured when people talk about those rumors, a bit rough around the edges." Rena says.

"Yea, certainly not your typical 'family that disappeared' story. Do either of you know anything about these disappearances? The kids and families that go missing?" asks Cael.

Rena and Rolin look at each other before Rolin speaks. "Not much I'm afraid."

"About as much as anyone willing to listen I suppose," Rena adds.

Wynn moves up in her seat. "But what do people say?"

"Just like children, always curious." Rolin says with a grin. He thinks for a moment scratching his face. "The regular, 'a family went missing over yonder' or 'the Frederickson's kid hasn't been seen in weeks.' Nothing really detailed, just a bunch of stories, too many to discount as rumor."

Rena leans in. "I've heard the same symptoms, but no one has figured out the cause. More rumors on that front as well. Some say slavers, others say sickness. I'm sure sometimes it's just a family moves on and doesn't tell anyone or they lose their child somehow and don't want to think on it. But all of these stories together? Too many to attribute to a random move or illness. No one near us has gone missing and so it's hard to really believe any of it. But once someone does, it'll become as true as the day is long."

Cael and Wynn glance at each other nervously and Rena catches their eye.

"You two know something more, don't you?" she asks, curiously and presses. "Come now, don't hold out on us."

Wynn shrugs. "We do—"

"Don't know anything. Just tales of people who have been taken." Cael cuts her off.

Wynn elbows him.

"Taken? What do you mean taken? Is there truth to the slave trading?" Rolin asks with interest.

Rena and Rolin both wait eagerly for an answer and Cael turns red with embarrassment as Wynn smiles devilishly. "I think what Cael meant to say is we have heard of people who have gone *missing*. He's just a little light around the head right now." She shrugs. "I'm sure you both have heard those stories. Maybe you've met some of those kids who have gone missing too. You never know." She stands and pulls Cael up with her.

"We should go find Landon before he calls the guard to search the city for us. He's always worrying." She takes out the purse in Cael's pocket and places a silver mark on the table.

Rena and Rolin stare wide eyed.

"Look at you two, dressed to the hilt and carrying purses filled with money. The life of royalty suits you well!" Rolin says with a hint of envy.

"Oh, trust us. It's only for now. We'll be on the road sweating and stinking by tomorrow morn. Cael more than me of course; boys are such smelly things," she says pinning her hair up and chuckling.

They embrace and say their goodbyes, promising to write and setting a time to meet again soon. As they leave the tavern and weave their way through dockside, they both begin feeling ill again.

"What is going on? Did we eat bad food?" Wynn asks, clutching her stomach.

Cael bends over and loses all he just ate into the ocean. "I don't know." He says, head burning with a sudden fever.

Wynn follows soon after. "Ugh, Finra save us. I feel awful."

Cael nods in agreement and pats her back as she finishes being sick. When she stands up, they both stare at each other, confused.

"I feel… fine?" Wynn says.

Cael waits a moment longer. "I do too. Moons above, what is happening to us?"

He opens his eyes wide. *"Our connection! Alek and Julia, they told us! Don't you remember?"*

Wynn hears his thoughts. "Of course! We haven't been connected! We've been having different thoughts and not communicating. I want to do something that you really don't like tell Rena and Rolin about us and then we get sick. It all makes sense. We got sick on the ship too when I wanted to learn more about the city and you didn't."

Cael rubs his face, exhausted. "So we're going to get sick because you are insufferably curious and I prefer to let well enough alone? Which one of us is going to change, I wonder..."

Wynn smirks. "We all need a bit of curiosity in our lives. Come now, you love hearing stories and rumors just as much as I do!"

Cael nods. "Well yea, stories are fine. But finding things out logically, firsthand, seeing things, that's how I want to learn. Not gossip and rumors and potentially getting ourselves into trouble. It doesn't matter. We can figure that out later. What do we do about this now? Alek said we should communicate and open ourselves up and that would help our connection."

Wynn stretches her hands out over her head. "Let's only speak in our minds until we find Landon."

"Deal." Cael says as they shake hands.

"Oh!" Wynn cries out. "If anyone else talks to us, let's try and only communicate by thoughts to them too!"

"Telepathically," Cael corrects.

Wynn nods. "Yes yes, telepathically. You're the insufferable one."

'Starting now' Cael thinks to her.

'Shameful! Beginning before a lady.' Wynn thinks back.

'If only there were a lady here.'

Wynn gasps and smacks Cael before he takes off back towards market square.

'Wait up!' she calls after him.

They slow down and communicate about things they see, getting used to their internal conversation. A delicious scent catches their attention and they head towards the market square where a vendor is selling cinnamon dusted sweet bread.

"What can I get for you two today?" asks the young lady as Cael and Wynn hurry over to her.

'Two sweet breads please!' Wynn speaks to her.

Cael shoves Wynn's shoulder. *'Move your mouth, you twit!'*

Wynn shoots a scowl his way, but luckily the young lady doesn't seem to notice. She hands them both warm sweet breads. "Three pennies each."

'Here you are. Thank you very much, Allison,' Cael says, reaching out to take his bread.

'Have a wonderful day!' Wynn adds

Allison smiles at them both and waves as they leave.

Wynn looks at Cael, excited. *'It worked! How did you know her name?'*

Cael shrugs. *'I heard her thinking about saying her name, but she never did.'*

'Ohh, I see. Maybe we should try listening to other people too?' Wynn thinks as they search for somewhere to enjoy their bread.

A play is starting in the center of the market on what looks to be a permanent stage. It's a perfect place to indiscreetly eavesdrop on thoughts, so they find an empty bench far away and begin eating their breads.

Looking around the market square, they silently agree on who to listen to and let the games begin.

'The weather is so wonderful, I think I'll go see David and take a walk aro...' Nope.

'I've seen this play a hundred times and it's still moves me to...' Next!

'The smell of flowers and candied pecans is amazi...' Not this one either.

They continuing searching for something of interest but soon grow bored. They finish their breads watching the play and enjoying the moment before giving up on the crowd and leaving.

'That wasn't what I expected. Didn't Landon say the cities are the worst for people like us?' Cael wonders.

'We're probably just not trained enough like he is. We have to actually think about hearing but he probably just hears everything nonstop. Let's try another conversation with someone.' Wynn thinks.

They wander around before settling on a stall of lovely flowers and Cael approaches. *'Excuse me my good sir, how much for a bunch of your healthiest flowers?'*

"That'll be a trink per flower, ten to a bunch so a penny for the bunch, young man," the vendor replies.

'Could we get some lovely blue flowers as well?' Wynn requests.

"Of course m'lady, that'll be a solid copper coin per flower. Would you like ten of those as well?"

'Quite expensive, but we'll take them.' Cael hands out a silver mark and a penny as the vendor hands Wynn two bunches of wrapped flowers. *'Thank you sir.'*

'Yes, thank you!' Wynn adds.

They walk away smiling before a guard in full armor approaches them. He takes off his helmet and reveals a kind older face. "Those certainly are lovely flowers. They suit you well, but I don't think I've seen either of you in the city before. Did you just arrive?"

Wynn too excited to stop, continues. *'Yes sir knight, we arrived only a few days ago and are in residence with the king.'*

'Where is your seeker?' the guard replies immediately without moving his mouth.

They stand in shock for a moment before Cael collects himself enough to respond, "I'm sorry, sir. We were just practicing."

Wynn, too flustered to respond, stares mouth open.

"It's alright, children. You do have a seeker I assume?" the guard replies.

They nod.

The guard sits them down on a nearby bench and kneels to their height. "It's alright to use your gift. But you must be careful using it so openly. It is ignorant to assume you're the only ones with gifts in this city of all cities." He closes his eyes for a moment. "You are joined?! I can see you've already spoken with Julia. She's very talented. More so than most. You should try and keep the games to a minimum while you're here. When on the open road or in a small town, you are free to use your gift unhindered. However, while in cities you must be vigilant; you must protect yourselves. You are very important if Emir Landon has taken an interest." He stands up and lifts them to their feet. With a small wave, he turns around and leaves.

'*Stay safe!*' he silently calls out

When the guard is out of earshot Cael speaks up, "Alright no more games."

"What? Why?! We just can't speak to people. We can still listen and talk to each other. Can't we?" Wynn pleads.

"No, I don't want us to get in trouble with the city guard and have that trouble reach the king," Cael says firmly.

"We have to agree on things, Cael. We'll get sick if we don't," Wynn says wryly as she sits back down and begins smelling the flowers.

Cael huffs. "Then you need to be fine with this decision."

Wynn continues smelling the flowers and rearranging them without acknowledging Cael. Their heads begin to spin and Cael falls back onto the bench, chilled and nauseous.

"Fine." He acquiesces. "But only listening. We shouldn't get too used to talking in our heads. I feel like people can hear us more. Maybe mind sound travels further than real sound?"

Wynn shakes her head clear of the dizziness. "Deal."

They continue walking through the city, making their way slowly towards the king's manor. Every so often listening in on a stranger's thoughts. Everyone is different, but much of the same. It's a beautiful day in a pristine city where everyone is happy. Perfectly dull for a pair of aspiring eavesdroppers.

The sun begins to set and they notice a commotion by the west gates. A group of guards rush past them and they watch as a guard captain dispenses orders. They decide to listen.

'*I want double shifts for the next week until this is cleared up. We've got threats of attack from Hector again and we don't know where he's posted his men this time. We've got our best trackers on the case and I'm confident we'll resolve this without incident, but we need to be prepared for anything and everything. Understood?*'

The guard captain pounds his sword against his shield and the small troop repeats the action back.

'War might be coming soon, men. I'll expect everyone to up their training times in maruleth warfare, and if you've been blessed twice over, sharpen your dakileth skills as well. DISMISSED!'

The group hits their shields once more before dispersing to their stations.

"Do you think all the guards are from the academy? Or just this one group?" Wynn asks.

"I have no idea, but it makes me wonder about this king. His advisors, his guards, they're all gifted. Why?" Cael asks thoughtfully.

As the last of the guards file out, Landon appears with a well-dressed older gentleman and a pair of guards wearing much different armor than those that just filtered out of the area.

"Cael, Wynn!" Landon says beckoning them over. "It's so good to see you both up and moving. You look like you're feeling months better."

Landon hugs them and steps back. "This is King Thokrin and some of his personal guard."

Cael quickly bows and looks up to Wynn who stares dumbfounded at the king. He pulls her down into a deep curtsey. "Our apologies, your grace, we should have recognized you sooner," he says still facing down.

They feel hands on their shoulders. "Come now, any friend of Landon's is a friend of mine. There's no need for all this royal rubbish," the king says before guiding them back up.

As they stand up, they begin taking the king full in. He is shoulders above Landon, probably ten stone heavier as well. Despite his aging appearance, he is still truly a tree of a man. If he hadn't offered such a kind and welcoming smile, he'd be a very imposing figure. But with the setting sun at his back and his strong stature, he appears very regal. They are lost for a moment in the presence of royalty and he looks down on them with his wise amber eyes.

"We were just about to dine, won't you join us?"

Chapter Thirty-One

They enter the dining room and are seated at a large table. The king and Landon are positioned at one end while Cael and Wynn sit at the other. A dozen serving men and women file into the room and begin placing platters and bowls filled with more foods than either of them had seen in their entire lives combined. Reds, oranges, blues, purples, yellows, and greens. All organized like a rainbow of food in front of them. Soft sweet pastries, juicy ripe fruits, steaming-hot tender meats, perfectly cooked vegetables.

A server stops near Cael and Wynn, "What else would you like to dine on this afternoon?"

The king waves the server away. "I think our guests would very much like to help themselves to what we have here. We all can today. Thank you, Neil, that will be all."

Even with the taste of stew and sweet bread still in their mouths, Cael and Wynn begin salivating at the sight and smell of the cornucopia of food lying before them. They wait patiently, wide eyed, and nearly drooling until King Thokrin takes his plate first. Not a moment later, they greedily fill their own with every edible thing they see. They start devouring food off each other's plates as they get hints of what the other is tasting. Barely able to control themselves, they eat with ravenous efficiency.

The king looks on, elated to see people enjoying the food. "It's not often we have guests that eat so thoroughly as you two."

He and Landon laugh as the children look up unashamed, juice dripping down their chins and smiling through their filled cheeks.

"Please continue, don't let us disturb you," the king says returning their smile before picking at his own noticeably more modest portion.

"Thank you again, Landon, for assisting me earlier. However, there is another matter which I would like to discuss." The king motions for the guards to exit.

Landon sips his wine and looks to the king expectantly. "Yes, Your Grace?"

As soon as the guards exit and close the doors behind them, the king puts his food down. "The South, Landon. They continue preaching their rightful claim to my throne to any and all who would hear it. They exclaim that a unified Liefland will serve all better than our divided nations. I continue to hold peace talks. I send envoys with gifts, but they are turned away or murdered. I want nothing more than a cooperative peace between our kingdoms, yet Hector pushes for war."

The children begin to slow their eating as curiosity starts to overpower hunger. They leisurely continue their movements without appearing suspicious but focus intently on the conversation across the table.

"The economy of the South has been struggling for many years. Their landlocked country would not prove such an issue if they hadn't provoked all of their neighbors. They are in the most privileged position in our world but refuse to see it. Rather than being diplomatic, they attempt to wage war. I am not my father and do not wish for war. But the state the South is in, they cannot tax their people any more, and the taxes they do collect are not enough to sustain them." The king says, irritation building in his voice the longer he speaks.

"Something must be done. I cannot continue sending envoys to their death. All diplomacy has failed. They've even begun brazenly raiding border towns with no fear of recourse because up until now there has been none. I cannot let these transgressions go, Landon. We must do something. I refuse to play the part of the weak ruler any longer." He says definitively.

"Your Majesty, please, we must remain vigilant. We cannot go to war, we—"

Cael cuts Landon off. "Why don't you just manipulate his mind? Your guards could do that, right? Or your advisors?"

Landon and the king stare at Cael for a moment, speechless.

Wynn chimes in, "We heard your guards communicating like we do and your advisors, too."

Landon goes red in the face, but the king laughs long and hard. "You're both very bold to say such things! If we were in any other company that would be a provocative remark, but young as you are we'll let it go. I am a man who appreciates honesty and forthright attitudes, in the right places of course. Hiding behind politics and niceties is very tiresome. It's refreshing to have youth step in and shake the branches free." He wipes his eyes. "It's true that we do work with the council here and it's for that very reason that peace has held so long. If it were my choice alone, I would have crushed the foolish war that Hector wished to create long before it came to this. But the council has its wishes that the Five Kingdoms remain five, and so I let diplomacy reign."

The king leans in and his visage becomes very serious. "You must keep this secret to our circle, children. No one else must know. If the citizens became aware of the academy and people with your gifts, they would fear you to no end. Finra himself would fear you. That fear will unquestionably cause tension and that tension will build into a rebellion. My kingdom cannot afford a rebellion. I have worked too long and too hard to create the serenity you see around you. Do you understand?"

Cael and Wynn nod their heads, but the king is still unsatisfied. "Vow to me here that you will remain silent on this until you've become one with the earth again."

"We vow it," they say, frightened, as they realize how much power this one man could command. Armies with soldiers both gifted and otherwise. Landon's words echo in their heads, 'What would a king do to keep a secret hidden?' Having the life taken from two unknown children seems suddenly very much within reason.

The king leans back in his chair, his seriousness falling away like a broken mask. "Well that's that, isn't it? No harm done and we're all on the same page. Excuse me, I have some other business to tend to. Landon, will you meet me in my chamber later this evening? I'll have my guard come get you." Before waiting for an answer the king stands up and exits the room.

Landon looks over at the motionless children, still shook from their encounter. "It's hard to explain to someone who hasn't met with royalty. They aren't like regular people. Not quite as different as we are, but the power they wield is much greater than ours. By your faces I see that you now know what a king *could* do to keep a secret. And a secret like ours is one truly worth keeping." He pushes his plate away. "I think it's time we make our exit as well, don't you?"

They quickly wipe their faces and chase after Landon as he leads them to the guest wing.

They pass a few servants cleaning the corridors and windows but find nothing exorbitant or useless. A few reading nooks, a small table with a few scattered chairs and a handful of bookcases are as extravagant as the decorations get. For a king's manor it certainly is less royal than many would assume.

They enter the guest room and Landon smirks seeing only two beds. "Just like old times, eh?"

Cael huffs. "Oh come on! I've had that bed to myself for days! Sleep with Wynn, she's had a bunk to herself for weeks now!"

Wynn gives a firm head shake in the negative. "Nope. Boys with boys, girls with girls. So unless Landon has a secret he'd like to share, he's sleeping with you." She finishes, pointing at Cael with a grin.

Landon plops on the bed without further argument. "Oooh, so plush! Come here, darling, and cuddle with me. I've so missed our time together." He spreads his arms wide motioning for Cael to hug him.

"You are an ass. No, you're whatever is worse than an ass. I just can't even think of right now," Cael says as he slumps onto a chair.

"An evil ass?" Wynn offers. "Or since we're in a king's manor we could go high class and call him a churl, or a toad. Call him a toad! A peasant toad!"

Cael chuckles. "A peasant toad? Can toads be peasants?"

Wynn stands indignantly. "Maybe! We could never fully comprehend the class structure of animals, especially toads!"

Cael shrugs. "Well then he's all of those things and many others." He sighs. "So what now?"

Landon waits patiently for them to finish berating him before rolling over, eyes staring at the ceiling, "I think, I think you two might have to finish this journey alone."

"What!?" they cry out together. "Why, what's happening? Where are you going? Where will you be? What will you do? Who will guide us?" They throw questions at him.

Landon waves his hands in a placating gesture. "Calm yourselves. It's King Thokrin. He wants me to do something that'll take a month, maybe more. And it might be dangerous... more than might, it will be dangerous. I'm stuck. I can't tell him no as he is royalty protected by the council."

"What do you have to do?" Cael asks as he and Wynn move over to the bed and sit next to him.

"He hasn't asked yet.... But *we* know that can't stop us from knowing," Landon says with a smirk. "He wants me to be the next envoy to King Hector to try and make peace. And if that doesn't work, he wants me to put down any thought of rebellion. But here's the line. I can't alter King Hector's mind. It's against the council's royalty accords."

Wynn looks to Landon startled. "So you'll be down there fighting without your magic?"

Landon nods. "Potentially. I'll still be able to manipulate my surroundings mind you, just nothing about the mind. But as an envoy I won't be able to do anything until an act of aggression is made upon me or the members of the party I travel with. The council has very tight rules when it comes to diplomatic actions. I've been able to have as much freedom as I do because of how closely I follow those rules, and I rather like the freedom I have."

Cael stares at his hands. "How dangerous will it be?"

"Aww you two really do care!" he says, scooping them up and kissing their heads.

They wriggle away and pin him down on the bed.

"So? Any chance that we'll get lucky and you die?" Wynn asks.

Landon sees them with concern in their eyes. "Come now, I'm not going to get hurt. This is just a long and boring errand that will almost certainly end with me coming back before you even reach Oarna." He sits up. "Besides, neither of you will have much to worry about because you'll have the king's own guard taking you to the border of Oarna where I'll have arranged for the royal family to take care of you until I arrive. If you're lucky, you might even see the White Days of Winter festival in Oarna *and* go to the royal winter ball. "

A knock at the door startles them. Landon gets up and walks over and opens the door. "Master Landon? The king would like to meet with you now. Please follow me."

"That was sooner than I expected." Landon looks over at Cael and Wynn. "This shouldn't take long." He says before leaving with the guard.

"How do you feel about it? About us traveling alone?" Cael asks.

"Not great, but not horrible. I just still don't understand why Landon has such an interest in us. It's really weird," Wynn says as she falls back on the bed and stares at the ceiling.

"I don't think it's weird," Cael says, falling back as well.

"Of course you don't." Wynn rolls over to face him. "Your family is still alive. Don't forget that we were *taken* by this mysterious academy and Landon works for them. He's nice to us, but why? Why does he care? It makes no sense."

Cael gets visibly upset. "He's protected us this whole time. He's been more helpful than we would get otherwise. And if he hadn't helped us, those Sephalim would have gotten to my family and probably taken me with them. You might not have made it out either."

Wynn cuts in. "Yes, I know! It could be much worse. We could have been beaten and dragged, but we're still going to pretty much the same place. Why doesn't this bother you more!?"

Cael sits up. "…. Because we have no choice? They have no choice? We're going to be taken either way. We get taken by people who hurt you more or people who choose to hurt you less. I guess I just chose to accept it. Why are you still so frustrated with it? We've lived each other's lives, I've seen everything. You should want this more than me. Why don't you? Your life was awful, even before the nightmares."

Wynn tries to find the words and gets flustered. "Because wrong is wrong and it shouldn't matter that we have no choice! We should still recognize that it's wrong and be trying to fight our way out! We could do it. We know enough now. I bet we could hide. Landon's leaving; we could run away and hide."

Cael stands up and collapses, dizzy and nauseous and Wynn sits up quickly, anger turning to concern, but falls next to him feeling ill.

"We need to stop fighting...." Cael moans before finding the chamber pot and puking. Wynn runs to the window and follows suit.

"I'm sorry," Wynn croaks half out the window.

"So we'll go with the guards?" Cael asks.

"Fine." Wynn drags herself out of the window and brushes herself off.

Cael offers a fresh handkerchief found in his pocket and they clean themselves up.

"It's weird how quickly we get sick and how quickly we recover, right?" Wynn says, thinking out loud.

Cael stares out the window to the stars. "Not really. Alek and Julia told us that we were meant to be one person or consciousness or however they explained it. We're caught in this awkward space where we aren't one but we can't be two. We get sick together so it must help reconnect us."

Wynn nods along. "Right... I think? It's so hard to remember when Alek and Julia were explaining everything to us."

"I have a hard time too, but I still get bits and pieces. Let's just try and agree on things and when we get on the road, we can try sharing senses and all the other stuff Julia said," Cael says as he plops into bed with a yawn. "But right now, I'm exhausted and ready to sleep."

Wynn shrugs and flops down in her bed yawning along with him. "Now that you mention it, I could probably sleep too."

Chapter Thirty-Two

The morning sun creeps through the window, slowly warming their still slumbering figures. They begin to stir as the sounds of robins and starlings trickle in from the garden signaling the morning's arrival. Soon the subtle songs turn to a peaceful chorus across the city.

Cael and Wynn gradually open their eyes when the scent of breakfast cooking in the kitchens not far from their room reaches their noses. Seeing Landon still in the depths of sleep, they stealthily creep towards the door and sneak into the hallway.

"Mmmm.. .pastries," Cael whispers to Wynn who still has her eyes closed. A smile growing on her face as she sniffs the air.

Her eyes shoot open, "And something else delicious, I think it's boar and eggs!" She whispers loudly.

They hastily slink down the corridors, trying to maintain silence until they enter the kitchens. The cooks and servants are stunned for a moment before one of the older chamber maids waves them in. "Come on then children. I'll fix ya a plate."

They thank her profusely as she sets a few slices of bacon and eggs with a deliciously puffed sweet bread.

"Maybe some of the rabbit as well?" Cael asks with a childish smile and big eyes.

Wynn mimics him. "And perhaps one of those wonderful looking Rosé pastries?"

The chamber maid huffs but the cook waves his approval. "You two're lucky that cooky here has a soft spot fer folks that 'preciate fine foods. And I suppose ya both are sweet enough ta ask nicely," she says, retrieving their food with a much friendlier expression. "Don't go making a habit outa this now, ya hear?"

They nod vigorously and head back to their rooms.

Dumping their plates on the table, they savor every bite. "Oh, that smells amazing!" Landon says creeping up behind Cael and swiping a piece of bacon off his plate.

Cael watches like a wounded dog as his bacon leaves the plate. "No!" He cries out, "Go get your own! Aww man... I wanted that."

"C'mon Landon the kitchen is right outside the door. Don't be an ass," Wynn adds through mouthfuls of food.

Landon feigns being hurt. "You two take your food way too seriously. It was just one piece!"

Cael and Wynn both eye him sternly before he throws his hands in the air. "Fine... fine, I'll go get my own damned plate. You guys are the asses." He mumbles.

He messes both their plates up with a fork before he leaves, but they don't even take the time to yell at him as they focus back in on their meals.

Landon returns a moment later with two full plates of nearly everything from the kitchens. They both gaze enviously as they look at their rapidly depleting plates and back to his gloriously filled ones.

"Nope," he says, sternly. "If you want more, you'll have to go beg the cook. Good luck by the way, because I think I took just about the rest of any extra he made."

Cael and Wynn finish their plates quickly and begin laying siege to Landon's extra plate.

"Hey! HEY! That's mine, you give that back right now! Not my sausages! The paaastrieeeeeeesss!" he yells as he tries to block the oncoming attacks and fails miserably.

He takes the rest of his second plate and dumps it onto his first and places his arm in front as a barrier while he inhales the rest of the food. Barely able to enjoy it but saving it from the thieves across the table who look on with mock indignancy. Once the food is all gone, they lazily sip their apple juice, fresh pressed from the garden trees. A comfortable silence builds as they each think of what the day will bring.

Landon is the first to break the silence. "Last night the king finally got around to requesting what we knew he would. So today I'll be heading out. Probably before noon, down to South Liefland. We'll meet with Hector's envoy near the town of Strawberry, along the border. We may end up heading down to the capital, Kelinburgh if we meet with Hector himself. If that happens, it'll be an extra few weeks total journey."

Cael, who had been balancing on his chairs back legs slams forward ungracefully with a loud thud. "Any chance you'll meet us on the road somewhere or are we going to wait for you in Oarna?"

Landon shrugs. "No idea. But if you go to Oarna, you'll stay in Rosé till I arrive and then we'll go on to Veirdeaux where a ship will take us to the Isle of Storms and the academy."

Wynn looks around at their room, clothes scattered, supplies littering the floor. "If you need to leave before noon, shouldn't we get a plan and start packing? Are we leaving today too? Who is taking us to Oarna again? Do you know them? I feel like we should be more prepared than this...."

Landon leans back. "We have some time yet, but you're right as usual. The king has arranged for his personal guard to escort you full across North Liefland to the border of Oarna. You shouldn't have any trouble on the road with his colors flying on the wagon and a retinue of the king's own. He mentioned you could 'depart at your leisure,' but I suggest today or tomorrow. You'll want to get on the road early. It might be best for you to wait until tomorrow morning to leave the city."

"So, shall we get you sorted on supplies and packed up?" Wynn suggests.

Landon nods, "We might as well."

They begin packing Landon's travel sack and putting in requests to the kitchen for hearty traveling foods of cheeses, breads, salted meats, and some fresher apples. They pack quickly and are left only waiting on the food so Cael and Landon begin playing cards while Wynn reads in the corner.

A knock on the door. Landon goes to answer and greets the rest of his envoy, a handful of well-dressed men and women all robed in the king's green and white colors with small travelling packs slung over their shoulders.

"That time already, fellas?" Landon asks, hiding his disappointment.

They nod. "We've brought the food from the kitchen you requested and our wagon is waiting. Are you ready to leave now?"

Landon glances back to his charges. "Give us a moment?" He calls to his new traveling party.

As the door closes they gather around the table and Landon begins nervously pacing, shaking his arms out. "Alright, this is it. I thought I was ready. Damn, this is tough. Every mission I'm sent on like this is hard to prepare for, but this one is different. At least the guards you'll be with are from the academy, but we can't know if they have kept up their training so if you guys have trouble with your connection, it'll be like you're at sea in a storm. Heh, I suppose you already were at sea in a storm. There's got to be another more fitting saying. You'll be in a river with no boat? In the mines with no light? That works."

Wynn and Cael grab his shoulders. "It'll be alright," they say together.

"We'll be safe; you'll be safe. Everything will be alright," Cael adds.

Landon wraps his arms around them again. "Remember to listen to the guards; they are academy trained. Follow their instructions but trust yourselves too. If something seems off, just make a run for it. The roads are dangerous far from the cities. Your guards will know what to do, just listen to them. But don't forget to trust yourselves! You'll have food. You'll have money for lodging when it's available and you'll have a covered wagon for those rainy days and nights. It's going to be an easy journey. Practice with the guards. They might not like that actually. Practice by yourselves if the guards aren't friendly. But make sure you listen to them!"

"You're like a mother hen protecting her chicks! We're going to be just fine! Go on now, you'll be less worried as soon as you're moving and out on the open road. You're making everyone wait while you fuss over us. We'll see you in a few months at the latest," Cael says and Wynn hands Landon his pack and shoos him towards door.

"It'll be no time at all before we see each other again," she reassures him as she opens the door and they hug once more before Wynn closes the door behind him.

"That was more emotional than I thought it would be," she says, wiping a tear away.

Cael does the same. "I think that's more me than you. I'm gonna miss that big dope. He helped us so much already, and, well I kind of felt safe with him. Now we're on our own with some people we don't know. Again."

Wynn pats him on the back. "It'll be fine, you dummy. We've still got each other! And that's really all we need, right?" she asks with a smile.

"Right." Cael says, trying to smile back. He heads to the bed and sits down on the edge.

Not as saddened at Landon's departure, but aware of the need to maintain their connection, Wynn sits next to Cael and shares in his concern for their friend and for themselves.

After a few moments she stands up. "We've got the day to do what we please, any ideas?"

"I could go for some of that cinnamon sweet bread," he replies with a sparkle in his eye.

They race out the door and collide directly with King Thokrin, all falling over onto the floor. His guards rush to help him to his feet while the group of advisors trailing behind gasp, startled by the mess in front of them.

"What in Finra's name are you two doing?! How dare you harm the king!" one of the guards says, glaring at the children as they get into a sitting position.

Once the king is back on his feet he scowls down at them. "You may be guests, but I will not tolerate this behavior. You two will conduct yourselves with class and dignity while in my home and especially while in my presence! Do you understand?!"

They nod, cheeks flushed with embarrassment.

"Out of my sight." He orders, still brushing himself off.

They scramble to their feet and walk hastily to the exit. As they reach the city streets, they breathe a sigh of relief.

"I'm beginning to think we should have left this morning." Cael says as they walk towards Allison's sweet bread in the market.

They again make the decision to listen to the thoughts of those around them, but Cael soon realizes that Wynn has a specific agenda in mind. He wishes only to practice, while Wynn begins searching for someone experiencing any type of grief, sadness or anger. Anything other than the constant dull happiness that everyone in the city so loudly feels.

"Two cinnamon sweet breads please!" Cael says cheerfully as they arrive at Allison's.

"Of course! No games today?" Allison replies with a knowing smirk.

Before they can ask what games, they hear her thoughts, *'Good luck tomorrow!'*

They walk away, stunned by their foolishness from the day before.

"Maybe we should just go back to our rooms and wait for dinner. It's afternoon already anyway. I feel awkward walking around with everyone knowing we've made fools of ourselves," Wynn says embarrassed.

Cael agrees but then shakes his head. "You know what? I'm beginning to think you're right. This place feels odd. Members of this academy thing are here as sweet bread vendors? Why? Something just doesn't add up. Let's go talk to the captain and Trep again. Maybe they'll remember something else."

They wind their way back down to dockside and spot the vessel they spent so much of their early journey on.

They run across the pier and up the creaky gangplank aboard the ship and call out, "Helloo! Anyone here?"

They open the captain's quarters and find it a mess of bottles and papers still littering the floor. They walk down to Rena and Rolin's cabin and sigh seeing all their luggage is gone.

"Didn't Rena say they were staying here for a few days?" Wynn asks confused.

"Maybe they got an earlier wagon?" Cael says but Wynn senses his concern.

"What about the captain and Trep? They could hardly move yesterday," she adds

Cael looks around at the deserted ship. "With Rena and Rolin gone, they probably just went to get some food down at one of the taverns."

Wynn shakes her head. "Something weird is going on here, Cael. And I know you feel it too."

He turns to her seriously, "Even if there is, what can we do about it? We need to look out for ourselves right now. Landon is gone so if something serious is happening we'd just be putting ourselves in danger. And if something serious isn't happening we'd…"

The creaking of footsteps come from the plank of the ship. They hurry topside and are relieved to see Trep and the captain coming back.

"Oh, Karif, look at them chillen. They come back to check up on us. Oh ya be sweet kids, right sweet," Trep says as he pats their heads. "Let me make something up for ya real quick like. I knows how ya like that duck I made!" He pushes his way to the stairs making his way into the galley.

'See! Look, they're totally fine,' Cael shares with Wynn.

'Maybe… I guess I was wrong,' Wynn responds.

"What brings ya back here, kiddos?" Karif asks as he guides them to his quarters and begins cleaning up, his arm fully healed.

"We just wanted to check up on you guys, make sure you were doing better than yesterday," Wynn says.

"Yesterday? We were right fine yesterday. What're ya on about?" Karif says confused, "Just worrying fer nuttin' I bet."

"Riiight… Where's Rena and Rolin?" Wynn asks as she hops on the bed.

"They was here earlier. They must've left on their trip," Karif says, picking up the empty bottles all over the floor.

"Do you think this place is weird?" Cael asks. "Maybe a little too… happy?"

"Too happy, now?" Karif says with a laugh. "How'n the world could that be a thing! Ya on about too happy! Trep n' I are fixin' ta stay here for the long haul. It's a right beautiful city, isn't it?"

"You're giving up sailing? Is it because of Brun?" Wynn asks suspiciously.

Cael feels what she's doing. "You shouldn't give everything up because we lost Brun." He adds.

Karif shrugs. "Brun dyin' ain't got nuttin' ta do with us stayin' here, kiddies. That was jest somethin' that happens at sea. I gotta accept it, we all do. Can't focus on all that bad!" He smiles back at them.

Wynn and Cael cautiously stand up.

"We should get going," they say before they run off the boat.

"Alright, you were right." Cael says as they hurry back to the king's manor. "Something absolutely is happening here!"

"It's probably why they have so many people from the academy. This place isn't a happy place. It's got to be some weird experiment that the king wanted to try! He wanted everyone to be happy so badly I bet they placed everyone under some… some happy spell or something!" Wynn suggests.

"Then why are we going back to the king's manor?" Cael says, panting heavily.

"We don't really have a choice. He'll suspect something if we just leave. We've got to pretend we don't know anything," Wynn says.

They make it back to the manor before dusk and try indiscreetly to enter but find Alek and Julia in conference with the king near the guest wing. They pretend not to see the group but the king calls out, beckoning them.

"Children, I wanted to apologize for my outburst earlier today. My advisors and I were having a rather heated argument about the errand I sent your friend on. The sudden embarrassment of falling over was like dropping a hot rock in a pot and I boiled right over," he says with an apologetic smile. "Will you forgive me?"

They bow and say, "Of course, Your Grace."

As they try to quickly exit to the bedrooms, Julia looks them over and laughs. "Oh dear, you two cannot be serious."

Alek starts along with her.

The king's expression becomes flustered as his advisors laugh openly. "Will someone explain what is happening right now?"

Alek turns to the king, wiping his glasses. "The children have gotten it into their heads that you've placed everyone in this city under some witch's spell!" He bends over laughing again. "The sheer madness of such a thing! As if that were even a real thing! A spell!"

Julia breathes in deeply to steady herself. "Children, you absolutely need to understand that there is no such thing as a spell. The academy does not have spells. We deal in sciences. Tangible things, things that can be explained."

Wynn gets flustered. "Then why is everyone happy, huh?" She demands.

She directs her question to the king himself who steps back slightly confused, "Well, that's explained easily."

Julia steps in front of Wynn. "Children, let's approach this logically. The city is beautiful. The economy is strong. There is food, money, entertainment, lodging and love for all. There are churches for all faiths. This is the perfect city. Why wouldn't someone be happy living here? You have all the evidence to arrive at a much more sensible conclusion right in front of you, but you are refusing to accept it. Everyone else here accepts it freely."

The king gathers himself. "Children have wild imaginations, and so they *want* for something to be unnatural and unexplained. Because that would be more fun than the simple, easy truth sitting right in front of you."

Cael and Wynn stare for a moment piecing the puzzle together.

"Then... but... well why did..." Wynn tries to find an argument and Cael puts his head down.

"We're sorry for accusing you, Your Grace" he says.

Alek pats his head. "You never accused anyone, my dear boy. It was only Julia who heard the fanciful thoughts bouncing around your heads. You have done nothing wrong. But you are going on a long journey tomorrow that will require you to toss aside your childlike wonder. You will need to be very logical to maintain your wits and ensure your safety. Understood?"

They nod their heads, acting properly ashamed.

The king cuts in. "Speaking of your guards, I haven't introduced you to them. Come with me and I'll do so now." He waves Alek and Julia away who bow and take their leave.

"These are some of my best men and I've taken the liberty of having your wagon stocked with provisions and money. You'll be allowed to take any of the clothes my royal tailors have created for you as they will be of no use to me," he says walking quickly down the hallways to the rear entrance. He leads them to the stables, following the raucous sound of a group of men playing cards.

"Guards!" the king calls out.

A small table of three men look around for a moment before hopping to their feet. "Yes, Your Grace!"

The king scowls at them. "These are your charges. You are to deliver them to Rosé, just on the border of Oarna. No harm shall befall these children while in your care or you will face the headsman's axe, do you understand?"

They salute on instinct.

"Very good. Enjoy your evening." And with that the king guides the children back to their room.

"I do hope you have a safe journey. And if you are ever in Ayverden again, please come see me. I would very much like to hear of your travels." He starts to nod a farewell to them but stops and let's his mind wander as he runs his hand through his slightly greying hair. "Perhaps we'll be working together once the two of you finish your training at the academy? From what I've seen, I imagine you'll both do great things there." With that he turns and departs, lifting a hand to wave without looking back.

They turn around and immediately lay eyes on dinner, already delivered but still warm. They look at each other and all at once their cares fall away as they dig in. They sip wine and brandy and devour what must amount to a full stone weight of food between the two of them.

Filled to bursting with food, warm and fuzzy from strong drinks, they stumble to the bed and pass out easily, barely a word or thought spoken.

Chapter Thirty-Three

"Get up."

"Hey… Hey wake up."

"Jean, these kids won't get up! Do we hit em or something?"

Cael and Wynn sit up on their hands, eyes still closed.

"We're up….We're up. Finra's beard, what is all the damn commotion?" Cael groggily asks.

"The king said ya'll needed to wake up early to get on the road, on a schedule and such."

Wynn opens her eyes as the realization that strange men are around them and Cael's eyes shoot open feeling her anxiety.

'*Relax, it's just the king's guard,*' Cael thinks to her. '*We're fine.*'

She unclenches her jaw and tries to make out the men in the darkness. "At least introduce yourselves. Don't just stand there acting like some thieves or kidnappers." She says, irritation plain in her voice.

Cael moves to light the lamps and the small warm flame perks to life illuminating the room. Three armored men stand just inside the doorway. Two are similar in height and build while one stands out from the others.

"I'm Cael and this is Wynn." Cael says rubbing his eyes while they adjust to the light.

"Fredrick, but everyone calls me Fred. That there's my mate Byron, and this big fella here is our fearless leader, Jean," Fredrick says.

"What's with the pre-dawn start, fellas?" Cael asks.

"The head honcho felt obliged to inform us of our departure time, which was being before the dawn sun lit the sky as ya'll were on quite a tight rope. Can't imagine it's that tight though, being as it's what? More'n a month out till we hit Rosé," Byron says with a slow bumpkin drawl.

The lantern begins to throw light onto the guards, Cael and Wynn take note of their features. The larger one, Jean, has a very serious look about him. He has a thick scar across his jaw where no hair grows making it easily noticeable when surrounded by his dark beard. He's at least two stone heavier than both Fredrick and Byron who appear strikingly similar in build. They both look to be a sight jollier than Jean as well. Byron's shoulder length light blond hair falls around his smoothly shaved face. Fredrick rubs his hands over his rough beard stubble and through his short brown hair. All are in the king's colored armor which must be standard issue as the sizes are ill fitted to all three of them.

"Do we get breakfast first?" Cael asks, stomach rumbling.

"We'll eat on the road. Get your things and move out," Jean orders, walking back into the hallway. Both Fredrick and Byron shrug as they follow him out.

"What a way to start the morning...." Wynn mumbles.

"An even better way to start the next month or two of our lives," Cael grumbles.

They pack up what little belongings they have into beautifully designed travelling bags, one blue and one brown, sitting on their table with a note from the tailor that reads, "Safe travels!"

"Aww, that was sweet of him!" Wynn says, feeling the soft fabric.

"Sweet of him certainly, but not very well thought out. Doesn't this feel like suede to you? That type of leather doesn't waterproof easily, and it'll get all ruined as soon as it gets wet."

Cael shakes his head. "It doesn't even really matter I suppose. We have a covered wagon and the thought is what really counts."

Wynn smiles at Cael's effort to stay connected and pats him on the back. "It's better than what we had!"

They pack the extra pair of clothing the tailor made them and their belongings from the start of their journey. The comparison between their own clothes and the royal ones is striking. So colorful, soft and smooth compared to the rough, dull, and tough fabrics they are accustomed to.

"Let's move!" Jean impatiently calls from the dark hall.

They hurry out and follow their escort to a wagon waiting near the stables. Four sturdy horses are hitched and raring to go. They climb in the back and Byron struggles to haul his armored figure in next to them. The large wagon tilts to either side as Jean and Fred get seated in front.

"We walk as soon as we're out of the city. We don't need the extra weight straining the horses," Jean calls back to them.

They stare out the back, feet dangling as the wagon makes its way down the streets, feeling every cobblestone as the wooden wheels pass over them. Such a wonderfully at peace city. Not perfectly built, no straight roads or paths, but trees and nature all throughout. It would be easy to imagine themselves living there. Public gardens and shows, friendly vendors. Perhaps they were wrong to think ill of the king, but even still… there is something different about the city.

The group is lulled into a trance as they bumble over the uneven cobblestone roads, staring at the starry morning sky above them. Soon they're awakened as the knocking of stones turns to the soft crunch of worn dirt marking the exit of the city. Jean halts the wagon and they hop out. They stretch their legs, already sore from sitting on the hard maple wood bed of the wagon. Glad to be on their feet for the moment, they soon dread the months of walking ahead of them and continue on in an uncomfortable silence. Cael and Wynn lag behind, still uneasy about the strange guards.

Their travels begin with a clear sky, not a cloud anywhere to be seen. After a short while of slow and easy walking, Jean calls over his shoulder, "Let's pick it up. You two are young enough to put in some hard walking."

The dirt road is easy on their feet and the open fields near the city encourages a pleasant breeze to sweep through making for comfortable traveling weather.

Once the sun is high and they're all warmed up by its rays, Wynn bumps into Cael. *'Want to practice?'*

He motions for her to be quiet and whispers, "These guys are from the academy, remember? Landon told us to be careful."

She shrugs. *'Well I'll just ask them if they mind. If they're from the academy, it's not like they'll be concerned. What's the worst they can say? No?'*

They decide to communicate with Jean, recognizing him as the leader. *'Excuse me, Jean?'* Wynn sends her words to him.

"What now?" His voice is tired and aggravated.

'Do you mind if Cael and I do a bit of training on the road? You know, alteration or communicating in our minds?' she asks.

Jean stops and turns around. "What in the world are you on about? What in the immovable stars is mind communication?"

Fred and Byron stare at Jean oddly.

"Hey mate, you alright?" Fredrick says to him.

Jean looks at them. "Course I'm alright, I'm just talking to the kid." He responds confused.

'Sorry, she meant telepathy or the maruleth training stuff. We're not really good at the names yet.' Cael adds.

Jean turns back around and continues walking, "Listen kids, I don't know or care to know what you're on about. Do whatever pleases you so long as you don't slow us down."

Fredrick and Byron look back to them and shrug. Cael and Wynn focus in on their thoughts and hear them thinking that Jean is probably tired, or hungover from the night before.

Wynn pulls Cael back. "I don't think these guys are from the academy."

Cael nods hesitantly. "Yea, that's pretty clear. Maybe the king thought we'd be safer on the road with regular people?"

Wynn agrees. *'Well the good news is we can practice!'*

"It feels weird. Maybe we should only practice at night?" Cael says nervously.

*'Oh, stop being such a worrier! You worry more than...
someone who worries all the time?'*

Cael smirks at her. *'Couldn't finish that one out, could ya?
Let's get to know our escorts first, then we can practice. Deal?'*

Wynn kicks her feet impatiently, *"Alright, deal."*

"So, John, how long have you worked for King Thokrin?"
Cael asks.

Fredrick and Byron laugh. "His name ain't *John*! He's from
Oarna, his name is *Jean*. It's like bean but it's got one've them
fancy long J's, not one of our 'peasant' short J's." Byron laughs at
Jean. "All that size and he's got a pretty. little. lady name."

"Alright now, quit ribbing on him. He's a sensitive soul,"
Fredrick says shoving Byron who trips in his large greaves. He
catches himself and goes to charge Fred who braces for impact.

Jean grabs Byron by the back of the breastplate and scowls
at them both. "Yes, I'm from Oarna, and unlike you fools we have
at least some honor and dignity. At least enough dignity to not get
stuck babysitting children for months on end. How in the moons
did you talk me into this? Can we just get back to walking?
Preferably in silence?" He sighs and continues leading the horses.

"Are you going to be like this the entire time? Only
speaking when you want to complain?" Wynn asks in frustration.

Fredrick calls back. "Naw, kids, we'll chat with you. Jean
there is the strong and silent type."

He acts out strength by flexing his muscles and Byron
imitates quiet by sneaking around the carriage to poke Jean in the
bottom. Jean swats him away in a huff. Fred and Byron chuckle
lightly.

"Ain't no sweat off our brow to shoot the breeze with some
youngins. It'll sure pass the time nicely. Let them questions flow
little one!" Byron adds

Wynn smiles and takes a deep breath. "How old are you?
Where are you from? Why'd you want to be the king's guard?
How'd Jean get that scar? Do you guys have any other scars?
Why's Jean so angry? Are you married? Do you have kids? Why's
your armor so big? Are all the armors that big?"

"Woooooow, slow down there kiddo! Sheesh, Bry, why'd
you have to go and tell her to assault us with all these questions? I

can't even member half the ones she asked!" Fred says, wiping his hair, "This is gonna be a long few months...."

"Naaah, don't worry 'bout them. I heard your words young lady and you bet I'll lay it on just as fast!" Byron takes a deep breath mocking her. "We're from Oarna just like the big fella but not a real fancy place, way outside all that class and in the sticks. Me and Freddo here are the same age and big ole Jean there, well he's likely a bit older n us but he never said nuttin' bout it. We're mercenaries so we get in all sorts of scraps, and Jean got that scar before we even met em, probably from scrappin' with some folk that deserved it on account of all his honor and what not. No kids or wives and... ehh, was that everything?" He ends scratching his head.

Fred and Wynn laugh at Byron and the speed that he spit out the words. Cael shakes his head slightly confused. "Hold on a minute, you said you were mercenaries? Before you were the king's guard or are you still mercenaries?"

Jean shoots Byron a dirty look but doesn't say anything and continues with his grueling pace. Fred rubs his hair embarrassed and Byron shrugs. "Might as well tell em."

Fred nods. "Well... The king there was mighty keen on sending you kids along with his guard, but he said he couldn't afford to let anyone go. Something about the war and what not. We just arrived in port, looking for work like all these merc fellas. War might not be officially declared, but everyone knows it's been brewing for years. They pay well for fighting hands, North pays better of course, but they both pay. Anyways, he asked if we'd pretend to be part of his guard for your sake. Paid us better than we expected so we were real fine with it."

Byron looks ashamed. "Didn't mean no harm, kids. Hope ya aren't over disappointed by it."

"No, no it's perfectly fine. I think our friend just thought we'd be with some other guards," Cael says, hiding his concern.

Wynn quickly adds. "But you guys seem great!"

"Dammit! Can we have even one moment without you all making noise!?" Jean says angrily.

Fred whispers. "I bet not all of us seem great."

He winks at them and Byron smiles but they return to their earlier uncomfortable silence.

Cael and Wynn practice their telepathy but quickly lose interest with nothing real to talk about. Being joined makes small talk pointless. They frequently play with the idea of alteration but hastily dismiss it out of fear their escorts would find it frightening or demonic.

The day passes slowly, with nothing to do but stare at the unchanging landscape. The same long stretches of open green fields and wide expansive wheat farms making it nearly unbearable. After what feels like days, but likely around midday, they come upon a large town.

Jean slows down as they enter the streets. "Let's make sure those fools at the castle actually packed us everything we need. We'll pick up anything we're missing here and head on out."

They begin combing through their supplies, taking stock of what they have.

Jean mumbles, "Idiots only packed enough for the kids… what did they think we were going to do? Survive on air and dewdrops?"

"Hey big guy, since the kids have caught on to us not being the king's guard and all, do we have to keep this armor on? I feel like a turtle in this thing," Fredrick says popping his head up and down in his breastplate.

Jean opens his mouth to yell again but stops as he fidgets with his armor. "It's not a bad idea, we might be able to sell em here too. Get some more spending money for our journey."

They finish taking inventory and note they'll need to double just about everything as the quartermaster really did only supply their wagon enough for Cael and Wynn and neglected to consider the three adult guards travelling with them.

Jean orders Fredrick and Byron to buy up some travelling food and Jean goes to sell their useless armor and purchase sleeping gear, clothing, and other necessary supplies.

"What should we do?" Cael asks

"Lead the wagon down this main road here to the end of town and wait. Don't get lost, don't stray from the wagon. And don't cause any trouble," Jean orders them.

Cael and Wynn hop in the wagon and direct the horses through town. Soon after they enter the main square they notice how much different it is here than in Ayverden. This town is dirtier, the people seem miserable, the buildings largely unmaintained. Passing through, they spot a huge stone wall near the center of town.

They slow the horses down and call to one of the vendors selling dried meats. "Excuse us, what's that large building in the center of town?"

"Piss off if ya ain't buyin' anything. I don't need no rich brats bugging me," he replies without moving from his seat.

"What's got you in such a foul mood? Can't accommodate potential customers?" Cael replies.

Wynn nudges him. *'Time to practice?'* she thinks to Cael.

He nods her on, *'Go on then.'*

'We aren't just any rich brats you oaf. I'm a witch, and if you don't tell us what we wish to know, I'll cast a spell on you!' Wynn thinks to the man

He huffs back. "Oh aye, certainly your grace. I should have recognized ya what with me bein' a witch too! Go piss off afore I get any more angry with ya."

Wynn closes her eyes and listens to the man's thoughts. She brings him into her clearing and, not being able to think of anything else, she reaches out and cover his eyes in her mind. A moment later the man yelps.

"What've ya done! Yer a witch! Yer a demon! HELP HELP!" he yells.

Cael frightened that someone will hear him, hops down and covers his mouth. "We only just wanted to know about the building."

"I know plenty, just gimme my sight back, I beg of you. Please kind witch, have mercy on a fool!" he pleads through Cael's fingers.

They release him and he breathes a sigh of relief before looking at them with pure terror in his eyes and making a wild run for it down the street.

Cael and Wynn exchange worried glances and hop back in the wagon as they hurry the horses to the far end of town and wait just outside the gates.

"Well, that could've gone better." Cael says wiping his hand off on his pants.

Wynn replies, "That was amazing! Did you see that, I blinded him! That's amazing, isn't that amazing? I can't think of any other way to describe it. It's just incredible!"

Cael turns to Wynn whose face is an image of pure joy and shakes his head. "You are a little scary, you know that?"

She makes a pouty face and he nudges her shoulder. "I'm just kidding, you nut. But honestly, should we be worried? That guy could be spouting nonsense all around town about how demons are coming. If we lose our escort, we'll have no way to get to Oarna. We don't know the way." Cael says as he watches the man, still running frantically through town.

"Who'd believe him. It's the middle of the day. He's definitely an ass; I bet everyone here hates him. Didn't you hear his thoughts? Some pretty hateful things floating around in there," Wynn replies as she hops down and sits in the grass under the shade of a large oak tree.

"Yeah, I guess," Cael says following her.

They sit in the shade for a while before Fredrick, Byron, and Jean make their way out of the town. They load up the newly purchased supplies and Jean calls for them to move out.

"Anything odd happen in the town?" Cael asks anxiously, hoping the man kept quiet.

Fred and Byron shrug. "Not really. There was a man who sprinted by me, tripped on a bag of flour and knocked himself straight out cold. But that could just be a typical day for that guy. He could be the town sprinter that knocks himself out cold at noon every day. I don't pass judgement," Fred says with a smile and Byron laughs.

"Out cold, really?" Byron asks and Fred nods his head, laughing along with him. Jean ignores the noise and sets up his usual pace for the road.

"What was that big wall in the center of town?" Cael asks.

Fredrick looks back at them. "Oh this is a good story kids, a right good story. Wait, do ya know anything about that king of yours? Thokrin there?" Shaking their heads 'no' Fredrick continues, "Right so this here king is a bastard son of Richard III who was a bastard in his own way, but a completely different meaning if ya catch my wind."

He continues, "Richard made everyone's lives awful, just ruining lives everywhere he went, a lot like me mum, but even *worse*." He shivers at the thought of his mother. "This fella was over taxing folks and taking all their crop for the war. Thokrin comes along and he'd lived poor, poorer than most to be sure. The people liked him bein' as he was one of 'em. When he took over, he wanted the people to not just hope that he'd make changes; he'd want 'em to know he'd do it. So he tore down his father's castle, tore down the university, and used them stones to build the walls around Ayverden. People had come to hate that castle and the school because only rich folk came and went from 'em. Thokrin told the people he'd not let a university in the capital city again, but the lords and ladies wanted North Liefland to have a place for education at least somewhere near the capital. What to do, eh? Them rich folk actually pooled their money and built a school, a fine one at that. And they put it right there in Hintersdale, hoping that bein' so close to Ayverden, it'd be taken well and good care of. The king wasn't havin' none of that, though. He cares for the people, but only one city in North Liefland, or anywhere is like Ayverden, and that's Ayverden. Oarna has fine places with plenty of resources, but there's still sad folk, poor folk, murderers. Not in Ayverden though. That king made the garden of the gods right here in North Liefland, so praise be to him."

"Here here!" Byron calls out. "Ya got ta respect a man that reaches for sumthin', and boy lad did he reach for sumthin' big!" He says, adoration in his voice.

Wynn, unconvinced, presses him for more. "How do you all know this? Aren't you from Oarna?"

Fredrick shrugs. "How does anyone know anything? You hear it from someone else."

"Over a few drinks!" Byron adds. "Speakin' of. Should we stop and drink a few ales 'fore we leave? When's the next town anyhow?"

"It'll be far enough sober, so no," Jean calls from the front.

"Now there's a man who just loves ta kill joy 'nd happiness," Byron sighs in disappointment.

The band of travelers continue their journey along the main road. Just before dark Jean halts and without any word of instruction the three of them begin setting camp for the night. Wynn and Cael watch, trying to stay out of the way of the familiar routine they have. Byron sets the fire, Jean scouts the area and gathers some wood while Fredrick starts setting up the bedrolls and preparing the food.

Not wanting to be useless, Cael and Wynn care for the horses, feeding and brushing before tying them off to a few trees near their wagon. They set on gathering up some firewood as well before helping Fred and Byron prepare and cook the food. They decide on something easier and cut up the fresh mutton and season it with dried rosemary sprigs. Looking over their vegetable supply, they leave the heartier root vegetables and instead decide to cook the softer peppers and tomatoes that the royal chef packed them and toast a loaf of bread.

Comfortably full, Fredrick and Byron chat idly stoking the fire while Jean rifles through the back of the wagon searching for something. On the opposite end of the fire, Cael and Wynn struggle to see what he's carrying in his hands. As he sits down, Fredrick and Byron stop their chatter and wait patiently.

Jean then begins playing a beautiful melody on an instrument that neither of them had ever laid eyes on before. It's similar to a lute or perhaps even a harp, only it has an echoing twang that sounds through the bowl, a mesmerizing sound. He tunes the instrument while playing a slow song that reminds them of a summer day in a market square. The cacophony of notes back and forth like bartering market goers. As he finds his rhythm, the music becomes faster, a dance on a midsummer night.

Somewhere, the music changed tone and despite the ferocity that Jean played, the sound was heartbreaking. A song straight from his soul, met and matched by wordless music released from within him. What loss feels like, played openly to the world around them. A breath of chill floats in the air, sinking into all listening and they are lost to their thoughts. Sadness deep inside wrenched from within them. Cael and Wynn cry silently to themselves missing Cael's family, and for the loss of Wynn's family long before they were taken from her.

Awoken from their trance as the song ends in a final emotional note, they watch as the fire dies down as if it were also waiting for the song to end. All wondering how long they were captivated but too preoccupied to truly care.

"Why's it always the sad ones, Jean?" Fred asks, wiping a tear from his eye.

"Some days I fear it's all I'll ever feel. But this telbir brings me peace, at least for a moment," he replies.

They all lay back staring at the stars losing themselves to memories and the eternity above. Cael and Wynn are able to share in their despair and for that, tonight at least, they are grateful.

Chapter Thirty-Four

"Can we just get going already?" Wynn asks impatiently.

"Fine, fine. Let me just finish marking this tree. If we get lost again Father will have our hides." Cael says as he carves a familiar symbol into the large oak by the stone path.

"Alright, let's go." He says before leading them further down the trail. The soft pitter patter of their leather shoes on the flat stones reaches far throughout the forest.

They are calm until they come upon a clearing with a small pool of water, long beautiful flowers encircling it. Cael quickly realizes the dream for what it is. "It's good to be back, isn't it?" He says jokingly as he drops their gear and sits on the ancient stone bench. He gazes at the splendor of the glade, trees cloaked in a gentle hue of gold.

Wynn's eyes are wild for a moment before Cael grabs her hand, "No one is here with us this time." He reassures her.

"Just get in you nitwit." Wynn says nervously, not wishing to stay any longer than they need to.

Cael sighs and follows Wynn as they both step into the pool without hesitation.

Wynn sits up on her elbows feeling oddly refreshed and even cheerful. She looks over at Cael, "Dreams again?" She says with a confused smile.

He pokes her shoulder, *"Careful."* He thinks to her, nodding to their slumbering companions around the fire. He takes his time on a long stretch before leaning back on his hands and staring at the morning sky.

"It felt different though, it felt like the earlier dreams. No fear, just... a dream. I wonder if someone is searching for us." He continues thoughtfully.

"I don't know... maybe we're just near someone who is searching in the area? The dreams were calm before they found us." She says, joining Cael as they watch the sun rise.

"Makes sense, those seekers must just be in the area and we're sensing them." He adds.

Wynn shrugs, brushing off any concern they have with a yawn that flows over to Cael and then to the rest of the group now waking and warming themselves around the fire. Wynn grabs a few apples from the wagon and tosses them around to the rejuvenated and cheery group as they pack up camp. Cael feeds and waters the horses. A hearty breed of Westrier, perfect for the king's own but a little large for their needs. All brindled stallions, except one. A gorgeous solid black mare. Similar in size, an impressive stature for a mare. Cael finishes hitching the horses and Jean looks around one last time before they return to their journey.

The long expedition they're undertaking has only just begun, but their early morning happiness turns quickly to afternoon boredom. Cael and Wynn, uneasy about practicing alteration or telepathy keep to themselves. Fred and Byron make small comments every so often about food or drink but also stay relatively quiet. Jean silently leads the company down the road. Not even the occasional passing traveler can manage to get a hello or even friendly nod from him. Despite the rest of the group's best efforts, the first impression of Jean always has the travelers quick to move along.

Another uncomfortable day of silence, stretching further along. Landscape unchanging, the same line of coniferous trees hiding the life behind it. The same flat ground for as far as the eye can see, which was very far on this cloudless, featureless day.

If Jean hadn't been so standoffish, perhaps Cael or Wynn could ask more questions, have a conversation about anything with Fred or Byron, or even Jean. But there was an easy silence between the three friends; one that Cael and Wynn couldn't seem to understand. It was one that likely came natural to a group of wanderers. Each left to their own thoughts, except for Cael and Wynn whose minds were connected like a doorway between rooms. With no task or immediate goal to focus on, all their energy turns inward.

Cael's wandering thoughts keep him content, but the longer Wynn has nothing to focus on the more easily Cael's random thoughts enter her mind, and the more frustrated she becomes.

'We've only been on the road for…. Moons above has it really only been a day?! I can't take it; this is maddening. I'm going crazy!' Wynn thinks out to Cael. He feels the same way of course, her feelings are strong enough to plant themselves firmly within him.

'I know, I know! But there's nothing to do. We just have to get used to this,' Cael responds to her.

'Easy for you…. Can you at least quiet your thoughts down? They're so loud!' she says

'It's just the way I think, I can't stop it!' he replies, getting irritated, *'Besides, you're the one who wanted this.'*

'Well, I didn't think it would be like this! We need to do something or we're going to get sick, I can feel it already,' Wynn says, suddenly feeling ill as they fight.

'Argh, we can never fight. This is impossible! This was by far the stupidest thing I've ever done in my entire life!' Cael screams in their heads, irritation outweighing his sudden queasiness.

'You're horrible!' Wynn shouts back.

They both fall to the ground and empty their stomachs. Jean stops the wagon and the three of them rush over.

"What's this? Did we eat something bad? It's probably goin' through the kids faster cause they're tiny. I bet we're next Bry. Oh man, I can feel it already," Fred says.

Byron's face goes green. "Fellas, I… I think I'm gonna—"

Fred and Byron bend over and lose their breakfast.

Jean looks on with disgust at the four of them hunched over a growing pool of liquid. "You imbeciles, it wasn't the food. We would've felt it long before now if it was. They got sick for some other reason." He eyes the kids curiously.

Cael and Wynn recover quickly, similar to their earlier arguments. It's becoming that as soon as they fall ill, their minds clear of any disagreements and they can think about nothing but discomfort, which fortunately works to realign them.

"There's a town not far from here where we can stop," Jean adds.

Byron stands up grabbing his stomach. "Good, cause I don't feel so well."

Jean shakes his head and mumbles, "Imbeciles, the lot of em."

He lifts Byron and Fred to their feet, leading them back toward the road.

'I'm sorry,' Cael and Wynn think together. They smirk at the timing.

As suddenly as that, the day once again feels lighter, better somehow. It's like a quick moving storm passed them by and the world is lively once again. They all feel happier, even Jean, surprisingly. They spot a family of deer and come to a halt, letting the small herd cross the road in peace. A big buck calmly leads the does and fawns across the worn dirt path, paying the humans no attention and acting as if they weren't even there. Birds sing all through the tall green trees, flittering across the open sky between forests on either end of the road. Smooth white clouds have drifted in and nestled themselves firmly amongst sheets of endless bright blue sky. A pair of chattering grey squirrels race each other through the short grass that guides their dirt path onward.

Lost to the frequent movements all around them, the day continues on easily. The earlier boredom gone and forgotten.

Thin pillars of smoke drift slowly into the sky, marking a small town ahead. Getting closer, they find a few decently made buildings lining the main through road while shabbier structures mark a separate winding road behind. The town, if it is large enough to be called such, could only be a stopping point on one's journey. Never the end and only very rarely the beginning.

"What is this place?" Wynn asks as they lead the wagon off to the side of the road.

Byron stands up straighter and clears his throat. "Ah yes young travelers if'n you'll look towards your left, your eyes'll fall upon 'Fell Tree Crossing.' So and such named for the fallen tree that be told to have stopped them original founders of this small town from continuing forward. And true! How could them folk ever hope to overcome such a monstrous barrier as a fallen tree?"

Fred has a wide smile and takes his cue. "Take care to observe the utter lack of smiles or general happiness throughout this small town. Why? You may find yourselves asking. Well, it's said that upon reaching adulthood everyone in this town is cursed with a curious condition known simply as 'poopie shoes' wherein they all appear to act as if they have large poops inside their shoes."

Cael and Wynn chuckle but Fred and Byron nearly fall over laughing.

"Oh that was a good one mate, lovely, pure genius!" Fred says.

Byron bows. "No sir, you was the one that wrapped her up all perfect! Poopie shoes?"

They laugh again.

Jean rolls his eyes and leads them into the only structure with any energy around it, the tavern.

"Three ales and two ciders." He looks at his group once more. "And a round of water, we're a thirsty bunch." Jean takes a seat at the bar.

The rest grab a few stools near him and turn to face the small crowd inside the tavern. Most patrons escaping the midday sun, or just escaping a bit of midday chores. Both are fine excuses to spend some time talking amongst friends, relaxing with a nice drink or a tasty snack before returning to the tedium of responsibility.

They throw back their waters easily. All thirstier than expected, which was typical of travelers with far out goals, stopping infrequently. Focusing on their ales, Fred and Byron keep chuckling to themselves about 'poopie shoes' and coming up with other witticisms for the town.

Cael and Wynn, whether unable to control their curiosity or unable to control their abilities, listen intently to the conversations of the other patrons. Two, in particular, draw their attention more than the rest. A pair of men, in field working clothes, lightweight cottons covered in sweat and dirt, speak quietly of a caravan that was raided by bandits.

"They was from the South, Pat. I tell ya here, they was from the South. No bandits round here with sword and shield, man. You got any brains left behind that thick skull?" an older balding man asks. He's got the look of a man who spent his entire life in the fields, thin muscle, not bulky at all, almost too thin. Not enough money to have food every day but just enough to spend a bit at the tavern.

"Oh Ham, you been saying them South Liefland folk'll be comin' up here to steal our livestock and burn our crop since afore good King Thokrin took his old pappy's throne. I bet ya been saying it since the South was called Vendre, ya old coot," Pat says, shaking his head.

Ham pounds his fist on the table drawing stares from all in the tavern.

"Sorry folk," he says loudly and waits for the noise to pick up before whispering, "The South still be Vendre, and they ain't never gonna let it go. Hector's got ties to both Liefland and Vendre. He's gonna fight Thokrin until they take their hands off his purse. I tell ya, me brother lives down that way. When our mum died, he told me a war is comin' and it ain't gonna be pretty. All these folk think the South is in the wrong, but they ain't know the half it. He told me they won't stop till Vendre is freed, the South be like slaves to Thokrin, boy! Why you thinkin' all these people been going missin' from round here? Why you thinkin' all these folk getting robbed round here? Huh? Well?" He looks at Pat expectantly.

"It's just the times old man, just the times...." he says attempting to sound more certain than he is. Cael and Wynn hear his worries. The stories he's heard time after time, all beginning to come together and make more sense the longer Ham speaks.

They turn to their drinks and Jean's eyes are upon them. For a moment, they're lost in his bright green eyes before Jean speaks up. "Hear anything interesting?"

"What's a Vendre? Or... where is Vendre? What's it have to do with South Liefland?" Cael asks.

The barkeep, entertained momentarily listening to Fred and Byron ribbing each other, now interrupts them. "Oh, I know Vendre. Family is from down south, but we moved up this way. Couldn't take all the talk about what was, who was, what did what and all that revenge stuff."

After a moment, Wynn impatiently asks, "So? What's Vendre?"

He smacks his head. "Right! A long while back, Vendre was a country. More to the point it was South Liefland. Surprised you kids never heard of The Great War. You fellas ought to be teaching these kids history! Can't let our youngins go on without knowin' things." He looks disapprovingly at the three adults. "My pap used to say all the time we can't never move on til we've taken count of where we been."

"Right, smart man he sounds like, friend," Fred says. "Can we get a couple whiskeys? The Great War sounds like it's gonna be a long story."

"And something ta eat, ifinnit please ya!" Byron adds

Jean rebukes them in a fatherly tone, "If you two get all sloshed *and* full, we're definitely not leaving this place tonight. No whiskey or no food, you pick."

They look at each other and promptly respond together. "No food!" They smile like children who just won a prize.

The barkeep pours a few glasses of whiskey and leaves the bottle on the counter. An impressively efficient trick to entice them to buy more.

"So. you know something of this 'Great War'?" Jean says loud enough to get the attention of the few stragglers left in the bar. He gazes out at the slowly quieting bunch, all waiting to listen to the barkeep's story.

"Wouldn't be much of a barman if I couldn't share my fair set of stories, now would I?" he replies with a grin. "Good business being able to take folks mind off the day and take 'em back a bit to a time when heroes were real."

"Heroes?" Cael and Wynn ask. "What kind of heroes?"

"The only kind, kids. The only kind…"

Chapter Thirty-Five

Weren't long ago, before our pappie's time and before his pappie's time, but not much before that. There were the Five Kingdoms, a lot like today, but one was Vendre. Now Vendre was a country of trading folk; the last kingdom to be found here on our side of the world. Long before that, all the folk came from Alisterra, but that's another story. Maybe another barman can take your coin while he tells that one.

The first of the King Richards of Liefland was a wild and ambitious man. Peace was shared amongst all Five Kingdoms, no wars in centuries, but King Richard wanted more than what this peace afforded him. Not just more, he wanted it all. He trained his warriors in secret and the greatest of all his warriors was Ser'rak. A mountain of a man, taller than any other before or after. Big as an ox and stronger than the strongest five others combined. Ser'rak was a kind, honorable man, sweet as honey to all who were before him. To this day no one can guess why he fought for King Richard's war, but he did.

It was a merciless slaughter when King Richard invaded Vendre, but it was a brilliant move. You see, Vendre was the youngest, least defensible and it was landlocked. Started out as just a big trading city long ago, and folk there pooled their money to buy land from all around 'em 'til they was big enough to be a country. Big enough, but no real army, no real ruler, and so it was simple and strategic to invade them first.

When they rushed the border, they didn't burn nothing; they just captured any who surrendered and killed any who tried to protect what was theirs. When they arrived at Vandre, that be the first trading post and namesake of their country. Not real creative folk being as they just changed Vandre to Vendre. Well y'see when they arrived, Ser'rak broke through the enormous gates with a *single* swing of his great hammer. The entire city shook from the blow. Many died of sheer fright seeing Ser'rak swinging his hammer and sending people flying through the air. Many more surrendered right then and there. Yet a few still fought as it was their home and lives that were being stolen, and they couldn't stand for such an injustice. Those that fought, well they all fell.

Victory was claimed. But it was just the first victory that Richard desired. His plan was to war with the three remaining countries, Kaldia, Oarna and Waylinn. With Ser'rak, he knew he would succeed. Richard didn't waste any time; he didn't want the other countries to become organized for he knew that was the only way he'd lose. He marched on to Kaldia, wanting to secure another victory to protect his flank. He sent his main forces to Felrikstead, the capital city of Kaldia back then. In a surprise attack, the troops stormed the gates, dispatched the city guards, and razed the city to the ground. Not a single structure was left standing. The army was in such disarray that there wasn't even a battle, no real defense at all.

Richard had split his forces; the strategic mind always at work, and he sent Ser'rak to Waylinn from Vendre. He wanted his own mountain to be the one that split theirs asunder. But the Wylaens retreated to their mountain fortresses and defended it soundly, even against the hammering of Ser'rak's mighty blows. They knew they could not defend forever so they sent runners to Oarna to prepare their armies for war. And they sent runners to the scattered Kaldaens and Vendrians, hoping to combine their weakened forces for a true stand against Richard's armies.

The runners to Vendre came across the still burning towns and found a young woman, Rell, her deep cobalt clothes and midnight hair melding into the blackened dirty ash around her. Only her face and furious eyes stood apart from the darkness. She had been out hunting when the attack came. Her town had honored her. They fought well but all had died. She was in despair, though she did not cry. She agreed to fight with the Wylaen people, but only after she tracked down the company who had lain waste to her beautiful village. For that village was under her protection and Finra help any man or woman who harmed her village.

And track them down she did. She waited for night, hiding in the rivers near their camp. As darkness fell she drowned them all one by one, silently. Pulling them from their beds, watching the life slowly flicker from their eyes like a fire just before it goes out. She smiled as vengeance filled her soul and when the deed was done, true to her word, she made haste to the Waylinn border. Quietly sneaking through to the fortress of Deldrin even before the runners arrived back.

Meanwhile, a Wylaen princess, Fwani, upon hearing of the destruction at Felrikstead, ran like the wind to find her friend Tuulen. They had often sought each other's counsel in guiding their countries as Tuulen was also a princess of Kaldia. Fwani had deep red hair, but in the sun, it almost came alive like fire. Her skin was dark as the bark of a tree as many of the Wylaen are, but her skin was not tattooed like the miners. Perhaps her most curious trait was yellow eyes. True yellow, almost like two dandelions or maybe buttercups.

And boy, was Tuulen something different completely. Pure white hair since the day she was born, white skin and eyes so deep brown you'd find yourself falling over staring at them. They were like opposites as opposite could be, but they loved each other as only sisters could. When Fwani found Tuulen, she was already busy burying her people before a storm that was brewing off the coast could roll through. It was a mighty storm, wind whipping through the open space where her city once was. Trees started to uproot in the forests nearer the storm. Fwani pulled her friend away and they ran, pushed by the wind to Waylinn faster than any could travel by foot. Together they burned encampments, they wreaked havoc and threw Richard's military into chaos, just the two of them. But they knew they'd need to do more to win this war.

So they made haste back to Deldrin. Meeting with the war council, they decided it was now or never. With Rell, Fwani and Tuulen, they had faith they could take on Richard's hero Ser'rak. Richard was confident in his champion, more than that he was confident in his armies who had much more training; he had groomed his people for this fight. They wanted this more than anything. They would become a single unified country spanning the entire continent. Eternal peace would be assured.

But his confidence was too great. He split his armies in half again, one to fight on the eastern front at Oarna and one to dismantle the defense mounted by Waylinn in the south. Ser'rak was brought to Waylinn to crush the last defenders.

The people of Waylinn had a simple plan. Rell, Fwani and Tuulen would battle Ser'rak while the combined might of the Waylaen, Kaldaen and Vendrian armies fought back against Richard's army. They hoped against all hope that Oarna would not fall, for it if did, the full might of Richard and his army would surely crush them.

And so the battle raged. Not much is remembered about the battle that waged behind them, for all eyes were on the heroes. The three women, stronger than any man, faster than any animal, and filled with righteous vengeance released a wrath unlike any other upon Ser'rak. The women divided and attacked him from all sides; Rell with daggers slashing and stabbing his body; Fwani charging axe in hand red with flame; and Tuulen with arrows flying so quickly in succession there was hardly space in between each draw.

An attack like that would surely have killed any dozen other men easily, but Ser'rak was not like any other man, or any other dozen for that matter. He stood fast against the attacks. His armor destroyed in the first onslaught. he threw it down and let loose a powerful cry that shook the ground. He swung his hammer once and Fwani was sent through the air. He swung his hammer a second time and Rell's leg was smashed to the ground. He swung his hammer a third time, sending it sailing through the air. It struck Tuulen squarely, sending her flailing across the ground. The women were stunned. How could Ser'rak be so powerful as to shrug off their attacks? But they did not lose hope, not yet. They stood again, bloodied, broken, but they stood. Tuulen grabbed Ser'raks's hammer and swung with all her might as he approached and as it struck his chest both she and Ser'rak were thrown backwards from the force. Tuulen lay unconscious, but Rell and Fwani saw their moment and scrambled over to Ser'rak, slashing wildly with animalistic rage. Ser'rak fought back with no other weapons than the hands he was gifted.

When Tuulen awoke, she looked to the heap of bodies in front of her. They all lay lifeless and she wept. The storm that they had run from in Kaldia made its way to the battlefield that day. It had grown into a powerful windstorm, a hurricane sending smaller tornadoes out from it. Tuulen ran to the safety of Deldrin, built into the mountains where no storm could destroy it.

The storm moved through with such speed and ferocity that it was gone shortly after the fortress doors closed. When they reopened them, the world was different. The armies were gone, the heroes that had lain motionless moments before had vanished with the wind.

Richard was furious when he heard of the battle, doubly furious that he had lost his champion. He was locked in a stalemate at Oarna, neither side giving in. Tuulen made her way to the front lines at Oarna and called for peace talks. She forced both sides to stop the needless fighting, to rebuild what had been destroyed. Richard demanded Vendre remain his as part of a greater Liefland, but Tuulen was steadfast in her refusal.

Though, after weeks of fruitless peace talks, the other leaders acquiesced. Richard would pay reparations to Kaldia, Waylinn and Oarna and in return he would be able to create a South Liefland where Vendre once was. The Vendrian people would still rule this new country, but they would pay tax to the North Liefland throne.

Shortly after peace was brokered, Tuulen disappeared, never to be seen again. Some say she succumbed to her injuries. Others say she died of a broken heart. Some yet still said she became a wanderer, looking for the bodies of those she lost. What became of her is uncertain, but what became of the world after is.

The people of Vendre are plotting their revenge, make no mistake. The fire of war will slowly fade; the coals burning out in time. But vengeance is like a coal that cannot be smothered. They will only grow brighter until they blaze once more.

And true, they're about to light again in Vendre. Just one bit of tinder and the world will light up once more with the flames of war.

Chapter Thirty-Six

The room returns to the hubbub of gossip and business
shortly after the tale ends. Jean sips on his third ale while Fred and
Byron are slumped over, faces level with the bar staring at the few
remaining drops of brown liquid left in the once full whiskey
bottle. Cael and Wynn's minds turn with thoughts of heroes and
legends.

"He thought he was doing the right thing," Jean says to no
one in particular before downing the rest of his ale.

"What's that now?" the barkeep asks

"Ser'rak. He thought the clearest way forward was
Richard's dream of one unified country. He thought he was doing
the right thing," Jean repeats before spinning around. "We'll clear
out that tab before these drunk fools pass out right here. We still
have a while of sunlight left before we need to set camp."

Jean pulls out the purse and takes a few coins out to pay for
their drinks and places another copper. "Thank you for the story."

Jean grabs Fred and Byron and slings their arms around his
shoulders before guiding them out to the cart and loading them in.
"You kids feel like stretching your legs or do you want to sit in the
cart with those loafs?"

"We'll stretch out." Wynn replies. "Our legs are sleeping.
They could use a good walk about."

Jean nods and leads them on down the road. The sun, still
high for the moment, has already begun to set. Enough time to put

in some good hard walking in before dark.

Cael and Wynn let their minds wander, losing themselves to their thoughts. Thinking of the old war and what it must have been like, wondering about Vendre and agreeing that King Thokrin should remove or reduce the taxes levied on their country. Daydreaming about becoming legends, of becoming heroes of a new war. Fantasizing about the love and adoration of an entire country, free from their own lives, meant for something bigger, the freedom of being rich as all heroes are. They are mesmerized by the descriptions they heard of the four heroes and their legendary fight. They all fought for what they believed in so fervently that they were willing to lose it all, to die on the battlefield.

"What is Ali....something? The place where he said people were from?" Wynn asks.

"Alisterra. A country across the sea, an old country. Peaceful place, or so I hear. Although there are tales of beasts that roam the borders, keeping travelers wary," Jean replies automatically while lost to his own memories.

"Oh. I thought there were only the Five Kingdoms," Cael says confused.

Jean pulls himself from his thoughts, sighing. "Five Kingdoms here, yes. But there are other lands beyond ours, many lands with many kingdoms. This world is much larger than almost everyone here knows. The people of Oarna see Alisterrans sometimes, so they are a bit more exposed, a bit more educated than the other kingdoms."

"Oh," Cael and Wynn say together.

"We can make camp here." Jean stops the wagon and they are surprised to find the sun already low. The pink sky sleepily pulling back the deep blue covers of night.

The forests on either end of the road squeeze in around them, marking the long stretches of uninhabited land to come. They manage to find a small clearing just off the road, perfect for their camp.

They go about their chores, filling in for Fred and Byron who are only now waking from their drunken nap, just in time for dinner. There is a slight chill in the air so Cael and Wynn decide on a warm stew that they throw together with some root vegetables and mutton. They let it cook slowly while they set camp and collect firewood. Jean scouts the area, setting a secured perimeter before circling inward, keeping his eyes peeled for game trails or anything edible they can harvest for their journey.

Fred and Byron stumble out of the wagon and notice a small brook that they collect fresh water from. Fred decides on some pine needle tea for the group. He and Byron sit back nursing their warm beverages and recovering from a little too much whiskey while Wynn doles out bowls of stew and Cael finishes brushing the horses.

"I've never had a hangover the same day as drinking...." Fred mumbles.

"Well, you both passed out in the back of a wagon while the sun was still high." Cael says simply.

"Drinking whiskey while traveling in the sun, you're likely dehydrated. Smart move." Wynn adds.

Jean chuckles softly. "The kids have you both figured out already."

Comfortably full, they sit back and relax. Notes soon begin to float through the air as Jean tunes his telbir. A quick happy song slowly lilts through the air, surrounding them with warmth almost like a blanket. They catch themselves drifting and wait apprehensively for the sadness of the previous night. But no such sadness comes this evening. The rhythm changes, slowly, subtly. Moving from a warm sunlit song to a midnight melody. It seems to create a bubble around them as the notes reach out only just far enough to be heard by those around the fire. It's a lulling tune, and they're deep into sleep before they even close their eyes.

A final note twangs through the air, startling them awake from their hypnosis. Jean stands up, quickly followed by Fred and Byron. They unsheathe their swords, following Jean's lead and search the darkness. A moment later five armed men leap from all directions and the clash of swords meeting rings throughout the clearing.

Before Cael or Wynn are aware enough to realize what is happening, Jean and his comrades disarm the attackers, but leave them largely unharmed. It's impressive swordsmanship for them to be outnumbered and still show restraint enough to not kill.

"Who are you?" Jean asks calmly, kneeling by the group of men who have all scrambled with their backs against the wagon wheels. He picks up one of their swords, inspecting the unkempt weapon.

"We're nobody's sir! Just farmhands is all! I swear it!" one of the men calls out from behind the others.

Fred moves forward as if to smack the man but Jean holds up a hand. "And what would nobody's be doing following us?"

Silence for a moment and Jean puts his hand down signaling Fred who rushes them. Before he can lay a hand on any of the cowering men, they all start blabbering at once and Jean holds his hand up again signaling the stop.

"One at a time. You there, you speak," Jean commands the nearest one, pointing the chipped, rusting blade at him.

"We's saw that money yous carryin' in the purse, sir knight," the man says quaking in fear. "We's just thought—"

He stops short as Jean leans in. "You didn't think at all, did you? None of you did." He says, glaring at them all. "You are men, blessed with free will, the freedom to choose who you will become. And yet you choose this?" He gestures to the group hiding their faces in shame.

"Look at you all. Look at yourselves!" Jean shouts, letting his anger run. "You are not born deranged. You are not born evil, but you so easily resort to evil action? What? Are your lives too difficult? The freedom you have too much? You can choose to do anything!"

He stares at them in silence until he composes himself and sighs wearily. "You are all cowards. We could easily kill you, you know. Yet I too have free will and with that I will choose to let you live. I afford you an opportunity to change. I wish to see you become more." Jean finishes and shoos them as if they were scolded children. "Leave quickly before I choose otherwise."

The men flee down the road leaving their shoddily made weapons scattered about the campsite. The group returns to their positions, slightly shaken. Jean picks up his telbir and sets it back in the wagon.

"That was..." Cael begins to say but Wynn finishes for them, "Impressive!"

Fred and Byron are surprised by the compliment. Byron quickly gets his wits and begins flourishing his sword. Fred laughs and smacks Byron's wrist causing him to drop his weapon to the ground, "Owch!" He scowls.

Fred turns to them "Was nothing, kids. Really, they was just farmers down on their luck hoping to make a quick bit of money,"

"Yes, that was what they hoped would happen, but not a single one of them gave thought to what would happen if things didn't go as they hoped. If someone was killed needlessly… They acted without thinking." Jean says, voice unsteady with anger.

"We know, friend. Not making excuses for them fools, not at all. Just letting these kids know they'll be safe with us," Byron says reassuringly.

Jean takes a deep breath, steadying his nerves and releases it in another heavy sigh.

"We know, brother." Fred adds. "Let's just call this one a night, eh?"

They all agree and lay back down staring at the cloudy night sky. Watching as the moon, alone tonight, peaks through the clouds floating far above. They find comfort by the warmth and light of the fire, but sleep does not come easily tonight. When they do find sleep, it will surely be restless.

Chapter Thirty-Seven

Cael and Wynn have fitful dreams. Seeing Wynn's family murdered, the house burning around them. Men chasing them through the woods, but their feet move slower than molasses while their pursuers chase faster than the wind. They're captured, laying motionless as they watch the life leave their bodies. Crying out silently. Arms outstretched, reaching not for themselves but to save the other. A strike of lightning flashes and their reflection lights up in a red pool expanding around them. They see the faces staring back at them are not their own.

Byron shakes them awake, "Wake up, c'mon now kids, it's just a dream."

They open their eyes as Byron and Fred return to tending the fire, some fragrant pine needle tea already set to brewing. Rays of sunlight struggle to peek through a cloudy sky.

Byron pulls out pork and eggs from their food stores. "Got to use it afore it gets bad, might as well brighten the mood, too." He throws the pork strips on the hot stones, cracking the eggs in a pan.

The immediate smell of cooking pork pulls Jean out of his easy slumber and he drowsily sits up and grabs a cup of tea. The group waits patiently for the eggs and meat to finish cooking before hungrily devouring it all. They sit for a moment more, enjoying the smell of the cooked food hanging in the air around them, before slowly getting up and going about their morning routine.

"Why do you think we haven't been dreaming as much? Do you think it's because we're connected now?" Wynn asks as she straps on her boots.

Cael picks his teeth, *"Probably. But I suppose before the nightmares, it's not like I had dreams every night... The dream we had last night, do you recognize those faces?"*

Wynn shrugs, *"I don't think so."* Her eyes fog over for a moment, *"Wait...I think I do remember them, but I don't know how. They're so familiar."* She shivers, *"I don't want to think about that dream anymore, it was creepy."* She says.

Cael nods in agreement, *"They were familiar but you're right. At least it wasn't the forest dream this time so we must be away from other seekers."*

Wynn sits up straighter, *"The dream... Should we try and see Arimel again. Maybe she has more to say? Why haven't we thought of that sooner?"*

"You're right... I almost forgot about Arimel. Why can't we remember her? Do you think something went wrong? What if she wasn't trying to help? If Landon hadn't been there to help, this whole thing wouldn't have worked. We should have asked more questions."

"I know, we sort of rushed into this. I want to know as much as you do so we'll go back and ask her tonight." Wynn decides.

She tosses everyone an apple to munch on and clean their teeth with. Everything packed and horses seen to, they set out.

"Do you think it's safe to be on the roads? Didn't they say more bandits from the south were coming this way?" Cael asks shortly after they begin walking.

"Do you have another way across the country?" Jean asks curtly.

"No... I just—" Cael begins but is cut off.

"You just nothing, got it? We keep to the king's road straight across until we hit Rosé and then you're someone else's problem," Jean says.

"You don't have to be an ass about it," Wynn says defensively.

Jean turns around quickly, temper flaring. "I'm forced to babysit children on a month's long journey while war brews all around us and you dare call me an ass?! Those not stuck in war are starving or if they're lucky they are murdered by common thieves hoping to steal enough to survive another night. What impact will taking you to Oarna have? None that I can see. At least when we're fighting in a war, we're fighting for something. Now we're fighting for nothing!"

Fred lays an arm on Jean's shoulder. "Brother, these kids ain't done nothing wrong. We don't always have to be fighting to be making a difference. Who knows, one of these kids might do something bigger than we ever could. Helping them might be the most useful thing we ever do."

Jean swats Fred's arm away and charges ahead.

Fred turns to Cael and Wynn. "Fighting takes a toll on our friend Jean there, he's always upset after a big one. Always. Just got to give him his space."

Byron walks up between them and puts arms around their shoulders. "He's a sight better'n he was afore, I tell ya. Wooh boy, you didn't wanna see him when we first met."

"Stop talking about me...." Jean growls from ahead. Fred acts out a lady peacefully combing her hair then suddenly looking shocked as she weeps into her hands, drawing a smile out of all four of them.

After they settle down, Byron speaks up, "It ain't all sweets and sheets out here though kids. If them fellas had been any kinda trained, we might notta been able to make fools outta em. At least not so easy. Towns is getting rougher and roads is scarier."

Fred adds in, "It's true enough. We heard rumor of the South making its way really far up on scouting trips. And when the South scouts, it raids too. They want to cause as much trouble as they can. The king's road is safest right now. It's pretty far away from the border and it's well traveled. We stay on this road here and we'll be true as the spring blooms."

"I'd hate ta think if'n them folk were military men. Boy, if we got caught up in a scouting party we'd be goners," Byron says, staring down the road.

They all set on with their thoughts. The shy morning sun decides to call it an early day as the storm clouds roll in. They briefly contemplate setting camp and waiting in comfort for it to pass them by but think better of it and push through. It could be a quick shower, or it could be a weeks long downpour and either way it won't help them to sit patiently and wait.

They duck their heads and charge forward as the wind picks up. The sky goes black as lightning reaches through the clouds. Grasping with thin fingers towards the ground, ready to strike down anything proud enough to grow taller than its surroundings.

They prepare themselves for the worst, but it passes them by, moving quickly on to a destination only the storm itself knows. They relax only then realizing they had tensed their entire bodies for the duration of the storm. Stretching with relief, they continue on in silence.

The next few days are strung together. It's seasonable weather for the month of Dekinlar as the summer comes to an end and fall begins to come alive. The group settles into a comfortable routine, but Cael and Wynn are still nervous around Jean. Not wanting to trouble their guide, they stay towards the back of the wagon.

The routine makes playing with their gifts easier and safer. With less fear of being caught, they walk out of eyesight behind the wagon and truly begin exploring their connection. After days of practicing, they decide to try something new.

'It's so hard trying to undo what Alek and Julia did,' Wynn complains as they watch the wheels roll forward from the back of the wagon.

'Yea, but man, am I glad they taught us how to just be ourselves again. I can still hear that noise....' Cael shivers, remembering the night of their joining.

'Yea yea, it was awful. But it's like they told us we can't use our left arm. You know what I mean?' Wynn asks.

'Of course, I know what you mean, you bubblehead. But you're right, we're so used to not using our left arm it's like we couldn't even if we tried,' Cael agrees.

'We're getting better at speaking in our heads though. That's something, but I'm not sure if it's the right something.' Wynn tries to organize her thoughts coherently enough for Cael to follow, but the concept is still difficult to grasp.

'Well, we're speaking the same way we would to someone else, so I'm guessing that's not what this connection is for. Remember when you spoke about quiet thoughts? Landon said something about it too; it's like letting our minds wander? We must have that connection because I understand what you feel and think. Even if I don't really hear the words, I have this feeling that I just get it?' Cael says, also struggling to explain the connection.

'Maybe that's it? We have this connection like we're always in our heads, but it's not a direct communication. It's like a gut feeling or something. It's too confusing. Let's move on to something easier,' Wynn suggests.

Cael nods his head in agreement. *'What about our senses? You took that one guy's sight away. Let's try and do something like that. Like I'll see from your eyes and you see from mine.'*

'I just covered that guy's eyes after I connected with him in my mind. It's pretty straightforward. It did make me a little dizzy though,' Wynn confesses.

They attempt to figure it out in their heads all day but can't quite get it to work. Wynn, at first reluctant to try, struggles to even see Cael in her mind. Cael encounters the same issues, almost like their minds cannot imagine them as separate beings and so they accept that they'll not be able to use the mind tricks that Landon had taught them, at least on each other.

'What now?' Wynn asks, irritated from their failure.

'We're thinking about this wrong. We're trying to do these things the way Landon showed us to do it on other people, but we're not other people. We're different now,' Cael says, trying to run through different scenarios in his mind.

Then, suddenly for both of them, it clicks.

'You were spot on about the arm thing!' Cael turns to her excitedly

Wynn matches his excitement. *'We just need to open our eyes! Your eyes are my eyes, my eyes are your eyes! We just need to find the muscles to move them!'*

'*Exactly!*' Cael agrees.

Shortly after their epiphany, they begin making progress. Blurry at first, they locate the muscle movement and are surprised when they finally can see.

'*It kind of hurts, but it's better if I close my eyes when I'm doing it,*' Cael says.

'*It's almost like I have dry eyes or I've been staring at the sun. Like a soreness and a prickling,*' Wynn agrees.

'*We probably shouldn't do this for too long, we don't know why it hurts. Maybe we're doing it wrong?*' Cael adds. '*I bet the instructors at the academy can teach us more.*'

Wynn smiles. '*I think that's the first time I've felt excited to get to this damn academy.*'

Cael matches her expression. '*Think of the possibilities! We could always see what the other sees; I bet we could smell and taste and feel and hear and everything!*'

'*We'll never get split apart now! If one of us gets lost, we can just see what they see and find them!*' Wynn says, recalling the night of the storm.

'*Yea, but we can communicate now for that stuff. You don't have to worry about getting lost because you can always talk to me,*' Cael reassures her.

'*This stuff is so much easier now that we're connected.*' Wynn says.

They become giddy realizing that they have achieved something they've been after for the better part of a month now.

'*What do you want to do now?*' Cael asks.

'*Well, we've got the mind stuff down, at least for each other,*' Wynn says.

Cael interrupts her, '*Which is different for us because of our connection so we really don't have the mind stuff down at all.*'

She nudges him. '*Don't be a sad sack. We have at least some understanding of it. But maybe we should go back to trying to play with the state of things. That will be so much more useful!*'

'*Yes!*' Cael replies excitedly.

"Alright, let's stop here," Jean calls from the front.

'*No!*' Cael deflates. '*Tomorrow, tomorrow we'll definitely get back to it.*'

They go about their routine with big smiles on their faces. Their enthusiasm and happiness spreads like wildfire to the rest of the group.

The constant walking, cloudless skies, and never-ending line of trees that had been closing in around them had encouraged them all to fall into a wandering stupor. Everyone had been waiting for a chance to simply feel good again.

Energetic for the first time in days, Fred comes up to them. "Hey, why don't we go for a quick hunt? A few of those farmers left their hunting bows when they ran away. We could make use of 'em around here, thick forests. I bet we'll see a deer right away!"

Cael and Wynn, already happy from their breakthrough, become ecstatic at the thought of hunting. Wynn, hungry for the chance to get her first kill since she shared memories with Cael, jumps at the opportunity.

They quickly agree to follow Fred along and he calls out to the guys, "We're gonna head out in them trees, see if we can't scare up some food real quick. You boys feel like joining?"

Byron hops up from the fire he just finished lighting. "Yessir, I could use me a change of scenery even if it's just the inside of what we been seein' the outside of for so dang long."

Jean sighs. "Don't take too long, we need to stay on schedule."

They walk the tree line until they spot a small opening. "Look here." Fred points out. "We'll follow this game trail, looks to be pretty active, and see what we can see. Not enough time to find ourselves a blind, but we can do a walk along."

"Fresh rabbit droppings," Cael whispers, moving aside some brush to show the group. "And some tracks heading that way."

"Look here, Freddo, we got ourselves a seasoned hunter if I guess right," Byron says patting Cael on the shoulder.

"Nice find! Take the lead, young hunter." Fred gestures Cael to move to the front.

They follow the tracks as far as they can, but don't manage to catch up with their prey. "I don't think we'll be able to find anything walking along with this many of us. We're too loud," Cael says.

"Still nice to get out and see the inside of this damned forest though. Vashir take the person who thought to make a road through the thickest forest in North Liefland," Fred says, spitting on the ground.

"We should get out more and hunt. Having something to do midday or end of the day would certainly help break up the boredom of walking," Wynn suggests.

"Agreed," they all say.

"Ought ta head back afore Captain Angry Britches comes out yelling for us." Byron says.

They make quick work of the trail heading out, not worrying about sound. Breaking through the trees they find Jean already tending the fire cooking some vegetables and salted meat. As they eat their sad meal, they all fantasize about the taste of a fresh kill. Being able to eat fresh food would do wonders to lift their spirits on this long tedious trek.

After they finish eating, Jean goes on first watch with a bottle of wine from Rosé, a purchase he must've made in Hintersdale. The rest of them warm by the fire as the summer sun sets over the tree line.

"So where you kids from anyhow?" Fred asks, stretching out on his bedroll, staring at the flames as the fire consumes the dead wood they found.

"I'm from Kaldia, which is just outside Rensfort," Cael says.

"I'm from north of there. We lived nearer to the border of North Liefland in the city of Menral," Wynn adds.

"Whew, Kaldia's a ways away. What brings you kids up here, and heading all the way to Oarna?" Fred says, interest piqued.

"We're going to a school near Oarna," Wynn replies vaguely.

Fred gazes up to the sky. "Oh heading out to Alundria? They say that's for the brightest minds of our time. The things they make out that way. Moons above, I wish I could understand just half of what they do."

"Fred 'n I ain't quite the brightest folk but we do alright. But Alundria? Now I'd give my left arm ta be smart like that," Byron says, joining Fred gazing at the sky.

Cael and Wynn decide not to correct them. It's better they think of somewhere regular people would go.

Fred rolls around onto his stomach and props himself on his elbows. "Ya know, those guys down there built up some amazing contraptions. I heard tale they dive down into caves in the ocean! Can ya believe that? Caves under the water!"

"Oh that ain't nothin, Fred my boy, they don't just go in them caves; they hunt monsters down there! And treasure, loads of treasure!" Byron adds excitedly. "What I could do with all that treasure. Lads if I had half the faith that Fred here does I'd be praying every night fer some damn treasure! Finra can ya hear me! Treasure please, sir!"

Fred kicks his shoe at Byron who dodges it easily. "Watch your tongue, brother. You don't want to end up reborn as part of Vashir's demon army, do you? Cause I tell you now, you keep blaspheming and you'll end up there sooner or later."

Byron waves his hand dismissively. "Oh now get off it, I was joking. Not that I believe none of that codswallop anyhow."

They all sit a moment longer in thought before Cael speaks up, "What about you two?"

"Well, ya's know about us bein' from Oarna and not havin' no kids or nothing. Got into merc work because it pays better for hardheaded folk like me and Fred," Byron says.

"We'd have done it even if we weren't so hardheaded," Fred adds. "Being a mercenary pays pretty darn well. At least it does compared to farming grapes or being a priest, or anything else we would've been able to do."

"We grew up together like brothers, same town and everything," Byron says with a fond smile.

"Why do you have an accent and Fred doesn't?" Wynn asks.

Fred chuckles. "His parents had awful accents. Byron is a poet compared to his family; I tell you right now."

"Really? What did they sound like?" Cael asks, interested to hear how much worse the accent could get.

"Real and true, Vashir take me now if I'm lying. But I can't do that accent like his folks do. I dunno if even Bry could do that. Can you, mate?" Fred asks.

"Aw ya'll are just awful, ya know that? My folk ain't even that bad. Sure, they ain't all smooth like King Fredrick here, but they get by and by alright. But naw, I don't think I could do a good nuff impression of pa to give it justice," Byron says with a shrug.

"Bry and I were brothers from the start. We fought all the time with each other and just about everyone else. When we was old enough, we didn't even waste time with other stuff, just right away signed up with a group hiring on bodies for some mercenary jobs. My old man wanted me to work for the church, follow in his footsteps and what not. I'm not really fit for that type of life, though." Fred says, laying back down. "Had some great times being a mercenary. Pretty easy money most of the time."

"Pretty tough money other times, though. Being a merc ain't all easy ya know. Loads've times ya get saddled up with some mercher caravan protecting em at all costs and whatnot. Well, bandits don't care up down or sideways bout yer life, they just want that money. It ain't fun or easy tryin' ta protect somebody else while fightin' for yer own damned life," Byron says with a yawn. "But we did alright fer ourselves. All them stories'll wait. We got to get some rest afore Jean comes over and beats us ta sleep."

They lay back in their bedrolls and stare at the night sky.

"We almost forgot again!" Wynn pokes Cael.

"It's so hard to remember her…" Cael thinks loudly. *"How did we even get to her?"*

Wynn shrugs, *"I think you got us there?"*

"I remember Landon's story. The magic one. We were… I was in your head? I was talking to you in your mind until we fell asleep? Right?" Cael rubs his head.

Wynn squeezes her eyes tightly, *"I give up. My head hurts. Let's try that… do the story thing."* She suggests.

"Alright." Cael takes a deep breath.

Chapter Thirty-Eight

Cael sluggishly opens his eyes to find the morning barely waking.

'Sorry!' Wynn calls to him as she whips the covers off herself and races to the wagon with a purpose Cael refuses to understand.

'Whaaaaaaat.... Why are you so excited this early?' he complains.

"I just wanted to practice a bit with the bow. I really want to learn how to use it. Remember, my parents never let me do anything fun like yours did. And I never had a bow when I was by myself either,' Wynn pleads to Cael.

Cael breathes deeply and uncovers himself as well. *'Fine. Grab two of them, we'll go find a stump or something and practice shooting.'*

They quietly make their way to the road searching for a moment until they find an old dead tree decently suited to their needs. Cael sets himself a few paces from the rotting wood and waves Wynn over.

'I taught Laena and Luther how to shoot, and you definitely can't be as bad as Luther was.' He smiles. *'We both have the same dominant side so just watch what I do. Left foot front, right foot out and back slightly. Grip the bow firmly below the shelf and raise it up so that your arm is even with your shoulder. Don't pull back*

just yet, you only need to look down the length of the arrow and find what you're aiming at.'

Wynn follows the instructions easily, but anticipation gets the best of her and she looses an arrow toward the tree. It flies wide and luckily falls short of the tree line, not being lost forever in the dense overgrowth. She runs to retrieve, it mumbling to herself.

'Are you going to listen and learn or are you going to try and lose all of our arrows?' Cael asks irritably.

'I should know all of this already!' she huffs.

'Why? Because I do?' Cael asks.

Wynn shrugs, *'Well yea... We should know everything the other does, right?'*

Cael scratches his head. *'We have the same memories, the same feelings, and apparently the same sleep schedule.'* He eyes her sternly.

Wynn smiles apologetically before Cael continues, *'But this is muscle memory. This isn't something that we transferred. You can probably recall my hunting, right?'*

'Yes. I can remember hunting.'

Cael nods, *'But in those memories, not even I remember how I did it. It's just something you get used to doing. Father never taught me like this. He just gave me a bow and let me learn myself. But, because I can feel your impatience, I know you don't want to do that. So, let's get back to it?'*

'Instruct away, master hunter.' Wynn offers a slight curtsey.

'Watch me. Place your feet, set your arms, find your target, draw fully back to your cheek with your three fingers, steady the bow, don't try and close your eye keep them both open and focus. Hold steady at full draw and when you're ready to loose, just relax your fingers and let the string move them out of the way for you.' Cael moves along with his instructions and they watch as he looses his own arrow and it drives into the trunk of the tree. Not quite where he was aiming, which he notes for the next time.

Wynn watches and follows his actions. She attempts to draw the bow fully, but the weight is too heavy for her and she struggles.

'Let me take a look at the bow for a moment,' Cael asks, reaching out and Wynn gives it to him. He draws it back without much trouble and gauges the weights of the bows.

"I don't think you can draw these bows. They're all pretty solid draws. I'd say five or six stone at least," Cael says out loud, noticing the group watching them from camp.

Wynn turns around to see everyone awake and watching them and she flushes red with embarrassment. Cael focuses on the bow, hiding his face while they breathe deeply and center themselves.

Fred walks over. "Too heavy, eh? We could make something real quick for ya, plenty of trees out here that'll do us just fine. Take the string from one of these bows here and set you up nicely with a bow your size." He offers.

Not being easily dissuaded, Wynn agrees quickly. "That sounds perfect, thank you!"

"You ever work with wood before, Cael?" Fred asks.

"Sure, I was a blacksmith under my father before we left for school. I've had my fair share of woodworking, not many bows, though, if I'm being honest. A handful at most, much larger than we'd need here and a lot more working than we have time to do," Cael says.

"Oh no, we don't need that. As a smith, you probably worked on war bows and longbows about your height, most likely a sturdier wood for draw weights in the ten, maybe fifteen stone range, right?" Fred asks and Cael nods his head. "Well, we'll just be doing something smaller, maybe half that size and a quarter of the weight. I can throw something together, if you don't mind of course?"

He poses it as a question so Cael replies, "Of course not, lead on."

"We just need a simple bow here, maybe a flat bow. We'll need ash or elm, even maple would do. Almost any hardwood actually," Fred says, rubbing his chin while eyeing the tree line.

"How do you know so much about bows?" Wynn asks.

"Oh, being a mercenary you travel with a bunch of interesting folks. One of them that Byron and I worked with for a few years had a love for bows and hunting. Shared it with me, but Bry never got the allure," he responds, scanning the trees.

"Ain't never had need of it neither, so there!" Byron calls out from the camp.

Fred makes a gesture towards Byron with his hand and Byron gives a shocked gasp.

"Disgraceful, sir!" he calls back to them in a playful voice.

"It needs to be dried up nice, but not too dry, so it'll be on the ground here. No rot though, needs to have gone down in the past month," Fred instructs.

"We'll look while we walk." Jean calls to them, "Let's get something light in our stomachs and be on our way."

"Aww do we have to, Father?" Fred whines, smiling at Jean who ignores him.

Byron passes around some hard cheese and venison jerky and they warm by the fire for a moment eating in silent anticipation. They break camp and clean their teeth with frayed branches and ash from the fire.

As soon as they set out, all of them keep their eyes to the road. Even Jean searches with them. It makes the day go by quickly. Before lunch they have a handful of potential staves for Fred to test.

"Can we make camp early so that Fredrick can start making me a bow? Please!" Wynn begs Jean who reluctantly agrees after everyone else begins pleading along with her.

They set camp with the sun high and Fred gets to work straight away. A few of the staves have knots or holes so he tosses them to the burn pile and focuses on the remaining ones. He stands them all straight up and presses down, watching for them to bow outward. He marks the center of the belly of each stave and moves on to the next.

Once he's marked the bellies, he quickly shaves the limbs until they bend evenly and pulls both limbs back with his knee against the belly gauging the strength. He decides on the hickory and goes about shaping the limbs with efficiency. The group watches intently as Fred works silently. Once he's managed to shape the wood, wide toward the center and thin toward the ends, he rounds out the grip, notches the ends and strings the bow.

He tillers it using a tree branch as a center point and makes slight adjustments, shaving pieces off until it's flexed equally.

He hands Wynn the bow. "Not perfect, but that'll do you nicely. It's about three stone and that's plenty for any deer in these woods. Trust me."

Wynn takes the bow with a childlike wonder in her eyes. "Thank you. This is beautiful."

"Moons above, man! You just made her a bow! It was so fast! How in Finra's green garden did you manage that?" Cael asks, eyes wide in amazement.

"That fella who taught me sure knew his stuff, I tell you now. It's not a perfect bow though. It's not treated for water and it'll likely start to loosen up, lowering that draw weight after a month or so. But it's good for now," Fred says, beaming with pride while trying to deflect the attention. "So what do ya say, Wynn? Want to go test her out?"

Without answering she giddily runs ahead to the nearest stump. She walks back a few meters and Cael is by her side.

"Just like earlier," he says as he places her body in the correct position. "Now find your target. Draw the string…."

She draws it back with just enough difficulty. He signals her to let loose the arrow and it sails through the air, right past the stump and far into the brush.

Wynn lets out her breath. Fred waits for her to be upset, but Cael and her jump in the air, thrilled she shot so well on her first true try.

They all take turns shooting on the remaining bows while Wynn continues practicing on her target. She becomes so intently focused on hitting her mark that Cael can hardly focus on anything himself so he gives up and stands by her side.

As dusk begins to fall, Wynn, sore from practicing for so long without rest, begins to regularly hit the stump. Not as clean as Cael would like, but perhaps clean enough.

"Just a little longer!" She begs as Cael pulls her away.

"You've been shooting for hours! Do you want to be able to go hunting tomorrow?" he asks like a parent teaching their child a lesson.

"Yes…" she concedes.

"Well then you need to rest! You can barely hold up your arms right now." He raises her arms and watches her struggle to hold them up.

"Fine! But you are taking me hunting tomorrow morning, bright and early!" she demands.

"A little huntress there, ain't she? Can't hardly wait to get her hands bloody, right good killer she'll be!" Byron says, ruffling her hair.

"So, a hunt tomorrow?" Fred asks, obviously amazed by the progress Wynn's made.

"If we go, it should be at least two groups to cut down on the scent and noise. There's bound to be some clearings near a stream we can post up by. You guys can hold one end and Wynn and I can hold the other," Cael instructs them.

"If we see a deer, I get first shot!" Wynn cries out.

"Really? You're ready for a deer on your first hunt?" Fred asks.

"Yes sir, more than anything! I've wanted to learn to hunt since I was really little, but… Well, it just never happened," she says, taking care to avoid mention of her family.

"She's ready," Cael says confidently. "If she has a clean shot." He adds.

"Alright, plans made. Let's eat," Jean says as he hands out bowls of beans and potatoes. "We could do with some fresh meat, we're down to our travelling food already."

They quickly finish their depressing meal, eager to get some rest and start their day early in the morning. To their surprise, for the first time in days, Jean pulls out his telbir and begins playing a light tune. He creates a percussion rhythm by tapping the body lightly with his hand and the beat allows the listeners to focus on the consistent sound as they are swept away in their imaginations. The soft music quickly pulls the group deeper into their thoughts. Without warning, exhaustion washes over them and they fall asleep.

Chapter Thirty-Nine

Cael and Wynn wake easily and well rested from their dreamless sleep. Not yet morning, the world is cloaked in a blue haze of mystery. It's the perfect camouflage to begin their hunt. Cael crouches over and taps Byron and Fred to wake them up.

"You guys ready?" he whispers.

"Mate, it's too early. You won't see a thing out there for days," Fred says as he rolls over.

Jean waves them off as he feeds the fire. "I'll tell them not to head out the same way you go."

Cael nods appreciatively and Wynn leads them out. The morning silence shatters as they enter the tree line. Branches, leaves, and pine needles litter the forest floor. Relying almost completely on their hands as eyes, they navigate towards the brook they found the day before. Their eyes play tricks on them in this light. Nothing is clear and the edges of everything start to blend together, all the same deep-shaded blue color.

They reach the water but stumble on rocks as they move upstream, trying to find any space big enough for them get a clear shot off. After a grueling hike through the dense forest, they find a small glade. A tree must have fallen years before creating a tiny space where grasses can grow, and the animals have made certain no other trees took its place by eating all the seeds.

None of the trees have branches large enough to support them so Cael and Wynn get to work on creating a small blind out of brush between a few trees. They take care to ensure there is an unobstructed line of sight to the brook and of the clearing ahead.

Cael breathes deeply, "Now we wait," he says as he sits down and relaxes against one of the tree trunks in their hideout.

Wynn eagerly searches the woods, focusing on any sound she hears and quickly whipping around to take a shot, while Cael reassures her over and over.

"It's just a squirrel, calm down."

"It's only a bird, you need to breathe."

The sun begins to stretch its rays over the horizon and a few streams of light reach through the forest. The quietest rustling, almost like a breeze blowing, catches Cael's ear. He looks out toward the brook to a beautiful doe bending down for a drink. His heart begins pounding with Wynn's excitement. The deer floats through the forest, barely making a single sound. They sit in awe as this magnificent creature, so perfectly made for its environment, meanders through the dense wood.

Cael places his hand on her shoulder as she readies an arrow to fire.

'Not yet,' he instructs.

Wynn's anticipation has both of their hearts pounding like a drum in their ears. The deer gets close to them but still Cael holds her shoulder. It's walking through too many trees. There's not a clear shot yet. He knows it'll go to the clearing; he feels it.

The doe reaches the clearing, half concealed by trees and begins nosing through some fallen leaves to reach the grass below. It all happens so fast. The deer looks up directly at them. Cael lifts his hand and Wynn looses the arrow. The deer jumps but it's too late; the arrow hits the mark. Straight through both the heart and the lungs. A truly perfect shot.

The deer moves to run but falls over. Wynn collapses, too excited to do anything. Cael walks over to the deer and pulls the arrow out and returns to Wynn, arrow dripping with blood. He presses his thumb onto the arrowhead and marks Wynn's forehead. "You're a hunter now."

They embrace and tears fall from their cheeks. They cry for her accomplishment, for the intense pride Cael feels for her and, above all, for the sadness that taking a beautiful life brings.

As they gather themselves, Cael leads her over to the kill and shows her how to field dress her deer. He instructs her as he guides the knife from the start of the stomach up to the chest and he points out all the incisions she needs to make. She dresses it well, taking care to not cut herself or the insides.

When she finishes, Cael picks the hollow deer up and throws it over his shoulders but Wynn stops him, "Let me do it? Please!"

He agrees, understanding how important this kill is to her. She struggles through the dense forest, falling more than a few times. Cael doesn't help her, but he waits patiently by her as she pushes onward.

As they breakthrough the tree line, they find the group still around the fire.

"She did it!" Fred calls out as he runs toward her.

Cael beams with pride and Wynn soaks in the congratulations that Byron and Fred heap on her, noticing the location of the arrows entry, they marvel at her first shot being so precise.

Jean pats her on the back. "Beginner's luck, but it was much needed luck. Well done, kid."

She graciously lets them butcher the deer while she sits down and relaxes from the hike out. Byron gets set to cooking the first bit of fresh meat they've had in more than a week. Not wanting to take away from the meat flavor, he puts it over the fire with no seasoning and only lets it heat up a bit before handing the first plate to Wynn. Fred leads them in a prayer to Finra before they happily shovel meat into their mouths.

They gorge themselves, eating more than any one of them expected. Becoming sluggish from the overdose of food, they decide to relax and smoke the rest instead of salting it on the road. Cael and Wynn, tired from too little sleep and lethargic from too much food, fall asleep while the others kick back and wait for the jerky to finish smoking.

They awake after midday. More clouds have rolled in covering the happy morning sun and bright blue sky with a sheet of disappointing grey. The group had already finished packing everything and waited for Cael and Wynn stow their bedrolls before moving out.

"Sorry," Wynn says, rubbing the sleep from her eyes.

Fred shrugs. "The way you pushed yourself I'm surprised you didn't rest longer. How are your arms by the way?"

"Not horrible, to be honest," she admits.

Cael rubs his shoulders. '*I think mine are hurting for you.*'

'*Really?*' She tilts her head in surprise. Cael nods and they realize at once.

Cael thinks for both of them. '*That's right, Julia told us any time we feel pain the other will too…. Oh man, that's going to be rough going.*'

'*I wonder what'll happen if we both get hurt. Does it make it worse because we feel it twice? Or is it the same, just split between us?*' Wynn wonders.

'*Or, maybe it's lessened because we both take a bit?*' Cael suggests optimistically.

"Hard ta believe that ya got em right through lung and heart on yer first try," Byron says admiring her luck again. "I tell ya now, my first deer weren't nothin like that. I gut shot that feller and he was in a right bad way. Pappy made me track it a whole day afore he finally gave up. Cleanin' it was bad." Byron shivers at the memory, "But wooh boy, eatin' that feller was awful. I'd sooner have Vashir take me than eat an animal that's been stewin' in their own guts fer a whole day."

"I remember that!" Fred says, chuckling. "Your dad made you eat that whole deer by yourself! He ate that thing for weeks straight. My mate here was sick the entire time. Couldn't do nothing."

"You shouldn't stress the animal out after a bad shot. You need to let it find peace and die. Chasing it a whole day made the animal suffer and the meat worse," Jean calls back.

"Truly?" Byron asks.

Jean nods and Cael adds, "That's what my father taught me. The animal panics and that keeps it alive. So when you finally kill it, it's almost inedible because it's just so gamey."

Byron looks down at the ground lost in thought. Fred pats his shoulder. "You sad about that deer? Don't stress, brother, it was a long time ago."

"It's just, I might not've been sick if that feller just died. I bet my pappy made me chase that deer on purpose, knowin' well and good I'd be stuck eatin' bad meat 'til I got sick," Byron says, frustrated.

Fred laughs and shoves Byron forward. "Should've known it wasn't about the deer."

"What? Oh... Well, life's life, Freddo, can't change meself!" Byron says, shrugging.

They walk on in a daze well into dark; the clouds above hiding the time of day. Preparing for the apparent rain, they set their bedrolls inside and underneath the wagon, foregoing the fire. Opting for their final apples as a small snack rather than cooking dinner, they curl up and wait for sleep.

"Should be coming up on Somewhere soon. Just in time too, we need to resupply." Jean says as they all drift away.

<u>Chapter Forty</u>

"Where are we? How'd we get here?" Wynn calls to Cael as she walks over to him.

The moon shines brightly above, masking all the nearby stars. They look around the clearing and realize it's not the moons light that illuminates the dark green trees or the deep blue spring, but the trees themselves casting a golden glow all around.

Cael sits on the familiar stone bench and sighs, "Back again… another seeker nearby?"

Recognizing the clearing Wynn stands still. "A seeker in the middle of nowhere? It doesn't seem right."

"This place reminds me of someone… Arimel? Stars above, what is happening? Why can't we remember her?!" Cael places his head in his hands in frustration.

"Maybe Alek and Julia messed around with our memories?" Wynn ponders.

Cael holds up his hand. "Do you hear that noise? It's like a tapping?" He says.

The sound of rain pitter patters on the roof of their covered wagon. Cael and Wynn are grateful they slept inside rather than underneath as they awaken from their dream.

"It's not so scary now that we're there together. It's almost beautiful." Wynn yawns as she rolls over, contemplating whether or not she'll return to sleep.

Cael makes the decision for both of them and sits up, throwing the bedroll off. "Aww, I'm glad I've got you too." He pats her head before jumping out of the wagon to go water the trees. Her eyes shoot open as she has the sudden urge to go as well.

"Hurry! I have to go!" She yell-whispers to him.

"There's a hollow stump over to the right, should do nicely for you," Fred calls from below. Wynn peeks her head down and sees him and Byron playing a game of cards under the light of a lantern. "Morning folks!" Byron greets her.

"Did we oversleep again!?" Wynn moans. "It doesn't even look that bright out yet."

"It's gonna be like this all day, rainy and cloudy. I bet it's right about time we usually get up," Fred says stretching out. "Bry and I were up early cause we had the meat scats after all that venison. Was a rough morning for sure."

"Oh, the young lady ain't needin' to hear all that in the mornin' ya foul mouthed twit!" Byron says as he smacks Fred in the head.

Fred smacks him back. "You trying to get whooped again, boy? I'll thrash you ten ways to Kurindal!"

They begin wrestling under the wagon, rolling over each other as Wynn giggles from above.

"Enough!" Jean yells. "It's too early for this. Pack up everyone. We're heading out."

Fred and Byron freeze as a twisted tangle of arms and legs. Both of them cry out, "No breakfast!?"

They quickly finish their morning routine and trudge along the muddy road. The rain, at first a drizzle, turns to a full downpour. It becomes hard to see, impossible to hear, and difficult to move as the wind picks up steadily from a strong gust to a constant roar. Cael and Wynn, unable to see too far ahead, concentrate on the wheels of the wagon so as to not get lost in the deluge.

A familiar crunch of leaves catches their ears, even over the howling wind and pounding rain. They instinctually turn to the sound and a flash of lightning illuminates the tree line. In that short burst of light they see the outline of a hooded figure. As the lightning fades and their eyes adjust, the figure disappears but the glow of a lantern still shines through the trees.

Cael shakes his head clear and rubs his eyes, satisfied that it was just his mind playing tricks on him. Yet Wynn is frozen still.

"It can't be..." She whispers.

Cael feels her words rather than hears them, *It was probably nothing, just our imagination. I can hardly hear you right next to me, there's no way there could be a dry leaf in a rainstorm, let alone us hear it crunching.* He thinks to her.

"No, Cael. That wasn't our imaginations. You may have my memories but those months on the run taught me that when those visions happen, the seekers aren't just close, they're searching for you." She replies anxiously.

They jump as Fred grabs them both by the shoulders and shouts, "What's the hold up kids? We gotta keep moving, we can't stay out in this rain much longer!" His voice only just audible over the thunderous storm.

"Sorry!" Cael yells back before guiding Wynn onward. *"Even if it wasn't our imagination who'd be looking for us? And even if someone was, we're safe with these guys. There's nothing for us to worry on."* Cael comforts her.

She nods, reluctantly agreeing, as they return to the dreary march along the road. They both try to force the image out of their minds by focusing on the monotony of moving forward. The unceasing storm pours down, sucking the heat from their bodies and chilling them to the bone. The wind pelts them with sharp stinging raindrops. They push through the day without stopping for anything.

Miserable and cold they trudge blindly with boots so thick with mud they only just notice the hard stone beneath their feet. The muffled sound of Jean's voice calls from the front as he points to a large tavern. Only steps away from them and still nearly invisible in the downpour. They pull their wagon out back and shelter the horses inside a barn, quickly drying them off before rushing inside.

Immediately, everything changes. The deafening rain is replaced by raucous laughter and music. The tavern is filled with life and warmth. The large barman moves over to them as they sit at a half-filled table nearest the music.

"Welcome to Somewhere, folks." He says.

"Somewhere?" Cael replies, brushing the rain free from his hair.

"We're in the middle of nowhere, but everywhere is somewhere. Made just about as sense as anything else," the barman says, looking over the group, "Rough traveling out there, eh?"

He asks the question on instinct. It's something he's likely asked to every patron in the tavern tonight.

"Any decent traveling is rough traveling," Jean calls over the music. "Do you have rooms left?"

"Just one, but it should do for all of ya. I'll have Tessy fix ya up some extra bedding. You folk look mighty hungry and thirsty. Just got finished stewing some lamb. We got a chicken roasting and Tessy's making some lovely, sweet breads and pies from peaches that come in on a wagon a few days past."

Fred stares at the man and with all the seriousness he can muster says, "We'll have everything you just said."

The barman eyes go wide in surprise but before he can move Byron adds, "An ewer of wine 'nd another of ale if it please ya sir! Oh 'nd some whiskey!"

Fred echoes "Whiskey!" In half a second they are patting each other on the back and smiling from ear to ear. The barman turns to Jean for confirmation, seeing he's the one holding the purse.

Jean sighs. "Alright."

Jean's word is followed by cheers from the table. They eat and drink until warmed through. Soon after Fred starts in on his whiskey he calls to the tavern, "This lady just got her first deer! Straight through the heart!"

There are cheers from around the room as everyone congratulates her.

'These guys are too much!' Wynn thinks.

Cael chuckles. *'I think they're just enough!'*

The music dies down and the musicians pack up their lute and drum, gathering the coins tossed their way, and move to the corner as a woman steps into their place. The barman and a few regulars hush the place to silence as she speaks.

"Ophelia isn't feeling well tonight." She says as disappointment rolls through the room. "She won't be able to come down. I know you were all looking forward to listening to her, I'm sorry."

The crowd grumbles in frustration before turning back to their tables.

"Who is Ophelia? A singer?" Cael asks his group.

"Not from around here?" The woman who made the announcement stands by their table, carrying an armful of some sort of cloth. "She's pretty famous, at least to all of us. Has stories more than most and makes even the slowest ones take you on a magical journey. It's like being in a dream or something." The woman gazes off for a moment. "But she'll be around again soon. We travel from here to a little ways into Waylinn. I'm her assistant Lira." She extends her arm and the table greets her.

"Well, being around such a famed storyteller, you should have some stories yourself, right?" Cael asks.

"Why not give it a go?" Wynn encourages.

She waves her hands dropping her bundle. She scoops it up, flustered. "No, I couldn't. That's Ophelia's thing! I get nervous, I'd stumble. I'm no good at stuff like that." She mumbles quickly.

"I know ya don't wanna tell stories tonight, but why not join us for a bit? Could use the company." Byron asks her with a charming smile.

"I suppose…" She brushes her messy dark hair behind her ear revealing stunning yellow eyes.

Fred drops his mouth open seeing her face, "Finra's…. Finra's… something… Great moons and… Your eyes are…. I can't stop staring, I'm sorry." He stumbles incoherently.

Byron smacks his friend on the back, "Don't ya mind us, he's got one of them speech issues. Hardly says a word without stuttering!" He smirks at Fred who swats his hand away.

"Oh I speak just fine! Don't listen to this fool. Please, please, sit! Join us, I insist." He pushes Byron into Jean and they squeeze over as he brushes off the seat.

Cael and Wynn move over, giving them extra space while Fred makes every attempt at wooing Lira.

"Stories would be really nice right about now." Cael grins at Wynn who matches his expression.

"You are insufferable when it comes to stories." She replies unable to fight his desire.

"Let's see who has a story to tell." Cael stares around the crowd as they peek into the minds of all they can see.

"How are you going to get them to talk?" Wynn asks.

"Simple! Just tell them they have a great story! I bet they'll think of one all on their own. All these fools are drunk as a sailor, they're waiting to be asked to share a tale!" Cael replies excitedly.

"Alright, quiet now! I'ven gotten a story'n it'll be a really good thing!" Their first victim stumbles onto the small stage. "I talk bout my love for the love of Darla. She's is my wiff... my wiff... my wife!"

"Oh no, take a look at this walnut!" Byron laughs, "Can't even speak!"

"I don't think this is what I had planned." Cael frowns.

"Let's get another one. I'm sure someone around here has a good story!" Wynn pats his arm.

As the night drags on, Cael and Wynn begin to forget themselves and their worries as they openly encourage the patrons of the tavern to share their stories. From tales of old gods to tales of lost love and seemingly everything in between. They run around from table to table, bringing wide smiles and laughter to all. Most hesitate but are inspired by the cheers from the crowd. Even Jameson, the barman, shares a tale or two. By the end of the night, Lira finds a bit of liquid courage to share her stories traveling with Ophelia.

"These kids is always getting stories from folks.... Ain't they, Fred?" Byron says with his face flat on the table.

"Your ares soo muuch in drunks thhat you canant eefen lift yer head up!" Fred finishes his sentence, almost surprised he made it through.

Jean eyes Cael and Wynn, their faces red from the wine. "He's not wrong. You two do seem to get stories out of people."

Wynn shocked at the accusation. "We don't take anything from people!"

"Nooo! He said we make people talk about stories and tellings!" Cael reassures her but she gasps.

"We don't make anyone do anything!" Then she smirks at Cael. "That he knows about!"

He puts his hand to his mouth. "Shhhh!"

Jean sighs heavily at the state of his group. He stands, about to leave them at the table, but looks down at the smiling fools and rubs his temples. He calls to the barkeep, Jameson, "Mind helping me with this mess?"

He and Jameson carry the motley crew into a room and drop them into their beds where they promptly pass out.

Cael and Wynn wake up in the morning confused and in a fog with a painful headache. They look around their small room, lost for a moment before the memories of the night before begin realigning in their mind. They stumble around Jean and move as quietly as they can past Fred and Byron who are cuddling on the other bed. They decide to get some fresh air outside while they finish waking up, hoping the cool morning air will alleviate their queasy stomachs. Sitting on the stairs they let their heads fall into their laps. The warmth of the morning sun reaching down to give them a bit of life.

"I think I've got something nice that'll clear you two up!" Tessy calls out as she walks up the stairs and opens the tavern door. "Come on in. I promise Aunt Tessy's medicine will set you right!"

They follow her, heads still hanging low and eyes closed, leaning on each other as counterweights to balance the other. Feeling for the bar, they find chairs and slump into them before collapsing their heads onto the bar top.

Tessy slides over a few mugs of some sweet-smelling divine nectar, straight from Finra's garden. They drink the mixture down and it's sugary and refreshing and… they rush out the door barely making it to the grass before emptying their stomachs onto the ground. Tessy follows after and rubs their backs slowly. "There, there, that's what it was meant to do. You'll feel bright soon enough."

They silently curse her until they stop throwing up. When it finally ends, they open their eyes and the earlier queasiness and headache begin to subside.

"Thank you!" they say in unison hugging her tightly. The rest of the group saunters down the steps seemingly unfazed by the night before.

"What's for breakfast my good woman?" Fred asks casually to Tessy.

"Glad to see the rest of ya are feeling right." She says. "We'll get some apples, bread, and cheese out quick. If ya want something a bit heartier, Jamie is already cooking some pork, fresh venison and eggs back there."

Byron eyes go wide as he turns to Jean and Fred. "Pork *and* venison *and* eggs!? In a tavern!? Wooh boy, this here is paradise fellas, I tell ya now!"

They sit at the table and drink ewer after ewer of water and munch on the flavorful cheese, fruits and bread before Jameson comes out with their main course. Fred smiles up at the big barkeep as the scent fills his nose. "My good man! You have outdone yourself this morning!"

"I don't do nothing out of kindness, only for coin. But thank you all the same, sir," he says as he drops the plate on the table. They dive into the steaming meats and sop up the juices with bread.

"Where'd that lady go from last night?" Cael asks curiously.

"Oh she left before the night was out. Got all flustered when she realized she had been there for so long. Ran off muttering something about that boss lady of hers." Fred says coolly.

Byron ruffles his hair, "They'll be others, mate. Plenty of others."

As they finish, Jean waves Jameson over and settles the debt. "Two marks, six coins and two pennies." Jameson rattles off the tab quickly. Jean pulls out three marks and hands them to him. "We're on the king's business, we can afford to pay a bit extra."

"Thank you kindly, sir," Jameson says appreciatively as he takes the coins and stuffs them into his pocket. "Anything else I can get you folk?"

They all shake their heads, but Jean asks, "Before we leave, how much for five baths?"

Jameson nods sagely. On long journeys the road has a way of punishing those who skimp on their hygiene. He points them to Tessy who leads them away.

After each one of them is feeling fresh, clean and scrubbed red, they toss on their cleaner sets of clothes before packing up the wagon. Jean hands Jameson another five coins. "It was well worth it. Worth more if I'm being honest."

In the bright light of day, Cael and Wynn notice it's not just a tavern, but a small town. They must live off the travelers that come through here as there's no large farms, just a small garden that Tessy is tending behind the tavern. The town is centered around Jameson's tavern as it's the largest and busiest building, which isn't overly large itself. A general store and horse breeder are the only other real buildings around.

They stop into the general store and are met with an older gentleman who complains incessantly about travelers, but decidedly refuses to give up his shop on account of the easy money. They purchase a resupply of traveling foods and extra arrows before leaving.

Jean stops and heads back in to grab a few medicinal supplies and herbs. "Now that we're hunting, I imagine one of you lot will end up getting hurt."

Jean counts out the remaining funds, "We're burning through this money fairly quickly," he says, brow furrowed while he plans out their route.

"How much is left?" Fred asks.

Jean replies quickly, "One stater, four marks, eleven coins, nine pennies and thirteen trinks left."

"That's plenty, mate. We won't use near all that." Fred says dumbly.

Jean pulls himself from his thoughts and stares at Fred seriously. "We're not even close to halfway through, and this money needs to be enough for us to get back to Ayverden."

"Oh, right. Well…" Fred says.

"Exactly." Jean replies as he turns and leads the horses on. "I shouldn't have been such a heavy tipper…We'll need to hunt regularly from here on in."

Chapter Forty-One

The days begin cooling, making their journey a bit easier. Summer is closing out fast and will soon be welcoming the crisp fall air. The group settles into an easy routine of hunting before they break camp every morning and putting in hard traveling during the days. Every so often they catch a glimpse of a hooded figure searching the tree line, yet no dreams come. They ignore the visions as a remnant of their earlier nightmares. A leftover of the fear they felt amplified by their connection. Rather than worry, they decide to make an effort to stay closer to their guards.

Thanks in part to their dwindling funds, hunts become frequent and a few weeks in Cael proves the most efficient with the bow. Without fail he returns with at least a small grouse, squirrel, or rabbit. After her initial 'beginners luck' as Jean put it, Wynn continues having trouble hitting her targets, but she and Cael practice consistently to make certain her skill improves. It comes easier to her than it would another, already having the knowledge she only needs to build the muscle and hone her reflexes.

Fred and Byron struggle to get up early enough to make a real go most days, but with Cael and Wynn returning with something regularly, they don't concern themselves overmuch. Jean plays his telbir some nights and on others they carry on friendly conversation to fill the time.

At night and during some days while traveling, they attempt lessons of alteration behind the wagon. They decide to

largely set aside their telepathy lessons on others to avoid any
trouble among their close group. The ability to heat and cool
comes easy, but Landon hadn't taught them any more than that,
and it's hard to grasp the reality of what they're doing. Despite the
difficulty, they refuse to give up. While they don't make any real
progress outside of their temperature manipulation, they are able to
alter temperatures with relative ease and speed. At one point Cael
starts a small fire inside the wagon, but they put it out before the
smell of smoke is noticed. Afterwards, they become a bit more
cautious, for a time, but quickly fall back into their experiments.

Soon the group runs out of conversation and walks on
mostly in silence. Byron, Fred, and Jean have worked together for
years so the silence they have is very familiar and routine. Jokes or
funny thoughts are the only things coming out of Fred or Byron's
mouths and even Jean smiles often. But other times Jean is lost to
his own mind, especially at nights. Cael and Wynn keep to
themselves in the morning while hunting and throughout the day
while practicing but also begin to feel the effects of traveling.
Boredom and fatigue are constant threats even when there is a task
to keep their minds busy.

Every so often, a group of travelers can be seen far behind
them, but they never quite catch up enough to walk together and
enjoy the company of new friends. The days begin blending,
cloudy days, sunny days; it's all the same. With nothing to break
up the travel except a random fallen tree that slows them down,
they all seem to be falling into more and more of a depressed state.

One sunny day like so many others, they walk down the
path feeling the ever cooling breeze flowing along, funneled by the
trees enclosing the road. All lost in thought, they hardly notice
when the tree line stops and a large field opens in front of them. A
lake to the south catches their attention.

"I tell ya all right now, I don't just want ta fish; I NEED ta
fish!" Byron says as he begins looking along the road for a branch
suitable for a pole.

"What're you looking for a pole stick for? We packed our
takedown poles right here, mate!" Fred says bringing out a few
pieces of wood, holes on either end where they plug the pieces and
twist in dowels to sturdy the entire pole. Lashing some line

together before anyone has a chance to speak the two of them are off running toward the lake. Suddenly, they toss their poles aside and quickly take their traveling clothes off before jumping into the water nearly naked. Jean and Cael unhitch the horses and let them roam the fields freely.

"Oh friends, it's beautiful! The sun must warm this sweet pool up all day long!" Fred calls to them.

Jean turns to Cael and Wynn who wait with hopeful eyes for him to make a decision.

"Well, we could use a bath at least," he says as he starts stripping to his underclothes and gingerly walking into the lake.

They rush passed him and dive in.

"WITCH'S BRITCHES MAN! THIS IS FREEZING!" Cael cries out as he resurfaces.

"Oh, it'll put hair on yer chest, boy, just enjoy it!" Byron says dunking him under.

Wynn swims over and tries to dunk Byron, but Fred gets to her first and dunks her under too.

They come up and spit water at everyone.

"You foul children!" Fred calls as he spits water back at them. "Take that!" He goes down for more water but inhales some and begins coughing wildly.

Everyone laughs and Byron smacks him on the back, "Ya ain't supposed ta drink the lake, ya donkey."

Jean walks out of the lake and grabs some soap root from the wagon.

"Here!" he calls to them as he tosses around some roots. "You lot smell worse than a pig farm."

They smash up the soap root and wash themselves.

"You don't smell any better... you mule deer!" Fred says.

"Mule deer?" Byron says with a smile. "Ya couldn't think of nothin better than, mule deer? What about King Stinkumus the third?"

"Or, Sir Jean the Soiled!" Wynn says laughing.

"He looks more like a Baron of Butts to me." Cael says smiling wide.

Jean grins slightly. "Ha ha, very funny. Now shut your faces and wash up."

They finish washing and lay out in the sun to dry while Byron and Fred set out fishing.

"Been a while since we fished, eh Bry?" Fred says, enjoying the peace.

"Mhm." Byron agrees with a grin, "Been a while." They relax sitting in the grass near the edge of the water, letting the serenity of the place overwhelm their thoughts.

After sunbathing, Cael and Wynn explore around the lake while Jean takes a nap on a rocky ledge jutting out into the water. They see life all throughout the lake and the many streams that lead to and from it. Not thinking about anything at all, they catch and release irritated little lake frogs and squirming violet salamanders.

They make their way back around the decently sized lake, but stop short hearing movement, a rustling in the forest just out of sight. They look in the woods expecting a vision but aren't able to make out anything through the dense growth. When they turn back around, they spot a full-grown moose with huge antlers calmly walking by them. He barely takes note before dipping his massive head down for a long drink. Marveling at its enormity, they slowly back away and continue around the lake, granting it a wide berth so as to now disturb him. They see the rest of their group watching the moose as well, but no thoughts of hunting him cross their minds. Everyone is at peace today, just relaxing.

Byron manages to catch himself half a dozen lake trout and Fred manages to catch none. Despite his lackluster haul, Fred is nothing but the picture of relaxed contentment while he prepares the fish with his best friend Byron.

Jean wakes up and mumbles to the group what they're all already thinking, "We can set camp here tonight."

They cook the trout with some wild leeks found in the field and enjoy the first bit of fish all journey. As they relax with full bellies sipping tea watching the twin moons rise full, Fred stokes the fire and speaks out to no one in particular. "It's odd that we haven't seen many travelers out this way, this being one of the biggest roads in North Liefland."

Byron picks at his toes with a fish bone. "Naw, it ain't that odd considerin' them folk that went missing."

"Oh, that's right, that whole family went missing on this road, what just last year, right?" Fred asks,

"Mhm, how I heard it anyway." Byron replies.

"One of those farmers over at the tavern in Somewhere told me something strange. I can't quite stop thinking on it." Fred continues, "said that it wasn't the whole family. One young boy made it back."

"Did he say what happened to his family?" Wynn asks, absorbed into the tale.

Fred nods his head and sips his tea. "He did… That boy said his family didn't go missing. They were murdered. Eaten up by a beast that roams these woods at night. A terrifying beast."

Cael and Wynn both stare unblinking at Fred, captivated by his words.

"What did it look like?" Cael asks.

"The boy said it looked like a man… until it changed. They were walking along this road, right by this here lake. Come to think on it, he said it was a night just like tonight. Fall was coming in on the wind, moons high and full in the sky, lighting their path. They figured they'd get some extra traveling done, being as bright as it was. They heard a noise just off into the woods and one of them men thought it might be a deer, an easy kill and they were real hungry." Fred takes a long sip of his tea.

"It wasn't a deer though. It was a man, an old man. His voice quaked as he pleaded for help. He said he was lost. The young hunter called his family over and they all rushed in to help the old man. Once they were all in the woods, the old man wasn't an old man no longer. He grew head and shoulders above them all, teeth stretched out to sharp points reaching past his jaw. Fingers shaped into claws and wings burst from his back!" Fred explodes his arms outward imitating the wings coming forth. "The family tried to turn and run, but it was too late. The beast cut them down and devoured them all. But one little boy was left in the wagon just outside the forest, hiding. Watching."

Leaves crunch in the woods startling Cael and Wynn. They search the darkness as the sound of footsteps and snapping twigs creeps closer. A man's form comes into view just in the shadows past the tree line.

"Please!" a hoarse voice calls out. "Please help me."

Cael and Wynn jolt upward and run away.

"Run!" Cael calls to Jean as they pass him. The sound of laughing slows their run as they turn around to Byron stumbling out of the woods, barely able to stand up. Fred rolls over onto the ground and Jean wipes tears from his eyes.

"Good one, fellas. I thought it was a bit much, but the kids seemed to eat it right up!" Jean says. chuckling softly.

Wynn huffs. "That was not funny! You shouldn't tell stories like that at night. It's scary!"

"That'd be the whole point, young lady," Fred says, dusting his pants off and gathering himself together.

"We weren't even scared. We were just going to get something out of the wagon," Cael says defensively.

"Oh really? Then why'd you yell 'Run!' as you bolted past Jean there?" Fred asks, smiling fiendishly.

"Fine, if you want scary stories, you'll get a scary story. There's a real tale about these woods that'll make your skin crawl and I'll tell it to you, tomorrow," Cael calls back before collapsing in his bedroll. "Stupid stories," he mumbles.

Wynn agrees. "Yeah, stupid stories."

The guys stay up laughing while Cael and Wynn work out a story in their minds for the following night. It takes them until the fire has burned down to smoldering coals, but they finally agree on what they'll say before they let the exhaustion of the day draw them in.

Chapter Forty-Two

As dawn breaks, they awaken to find that the group who had been trailing them for a week or so had passed them in the night. Still visible just on the horizon, Jean becomes irritated at their slow pace.

"We need to make good time here. Our job is to get these kids to Rosé *before* this other guy, not after," he grumbles.

"Landon won't mind if he has to wait for us," Cael says, trying to keep the friendly pace they've maintained.

"The man who pays us, who is also the king, minds. We follow orders to get paid," Jean replies simply.

They break camp and set a grueling pace, but soon Jean eases up as he recognizes his group becoming winded quickly. Not long after they begin their midday rest, another group of travelers passes them and Jean begins his grumbling with renewed vigor as he forces them onward.

They have nearly no time to think over the next few days as Jean keeps pushing them harder and harder. Their hunting is left to a few moments in the morning and they barely manage to spot a small bird or squirrel before Jean calls them back to the road. They sleep exhausted and dreamless with the only blessing that their visions stop. Few words pass between them other than their taskmaster's occasional, 'Hurry up'.

Exhaustion seeps into all of them as the days drag on.

Finally, a frustrated and tired Fred throws his hands in the air, "What are you doing, mate?! Why are we pushing so hard?! You still mad about those folk that passed us near a week ago? Who cares! I'm done. I'm not letting these horses walk a moment longer and I'm letting these kids sleep. You're turning into Vashir over there, man! Just relax, please!"

Jean turns to his group. It's only midmorning and they're all sweating heavily and filled with exhaustion. Even the horses are panting from lack of rest and the tough traveling. He sees their faces, too tired to even think and calls back to him, "Fine. A day of rest, but then we're back to it."

Fred stares at Jean. "No, mate! That's not what we're doing!"

Byron puts his hand on Fred's shoulder and looks at Jean. "Friend, ya know we always got yer back, but this ain't right. We can hardly feel our toes and I tell ya now we ain't gonna keep at it like this. Fred's right. We can't keep movin' and these kids can't neither. Look at em, they hardly had a word said between 'em since that night at the lake. We ain't gotta rush, it ain't a race. Ya turned to a monster, brother."

"I'm no *monster*, brother." Jean spits venomously. "I'm the only one who with any sense around here! We're so far behind because of all these stops and dragging our feet every damn day. I feel like I'm the only one who wants to get this job done! We're doing what we said we would. We need to get these damned kids to their damned destination so we can get our damned money and continue on with our damned lives!" Jean says fuming.

"Well, then you can continue on your own damned self and the kids will stay with us," Fred says angrily as he starts setting up camp.

Jean screams to the sky and stomps off alone while Fred begins smashing their gear to the ground angrily setting up camp, throwing bedrolls around and tossing bundles of kindling into the dirt.

The horses become skittish from all the yelling, whinnying and rearing. Cael and Wynn unhitch them and calmly brush them down until their nerves ease enough to let them roam around the tree line grazing on small grasses and twigs.

They return to camp and find Fred still muttering to himself, knocking things over. Byron, in his casual aloof attitude, goes about picking up all the mess Fred makes while setting up camp neatly.

"Let's just leave this all here for a bit and why not go for a hunt? Enjoy the day? We could explore the area, maybe get ourselves something good for lunch?" Cael suggests, trying to take their minds off the conflict.

Fred huffs to himself but takes a deep breath in. "That actually sounds like a good idea," he admits.

Byron smiles gratefully to Cael. "That it does, friend," he says before gathering their bows and passing them around.

Thy silently enter the tree line and decide to split into two groups. Cael and Fred head in a general eastward direction while Wynn and Byron take the west. Fred concentrates quietly on the forest, eyes searching the area for fresh signs of life. Byron, not being as avid a hunter, just casually walks along with Wynn.

"Ya two holdin' up well enough?" Byron asks her as he touches a deer track in the mud gauging its age.

"Of course! It's been really great so far, we've hunted and fished and Fred made me a bow!" Wynn says trying to find the positives. Byron looks at her with his eyebrow raised and she hears his comment before he says it.

"Alright, it hasn't been *great*.... But it's not been awful, truly! It's just. Well sometimes. Hmm." Wynn stops trying to find the right words to navigate the conversation.

Byron offers his own thoughts. "Jean can be a right ass sometimes, little lady. No need to try 'nd dance round it." He says simply. "But I tell ya now, that ass has saved our asses more 'n once, and he'll likely save em a few more times afore we're done. He's a bitter man; rough life I s'pose. We all got pasts. We just gotta know that when he's bein' an ass, he don't mean half it. He just don't know how to really talk about it."

Wynn nods. "I guess, but—"

Byron holds up his hand to his mouth gesturing for quiet. They listen and hear something rustling around. A distinct gobble before a big tom turkey walks right into their path without a care in the world followed by a handful of hens, clucking as they walk by. Wynn and Byron raise their bows and fire.

Cael, not wanting to break the concentration of his partner, walks in silence. He tries to focus on Fred's thoughts to hear what he's thinking about but it's difficult for him to walk and listen at the same time.

"Thank you," Cael says after they've walked on for a bit.

"What's that now?" Fred says, waking from his concentration.

"Thank you for saying something and giving us a rest. It was rough for a while, I can't even really remember anything except us walking these past few days," Cael continues as Fred guides them through the woods. "So thank you. But I'm sorry that you both fought over it. I'm sure this isn't the easiest job for mercenaries, babysitting a couple of kids, but Wynn and I appreciate it very much."

Fred stops and grabs Cael's shoulder. "You don't need to apologize. Jean had it coming. You weren't the only ones getting tired. Bry and I had already talked about it. We were dying a slow death." He pats Cael on the back and continues walking.

"Jean's a born leader. He's got all these ideas rolling around in his head, but he just doesn't tell anyone anything. He's always trying to hold all the problems in the world close to himself. That wears a man down after a while. Every so often he just loses it." Fred stops a moment, picking at some broken twigs. "Even without all that, we're a traveling family now. I'm surprised we've only had a few fights. Families love each other one moment and hate each other the next. It's the nature of being so close for so long."

Fred turns back with a smile to Cael and his eyes open wide as Cael looses an arrow right past his face. He whips around to find a rabbit pinned to the ground. "Damn, man! You scared the religion right out of me!"

"I'm sorry! I saw him and I took the shot without thinking. I promise I would have never taken it if I might have hit you." Cael reassures.

Fred eyes him suspiciously for a moment and then laughs. "Alright then, little brother! At least we'll have something good to eat for lunch."

On their way out, Fred manages to get a grouse and a squirrel on his belt while Cael gets a squirrel as well. They all exit the woods near the same time and cheer seeing the other's success. They clean their kills as a group and set about smoking most of the meat while cooking a bit of everything fresh. Fred leads them in giving thanks to Finra for their hunt and for their family.

Sitting back and enjoying each other's company, they let the chirping sounds of birds and the crackling of their warm fire lull them into a comfortable post meal daze. After a short while of peaceful quiet, Byron brings out a deck of playing cards.

"Any of you folk wanna play some cards?" he asks, shuffling the deck.

Fred sits up suddenly, awoken from his nap. "What's that now?" he mumbles, looking around.

Byron bonks him on the head. "Cards, friend, you up for some cards?"

Fred rubs his head and nods. "Sure, a game sounds nice right about now. Good way to pass some time."

Byron eyes Cael and Wynn. "You two know how to play anything?"

They shake their heads.

"Nothing special. Garden is about it. I don't think either of us have ever played cards seriously," Cael replies, his interest piqued as he and Wynn scoot closer.

"Not a surprise," Fred says sucking his teeth. "Card games are usually friendly, but some folk love to bet. I'm sure your parents didn't want either of you getting dragged into something where you'd lose your purse over a silly game."

Byron gasps. "Silly game, Freddo?! How you gonna call our favorite thing a 'silly game?'"

Fred shrugs, "Sure, it's our favorite thing to do on the road, but you have to admit it's a no skill game."

Byron's eyes go wide. "No skill?! Brother, I tell ya now, this game takes more skill n' most."

Fred puts his hands up in a conciliatory gesture. "Alright now, mate, no need to get testy. Let's just play something easy?"

Byron thinks a moment. "Caravan is right easy, and it fits too."

Fred agrees. "Alright, you want to explain the rules or should I?"

Byron waves his hand in front of him. "Teach away, Freddo."

Fred sits up and Byron hands him the deck. "Alright, kids, a typical deck has one hundred cards which is what we've got here," he says, splaying the cards out in front of him. "Five sets of twenty numbered cards, each set being colored a different country. So here we've got Kaldia." He shows a yellow set. "And here's North Liefland, South Liefland, Waylinn and Oarna." He finishes splaying a set of green, blue, red and purple cards. "Face up, they're all different, but face down?" He flips the cards over. "They're all the same. See?"

"So how do we play the game?" Wynn asks getting impatient.

Fred holds his hand up, "I'm getting there."

Byron laughs. "Well hurry up then, friend! Yer takin so long I'm settin' up to sleep over here!"

Fred huffs. "They haven't ever played before; they need to learn the basics."

He continues, "The game is simple. We shuffle. Each one of us will get fifteen cards and we'll work in teams of two. Each team will set down five cards and the total of those five cards need to be higher than your opponents' five cards or you lose that hand. The winners get to keep one card from either of the played hands and the rest are discarded. Each team then draws two cards from the deck and plays the next hand. If a team loses three in a row, they get to draw any card from the discarded pile. First team to have less than five cards total loses."

Byron leans in. "Any questions?" He smirks.

The games are slow at first as Cael and Wynn try to over strategize each hand. Guessing if the other team will underplay their hand or put all their high cards down at once. Soon they get into a nice rhythm.

'Hey! Don't cheat!' Cael thinks to Wynn, feeling the subtle changes in his hearing and thought pattern that tell him she's been listening in.

'What!? How dare you accuse a lady of cheating!' Wynn tries to look insulted but chuckles to herself.

The game devolves into a mind game between the two. The early attempts at altering thoughts prove futile and they soon only try and block the other from listening or feeding false information. Byron and Fred watch as the two giggle to themselves while having difficulty concentrating, but they brush it off as a joke between them.

After Wynn manages to best Cael a few games in a row, Cael gives up and scowls at her.

'Cheater!' he thinks to her as he tosses the last few cards he has in the pile. Wynn and Byron cheer and Fred congratulates them.

"What's all this then?" Jean says walking toward them.

"Jean!" Byron calls. "Welcome back, friend. Where'd ya get off to? I tell ya, these kids been playing a mighty game of Caravan while you was gone. Sharp minds here, fella, sharp minds."

"I'm not surprised by that," Jean says wringing his hands, "I... " He clears his throat. "I wanted to apologize for... Well, for everything I suppose. I don't rightly know what had taken me over. I suppose I'm just not truly used to taking my time. We work really quickly and move from job to job and all this time where it's been just us doing nothing it's..." He goes silent for a moment. "I'm sorry."

Fred stares at the fire for a long breath, thinking on Jean's words. After a moment he hops up and smiles. "No harm done, brother!" he says, shaking his hand and then they embrace. Byron hops up too, joining in.

Jean pulls back and looks on to the kids. "I'm sorry to both of you as well."

Cael nods to him. "Care for a game?"

Jean smiles. "That sounds wonderful but first, something smells even more wonderful. Did you all go hunting?"

They tell him their hunting tales as he packs his plate and fills his belly with good fresh meats. Savoring the diverse selection and congratulating them all. They pick at a few leftovers while they wait for him to finish.

"So what are we playing?" Jean asks.

"Anything but Caravan…." Cael responds, still sore from his losses to Wynn who smirks back at him victoriously.

"That's about right, Caravan can't be played with five either way. You know, I haven't played Five Kingdoms in a while." Jean calls out to the group. "How's that sound?"

"I'll play anything." Fred says.

Byron nods along, "Five Kingdoms, boy now that's a fun card game. No more hand holdin', kids, this game is every man fer his own self." He catches Wynn's eye, "Or lady, of course."

Jean looks at them. "New to cards?"

They nod. "Five Kingdoms is traditionally a betting game, and it can only be played with five players." He turns to them one by one holding up a finger for each. "Which makes it a perfect game for us."

"Like Byron said, this game isn't a team game. Each player gets the entire set from a kingdom. It doesn't matter which kingdom you get because before long we'll all have pieces of the other sets. We shuffle our sets and lay them face down in a stack. We draw five and hold them in our hands. Once we have our hands, we'll all play a card together and the highest card takes all others. If there are matching cards, those players will then skirmish between each other. Laying down an additional card drawn blindly from their face down cards. The winner of this skirmish wins the hand. This can continue for as long as two or more players have matching high cards. The winner will place the won cards in a second pile and we'll all redraw until we have five cards in our hands again. The winner is the first to have another kingdoms entire set in their pile. Betting is done at the start of the game, none during. Winner takes all. Betting doesn't matter for us as this is all in good fun. Let's play!" Jean rattles off the instructions quickly as he hands out the sets.

The game is easy to pick up, which is good for Cael and Wynn as it's also very fast paced due to the simplicity. They quickly fall back into their mind games. Unlike the first game though, they immediately begin by losing every round, and soon every game. Wynn is blinded by her success against Cael. Her ability to shelter her thoughts has improved substantially. However, Cael notices the others winning decidedly against the two of them and chooses to change his tactics. He sets up a lesson plan of sorts in his head on how to smith a sword starting from ore through finished blade and begins rattling off the instructions to Wynn, hoping to assault her with an abundance of thoughts. While he proceeds with the effortless lessons, he searches the group to see what cards they have and are playing, aiming to win against them alone and hoping his efforts beat out Wynn on the side.

He sees Jean playing a twelve, Byron and Fred both strategically playing lower cards of five and six for the chance to draw higher ones next round. Cael looks over his cards. He only has a fourteen as a high card. He plays it and hopes his plan for Wynn works.

Success! Wynn, unable to concentrate on anything with the barrage of lessons on smithing filling her mind, throws a twelve down. When she sees Cael's fourteen, she scowls at him.

'No fair! That's not fair! You can't keep doing that. It's annoying!' She whines to him, but he shrugs and smiles her own earlier victorious smile back at her. She huffs but sets her mind on ignoring him. They struggle to beat each other but also the others. Wynn, catching on to Cael's new strategy, turns her attention to the other players. But soon Cael begins confusing Wynn by filling their minds with false information on the other players, yet Cael can easily determine what he's falsified while Wynn becomes frustrated.

The rounds end up being split between them as Cael adjusts his own strategies to defeat Wynn who is always playing catch up despite her greater telepathic ability. Jean, Fred, and Byron end up sitting back, losing their decks and watching the intense battle as it comes down to Cael and Wynn. Cael tries to find new ways to split his thoughts and alter his senses while Wynn finds new ways to focus in on the truth.

Cael soon tries only to throw the same card Wynn does in hopes that the blind luck of the draw will help him win the game. His strategy pays off. They both throw down tens and choose a card from their face down piles. Wynn drops a nineteen and Cael pulls a twenty, winning him the round and the game. She scowls but congratulates him along with the rest of their group.

'Good game... cheater,' she thinks to him with a smirk.

He smiles back with a shrug. *'That was all luck; you had me straight out if I hadn't closed my eyes and prayed the last few hands there.'*

"I tell ya now. I wouldn't wanna play a bettin' game with neither of you kids!" Byron says as they sit back and relax.

"Seriously! That was impressive to watch! I've never seen a game of Five Kingdoms end up like that, such a huge back and forth. You two know each other way too well. It was like you were in each other's heads!" Fred says, impressed.

"Almost just like that, wasn't it?" Jean says, "Well, what's next? I'm getting a bit hungry again. We've been playing so long the suns setting here."

The group gazes up at the sky.

"First time we've been able to enjoy the sunset in weeks it seems." Fred eyes Jean with a grin.

Jean kicks a bit of dirt at him and mumbles, "Jackass." Before returning a smile of his own.

They enjoy the view as the sky changes slowly from the perfectly clear blue of the day to bright purples and calm pinks before the sun hides itself below the horizon leaving a deep sapphire sky hanging overhead. A sky speckled with an infinite number of stars, all much clearer on this moonless night.

They pick at a few of the smoked meats, still tender and delicious while they watch the natural show unfold above them. Listening to the forest chorus slowly die down before they sleep for the night.

"How about some music?" Jean says as he goes searching through the wagon.

"You know, this dark night reminds me of something," Cael says as he elbows Wynn.

She looks up at him and immediately smiles deviously. "What's that?" she says with the perfect amount of interest.

Jean settles back down, realizing what they're up to but deciding to let them have their moment.

"My grandfather used to travel up this way. He was a smith just like Father is. These dark nights always remind me of a story he used to tell," Cael begins his tale and the group leans in around the fire.

"These long stretches of road always play tricks on your mind, especially at night and even more so when the moons leave the sky. My grandfather used to say Vashir takes one of the moons each week so that his demons can leave their caves. Afraid of the light that Finra shines from the sun and moons, they hide just outside of vision. They call out to us with the hope that an unexpecting wanderer will seek their voice in the forest or in their caves. But once per month Vashir manages to steal both moons from the sky. A night of near total darkness, perfect for the demons to stalk their prey freely. An evil presence is all you feel before you're taken, never to be seen or heard from again." Cael drinks a long sip of his tea to soothe his voice and the tension builds as even Jean leans in, interest piqued.

"He was walking through one of these long stretches, and just like us he found himself far away from everything on a quiet, calm, moonless night. Now back then, all my grandfather truly believed in was the strength of the steel he himself had forged. He didn't believe in demons or Vashir, or even Finra."

Cael leans in towards the fire, warming his hands. "The group that he had been traveling with decided to settle in by a warm fire, seeking the shelter of its light. Yet he chose to keep pushing through. Oddly energized and wanting only to get back to his beautiful wife, he continued down the path. It wasn't long after he left his companions that he began hearing a woman's voice. She whispered in the darkness; she called out to him. He searched the tree line but couldn't see a thing and so he set one foot in front of the other and continued. His horse became anxious, rearing up every few steps, eager to get back to the light. He calmed his horse, but he felt a chill behind him, the hairs on his arm and the back of his neck stood straight. He turned slowly and saw her. A woman's face, only her face, pale as the moons, right in front of him. She was cloaked in darkness. 'Come, Edrin,' she called to him as she floated back into the darkness of the forest. She sang sweet words that had no meaning, but they pulled him. His horse moved slightly, breaking the spell he was under. He shook his head and ran back toward the fire light of his friends. He called out as he drew closer, but no one answered. He ran to them, all sitting by the fire. But they did not move. They stared blankly into the flames, even their horses were frozen in time. Not a single breath left their lungs. They were all dead, but there was no blood. No wounds on their bodies. Eyes all wide, still staring. My grandfather grabbed a torch and ran as fast as he could.

"He knew she was following him. He heard her song. He heard her whispering to him, 'Come, Edrin. Come.' He blocked his ears and ran full sprint until morning only looking at the ground. When morning light began to break the darkness, he looked up and was surprised to see that he was sitting. Staring at the fire in front of him. He looked around and saw all his friends, unblinking at the flames, still as stone. He heard a laugh echo in the forest behind him. The fire, roaring before, was now nothing but coals."

A laughter from the forest behind them causes the group to sit straight up in fear. In the silence, Cael and Wynn douse the flames to coals. Fred and Byron shiver and Jean stands up about to shout, but they weren't done yet.

"Someone's been telling stories about me," A voice drifts from beyond the trees. Wynn concentrates on putting the image of a face in the woods. They all shoot up and draw their weapons. Before Cael and Wynn can laugh, the sound of dozens of boots charging through the woods shake them from their story. In barely a moment, men are upon them all.

Fred and Byron, glad to have something tangible to focus on, throw themselves at the attackers.

"Hide!" Jean calls to Cael and Wynn as he runs to help Byron. They hide under the cover of the wagon, frightened and stunned. Too many men and women to count fill the field, fighting with sword and arrow. A pair of men tackle Byron to the ground and begin slashing their swords down. He manages to get his sword in front of him to block most of it, but he's being cut from above and blood spills from his arms as their blades reach deep into his leather.

Jean dives towards the two men, throwing them off Byron. He dispatches them swiftly and runs to help Fred who is dueling two fully armored women with longswords. One drops a blow from above and Fred parries, but the other slices low and cuts a large gash in his leg. He manages to stay on his feet, only barely able to defend himself. He throws himself wildly at one, catching her off guard and drives his small dagger through her breastplate. The other falls on him with a slash of her sword. He dodges but she descends with a flurry of blows from her gauntlets. His head is battered against her iron hands and the ground below. Jean grabs her by the legs and swings her into an oncoming group of three more men. The men fall to the ground and Jean lifts Fred up while the others scramble to their feet.

Cael and Wynn stare numbly at the scene in front of them.

"We have to do something! We can't just sit here!" Cael cries before charging shoulder out into the group of men who stumble back before focusing on him. Without thinking, he grabs their armor and concentrates on its structure. He heats them up to red hot and the men scream out in pain as they try and tear off their metal plates. Fred stares at Cael in disbelief, confused, but Jean turns them both to fight four men dismounting off their horses with shield and sword, an armored cavalry.

"Retreat!" A voice calls loudly through the field and the attackers are a mix of confusion. Some begin to withdraw before one of the men points to Wynn. "Get her!"

'I tried!' Wynn calls to Cael.

'We need to do something else! Blind them, something!' Cael thinks back.

Cael runs to Byron and lifts him up as they both grab swords and begin defending against another pair of lightly armored men. They parry blows left and right, but they are outmatched. Cael, unable to reach the men, heats his own sword and slices through the attacker's sword and armor in one blow. Byron, too dazed to notice, continues his defense against the other man who puts all his weight into a swing that cleaves Byron's right leg from his body. Byron goes limp and Cael drops him before diving on the man and turning his helmet around, confusing him and stabbing wildly with his sword.

A voice calls out over the clang of metal, "Don't harm the An'aith!"

"*An'aith?*" Cael begins to think.

"*There's no time! We need to focus!*" Wynn forces his attention back to the fighting.

Cael picks himself up and turns to see Jean still defending against four men, but Fred has fallen to the ground, his arm twisted unnaturally. Cael runs to help but is tackled. His arm is cut by a loose dagger hanging on the hip of his attacker. He cries out but fights back, blocking the blows from above with his sword. He pulls the dagger free off his attacker and thrusts upward just as an iron fist rains down from above. The armored body collapses and he sees it's a young woman. She gasps for air before going limp.

Cael pulls himself to his feet and searches for Wynn. He hears her and feels what she's doing, finding her still under the wagon focusing. She concentrates on the men. She can see them clearly in her mind and she begins telling them they can no longer breathe. It works quickly. They watch as the men struggle to breathe, scratching at their necks. Jean takes the upper hand. He disarms two swiftly and quickly dispatches the other two with a thrust to the chest plate and as he pulls his sword free he spins with the momentum and cuts high at the final of the four who falls to the ground lifeless. The last of the men surround Cael and Jean. Wynn, still safe under the wagon, rushes out and grabs her bow, quickly releasing arrow after arrow at them all. The bow causes enough chaos to give them a chance.

As they fight, Cael and Wynn begin communicating effortlessly. We see more now, more than is possible, almost floating above the field. Wynn's positioning further back allows Cael to always be in the right place, blocking every blow. Wynn looses arrows that are perfectly timed to hit the attackers just as they are parried and off balance, sliding in between armor and through leathers. They are lost to the battle, allowing full control. Cael moving gracefully, easily blocking or dodging each blow no matter the direction they come. A perfect harmony encompasses them as each action is in complete sync with the other. If they weren't fighting for their lives, it would seem like a dance, almost.

Suddenly, they both go cold, their bodies slow, they can no longer breathe. They look at a man who stares at them unflinching, crushing their lungs, freezing them solid. Their bodies are lifted into the air and they hang helplessly. Jean charges at the man just before the world goes dark around them.

Chapter Forty-Three

Jean stares out over the battlefield that was once their campsite. Twenty or more men and women had attacked them. An impossible defense, but still they held. He checks for signs of life among the fallen and finds many still breathing and conscious. He binds and props two up near a rock and lights a torch from his fire. He searches their faces, wondering why they targeted a group of travelers.

The prisoners sit silently, one calm and strong while the other is anxious and jittery. The night hides most of the chaotic scene beside them but their eyes still dart to the motionless shadows marking the bodies of their comrades. Jean follows their gaze as Fred begins to stir, pulling himself up with his sword arm, holding his left arm close. He winces as he limps over to Jean, sight fixed upon the tied-up prisoners.

"Why?" Fred growls as he gets close enough. Neither answer. "Why!?" he shouts, "Why!? Give me answers now, dammit!" He waits for only a moment before raising his sword. "Tell me now."

Still they sit silently, the anxious one shivering in fear, eyes wide and locked onto the sword in front of him. Fred looks at the frightened soldier and lets his sword fall swiftly onto the other. He wipes his sword off on the grass, never breaking eye contact with the fearful man who begins crying, "Tell me why you attacked us. Tell me what in Finra's good name is going on here!"

"Please! Please I only did what was right! Please don't hurt me!" He begs his captors.

"'What was right?' What are you on about?! Your people damn near killed us!" Fred shouts.

Jean looks on, letting his friend interrogate. Cael and Wynn stir just out of sight, regaining consciousness. They decide to lay still where they are, listening to the argument.

"We were told you're all evil! You're working for them. We had to do what was right! I only did what was right! They hurt my family. I had to fight back! I had to! I only wanted to do what was right!" the prisoner continues pleading.

"Are you talking about the witchcraft we saw tonight?" Fred leans in as realization dawns on him. "I saw those kids do impossible things…. Is that what you're talking about!? We don't work for these demons! Vashir may have wrapped his corrupted claws on these poor children, but he hasn't reached me!" Fred pounds his chest righteously. "I walk in the forest of Finra. I was born of Veera, holiest mother!"

Fred begins praying loudly.

Jean pleads with him. "Fredrick, please, we need to know what's going on here." He turns to the prisoner but Fred grabs Jean by the shoulder. "We know what's going on, brother. We saw Cael turn metal to fire. I saw Wynn steal the life out of those men before you, and I know it was her that called that demon to our fire earlier!" Fred looks over to where the children lay unmoving.

"What are you doing?" Jean asks following his eyes.

"We've got to, brother. We have to stop Vashir's corruption from spreading. I didn't think it was real before when my father would talk about it. But we saw it tonight with our own eyes. It's all real… my father was right, everything he said was true. And they are evil! You heard this man. He said we were evil just for helping! We have to atone. We have to do what's right! What they've done, it's not natural. They are evil! You have to trust me!"

Jean stands up and blocks Fred's path. "If this man is so pure and his actions so righteous, why did he have people granted with abilities to do the same impossible things that these kids did? Can you answer me that? Why is his group of cursed men and women holy but our two demonic? Can you answer that?"

Uncertainty and confusion creep into Fred's thoughts for only a moment before he pushes it aside. "They've already gotten to you, haven't they? They are evil, man! Open your eyes! People can't do what they did! They shouldn't have even survived this, none of us should have!"

Jean nods his head. "Exactly! None of us should have survived, but Cael saved you. He ran to help Byron as well! We would not have survived this without those children. Wynn saved my life, and they helped me fight off the rest of these men and women when you and Byron lay unable to fight. They saved us."

Fred shakes his head. "No! No no no! You don't understand! We wouldn't have even been attacked if it hadn't been for them! They saved us from something they caused!" He turns his head back to Cael and Wynn. "They need to die."

Jean steps in front of Fred and puts his hand on his sword, "They're not even grown yet. Cursed or not, demons or not, they're just kids. There is hope for all man. Can there not be hope for these children as well? Can you not learn to accept them? They cannot be evil. We have traveled with them for months, they are good and true, can you not see that?" he pleads.

"I see nothing of that left in them. They are darkness and wrong. They are unnatural. No one and no thing should have that power. I will kill them, with or without your consent." Fred goes to move passed Jean, but Jean unsheathes his sword and holds it out front.

"I will not allow you to hurt these two. They are not cursed. They are our charges! We may not understand what's going on here, but we gave our word that we'd deliver them to Oarna. If they truly were demons, they wouldn't need our help! Think man, please! I cannot let you hurt them." Jean begins shaking as he holds his sword to his companion of so many years. He breathes deep, regaining his composure. "I will not let you." He says calmly.

"You choose them!?" Fred yells, his voice quavering. "Look at Byron, look at him! We were brothers, all of us! We trusted you, we followed you! Now you choose them over us?! We loved you!" He throws his hands in the air, wincing in pain.

He continues, his frustration building, "Byron is dying because of them. Man, you can't choose them. I won't let you choose them." Fred charges at him and Jean easily dodges his attack and punches him in the jaw. Fred falls to the ground, tears in his eyes, "I loved you, brother…"

Fred crawls over to Byron who still lays unconscious. Breath shallow from severe blood loss. He struggles to lift him. Jean helps put Byron in the back of the wagon. Fred rounds up the horses and begins hitching them silently while Jean watches, still stunned and emotional.

"I just need enough to get these two to Oarna; that's all I ask," Jean says to Fred who climbs into the seat and turns away as tears roll down his cheek. He waits as Jean unhitches one of the horses and unloads a bit of food.

He finishes gathering supplies and looks up at Fred, both frustrated with each other, both not knowing how to fix it. Jean goes to say his farewells, to wish his brother safe travels, perhaps to tell him he loves him one last time, but Fred ushers his horses onward without another word.

Jean walks over to the bound prisoner who is still sobbing, head bowed and fearful for his life. He unties him. "Gather your group and leave us in peace."

The man rubs his wrists as he stares at Jean in disbelief. "I'm… I'm sorry. I thought you were…. We thought you were working for the praetors. I didn't want any of this. I only did what I thought was right. I just didn't want anyone else to get hurt like my sister." The young man gets to his feet and looks at Jean, "Thank you for sparing us, thank you. I was wrong. We all were. I'm sorry."

Jean sits by their fire pit, only a few coals left smoldering. Cael and Wynn make their way over to sit near the warmth and light as well, watching as the young man goes body to body searching for those still alive enough to help him. Some argue angrily when they awake to realize their mission is incomplete, but the young man persuades them to all leave as peacefully and quickly as possible. They carry their fallen comrades to the horses and ride away, leaving an empty road.

The three of them are left alone in the darkness and silence. Left with few supplies and one horse to carry everything they own. Left alone but left alive.

After a long while lost to themselves and the darkness around them, Wynn lifts her head and faces Jean. His eyes glazed over, staring into the coals as the last bit of life leaves them.

"Why did you defend us?" she asks quietly, her voice shattering the slowly growing silence around them, startling Jean awake.

Jean doesn't respond right away. He waits a few moments before taking a deep breath and sighing. "Most of the time..." He pauses, "The why of it, doesn't really matter. Knowing these things changes very little." He goes quiet before looking back at the empty field. "Fred asked why those people attacked us, but their answer wouldn't have changed his mind. He knew as soon as he saw you both doing things, things he thought impossible, the only explanation he'd accept was that you were evil. He needed it to be evil. Evil things are allowed to be unexplainable."

Wynn presses him. "But sometimes the why does matter."

He sighs again. "You're right, sometimes, for us at least, the why does make all the difference. I suppose it was a choice I made in the moment. Because for whatever reason, I still have a sense of morality. I still have a ridiculous notion that everyone deserves a chance no matter what evidence is lain before us. We should all be given the chance to defend our actions before our life is taken. I've seen how man reacts when faced with something different. I've seen how the ignorance of a person leads to an unrelenting fear. And sometimes that fear leads to a dangerous end. I defended you because it is what needed to be done."

Cael stares into his hands. "We aren't monsters... and we aren't evil," he says numbly. "We never asked for this. We didn't want to be different. We weren't given a choice."

Jean nods. "I figured." He goes to say more but closes his mouth and stares into the fire.

"I don't know what else to say. Thank you for helping us," Cael says reaching out to shake his arm.

Jean grasps it firmly before rolling onto his back. "Get some sleep. We've got a long way still to go."

Chapter Forty-Four

They awake with the sun, its warm rays heating their bodies. Jean, already nursing the coals of their fire back to life and setting some tea on. Their first thoughts are of food, but as they rub the sleep from their eyes, they are almost surprised by the remains of the battle from the night before strewn out all around them. In the small area that the fighting took place, it's as though a rainstorm moved through, the ground muddied and red, grass torn up and a stampede of footprints scattered throughout. Weapons and pieces of armor still litter the ground, their owners having long since fled.

Jean hands them their mugs of tea and they sip for a moment before their surroundings get the better of them. They stand up and wordlessly agree to move on from the depressing scene. They travel quietly and easily. With one horse and few supplies, breaking camp is much quicker than they had become used to and are relieved to move out so soon.

No words pass between any of them, spoken or otherwise. Cael and Wynn still confused from the night before, and with an odd pounding pain in their heads, decide to refrain from using their gifts. They agree it's for the best either way as they don't know who might be following them. They aren't certain of how those people found them but are sure using their gifts so flagrantly was why they attacked.

They set a brisk pace, not grueling as it had been before, but not lazy either. A cool autumn breeze pushes them along their path, keeping the sun's heat from draining their energy. It's a comfortable day to travel, but the silence between them is uncomfortably loud.

Jean stops a moment to dig around for some of their dried meat from the day before and passes it around. Only a day has passed, but it seems a lifetime ago when Byron and Fred were laughing and joking about everything.

They numbly chew the jerky and continue on their way. None of them want to stop now. They all want to push until exhaustion pulls them to sleep. Anything to keep from remembering.

The days drift by, one foot in front of the other. Sadness kept at bay by the constant travel. It's as if they're not truly alive, only watching figures that resemble themselves march along a never-ending road. Stopping only to buy food in a small trading town or to hunt along the tree line. Never just to speak, never stopping just to enjoy the day. Jean... he doesn't remember the man he used to be. If he did, he would help them. Lost, like the others. Forgetful, like the others.

Weeks pass without a thought. Jean looks over to Cael and Wynn as he hands around some fruit they purchased off a trader a few days before. He realizes it's been near a month since he's seen them. None of them have focused on anything but moving. It's as difficult for him as it is for them, but he has lived this life before. Just a memory, that's all it would take.

"Why don't we set camp here for the day?" His voice dry and raspy from disuse. They nod their heads sullenly as they go about setting camp without a word.

They sit down with the sun still high and far from setting. It's too much time for remembering. They are all anxious to be moving, their feet so used to the motion that Cael has to rub his legs to keep them from kicking uncontrollably out from under him. Soon Wynn's legs begin jittering along with his.

Jean boils some water for tea to warm their hands, which are already getting cold as the gentle breeze steals the heat from them. Once the tea is ready, Jean passes around their mugs and they sit watching the leaves fall around them.

"I'm sorry," Jean says suddenly. Cael and Wynn are startled out of their silence but can't bring themselves to speak, so he continues, "I should have watched you both. I let you fall away, and I'm sorry." He bows his head. "It's been so long." He shakes his head and turns back to them. "I can't let you lose yourselves. I've lost my way, so much so that I don't think I could ever be the same person. You both have experienced things that you shouldn't have at such an age. You'll become stronger because of it, but you mustn't mistake that void you're in now as strength. You must accept life, not dismiss it. You cannot hide away like you are right now."

"I don't know what to do…." Cael says, his voice rough and heavy with emotion.

Wynn puts her hand on his shoulder. "We." She adds, "We don't know what to do."

"We killed people….I don't even remember doing it. It's like I was in a nightmare, watching myself kill them." Cael says looking at Wynn, tears filling his eyes. "Fred was right, we are monsters."

Wynn looks to Jean, tears streaming down her face. "Why us?".

Unsure of what else to do, Jean embraces them and they cry together. They cry until the night reaches them. For the lives they took and for the friends they lost, they weep. More than that, they cry trying to find a reason for their own lives.

Jean holds them close until they fall asleep, and for a long while after. He stays up alone, silent tears glistening by the light of the fire.

When the morning comes, despite their sadness, they begin to feel better. The smell of autumn is in the air, along with the wafting scent of salted pork and apples that Jean is frying up for breakfast.

"That smells good," Cael says, struggling to free himself from his bedroll.

"Really good." Wynn agrees opening her eyes as well.

"I was hoping more for a 'wonderful' or 'fantastic,' but 'really good' will do." Jean manages to smile at them as he scrapes breakfast into their bowls. They eat slowly at first, but soon begin shoveling the food into their mouths almost with as much enthusiasm as they had before it all. The saltiness of the pork and sugary sweetness of the apples mixing perfectly.

After satisfying their hunger and going about the morning routine, Jean calls them out of their thoughts, "Hey, sit down for a moment."

"What's on your mind?" Cael asks as they sit on the ground.

Jean shrugs, unsure of what to say. "I don't really know how to handle this whole thing. But we can't pretend like nothings different."

"So, you want to talk about it?" Wynn suggests, "Like, talk about how we feel?"

Jean points at her and nods vigorously. "Exactly, yes, how we feel! Feelings, thoughts, that whole thing."

Wynn turns to Cael expectantly but he shakes his head. "It was your idea, you go."

She rolls her eyes. "Fine."

She thinks on it, looking around for a short while trying to find the words. "I'm not sure how I feel. I mean, I can feel how Cael feels, but I can't tell how much of that is mine and how much is his."

"You feel what the other feels?" Jean asks curiously. They nod their heads shyly. "And you can't separate the feelings? Can you hear the other's thoughts as well?" He continues with more interest. They nod again.

"It is amazing what he's done…" Jean mumbles but quickly continues, "What about the story you told, I've seen your power over fire, but the voice we heard and face we saw, you did that as well?"

Wynn nods. "That was me. Cael is better at altering heat but he has trouble with focusing on the mind." She says nervously. "Which is weird because before we were connected he was better at that and I was better with the heat stuff."

Cael agrees. "You're right… I almost didn't remember. Something in us must have crossed that night."

He sighs, letting his head fall back as his eyes gaze out at the sky above, "You know, I haven't felt myself since then. I feel, kind of scared all of the time. Or anxious, it's weird."

Wynn slowly nods her head. "That's how I used to feel all the time…. Since that night I've felt happier, more confident, I guess stronger in general. I don't want to feel how I used to, but I don't want you to feel that way either."

Cael grins. "Well, I don't want to feel this way either. you doof."

"What's this night you're on about?" Jean asks.

"That, my good man, is a long story," Cael says. He and Wynn dive into their tale. Telling everything from the death of Wynn's family and her life on the run to Cael's fateful encounter with Landon and their meeting. The rebel group chasing them. The voyage on the ship and the night of the storm. The fear they felt and the help they received from someone.

Jean, listening closely and nodding along as if none of what they were saying was unusual. "So you're bound forever to each other now?" he asks at the end.

"I suppose," Wynn says, shrugging.

"Interesting," Jean says scratching at his chin. A beard growing thickly now, showing the time traveling. "Let's step back. I think we're getting somewhere but we've missed a crucial piece. It's easy to forget in the moment, but it'll sit like a stone in us if we choose to ignore it."

"Yea, I know," Cael mumbles. "We hurt people."

Jean shakes his head. "No, we didn't just hurt people. We killed them. And *that* is something that lives in us forever. We are cursed to bear that burden for eternity. Some don't have as much difficulty as others, but often I feel I carry an impossible weight. Maybe it'll help you two to talk about it?"

"It wasn't hard at the time. We did what we had to so that we could survive. And we tried to protect you all, too," Cael says.

"I feel bad thinking about it, but it hurt more when Fred called us evil monsters. He wanted to kill us so badly…. Landon said that we have a 'gift,' that we're stronger than everyone else. But we've done nothing but hide and be scared since we were told about it," Wynn says, getting angrier as she speaks.

Cael nods his head. "When Fred said that he wanted to... to kill us, it was so unreal. We were friends. We played games and sang songs. We ate together and traveled together... and just like that, without even talking to us, he forgot all of it and just wanted us dead."

"It's going to be hard for you both because of the abilities you have and the trouble it'll cause." Jean agrees. "It might get easier when you're among others like you. But out here, well let's just say people are scared of anything different, especially when that difference comes with power such as yours."

He sets some more logs on the fire. "If it helps, I don't think Fred was thinking right. If I had to guess, I'd say he regrets the way he acted, even now. But he'll have to live with his actions that night just as we all will. He's a good man, but religion preaches these myths about gods and right and wrong. When someone takes everything without question as Fred does, the lines of good and bad are very definite, very strict. If you are what is deemed 'regular,' you can be good. If you're different, as you two are, the only explanation is that you're evil or wrong. It's much like the story of Vashir. Even in the stories you've heard, he's just a man struggling with emotions of jealousy and anger. Finra clearly had the power to fix what Vashir had done to the wolves, but still he cursed his creation and banished him." He kicks his shoes off and warms his feet by the growing fire while sipping some bourbon.

"So you see, even the most evil person in your religion is just a misunderstood man. And even the god you pray to was ignorant of the differences Vashir possessed. In the stories Finra is logical; he's not emotional. Well, he has emotions; I can't deny him that. But, in the stories at least, he doesn't feel things like man does, he is a 'god' after all. And so man, being different, is difficult to understand and thus easy to criticize and demonize, as you see with Vashir."

Cael and Wynn nod sagely as they grasp bits and pieces of what Jean tells them.

"Vashir wasn't bad, then?" Cael asks.

"It depends on who you ask, but I don't see him that way." Jean shrugs.

"Well, what are our chances then if not even Finra could overcome the differences that he himself created?!" Wynn shouts, throwing her hands in the air exasperated.

Jean laughs. "I told you it's going to be hard for you both! But there's hope still, I think." He leans forward. "Take Fred for example. He might not have reacted so harshly if we *hadn't* been traveling for so long together. He trusted you both just as you trusted him. When it was shown that you were not who he thought you were, he felt betrayed." He raises his hands in a calming gesture, "Now, his betrayal was without a doubt much worse, but it was coming from a place of anger. Your betrayal was coming from a place of fear."

"So we're just supposed to tell everyone we meet that we can do these things and let them decide there and then if they want us dead?" Cael says sarcastically.

"No, of course not!" Jean waves his hands, "But perhaps when a friendship starts to build it would be a good idea to give a hint of at least *something* of what you can do. There are those living out in the world who openly show their abilities. They are ostracized, that means they aren't really accepted, but they still are out there openly and aren't getting killed or having mobs beat down their doors," He replies easily.

Cael thinks a moment. "Like the Draisek in Rensfort."

Wynn adds, "Or even just the traveling fortune tellers. They're out there openly. We could show a little of our gifts to people, that way they know at least we're different."

Jean nods. "Exactly, my children, exactly."

"Why didn't the academy guys just think of letting everyone know a little bit about us?" Cael wonders out loud.

"Right, about that group there, you said you're being taken, correct?" Jean asks and they nod. "Well, what about those folk in the woods? There was a few of them that could do what you did. If all of you kids are taken, how is it there are some out there running around in the woods?"

"We all get taken I suppose. But some get taken by seekers from this academy and others get taken by the Sephalim group that attacked us." Cael says.

"What's the difference?" Jean asks, interested.

They shrug. "Well we know one kills people. That's how my family died." Wynn says

"But Landon did say the seekers hurt people too." Cael adds.

"Well, if there was another group that didn't make you go, would you join them instead?" Jean asks.

Wynn opens her mouth to agree right away but Cael stops her.

'They'd find us.' He reminds her.

She sighs. "He's right, they'd just find us. I was on the run for such a long time and they still kept following me. I don't know how those people haven't been found yet, but I'd bet there's seekers looking for them right now."

"You're likely right. If there are folks that can track magic and such, they'll be caught pretty easily what with all the magic being used there. And I can understand the need for secrecy. You folk are just a new kind of different, and your kind of different is certainly cause for secrets," Jean says.

They sit by the fire warming themselves, all floating through their own thoughts. Cael stares at Jean, calmly sipping his whiskey. "Why are you different than everyone else? Why did you accept us so easily when Fred and Byron didn't?"

"Well, firstly, Byron likely would have accepted you. He doesn't think too hard on differences, so long as you're friendly to him, he'll be friendly to you. As for me, well, I don't much care about differences either. I suppose now I really prefer people that are different. They're less inclined to prejudices, more rational, they are usually better folks all around." He looks up to the sky. "Years ago I was in a village. There was a fierce drought and all the crops had died. A young woman had just moved up from Waylinn. She had been of the mining families but wanted a different life. The Wylaen people are dark as trees, but their miners are pale as ghosts. Those miners tattoo themselves with fungi that grows down in their caves. It feeds off the metal found inside Pelhara, and it actually lights up. I'm not quite sure how it works, but it feeds off the Wylaen people and continues to glow. Something to do with the metals in their bodies. Part of the reason they're so sturdy I'd guess. Anyway, the folks in a nearby town thought this woman was a witch on account of her glowing tattoos. Of course, right? What other explanation could there be. And as luck would have it, the drought happened on the first year she arrived. Worst drought in memory, too. So, the folks mobbed together from a neighboring town, marched on her farm and killed her and her family, burned their whole village to the ground. All because she was different. They didn't care to learn about her. She didn't even have powers like you two do. She just looked different. Every single miner in Waylinn has these tattoos, every one of them. But they didn't care to ask Lenore anything. They didn't even say a word to her before they threw their torches...."

Jean goes silent for a long while before he lifts his head to Cael and Wynn staring at him expectantly. "Well, that's enough stories for today. We all feeling better?"

"I think you've got a lot more to say." Wynn encourages Jean but he shakes his head.

"Perhaps... But not today!" He smirks. "Let's get on our way."

Chapter Forty-Five

They break camp and return to their journey, feeling revitalized and light. The burden of forced silenced now lifted, they are free to enjoy the comfortable silences between friends, almost as if Fredrick and Byron were still with them.

Days pass easier, and soon they're all out hunting again, supplementing their dwindling food supply with much needed fresh meat and any vegetables they scavenge on their forays into the woods.

They're awoken early one morning with the first snowfall of the season. They gaze at the peaceful scene and Jean joins in on the moment. "It's beautiful."

They sit, lost in the falling flakes.

"I've been trying to think of some way to pass the time so that traveling isn't so dull. Is heating the only thing you can do with your gifts or can you do more?" he asks.

"Besides the mind stuff, heating things is pretty much it. Cael's been trying to do more, but our connection doesn't really work like I thought it would for learning," Wynn says.

"Yea, I think that has something to do with Alek and Julia helping to split us. But I've been working on the cooling side of things. It's a lot easier than heating actually, at least for me," Cael explains.

"Why don't we play a game with your gifts? You and Wynn can try and clear the road of snow ahead of us. The one who clears out the furthest will win," Jean suggests.

"What do we win?" Cael asks excitedly, realizing he has the upper hand in this game.

"A good feeling?" Jean says with a smirk. "We don't have much left as a reward. How about a point system? At the end of our trip, the one of you with the most points can have my favorite dagger." He pulls out his ornate dagger. The pure white handle and blackened blade appear shiny and new but there are scars in the working that seem older than time. A blade he's carried with him since before the fall of our home.

They reach for the dagger, in awe of their potential prize. Jean puts it away smoothly into its sheathe before they touch it.

They quickly nod their heads. "Deal!"

"This first game is simple. You just need to clear your half of the road of any snow. The one who can clear the furthest out by the end of the day wins. Easy, right?" Jean instructs.

They look at him dumbly.

"We can't do that yet." Cael says.

"We can only alter things that we touch, so unless you want us to see who can stretch out the furthest on the ground, I don't think this game is gonna work," Wynn adds.

"Well, I suppose it's time for you both to try harder then, isn't it?" Jean smirks at them and begins walking along. He stops a moment., "Excuse me, children, there appears to be snow beneath my boot. I'm sure it's a small mistake on your part, but please don't let it happen again. If it helps, I'll let you lead for the first half of the day and I'll lead the latter half," Jean says, waving his arm out in front of him, allowing them to pass.

They huff but are quietly excited to begin practicing again. It has been weeks since they've even spoken and time beyond remembering since they've been able to practice openly.

As expected, the day moves quite slowly. Both Cael and Wynn start out able to heat their hands only. As the day drags on they become frustrated with their lack of progress, and also being bent over like a mule with their hands in the snow. Out of that frustration, Cael makes a connection and Wynn follows his lead. He notices an infinite amount of tiny pricks along his body and realizes he's only been focusing on the heat in his hand, not the heat all around him. Using his hand, he directs the vibration outward, agitating the air enough to almost see it begin to heat. Finally able to walk upright and still melting the snow, he sprints ahead clearing the road with a wide smile plastered on his face.

Wynn, elated for Cael, frowns at her own progress. Avoiding a disconnect she returns her focus to the task. Still unable to find the muscles to create the pulses that Cael does with ease, she joins Cael within himself. Feeling the movements he makes and mimicking them. For a moment, Cael doesn't realize she's helping and the heat reaches meters out in front of him like a blast of hot air. He laughs in shock, but then feels Wynn's thoughts and movements along his own. "Hey, that's not fair! You can't cheat like that!"

Wynn stops focusing on Cael and copies what she felt and is relieved to see progress of her own. It's difficult and her muscles tire quickly, but she's able to stand and heat the air along the road.

They break for lunch midway through the day and enjoy a much-deserved rest for their aching muscles. Sticking to his earlier plan, Jean takes the lead after lunch and both Cael and Wynn struggle to heat just past his feet but are able to maintain the distance.

They spot their first traveler in days on the horizon and quickly stop practicing, hiding their hands behind their backs in guilt.

Jean looks at them confused. "Why are you stopping? My feet must not get wet!" He jokes.

Cael points at the group of travelers, who appear to be merchants, heading their way. "There's people coming, shouldn't we stop?"

"Nonsense!" Jean says indignantly and pushes forward. Wynn swiftly melts the snow beneath his foot before it hits the ground and they continue walking forward.

As the travelers pass they slow down. "Good travels?" They call out.

Jean responds, "The finest! Safe roads from here to there."

They stare at the ground behind him seeing the brown dirt highlighted by the pure white snow on either side, "How?" One of them starts to ask but Jean follows their gaze and shrugs. "We run hot I suppose! Safe journey friends!"

They pass on, rubbing their heads, confused.

Cael and Wynn laugh, lost for words and amazed that they didn't think anything of it.

Jean turns to them "All you need to do is act like it's normal. Confidence! Be sure of yourselves and everyone around you will just assume nothing is wrong. Even if it's something completely unexplainable, they'll only assume it's a normal thing they've never seen before." He shrugs. "Sure, when they tell people that some folk melted the snow off the road others will think them insane, but that's not really our problem, is it?" He smiles devilishly.

They continue playing their game and by the end of the day Cael manages to maintain his lead over Wynn, extending out an impressive four meters while Wynn struggles to reach just under three. Even losing, Wynn is happy with her progress and proud of her growth.

"Tomorrow we'll do something different," Jean says as they stop for camp. "But now that you two can easily heat things, making camp should be a lot easier."

They are met with a new game the next day. Jean, recognizing that Cael excels with the physical alteration while Wynn excels with her mental abilities, decides to change the layout of the challenge so that they succeed evenly.

As they break camp in the morning, Jean gives them their instructions. "Today, you will be trying to trick me as Wynn did during your story. Which by the way, was very well done. Had it not been for the uninvited guests I would easily give you the win on scary stories." He grins. "But that's neither here nor there. We must focus! You'll be attempting to show me something that is not real, but I must believe that it is real. I'll suggest animals as we see them frequently. I'll call out whether I believe what I'm seeing is real or not and you'll both tell me if it was indeed you or reality. Deal?"

They agree and set about their new game.

Mental exercises remain difficult for Cael, but the concept is easy to grasp. Imagining something in their minds, they only need to feel Jean with them. The clearer they can imagine the object, the clearer Jean sees them. The trouble lies with recognizing Jean's thoughts and focusing on them. Wynn, already practiced, begins right away. While she's able to show Jean these images, the animals act unnaturally or are completely still, like true painted images. He easily dismisses them as fakes.

Wynn becomes frustrated and tries to imagine animals being overly animated, but the reality doesn't translate. Her squirrels float too long, or her rabbits don't move as they hop. Cael, still struggling to even find Jean's thoughts while they move, gets frustrated.

"This is ridiculous! I need to sit down or something. I can't concentrate on moving and the mind clearing thing!" He complains loudly.

Wynn feels his frustration and puts the game aside as she teaches him instead. With her skill advancing quickly, it's not difficult for her to join Cael while moving and instruct him. *'We can talk in our heads easily, but we haven't had to imagine others since the ship really, so it's easy to forget how. You just need to feel the thoughts. They're there; you only have to find them. It's like a wave, almost like a tickle every so often, but it's consistent. We know Jean, you only have to listen for him.'*

Cael tries but fails. *'I don't even understand what you're trying to say. How do I listen for him?'* He asks.

Wynn thinks on it. *'Pretend you can hear him. That's what I did at first, but soon even when I thought I was only pretending, it was actually working. It won't feel real, because it's just so weird to think about. But it is real, that's the crazy part!'*

Cael tries again, sarcastically pretending to hear Jean. He imagines a rabbit hopping near Jean and hears Jean call out, "Fake."

He stops and stares at Wynn who has a smile ear to ear staring back at him, "You did it!" She cries out and he hugs her, "I did it! Thank you! Moons above I did it! How in the world did that work?!" He asks excitedly and Wynn shrugs, "No idea, but it works!"

"Ah, so Cael has finally joined our game?" Jean calls back to them, "Congratulations, kid, now you both need to work on the realism."

They nod and set their minds to work as they walk. Wynn watches the world around her trying to capture the movements of the animals in her mind and soon she's done it. She pictures a squirrel jumping from the trees and hears the increasingly rare "Real" from Jean. She calls back for the first time, "That squirrel was me!" She points to it as she lets the image fall and it disappears.

"Good. Go again. Another animal this time." Jean instructs.

Cael follows Wynn's earlier mistakes, although the animals in his mind are more realistic, they don't react the way they should at seeing humans and Jean spots them immediately. "Cael, your animals are like in a dream. They're real, but they don't see us. You need them to see us."

The day progresses along with their skill. Soon Cael and Wynn have both moved on from squirrel and small birds to rabbits and turkey. As the sun sets Wynn manages to get a deer to react correctly and Jean congratulates her. Cael struggles to imagine the grass and brush moving with the deer as it flees into the woods and so Wynn prevails. "One to one!" She says smiling but exhausted.

They sleep dreamlessly and wake up feeling groggy with pounding headaches. The stress of the day before taking its toll on their minds. Jean sees this and allows for a day without games to rest.

They fall into a happy routine playing their games. Heating and cooling objects at various distances and imagining people or animals, even moving to placing small intricate objects in Jean's open hand. They have difficulty fully tricking his mind into feeling weight, but the image itself gets better over time. The games continue and they take wins evenly between them. After a week of games Jean begins acting distant. Still encouraging them but not as interested in playing, and slow to smile or laugh. A much different person than they had become used to recently.

They stop for the day and rather than play his telbir as he had been, he sits alone in thought. They set camp and cook some of the fresh game they caught that morning and try to give Jean his space, unsure if he's simply feeling ill or getting bored of the games, or something else.

As they bed down, Jean sits alone, thinking. They wonder about what but decide against invading his privacy and instead agree to talk to him in the morning. He is changing, remembering more of himself. Who he used to be.

When morning arrives, Jean, still awake or never having slept, looks to them as they open their eyes. "I wanted to ask you both a favor." He says anxiously, "I think… I'd like to go see someone."

Chapter Forty-Six

They veer off the main path down what appears like a game trail, but slightly larger. Perhaps it used to be a road but grass and weeds have retaken most of what was. The day feels different. Without their games time takes longer to pass. Jean is quiet, reserved, and determined to move on quickly. They don't stop for lunch as Jean presses on in an apparent trance by this new mission. Cael and Wynn become anxious. Unsure of where they are going or what's to come, their imaginations run wild with all manner of inane possibilities.

The sun begins to set as they reach an open field and a grassy road. A village comes into view in the distance and Jean sets their path directly toward it. As they grow closer, the village seems to deteriorate before their eyes. No longer a village. Perhaps it was years ago, maybe even decades ago, but no soul lives here now. It's burnt fully and only charred corpses of buildings remain. Plants have begun to grow within the hollow structures and vines wrap themselves up the blackened beams creating an eerie sight in the dimming light.

Jean pushes on quickly through the ruins of the village. Directing them to a field off to the east, just behind a fallen home. There they find a makeshift graveyard filled with hundreds of graves. None of the typical stonework or fencing surround it, just sticks marking each grave in the traditional tree shape. All except two graves are marked with shaped sticks, and these are covered in stones with patterns carved in them. Jean kneels down by these graves and bows his head for a long while.

As the sun sets fully, the moons peek out on the horizon lighting the stones in silver. Jean begins speaking. He talks to the graves as if their residents were still alive. He apologizes for being away for so long and spins tales of his journeys through the world, the battles he's fought and how he's missed them terribly. Cael and Wynn let him pay his respects in peace. Walking to the far edge of the burnt village, they decide not to make a fire here and instead wait patiently in the moonlit fields.

After a time, Cael and Wynn return to Jean. He sits silent and still by the stones, staring at them. Cael places his hand on Jean's shoulder and he startles, stunned that anyone else is here with him. He shakes his head, clearing it of the distant memories.

"I'm sorry. I lost myself for a moment. Are you ready to move on?" he asks quietly as he stands up, shaking his legs free of the numbness. He steps toward the center of the town, but Cael and Wynn walk toward the graves and pray silently for the fallen. Promising to watch over Jean as long as they can.

"Thank you," Jean says, tears threatening to fall. He rubs their heads and turns away, leading them down the road not wanting to disturb the dead any more than they need to.

They set camp a short walk away. Cael starts the fire and Jean begins speaking as the flames grow, "Years ago, I was a traveler. I was searching for something, anything, to believe in. I was lost. I traveled longer than even I can recall and further than most. That whole journey is faded in my memory. The first full moment I can recall is seeing her. I was in Waylinn when I woke from my daze. I saw the love that all had for her, and the love she had for all of them. She helped everyone so easily, and without care for the burden it placed upon her. I was a shell and didn't know what to say or how to act but it didn't matter. She saw the person inside of me, the man I wanted to be, not the lost soul that had spent eternity searching. She loved me for it. She gave me new meaning, a purpose to live. She wanted to travel as I had and so we did. I took her everywhere I had been, and we loved every moment of it. From Alisterra to the Desert Bair, over the Broken Mountains and far beyond. We wandered from Kaldia to Oarna to Alundra and the depths below. She smiled every day, and it breaks my heart to remember that smile."

Jean takes a moment to steady his voice. "She became pregnant. Neither of us knew so much joy as when our daughter was born. Lenore wanted me to name her, but I could only think of a name from another life. Jestine. And she was perfect. Her hands and feet were perfect. Her nose and eyes and her funny little ears. Her cheeks and mouth and stubby chin. She was beautiful. Lenore wanted a place to call home, a place to raise our child. And we found a small village. It wasn't perfect, but everyone there was loving and caring. They had all wanted a place for a second chance, and we couldn't think of a better community to settle. But Lenore was different. Her differences meant nothing to the people close to us, but it was more than enough to cause others to hate."

"When they came to burn down our home, I was farming in the fields. By the time I had made it back, it was too late. Our entire village protected them, shielding my family from the attacks with their lives. Nearly all died trying to save them. I threw myself at the mob and went mad with fury. I struck them all down. When I opened my eyes, only a few from my village remained. But my child and wife were lost. We dug graves for many days and when we were finished, we all went our separate ways without so much as a goodbye. I regret that even still. Yet as broken as I am today, I was lost to everything back then. Without my love, I had no purpose and so I wandered. I walked until I found someone had put a sword in my hand. When I finally looked up I found myself in the middle of a battlefield. I moved on and when I looked behind me I found a few stragglers had decided to follow. Fredrick and Byron have been with me since then. I walked on and their laughter guided me; their love helped me come alive. We chose to be mercenaries to help, but I never wanted this life. I was scared to think about any life without my family and so I chose not to think." He wipes his eyes, "But it took travelling with you two for me to actually remember my family. It was hard, and I took it out on you both. For that I am truly sorry, but I needed to walk this path. I needed to remember them, to speak with them."

Cael and Wynn feel Jean's emotion and they are struck by it. Tears fall freely down their faces and patter along the dirt. Jean hugs them and they sit in silence by the fire.

"What will you do now?" Wynn asks, staring at the ground.

"What do you mean? I still have a job to do, don't I? You both need to get to Oarna. We've still got hard traveling ahead." Jean says.

"You never wanted this life, you just said it. Will you continue wandering alone or will you settle down? Try and find a way to live again, to be happy again?" Cael presses him.

A long silence passes. "I'm not sure. Seeing our village, it's hard, but I think it helps. It reminds me of the happiness I had with them. They'd want me to be happy. Lenore always wanted everyone to be happy."

"Will you live in Oarna? That's where you're from isn't it?" Cael asks.

"Oarna wasn't always my home but maybe... I don't know." Jean replies, thinking. "Being with you both... it has me thinking of a time long ago. A time I have chosen to forget. Perhaps I'll travel a bit more. Or perhaps I'll rebuild our home. Then our village after that. I could build a place where any who desires peace need only trade peace in turn. A place that will honor the memory of those who lost their lives protecting the ones I loved. A place where Lenore and Jestine would have been proud to live."

"Perhaps one day you'll find happiness yourself here," Wynn says. "And maybe you'll find love again."

Jean grins. "Slow down there, young lady. I'm not a man who's ready for a family right now." He sighs. "But I think one day, years from now perhaps, I could try to be a man that *might* be ready again."

"You'd make a wonderful father," Wynn says as they lay down to sleep.

Chapter Forty-Seven

Rested and renewed with the morning sun, they set off back to the king's road. "So what is this academy like?" Jean asks, pushing his way through the overgrown trail.

"We have no idea. Landon's told us a bit, but we haven't asked about it," Cael says.

"Well, what do you hope it's like? Are you excited to finally be done traveling? Oarna is just south of here. I imagine we'll be there in a few days. Certainly before the week is out," Jean says.

"Really? That soon?" Wynn asks, suddenly saddened.

"True, that soon," Jean says evenly. "Well, what of this academy then? What do you hope you'll find there?"

"I think we're both just really hoping to find a way to get out," Cael says, "We're hoping to learn as much as we can and then to leave as soon as they allow it."

"How long must you stay?" Jean asks curiously.

"I think Landon said it's kind of a permanent thing. But he said a few people get to travel outside, and some even get to visit their families," Cael replies excitedly.

"Permanent? So you'll be with these people forever?" Jean presses.

"That's what we were told," Wynn says. "And Landon said it was more strict, kind of like some military thing, so it's not like a university where we'll get to learn everything. It'll probably be really awful, very scheduled, marching around and stuff."

"That does sound pretty awful, but I would assume they'd teach you all manner of things so you'll get some education, right?" Jean says.

"Well yea," Cael says, running his fingers through his hair. "Landon said we'd likely learn everything we would at university. They even allow us to choose the position we'd like to be in."

"And they'll be more kids like you, right?" Jean adds.

"Yup," Wynn replies.

"So, you could make friends, have fun and all the regular kid stuff, just at a military academy rather than university. Right?" Jean says, clearly trying to make it sound better.

"Well yes, I suppose." Cael shrugs. "I mean, we've gone back and forth between sort of excited and really dreading it. But the middle of that line isn't a happy place. Mostly we just put it out of our minds."

Wynn nods. "We're still alive and if this place isn't pure evil, then I suppose we'll be able to take something good from it. An education and control over our abilities."

"Can other people do other things or is what you guys do about it?" Jean slows down as he reaches the main road and they stretch for a moment welcoming the suns warm rays.

"Landon said we could do both things, so I think we could do about everything." Cael says and Wynn adds, "But we can't do really anything yet. Remember when Landon showed us his memories? That was amazing. He told us there's so much we can do."

Jean chuckles as he continues on down the road. "Sounds like you're getting excited again. What kind of things can you learn to do?"

"Landon said we can make people do what we want, and we can take their memories or give them other ones. And we can take their senses or make their senses work for us, kind of like when we show you things but way more," Wynn rattles off.

Cael jumps in. "And we can alter things, like their state or something. He said that ice and water are different states and everything can be altered like that. He stuck his hand through stone! I bet we could do a bunch of stuff with that."

Jean looks at them impressed. "That's all wild to me, but after what I've seen you both already do with no training, it sounds attainable. So, after you learn how to take over the world, what will you do?"

"We choose a position and then we work for them I suppose. Like an advisor or researcher or seeker or anything really, but we'd have to be working for them," Wynn says simply.

Jean shakes his head. "No I mean after all of that. Have you thought about a family or anything?"

"We can't see our family unless we get a position that travels a bunch like Landon's. But for most people they'd never see their families again because of the memories being taken or..." Cael stops.

Wynn finishes, "Or their parents being killed."

Jean shakes his head again. "I get that part. I mean your own family. What of love? Marriage and a home, children, and friends. You know, lives of your own. You find someone to love," he says, pointing to Cael. "And you find someone to love," he says, pointing to Wynn. "And you settle down happily ever after and such."

They blush.

"That's not something we've ever really thought about. Not recently anyway," Wynn says.

"Before all of this, I thought my life was already planned. I was probably going to marry Laena and be a smith like my father. Live close enough to my family to visit and see my brother and his family. My horse Clout would live with us and grow old. But now, it's... I suppose I think about the future as me getting back home so everything can go back to normal," Cael says grabbing Wynn's shoulder. "With Wynn of course."

She rolls her eyes. "I'll just be a spinster in your spare room then?"

Cael shrugs. "Well no, the spare room is for Clout. You'd have to live in the barn." He laughs and she swats him. "Oh, I'm joking and you know it. We're going to be together forever and that's the truth."

Jean smiles fondly at their immaturity. "It's easy to forget how young you two are. Especially after a journey such as ours.... You really should never have had to go through these things. You more than anyone, Wynn. Losing your family and being alone for so long, even before all of this?" He sighs. "That's a life no one should have to bear. But you've found a companion in Cael and a friend in me. Love will come to you easily, and you'll be turning away men like a princess turning down suitors."

"What about me!" Cael says.

Jean laughs. "Oh, you'll be fine growing old with Clout while Wynn lets you both sleep in the barn."

Wynn joins in laughing and they wander down the road as it turns southerly.

They crest a hill and notice the ground still green with grass. From their vantage point, they can see nothing but rolling hills and a winding path down to lush fields, still colorful despite being so late in the season. Jean points beyond another hill. "Just over that hill is Oarna. From the border, we're only a few days to Rosé."

The days pass too quickly as they try desperately to enjoy the final moments of their long trek across North Liefland. Remembering all the things they've seen and done, but in spite of their best efforts they can't stretch the final days any further. Before any of them are ready, they cross into Rosé. Fields of recently picked vines line the road to the city. A surprisingly warm sea breeze greets them as they walk amongst wildflowers still in bloom.

They marvel at the beauty and the warmth. Both are so used to harsher winters further north and west, that the warm reprieve is welcome.

"Why don't we go grab something to eat? I can show you Rosé and we can enjoy the time until your friend arrives?" Jean asks and they quickly agree as they pick up the pace towards Rosé.

As they enter the city, a familiar voice calls to them, "Finally made it, eh?"

Chapter Forty-Eight

They whip around to find Landon sitting at a café just inside the city walls. Cael runs over to him and Wynn follows after.

"It's been a long while, hasn't' it? Look at you both, you look so different already!" he says, holding them at arm's length to get a good view.

Cael looks at his face and sees a fresh scar along his jaw. "We're not the only ones who've changed. What in the world happened there?"

Landon brushes it off. "Oh that's a story for another day." He turns to Jean. "You must be one of their guards. Thank you very much for caring after them on their journey." He reaches out his open hand and Jean grasps it firmly.

"It was no trouble at all," Jean says, moving back slightly. "Well, I suppose I'll be on my way."

Wynn grabs Jeans shoulder. "No! You can't leave yet! We only just got here and you were supposed to show us around! Please stay? We can finally relax at the end of our journey. We deserve a good rest anyway, and a nice hot meal!"

Cael nods in agreement. "There's no way you're leaving yet!"

"I guess that's settled. There's just no other option but to stay. How about it?" Landon asks.

Jean sighs but lets a smile peek out. "Alright, you talked me into it. There's a great place down by the water. It might be a little late in the season for us to be near the ocean, but it's my favorite place in Rosé."

They follow Jean through the gorgeous city of Rosé and take in the sights. The white buildings are spaced perfectly along the straight and smooth roads that create a stunning pattern. There are flowers and gardens everywhere, contrasting beautifully with the white structures all around. Trees dot each cross street and large spaces are reserved in the center of the city for manicured grass and fruit trees. People meander through small walking paths or sit on benches, it's as if the whole city is on its own time schedule.

"It's beautiful," Wynn says. "I would have never guessed that just a day ago we were sloshing through wet snow with cold winds whipping by."

"Rosé is in a unique spot. The warm waters off the coast keep chilled air away at least for a while longer. It's also surrounded by hills and mountains. We didn't really notice too much but for the past few months, we've been steadily rising with the land. The higher up we went, the colder it got. It's not winter quite yet, but it sure felt like it up there." Jean says.

"Going from winter snow to a seemingly beautiful spring day is what Rosé is known for." Landon adds, "It's such a rare place that people come to visit from all over. It's one of the few places on this continent that offers such an experience. Another is the Broken Mountains in Waylinn."

They marvel at the beauty of the city and watch as performers act out a play in one of the open gardens. Music filters through from all around, but unlike other cities it all works to come together in a larger rhythm. Almost as if from anywhere in Rosé you could hear the same music.

"Ah, here we are!" Jean says as they come up on a small building separated from the rest. Benches and tables overlook a warm sandy beach. "Madeline's café, it's just as I remember. The bourguignon is stupendous!"

Jean leads them to a small table in between lovely flowering trees and a woman comes up with a smile, "Fierce Jean! You have returned to me!" She plants a kiss on each cheek and

Jean stands up to embrace her, "Madeline! These are my companions, Cael, Wynn and their good friend Landon."

Madeline kisses each of them as they are introduced and holds Landon at arm's length. "Ah, a handsome man!" Landon blushes and Jean pats him on the back. "Fear not, my friend. She does not bite."

Madeline swats at him. "Oh, Jean, you are terrible!" She gasps in delight. "I just made some of your favorite beef bourguignon! I will get the wine and bread!"

She quickly returns and sits alongside them, "Celia! I have guests, thank you!" She calls to a young lady bustling around who barely acknowledges her other than a slightly indignant huff.

"Jean, you are so different? How did this happen? You are… not so fache, you are happy?" She asks.

Jean laughs and Cael smiles at Madeline. "We've fixed him, quite a job to be honest." He says and Madeline laughs along with Jean.

The wine comes out and shortly after taking a drink, the warmth of it rushes to their faces and they become bubbly. They talk of nothing and everything. The food comes and even the delicious beef bourguignon can't stop them from talking and joking.

After spending the better part of the day in their company, Madeline stands up and places a hand on Jean to steady herself. "Oh, the day has forgotten us! I must get back to helping Celia." Just then Celia walks by and snorts loudly. Madeline shoots her a glare. "I'll bring over some caffe to help you settle." She says turning her friendly eyes back on the group.

They allow a warm moment of silence as they lose themselves in the beautiful sights all around. The sun setting beyond the mountains and the moons cresting over the water. Madeline returns with small cups of coffee and a kiss on the head for each of them. She waves farewell as she returns to her duties.

"So how was your journey?" Landon asks after a while. "Oh, and where are the other guards? Are they already returning?"

Jeans expression changes for a moment to sadness. "That is quite a long story."

They regale Landon with their journey from start to end and he becomes furious upon learning that the king hired mercenaries to escort them rather than his own personal guards. As the story goes on, Landon's face goes from anger to happy at the stories of Wynn's hunt and the fun they had on their journey to an instant of shock at learning Jean's knowledge of their skill. He listens intently, asking few questions, and paying close attention to Jean the entire time. They leave out mention of Jean's village, almost without thinking as the personal nature seems outside the scope of their journey.

"I cannot express my gratitude thoroughly enough, my friend," Landon says to Jean. "You've not only kept them safe; you've done the last stretch alone. I never would have imagined them being attacked like you say, and I cannot even begin to fathom how you all overcame those odds. I am grateful and indebted. How can I ever repay you?"

Jean pats Landon's shoulder. "These two did as much for me as I did for them. Perhaps more so. If you wish to repay me, take good care of them and maybe bring them for a visit once they finish their training." His eyes rest on Landon's jaw. "Ah, the new scar! How came you by that, friend?"

Landon rubs his fingers along the new addition to his face, "Oh, this … That, my friend, is a story for another time." He gazes out at the stars. "I almost don't want this night to end, but I must get them to the docks early. We set sail for the isle tomorrow."

Jean waves his hands. "Say no more. There's an inn not a stone's throw from where we sit. This late in the season they're bound to have rooms."

They walk along the roads breathing in the seasonably warm night air and listening to the waves crash along the shore. Completely at ease and still toasty from the wine, they all wish to continue the night, but the moons are high and night will not last forever. Jean walks into an inconspicuous building, more a home than an inn. A rowdy crowd is playing games in the adjoining room. A burly man walks over with a smile.

"How many rooms?" he asks.

"Two should be fine. Do you mind sharing with me?" Landon looks to Jean.

He shakes his head. "Of course not!"

They navigate the winding stairs to their rooms and

collapse into their beds. Before even the softness of the pillows meet their face, they are whisked away to warm and happy dreams.

Chapter Forty-Nine

Morning comes and with it a bright sun and warm breeze over the ocean.

"Oh man, my legs feel broken…." Cael mumbles as he gets to his feet and stumbles about his morning routine.

Wynn sits up, eyes still closed, "Mine too…" She falls face first back into the pillow. "I just need to sleep more. Please let me go back to bed, I'm tired."

Cael walks back into the room stretching his legs. "Come on, it's morning already. Time to wake up." He starts to shake her and she jumps up feeling a sudden urge to pee.

"Wow, I've never seen a room like this before. It's so clean!" Wynn calls from the washroom.

"Hurry up, come look at this." Cael says, staring at a beautiful knife placed on a nightstand in between both of them.

"Is that the dagger Jean was going to give to the winner?" Wynn asks stumbling back into the room. She takes it in her hands and examines it.

"Yup, I guess we tied," he replies. Wynn hands it to him and he investigates the grooves and craftsmanship. "It's sharp." He says, running his finger lightly along the blade. "It's seems old, too. Really old. I don't think I've ever seen anything like it but it reminds me of something… It's so familiar."

"Yea." Wynn says watching the light bounce off the dagger, "There's something different about this..." She stands up. "We should ask him about it. It's clearly important to him."

She leads them out the door and down the hallway to Jean and Landon's room. They find the room empty and shrug as they head down to the bar area.

They spot Landon speaking with the owner and paying for the rooms.

"Hey, where's Jean?" Cael calls out.

Landon holds up his hand while he finishes his conversation and turns to greet them.

"Wow, what happened to you?" Wynn says, seeing a large bruise across half of his face.

"I fell out of bed this morning and smashed my head on the ground. Your friend Jean woke early and startled me near to death before he took off!" Landon rubs his face as he talks.

Cael and Wynn stare stunned, shocked to hear their friend of so long would leave without saying a word.

"But why so sudden? Why not say goodbye? Why give us this gift and leave?" Cael asks, confused.

"It doesn't matter. He's gone and we've got to get a ship," Landon says abruptly as he leads them out the door.

"Jean traveled with us for months, longer than we traveled with you even. He wouldn't have just left like that. I know he wouldn't have," Wynn says becoming irritated at Landon's dismissal.

"She's right, Landon. Did Jean say anything to you before he left? Like why he was leaving or... anything?" Cael adds.

Landon shrugs. "Something about a knife." He looks to Wynn and spots the dagger on her hip, "Which it looks like you've found, so everything is settled." Stopping suddenly, Landon takes a deep breath. "I'm sorry that your friend left. Truly I am. But we need to get safe passage out of here. Oarna is probably one of the safest places, but that doesn't mean it's safe. Hearing what happened to you on the king's road made me really nervous. We're so close to the end of this journey and the start of your training. We should be excited! The start of something so much bigger than you can even imagine is so close." He grabs them by the arms and offers a big toothy smile. "So let's go!"

"It doesn't feel right. Jean isn't like that!" Wynn yells in frustration.

"You're hiding something. We know Jean, he wouldn't just leave." Cael adds.

"This same Jean who was prepared to leave moments after you arrived in the city? It was all your pleading that encouraged him to stay in the first place. I know it might feel wrong, but he said he didn't want to do all the sad farewells. He went to give you both some kind of gift and then he left without another word. He did seem upset if that helps." Landon explains.

"Fine, I suppose." Cael mutters. "But it still doesn't seem like him."

They sigh and try and push Jean out of their minds as Landon speedily navigates through Rosé. Keeping the coast close, he spots the docks and makes his way to a small building.

"Is the Isle transport in?" Landon calls to a large man with a long black beard sitting inside the small building, making him appear even larger in his tiny window. "No. She left a few days ago."

"Well, we need to get these kids to the Isle. Are there any ships that can make the voyage left in port?" Landon says, getting impatient.

The harbormaster smirks at him. "No."

Landon throws his arms up in the air. "Well, what do we do now?"

The large man turns back to his papers. "You could swim."

Landon suppresses the urge to hit the man, but instead grits his teeth. "Where is Piers?"

"It is not my business to keep track of where the prince is," the man says without looking up.

"Well then what is your business!?" Landon shouts.

The large man calmly steps out of his tiny hut and stands at his full height. The change is so sudden that they all move back. "My business," he says stretching out, "is these ships here. It would seem your business is elsewhere."

Landon looks for a moment as if he would move on the man but thinks better of it, instead stomping off back towards the center of the city.

"Apologies, sir." Cael says to the man.

"We're in a bit of a rush, don't mind him," Wynn adds before turning to follow Landon.

The large man calls after them, "Try the City Stage, near the Loaf and Ladle. He's usually around there."

"Thank you!" They call back with a wave.

As they catch up to Landon, he quickly snaps, "I heard him, the ass. Why couldn't he just tell me that himself when I asked?"

"Well, with an attitude like that it's no wonder," Wynn snaps back. "You've been acting awfully weird. First Jean disappears and you have this suspicious bruise and now you're getting all angry at random people?"

Landon whips around ready to yell and sees Cael and Wynn shirk away. He drops his head and takes a deep breath. "I'm sorry, you two. I promise I'll tell you what's going on as soon as we're safe." He scans the city looking for a landmark. "As soon as we can get a damned ship out of here." The scent of flowers and fresh bread lead them to a garden, just beside is a sign that reads 'The Loaf and Ladle.' "Ah, there it is. Come on, let's hope Prince Piers is somewhere around here."

They follow the cheers and listen as a storyteller spins a tale over the noise of the crowd. Turning a corner, a stage comes into view centered in a garden and a small group of marketgoers take a brief moment to enjoy the show before going on about their days.

"She had nothing of value left, but she offered the one thing we always carry with us. Her love. And Leonidar gave her his love in turn, and so they lived on happily. When Princess Faer'dre was granted the crown of her people, they also granted Leonidar a crown for the love he had for their new queen. They ruled alongside their subjects, not over them. Everyone was heard and everyone was free to live and love," the storyteller narrates the tale as his actors play it out upon the stage. "The peace that King Leonidar had fought for was long lasting until one day, he mysteriously disappeared. But that is a tale for another time. Good morning Rosé!" A smattering of applause ripple through the gardens.

"I've never been one for these fairy tale plays, I prefer the real accounts," Landon says to them without thinking as he searches the crowds bustling around the market square. He spots a large group of well-dressed individuals. "If he were anywhere, I'd bet the house I don't have that it'd be in the center of that crowd."

"Oh, you embarrass me, Jacques! It was not like that at all, I swear by it!"

The crowd laughs and a beautiful young man with dark hair and features, rather shorter than the rest but impeccably well dressed, calls out, "Landon, my good friend. Come here my dear, you absolutely must tell of the time you helped save my father!" He grabs Landon's arm and without word or question puts him on display for all the group to see.

"He's not much to look at," one woman says examining his clothes closely.

"Saved your father? The king, truly?" Another calls in surprise.

"Unbelievable! You must tell us," a man cries out.

The overly perfumed crowd circles around them and begins poking and prodding at Landon. He masks his irritation and wriggles away from the grabbing hands. "Yes, well, perhaps another time. Your Highness there is an urgent matter with which I desperately require your help."

Piers laughs smoothly. "Ah, such is the life of royalty. Adieu my subjects, your hero will return after saving the day yet again!"

Once Landon manages to separate the prince, he makes his request immediately. "Your Highness, our vessel has already left for the isle, but we cannot wait for the return. We must leave before the winter festival."

Piers gasps and claps his hands. "The winter festival! It is so close, yes? You will stay; it is settled. We will leave for Vierdeaux at once and you will accompany me to the festival as my royal guests!"

Landon shakes his head. "Piers, you are not hearing me. We *must* leave *before* the festival. Our journey is to the Isles. We cannot wait for winter to begin; the waters are rough as it is with the storm raging. The winter months are too unpredictable with the storm pulling in warm waters from the southern seas and..."

Piers sighs and waves his hand. "I do not need a lecture; don't be so dreadfully boring. You will stay; that is final. Once the winter festival has concluded, if your ship has not returned, I will lend you one of my personal ships and they will help you sail." He claps his hands. "Come now! To Vierdeaux! We only have a few days to prepare and you all certainly need every bit of help me and my couturiers can offer." He says eyeing them scrupulously.

Chapter Fifty

Prince Piers leads them to the harbor and greets the harbormaster quickly. "Ganlin, my dear fellow, please you will assist us, yes? We sail to Veirdeaux. Are the royal matelots still docked here with my vessel?"

Ganlin sighs as his eyes fall on Prince Piers. He scans through his manifest. "Yes, the 'My Sister Is A Dog' is still docked and the crew is ready to sail."

Cael and Wynn smirk and Landon laughs out loud. "Was that for Princess Emilia or Princess Elise?"

Piers thinks a moment. "Elise? No, it was Emilia. I can't recall. It does not matter; they are both dogs. Come, come, we waste no more time thinking of those animals. We prepare for the celebration!" he says, following Ganlin to his ship.

Written clearly on the side of the largest and whitest vessel they'd ever seen are the words 'My Sister Is A Dog'. Piers grins as he points to it and repeats the words loudly for all to hear. They board the ship and Ganlin smiles to Cael and Wynn, throwing a scowl Landon's way who gifts a scowl in return.

Piers shouts, "To Veirdeaux!" and at least a dozen sailors begin running about preparing to depart.

Piers leads them to a comfortable cabin overlooking the cobalt blue water. A servant rushes in and pours a fragrant wine for them. They relax sitting in beautifully colored plush seats surrounded by wide glass windows. More furniture than a small army could hope to use is placed decoratively around the main recessed floor.

Piers throws himself into the center lounge chair. "This is the worst part. It takes so dreadfully long!"

Landon sits them down on a larger couch. *'It's not long. We'll dock before lunch,'* he thinks to them.

The servants rush back and forth with healthy plates of fruits, cheeses and breads, constantly filling up their wine glasses as they stare at the ever-growing city of Veirdeaux out the windows. The first part of the journey the city grows slowly, but towards the end the city seems to burst from the water itself. Starkly contrasted to Rosé, which has very small buildings with none taller than a few stories, Veirdeaux has enormous structures throughout. Some requiring truly marvelous architectural feats. As they draw nearer, they notice that the royal castle is placed on a cliff overlooking the surrounding city. It's easily twice the size of Ayverden or even Rensfort. The city expands out from small ports and rises quickly on the hills to where the furthest back is equal in height to the castle itself.

Unlike Rosé which is specifically designed with straight lines and long roads, Veirdeaux looks like a forest after a fire. Darker colored buildings placed with no plan or ideas, chaotic and random. Rosé being white and green, clean and organized, Veirdeaux embraces a darker coloring and seems to expel any sign of nature within its borders.

Cael, Wynn and even Landon move to the front of the ship to stare in awe at the sprawling city lain out before them. Docking the vessel Piers sighs heavily, "Finally. This ship is so slow, we absolutely must commission something faster. Come now, don't stare like peasants. You must play the part of royal guests if we are to have any fun at all. Follow me." He instructs.

Piers leads them off the ship and through the port to a gilded carriage waiting just off the busy street. "Your Highness, I was not expecting guests. Shall I fetch the larger carriage?"

"Nonsense." Piers shakes his head. "Have you seen my guests? We cannot wait a moment longer! They look truly awful from their travels. We can squeeze in if we must."

The driver bows his head. "As you wish, Your Highness." He jumps from his seat and opens the doors to a reveal a thoroughly spacious wide cabin with ample room for them, and more if necessary.

"Sit over there. You're all so unkempt from your long journey." Piers grimaces. "Robert! Have the stable hand clean this carriage as soon as we arrive, yes?" He calls through the window.

Piers slouches down in his seat and stretches out as the carriage begins bumbling down the cobblestone road. Cael and Wynn, placed on either end of Landon, stare out the open windows as they make their way up a private path. Winding up the cliff, the driver navigates back and forth up the steep climb. As they rise higher, they see the north side of the city in full below them. The entire city is on an enormous hill, almost a mountain, stretching back and up for at least half a day's walk. The sight overwhelms them.

"You could live your whole life here and never have a need to go outside the city," Cael says in wonder.

Piers peeks out the window and frowns. "Who would want to spend their whole life living down there? Rosé is truly so much better. I've asked Father to move the capital to Rosé, but he refuses, going on and on about tradition. Who cares about tradition!? Rosé is beautiful. Veirdeaux is disgusting!" He shivers at the sight and closes the blind. "At least the royal grounds aren't as unseemly as the city."

The carriage comes to a stop and the doors open. Robert helps Piers down and then offers his hand to Wynn while Landon and Cael hop out the other side.

"You there! Get these poor souls groomed properly. Robert! Don't forget to wash out my carriage." He gives Cael another glance. "Best to be safe, wash it twice then, yes?" And without another word he disappears into the castle.

Cael turns to the driver. "We're sorry if we've dirtied your carriage, Robert."

He waves his hands. "Oh, it's not my carriage and you've dirtied nothing. Also, my name isn't actually Robert. That was the driver before me, or perhaps before him." He bows. "My name is Benjie. Pleased to make your acquaintance." He shakes all of their hands. "This here actually is a Robert, at least I believe so. Robert!" He calls to a very well-dressed man looking down his nose as he orders others about. "I believe Piers wanted his guests groomed and given proper garments for the winter festival. He yelled at one of the guards, but I'm sure he'd have wanted you to handle it." He turns back to them. "It was a pleasure. Enjoy your time here!" And he climbs back in his seat and leads the carriage along a road leading to the east of the castle.

"So is your actual name Robert or is that just a name they've given you?" Cael smirks.

Robert sneers out, "It is my actual name, so far as you're all concerned." He fixes his shirt collar, "I cannot begin to imagine why Prince Piers has deigned to give you royal guests status, but it is not for me to question. Follow." He quickly turns and hastily walks through the large castle doors.

As they pass through a second set of doors, they are met with an amazing transformation. A city within the castle. The bright clear sky visible above with open gardens and roads leading to inns, taverns, café's, market squares with vendors selling all manner of luxurious goods. The closest garden has an enclosed stage where a musician performs on an instrument of unknown origin to barely a handful of extremely fashionable listeners.

Cael nor Wynn can comprehend the sheer size of the castle walls that surround this small city. Lanterns are lit all along adding artificial light to the natural light of the sun directly above. Manicured trees sprout from every corner and colorful flowers line the walking paths, blooming even out of season. For as much chaos and randomness lies below, there is order and structure here in turn. Open air and gardens in equal part to the buildings and vendor stalls.

They have only a moment to take in the sights before Robert leads them to the interior of the castle once again. Their eyes take a moment to adjust to the poorly lit hallways. "You there!" he calls to a young servant, hands full with supplies. "Bathe these *guests* and send them to Nero for tailoring afterwards. Understood? Good."

"But!" the boy calls back as Robert disappears down the halls and through another door. "Well, ain't that dandy." He sighs. "Alright then, c'mon folk. Let's get you tidied."

"Name's Kit, but all them important folk take to callin' me boy. Not that I mind. Well, I suppose that I do mind a bit. Ain't nothin' wrong with minding, mind you." He opens a door to a room with bathing tubs and wash bins. "Just need to run down and get some hot water. I'll grab some ladies for the lady as well."

Kit returns along with three irritated women being dragged behind him.

"This here's the one. Work your magic," Kit says, waving them in.

The shorter, wider of the three huffs and swats his head. He winces and catches Wynn's eye. "Not that you need any magic, mind you." He dumps a small pot of hot water into the large tub basin and scratches his cheek, eyeing Cael and Landon. "Gonna need a bit more help, ain't I?"

The three ladies drag Wynn into the adjoining washroom and servants funnel in pot after pot of hot water for her. They strip her down and begin bathing her.

"What wonderfully perfect skin!" a woman in a dark yellow dress cries as she settles down next to Wynn. "Are you from Yselden? Piers brought you here? Emilia and Elise will be so jealous at your hair! Oh, we must style it wonderfully!"

The slightly older woman shoots a dirty look at the youngest one in yellow. "Anastasia! We are ladies-in-waiting and we must act accordingly! You cannot act in a petty manner especially toward Her Highness."

Anastasia bows her head. "Yes ma'am." She looks up quickly. "Oh, but we will still style it wonderfully?! Please Arabella!"

"Of course!" Arabella cries out. "We can't let our guest looking anything less than flawless. Annie, you scrub her. Lette you take nails and I'll go talk to Nero. He'll be over the moons with excitement at her coloring. I can't wait to see what he does!"

Arabella runs through Cael and Landon's room as a handful of servants pile in to groom and bathe them.

"As weird as it is to be bathed by a dozen men, it's actually pretty nice," Landon says as he leans his head back in the tub. The servants grab his hands and feet to begin cleaning and cutting his nails. "Ahhh.. perfection," he mumbles as he slumps down into the steaming hot water.

"I'm not so sure, do we really need all of this? Did we stink that badly?" Cael asks, unable to get comfortable with all the hands reaching around and pulling at him.

A few men laugh. "You, sir, are dirtier than the royal hounds after a hunt. Now relax a moment, you are too stiff!" One says pushing hard on Cael's shoulders.

"I was frustrated with all the delays, but, lad, I'm almost glad we came here. Almost." Landon says sinking deeper into the tub before the men hoist him back up to comb and trim his beard.

"Easy for you to say." Cael growls as the men laugh at his chin and lip whiskers.

"Phillip, what in the world do you expect of me? I cannot work with this! He has nothing! He is a man child!" The man pulls at Cael's chin. "A woman would have more!" They hurl insults as they prepare to shave his chin.

Another man pulls out a bit of charcoal. "Ah, you underestimate my cleverness! He has very tiny hairs, we can color them!"

Cael pulls back as the men hold him down and rub charcoal across his upper lip.

"Hold still!" Phillip calls out. "Almost done!"

Landon begins laughing so desperately that he starts crying at the sight. Cael's hair is nicely styled long and straight by his ears, but a severely out-of-place, thin, coal-black line runs across his lip. Landon quickly looks at his reflection in the mirror to compare and sees his beard trimmed close to his face and hair left long and straight by his shoulders. "I look fantastic! You've done marvelously!" He pats them on the back and laughs again watching as Cael is painted.

"Voila! He is beautiful!" the men call out and clap as they finish struggling to put the finishing touches on Cael's mustache.

"Indeed!" Landon adds with a final chuckle.

After being bathed, perfumed and manicured, Wynn is dressed quickly in undergarments and thrust into a plush chair. A plethora of tools and powders lie in front of her.

"Lette, pluck those hairs, layer her face and add a touch of rose above the cheeks. Let's add some color to those lips. Annie, should we plait her hair back? Maybe a cross braid, or cornettes? What did Elise ask for the other day, ramshorns?"

Annie shakes her head quickly. "Certainly not cornettes, she's so young! Plaited to the back, or straight down? Elise wanted her hair braided and crossed in the front, perhaps that? I know! Let's try it all and see which one is best!"

They giggle and get to setting her hair while Lette grumbles about which coloring to use.

After finishing, Wynn comes out of the room and stares at Cael for a moment before laughing uncontrollably. He looks at her and laughs as well. Her eyebrows and upper lip are plucked and red all around, slightly raised and clearly painful. It's as if she's been stung a dozen times by bees.

"What are you laughing at!" she says indignantly, holding a mirror up for them to see each other.

Cael furiously wipes off the charcoal while Wynn gingerly touches her abused face.

The servants drag them through the castle in their undergarments to a room filled with cloth and linens. They sit in anticipation as a small oddly dressed elderly man with wild gray hair scrutinizes their appearance silently.

"You. Stand," he calls to Landon while his assistant runs to grab a stool and measuring stick. Nero climbs atop the stool, barely coming up to Landon's shoulders.

"Interesting," he says as he takes Landon's measurements with a marked thread and jots down a few notes. "Very well. Next."

He moves to Cael and the assistant pulls Cael to his feet and presses his knuckles hard against his spine forcing him to stand straight and tall.

"What is on your face, son?" he asks as he raises to eye level on the stool.

Cael blushes, wiping hard at his lip. "Coal, sir. For a mustache."

The edges of Nero's mouth curve into a slight smile. "Yes, of course. Very well. Next."

He moves to Wynn and she stands straight up, holding her arms out as he takes her measurements. When his eyes meet hers, he gasps. "Veera's soul! You are the Yselden girl! What is this on your face? No absolutely not! You will have no powder conceal your beauty. I must get to work right away," he cries as he hops off and makes a few notes but turns back to Wynn. "If any brainless monster tries to color you again, you tell them that Nero will whip them if they do. Yes?" And he rushes to a back room.

"Well, if we've had enough fun embarrassing me, I think I'd like to go die now," Cael says, standing up and walking out of the room.

Nero's assistant runs out and drags Cael back in. "No. Sit please," he says, shoving Cael back down.

The assistant rummages through closets and drawers, checking his list every so often before carrying an arm-full of clothes over to the group. "Please, dress." He hands them all gorgeous sets of clothes that fit surprisingly well for not having been tailored to them. Cael is handed a classic dark burgundy with silver accents and Landon is gifted a brighter set of grey and red while Wynn puts on a long thin deep sapphire dress extending to the floor.

After getting clothed, Landon licks his thumb and wipes the remaining coal smudge from Cael's face. "It's all in good fun, lad." He says with a smirk.

Shortly after leaving Nero's room, Piers walks by, already with an entourage of older ladies and gentlemen hoping to curry favor with the royal family. He stares at them confused. "Nero made those for you? He's certainly losing his touch. Those are so ill fitting!" He sighs. "Well, I suppose you do look better than when I found you, come along then," he says, grabbing Cael and Wynn's hands and pulling them over to the large group.

"Everyone, these are my guests for the winter festival! Cael and Wynn, all the way from Kaldia on dreadfully important royal business. They almost couldn't stay for the festival at all, could you imagine!? Luckily, I managed to convince them." He turns to Landon. "And of course you should all have heard of Landon, council to my father and having saved his life at least once," his voice goes lower. "that we know of!"

The group looks justifiably astonished and even Cael and Wynn appear surprised. Just as questions start being thrown their way, Piers waves his hands. "We must be going, thank you all!"

Piers parades them through the castle and courtyard, giving short brief introductions to every dignitary and person of note. The details of who they are become more and more fascinating but are all just vague enough that each group is left with questions and wanting to know more. At first, they were on royal business from Kaldia and soon they've traveled all over the continent working with every royal family and even having been to the courts in Alisterra and Alundria. Landon, council to the king, becomes bodyguard and then heroic savior of the country. His feats are stretched to the limit, fighting off dozens of guards barehanded and reaching into the mystical with battles between man and monster in the Waylinn jungles.

The three of them are truly impressed with themselves by the end of the day. With the introductions over, Piers puts them in one of his spare rooms in the royal wing directly next to his. "So that none bother you" He says, giving an easy excuse.

As soon as the doors are closed, Landon chuckles. "What a day... This room will likely give us even more allure than all of the stories that were told."

A knock on the door and a servant appears. "Is there anything I can get you?"

Wynn smiles and lays back on one of the beds. "Food! Please!"

Landon and Cael nod vigorously in agreement.

"As much as you can manage at this point," Landon calls as the servant bows and rushes down the hall.

After eating, Cael looks in awe around the room they've been given. "This is bigger than my whole house." He leans back in his chair. "But man, could I get used to it."

Landon knocks his chair back and Cael falls onto the floor. He laughs. "Well don't! Because the food and lodging at the academy isn't anything like this, I assure you."

Landon then leans back in his chair and Wynn kicks the legs out from under him and laughs. "Ass." She says looking down at him. Cael laughs with her before both he and Landon try to pull her down as well. She dodges their hands and quickly runs away.

"Peace! Peace!" she yells as she is chased around the large room.

"Alright, alright," Landon says out of breath. "I give up. I'm too full. Let's just relax and get ready for tomorrow. I'm sure Piers is planning plenty more running around for us."

Chapter Fifty-One

The next day is just as Landon predicted. Piers continues to parade them around, making brief but outlandish introductions. Describing elaborate missions and impossible feats to everyone who arrives. Piers' smile grows throughout the day with each new introduction and his happiness turns to pure euphoria when even his sisters' royal guests excuse themselves to join the crowd hearing of Cael, Wynn and Landon's adventures. Before the day is out Piers ensures that all eyes are on his guests and they can hardly move through the castle without hearing tales being told in hushed whispers.

The upcoming festival has the castle humming with energy. All manner of people coming and going, making last minute arrangements. Larger stages are being set in the courtyard along with a full tournament grounds. Vendors pile into the market square and even smiths begin setting up shop to work on armor and weapons for the dueling and jousting events. The castle is decorated fully with trees and paper snowflakes. White flowers are shipped in from the south and placed around the entire castle with florists specifically staffed to ensure they stay bright and lively throughout the festivities.

Piers leaves them as night falls to make his own preparations for the following day. The winter festival finally upon them, they call it an early night as well.

Morning arrives and the excitement of the festival fills them with a nervous energy. They dress in the clothes that Nero's assistant had sent them the day before and make their way to the grounds. People from all over the continent, perhaps even the world, are crowding eagerly around the stage. Too many faces to count and they all whisper when they lay eyes upon the three of them.

"The king will come speak and then the festival will begin. There should be a few plays, perhaps a musical display and then the junior tournament will begin. That should take a day or two and then the real tournament will begin taking near the rest of the time. A champion will be crowned the day before the feast. He or she will receive accolades and a place of honor as well as they're choice of partner to dance with at the ball," Landon says quietly, trying to mask his own nerves.

They stand for a long while staring at the stage, trying to blend with the crowd, before trumpets sound and the king and queen walk out, followed by their children.

"Welcome, all, to our winter festival!" The king opens his arms wide as applause and cheers echo around the courtyard. "I have been fortunate enough to rule over one of the most beautiful countries with the love and respect of my people. For that I am ever grateful. Each year when we celebrate the winter festival, we mark a new year that has come and gone. We recognize growth and new life to be had. As we watch the leaves fall, we remember our loved ones who have returned to the earth. As we watch the snow fall, we are thankful for the year of hard work that allows us to continue thriving while the ground is purified. When the leaves bloom once more, we work harder, we push farther, and we aim to be better. To be more. Just as the tree grows ever larger, reaching ever higher, so must we. We will be better men and women, fathers and mothers, farmers and kings."

The crowd applauds as the king gazes out over them and gives the slightest wave of his hand. Just then, it begins snowing. The crowd goes silent, staring in awe for a moment before cheering in excitement. Few noticing the men and women launching snow from the castle walls. The king calls out above the oohs and ahs, "Let the festival commence!"

The crowd applauds once more as the king and his family walk off the stage to the sound of trumpets. Musicians hurry to their places and music quickly begins filling the air.

"Nice touch," Landon says thoughtfully as he stares at the last few snowflakes to fall down. A couple larger chunks hit some of the crowd marked by areas of laughter. "Let's take a look around?" Landon suggests.

They wander through the courtyard watching as crowds begin gathering nearer to the stage, enjoying the music. Another crowd gathers around a horse track where races are preparing to be held. They continue down the length of the yard into the market square and find the majority of the guests are shopping, relaxing near the multiple water fixtures or listening to stories by the taverns.

Landon buys slices of apple pies and as they meander through the crowds a story catches their ears. They settle on one of the many benches placed out and listen in as a man begins his tale accompanied by a lute.

"Gather round and listen well for I have a rather intriguing story to tell.

Long ago and very far away, there was a princess locked all night and all day.

She cried for help and wept to be free, but alas no savior did she see.

A monster had stolen her from the good king, a curse he placed upon her name and sealed it with a ring.

He broke through the gates and quickly fled, the king ran to his men and screamed 'off with its head!.'

The beast rushed to his tower and kept her inside, he shouted down to his pursuers, 'She will be my bride!'

The men laid siege to the tower but no stone did break, for all their efforts they went home in heartache.

Their king did weep and pleaded for help, from the farmer plowing field to the scribe stacking shelf.

Many did hear his cry and many did come, but all did fall to the creature. All, save one.

A thief crept into the castle to pray on despair, he hoped to steal the king's treasure and vanish to thin air.

He stuffed his pockets filled with all he could carry, he then quickly planned an escape not wanting to tarry.

But he was not alone that night, not even quite, for the king was there watching and was surprised by the sight.

A thief like this could be what we need, where others had failed he surely would succeed.

He walked from the shadows and stood staring at the thief, who took one look and his face was stricken with grief.

He fell to his knees and begged for his life, but the king pulled him up and made him a knight.

He told him all he took could be his if he would do just one thing, save his daughter and break that damned cursed ring.

The thief laughed at his luck and quickly agreed, what more could he want what more could he need?

He sped to the tower and planned his heist, wasting no time he thought, 'this happens tonight'.

He climbed the walls silently and taking great care, until his eyes laid on the princess so beautiful, so fair.

He looked in the windows and that's when their eyes met, she fell in love while he fell to his death.

The creature grabbed him by his hands and threw him from the tower, but all the way down the thief laughed with his power.

He had stolen a trinket from a wizard long ago, and he wore it around his neck and his fall did slow.

You see the amulet he wore made him silent but also light, like a feather from a bird in a midsummer flight.

He floated softly to the ground and again made his way up, the creature threw everything from tables to chairs, even a cup.

The thief could not be stopped for he was in love, and his love was right there, mere meters above.

He kept climbing and reached the window once more, this time he was ready and had a secret in store.

The beast leapt at the thief but he just missed his grasp, and the thief took his dagger and stabbed it right in the ass.

The monster roared and the thief lunged again with his knife, the monster fell backwards out the window and clear out of sight.

He fell to his death and no trinket saved him, a suitable ending for a monster so grim.

The princess was freed and the king's gratitude was voiced,
the thief asked for her hand and the kingdom rejoiced.

They married that day and lived ever after, happiness
abounded along with their laughter.

We see thieves and the poor struggling en masse but
remember the thief that triumphed with a dagger to a beast's ass."

Roars of laughter erupt at the story and the three find
themselves laughing right along with the crowd.

Landon tosses a few coins towards the performers and they
walk away. "That story started out horrible, but the ending." He
chuckles. "I did not see that coming!"

They disperse with the crowd and navigate slowly through
the market enjoying the entertainment and interesting foods. Soon
Landon starts to loop around towards the track to watch the races.
On their way they pass the tournament grounds where a few young
entrants spar amongst themselves.

"My royal guests!" Piers voice calls out from behind them.
"I see you're interested in the tournament! It would be absolutely
wonderful if the two of you joined in the junior duels!" He claps
his hands and a few words of agreement come from the group
following him.

Landon steps in front. "I'm sorry that just won't be
possible. We're still very exhausted from our journey and it would
not be fair for them to duel at such a disadvantage." He says
protectively.

Piers scowls at Landon. "I did not ask you for your opinion.
Cael and Wynn are both accomplished in their own right and can
answer this for themselves."

"I'm interested," Wynn says quickly and Landon shoots her
an angry look.

Cael nods his head. "Might as well."

Piers claps his hands. "Wonderful, simply wonderful! I'll
have the royal armorer outfit the both of you. Landon can show
you to the tournament administrator." He turns to his group. "Let's
go get comfortable! The tournament should begin shortly!" He
makes a quick exit towards the royal viewing area.

"What is wrong with you two?! What are you thinking joining a tournament?" Landon shouts at them as he leads them along the fencing.

"We're more than capable of handling some brats," Wynn shoots back. "We've done much more than that already."

"I don't care what you're capable of!" Landon grabs her. "Did you stop to think that maybe you'd lose control and use your gifts in front of an enormous crowd?! Did you think that perhaps if you get hurt, Cael will also get hurt and there would certainly be questions?! What happens if you win? Absolutely nothing. What happens if you lose? Nothing. So why take the risk? Why risk everything for nothing?! You're so blinded by your overconfidence that you aren't even considering that there are clear and dangerous consequences!" He huffs and lets her go.

"We're sorry; we didn't think of that. We can just go and tell Piers we changed our minds, right?" Cael says, stepping in between them.

Landon shakes his head. "No, that would likely just cause more problems.... We need to hope that you either win easily or you lose by submission and not injury." He sighs and drops his head in his hands. "Come on, let's get you outfitted."

They secure time slots for their fights and a runner manages to track them down with armor from the royal armory, already fitted to them. Landon ties off their suits and checks for any imperfections. Cael picks up the wooden sword and shield and weighs them out while Wynn mimics his motions.

Landon watches Cael move and sees Wynn matching his movements. "This might actually be interesting to watch," he admits.

"I just hope we don't do anything stupid without thinking," Cael says, swinging his sword back and forth.

"Too late," Landon says. "But it might not be bad; just be careful and stay in control. If you feel yourselves becoming emotional and angry, just submit. You absolutely cannot use your gifts in front of this crowd." He stands up and squares Wynn's shoulders. "Alright, you two spar together. You've got a while before either one of you is called up and it needs to look like you're warming up."

They try and spar, but they match their movements exactly each time, so it appears more a choreographed dance than a sparring match.

Landon stops them. "At least make an attempt. Try not thinking so hard about it. Alek and Julia told you that your conscious connection isn't deep yet; it's only on the surface. Only the spoken thoughts, so stop thinking so loud. Move without thinking; let your instincts take over."

They follow his direction, but they appear to continue their dance so he stops them again. "Move faster! Faster! Stop thinking just move!"

Moving faster helps them to disconnect and they begin appearing more natural in their movements. Just in time for Cael's first duel.

"Cael of Kaldia, royal guest to His Highness Prince Piers," the announcer calls out over the crowd. "Lorento Tiempo Rafiele Maleco Hilleduedo, first born of Lord Hilleduedo, Baron of Venisteo and Advisor to His Royal Majesty of Oarna."

"Finra's beard, man! How many names does this guy have?" Cael mumbles.

"It doesn't matter. Everyone in Oarna of note is titled with advisor to the king; he's just some noble's son," Landon says. "Go to the announcer. He'll lay out the ground rules."

Cael walks over and spots Lorento entering the tournament ring as well. Thin build, taller than Cael and wearing what appears to be a lighter plate.

'His arms are longer than your legs!' Wynn laughs.

'Well yea, he's really tall,' Cael thinks back.

'He's tiny though, you've got this!' Wynn cheers.

'Tiny, but really fast I bet. Look at that armor. It's barely a plate at all; it's so thin,' he replies.

'Well, then hit his plate! Crush him! Smash it to bits!' Wynn's energy is contagious and quickly gets Cael wound up and ready to go.

The announcer points them to their starting positions.

'I didn't hear the instructions! What were the rules?!' he thinks.

Landon cuts in, *'No thrusting and when you're disarmed, there is no fisticuffs; you just lose the duel.'*

The trumpets sound and Lorento charges quickly at Cael, slashing his sword at the neck and head. Cael dodges quickly and throws his shield in front of his face. Wynn tries to feed him what Lorento is doing but he's being beaten back handily by the longer reach. Every time Cael brings his shield down a moment, Lorento slashes again.

Cael, unable to concentrate on anything but blocking and dodging is at the mercy of Lorento's speed and reach. Wynn concentrates for them both, forcing her way into Cael's mind and binding their sight together. Immediately Cael is knocked down in the confusion but quickly scrambles to his feet. More than just two sets of eyes, the blind spots in their sight are filled in, creating a flowing tapestry of the field. He begins moving with inhuman precision having complete knowledge of Lorento's movements as they happen. Lorento swings to the neck again and Cael dodges quickly and slashes to his chest. The heavy thud dents his plate and sends Lorento staggering backwards. Cael rushes him. Lorento thrusts his sword at Cael's chest, but it is knocked easily away by Cael's shield. Cael spins around, using his momentum to slam his blade into Lorento's chest plate once more cracking it along the center. Lorento is knocked over unable to catch his breath. The announcer calls out Cael's name and cheers from the crowd fill the courtyard.

"Why didn't you do that from the start?" Landon asks as Cael stumbles his way over to them.

"I didn't do it, Wynn did. I wasn't even thinking," Cael says, winded.

"It's better this way to be honest," Landon muses out loud. "If you both fight too well, it'll look odd. If you don't fight well enough, it'll look odd. I reckon it's best to take a few hits before making that connection happen to avoid suspicion."

They relax and watch as a slew of other duels take place. Dozens upon dozens of fighters come and go. Some truly spectacular swordsmen, for being so young, dueling amongst the less trained entrants, making quick work of their competitors. Despite the number of contestants dueling, it's not long before Wynn's name is called.

"Wynn of the Yselden Province of North Liefland, royal guest to His Highness Prince Piers." The announcer waves Wynn over and begins calling her challenger, "Edurin Isenthril, third son of Count Menthel Bwakalin Isenthril, His Royal Grace Duke Keldin of Alundria and Advisor to His Royal Majesty of Oarna."

Cael whispers to Landon, "When do I get a fancy title to wave about?"

Landon rolls his eyes. "I'm telling you, these names aren't important." He pauses in thought as he stares out at Wynn listening to the rules. "Hey, she's better at telepathy than you, right?"

Cael nods. "Yea, so?"

Landon turns to him. "Well then, shouldn't you be already trying to make the connection with her? It didn't take her long, but it might take you a lot longer. If she needs help, she won't be able to clear her mind when she's defending herself."

Cael sets himself about making the connection immediately while Wynn waits for the round to begin. The trumpets sound and Wynn is the one who rushes Edurin. He's caught off guard by her charge and she swings wildly. He parries her blows quickly and then stands defensively blocking and parrying easily as he relaxes from the initial attack.

Wynn's lack of training shows and Edurin begins fighting back, blocking and slashing. Landing solid blows on her armor and knocking her backwards. He leans in with lighter feet, taking an offensive stance as he swings his sword and shoves her with his shield. He's stocky, a lot of muscle and weight behind his strikes.

'I could use... some help!' Wynn struggles to reach out to Cael who in turn is struggling to connect.

Edurin rushes Wynn with his shield up and she's thrown to the ground just as Cael finally manages to navigate their thoughts and share his sight.

Just as it was with Cael, she begins moving smoothly and gracefully instantly. It's like watching a completely different fighter as she regains her offensive pace. Rather than taking Edurin's solid blows with the shield, she opts to dodge all of them. She uses the sword like a hammer, raining blows on his outstretched arms as his sword passes by her, a few breaths away from her face or chest. He quickly exhausts himself and after the continuous blows to his arms, he can barely raise his weapon. Wynn lands a solid kick to his chest and he falls over. He kneels, submitting and the announcer calls Wynn's name out victoriously. She collapses to her knees and cheers rain down around her.

Wynn walks out of the ring of her own strength, but Cael is right by the edge to take her weight as soon as she breaks that threshold. "Took long enough…" She winces as she sits down and they begin untying her armor to reveal impressive bruises already showing green.

"You're young. It'll heal in a few days." Landon says more confidently than his face shows.

"I just couldn't concentrate. I was seeing you, but I couldn't make that connection," Cael says apologetically.

"We'll just practice more," Wynn says, reassuring him. "But right now I just want food and sleep, so carry me to my food!"

They wrap her arms around themselves and help her to her feet.

Piers runs to them. "Absolutely fabulous! That low-born churl Edurin deserved everything and more! To be defeated so handily by a maiden so fair! He'll never hear the end of that, I assure you all! Truly remarkable, you are both even more accomplished than I had given you credit for. Lorento will certainly be hesitant to call me a prissy princess ever again! This is the most perfect day ever!" He stops as he sees Wynn. "Oh dear, that looks dreadfully painful. Robert! Robert!" he calls over the crowd until one of the many non-Roberts answers his call.

"Yes, your Highness?" a younger man says with a short bow.

"Robert, please take my royal guests to our healer. Surely we have one somewhere around here? Make certain that these two are fighting fit for tomorrow!" He waves them off. "Heal well! I'll make certain everyone knows of your impressive skills!"

Not-a-Robert helps assist them through the castle to a room rife with antiseptic smells and a multitude of grisly looking tools. "Doctor Miamek! Prince Piers has requested that his guests be cared after by our staff."

A middle-aged woman peeks out of the back room. "Ah hello, Timothy. I'll be right with our guests, you may leave."

Timothy bows and exits the room, leaving the three of them standing awkwardly waiting for the doctor. She returns after a moment and examines them. "The newest toys of Prince Piers, I imagine? He's got the two of you fighting in the tournament clearly. But why aren't you?" she asks, eyeing Landon.

"I'm not the newest." He grins back at her and she nods quickly.

"Of course, of course." She works her way down their arms and legs feeling for fractured or broken bones before moving to their chests and abdomens. Methodically applying pressure and asking them to breathe as she listens close to their mouths.

"Nothing too severe. You're in luck, as it so happens is quite often the case around here, that we have some rather helpful rare plants." She rifles through some drawers and cabinets in the backroom before returning. "This is aloe, quite effective for bruising. Keep the bruised area raised and apply aloe to cloths and heat. Wrap the heated cloth around your bruised area and you should feel a reduction in pain immediately." She instructs handing them a thick clear liquid. "I could give you some herbs to make a tea that would increase your energy for tomorrow? I imagine he'll have you fighting again?"

"That's the plan." Landon says, "And we'd be very grateful for any help. Perhaps something that could aid concentration?" He nods to Cael. "Our friend here has an awful time focusing."

She moves to the back room and returns quickly with two packets of herbs. "Concentration. Energy," she says holding them up one at a time.

"Thank you," Cael and Wynn say, holding out their hands.

Doctor Miamek places them in their palms and closes their hands. "Good luck," she says with a hint of a smile before rushing out to the back room again.

"What an interesting woman." Landon says, eyes lost in thought as they walk into the hallway.

"But very helpful, and hopefully knowledgeable." Cael says, looking at his packet. "Do you think it'll really help my concentration? How would that even work?"

Landon shrugs. "Don't question it, just pray that it does."

Wynn nudges him. "It'll work, but you probably won't even need it. You did it today, a little late" She teases, "But you still did it."

They make it back to their room and set Wynn down on her bed. "Food... Please!" She calls out as she collapses backwards.

A knock at the door startles all of them. Wynn sits up on her elbows and Landon opens the door.

"Can I get you anything?" A serving boy asks.

"We just... How did you...? Are you only waiting on us?" Cael asks, at a loss for words.

"Of course, sir. Each royal guestroom has their own servants. Was there something wrong? If you'd prefer privacy, I could leave this post vacant. I do apologize if we've caused you trouble," the young boy says bowing slightly.

"No, not at all. I was just surprised," Cael says.

"Fooooooood!" Wynn calls from behind them.

"We're very hungry, could we get whatever the chef has cooking? Also a pot of hot water would be helpful." Cael says.

Their serving boy runs away towards the kitchens.

"That's convenient!" Landon says, closing the door.

After eating and wrapping themselves in the aloe covered cloth, they all sit back and rest, agreeing to wait until tomorrow to test their teas. They quietly relax while dinner sets in their stomachs before letting sleep steal them away.

Chapter Fifty-Two

"That aloe worked well, I'm a little surprised," Cael says, touching his quickly healing injuries.

Wynn takes off her bandages to reveal a similar sight. "Wow!" She pokes the small bruises. "They don't even hurt that bad. That's a good sign for the teas she gave us."

"Speaking of, you should probably drink those now. I think it's later than we thought. There's no view of the sky inside so it's really hard to keep track of the day," Landon says, peeking out their door.

They stir up their tea packets in some hot water. They each smell their tea and gag.

"Chug it?" Cael says, plugging his nose.

Wynn nods in agreement as they down their teas and grimace even before the flavor hits their tongues. Cael stands up a bit straighter after finishing. "Mine wasn't that bad. It smelled awful, but the taste wasn't even close to the smell."

"Lucky! Mine tasted exactly like it smelled, which was a dirt fungus combination," Wynn says, spitting a few leaves out of her mouth.

"Alright, that's done so let's get going. I need to get my bearings. I feel like it's way later and if you've missed your fights, you'll forfeit," Landon says ushering them outside quickly.

They make it to the grounds and the fights are in full swing. Landon runs up to the tournament administrator, Mathys. "Did Cael or Wynn get called yet?" he asks anxiously.

"Not yet, Wynn is fighting shortly," he replies without looking up.

They find a few open seats for the participants and watch the bouts. It becomes painfully clear that the caliber of fighter has increased substantially as only the winners of day one moved on. While the first day many of them had won their rounds handily, this day finds all fighters struggling to win out against their opponents. Rather than appear less skilled, each contestant seems even more accomplished with their weapons than before as they are pushed to the limits of their abilities.

Luckily, the introductions are shorter. "Selin of Oarna and her opponent Wynn of North Liefland!"

Wynn and Selin enter the ring and Cael immediately begins attempting to connect. Selin is slightly shorter than Wynn, but clearly more solid. They shake hands and are sent a few paces away. Cael's mind, uncluttered from all his thoughts, is easily manipulated into connecting with Wynn. Before the round even begins, Wynn has their full vision at her disposal.

'*Nice to know your tea worked. Now just to see if mine did!*' she thinks excitedly.

As the trumpets sound, both Selin and Wynn charge each other. They swing their swords smoothly and with purpose, blocking the incoming blows easily. It's instantly clear that Wynn would be outmatched if she didn't have her expanded vision.

Wynn's nerves and increased energy get the better of her. Rather than waiting for an opening she continues going blow for blow with Selin. Both appear at a stalemate, but Selin blocks Wynn's sword and rather than aiming for her chest she cuts low and lands a solid thud against Wynn's leg causing her to stumble to her knee. Selin takes advantage and kicks Wynn in the chest and she falls back.

'*I can feel your exhaustion,*' Cael thinks.

She replies, '*You don't say?*'

'*I'm going to try something.*' Already sharing sight, we concentrate on her arms, feeling the movement and weight in our own.

Wynn stands up and her arms begin moving of their own accord. She blocks quickly and cuts with a force she didn't know she had. Selin is caught off guard by the sudden change and staggers backwards as they land a fierce blow to her sword arm.

Rather than anger, Selin composes herself and grasps her sword in her left hand and swaps her shield to the right. Her blocks become awkward but focused more on deflecting rather than absorbing. The battle continues with Selin impressively holding her own even in her weakened state. They charge her shield down and as she braces herself Cael drops the shield from Wynn's hands and grasps their sword in both and cleaves a mighty swing down upon Selin's thigh and she collapses.

The announcer calls Wynn as the victor while she helps Selin to her feet.

"Well fought," Selin says through gritted teeth, "You have a vigor in you I couldn't match." She limps with her weight on Wynn's shoulder, clearly in pain.

"You are stronger than you realize," Wynn says to her. "I wish I could tell you how strong you truly are." She admits, "Well fought."

The crowd cheers for both contestants. Wynn returns to her seat and sighs as she plops down. "She is a monster. If you hadn't taken control of my arms that would have been a quick fight."

Landon's eyes go wide in surprise. "You controlled her arms? I thought you both only could share sight?"

"He just did it, so I guess we can," Wynn groans, still out of breath.

"I didn't control your arms." Cael says confused.

Wynn stares in disbelief before shaking her head, "What are you talking about? Of course you did it, you even said you were going to try something, remember?" She smacks her forehead, "It must have been that tea! You probably just did it all without thinking."

Landon pats him on the back, "It had to have been you, lad. I can sense your exhaustion. I'm just surprised that you could manage it. That tea must be something powerful."

Cael shivers before putting his thoughts aside, "You're probably right. My arms are sore, my head hurts." He rubs his temples, "My fight is going to be rough…." He sighs.

Right on cue the announcer calls out, "Cael of Kaldia and Olam of Waylinn!"

Landon shrugs. "Good luck!"

Wynn shakes her head and sets on connecting with Cael. Before he approaches Olam to shake his hand, he's already seeing the full field. He marvels at the precision of his sight. The second set of eyes clearly providing a real advantage. Olam is much shorter than Cael, likely a bit older as well but not as stocky. He can't see into his helmet but there is a faint glow in the darkness. The sun directly above drowns out most of it, but the blue hue is struggling to be seen.

They greet one another with a slight bow and the announcer quickly rattles off the rules before sending them to their marks. The trumpets sound and Olam charges forward, feet leaving deep divots in the dirt. His speed is incredible and Cael only just barely manages to spin out of the way. The corner of Olam's shield cuts deeply into Cael's armor as he rushes passed. Olam sets his feet and slows his pace, taking a slightly more defensive tone after his charge missed.

Cael approaches and begins landing blows easily, his swordplay far better than Olam's but his hits are shrugged off. Cael begins putting his full force behind each blow, but Olam barely moves. Dent after dent into his armor, chips of metal begin flaking away from the wooden sword blows. Olam strikes out but misses every time. He charges again and Cael dodges, but his expanded vision is suddenly clouded.

'I can't see him. You're blocking my sight.' Wynn calls to him, but it's too late. Olam slams Cael in the chest with his shield. While Cael is off balance, Olam throws a punch straight to Cael's face.

Landon catches Wynn before she collapses fully and sits her down as if she were sleeping. Olam tosses Cael over his shoulder as the announcer calls out Olam's name to cheers.

Olam carries Cael to Landon and places him next to Wynn. "Right strong lad and quick with that wooden blade there. I was right near the end of me stones, too. Good on him, but ya can't fight a Wylaen, eh?"

Chapter Fifty-Three

"I feel like I've been hit by a moose...." Cael says, rolling over onto his side and throwing the blankets over his face.

"What happened to us?" Wynn mumbles through her pillow.

"Exactly what I thought was going to happen, but I suppose a lot later than I expected it to." Landon calls from his chair.

"What does that even mean?" Cael's muffled voice comes from under the blankets.

"You were knocked clean out by Olam, who by the way thinks you're a very skilled swordsman, which I don't agree with. And he also said that there's no fighting with a Wylaen, which I do agree with. At any rate, you being knocked out caused Wynn to lose consciousness. You've both been out for... a day? Maybe a bit more? Damn these rooms, I can't tell how long has passed!"

Wynn shoots up but grabs her head as pain radiates through her. "Did I miss my next match?"

Landon laughs. "Of course you did! You were both unconscious for at least a day! I told the tournament administrator that you forfeit as soon as Cael was taken out. I'm sure rumors will be floating around about that on top of everything else...."

Cael sits up. "Don't tell me that Piers has been—"

Landon cuts him off. "Yup. He's been telling all manner of story about both of you."

Cael and Wynn both fall back and groan.

"It's courtly gossip. It'll fade as soon as we leave. I would bet everything that your names will be forgotten in a matter of weeks."

"Thanks," they say, holding their heads.

"We can't connect for so long…. This is unbearable," Wynn says

"Well, it's either the strain of holding a connection, or the concussion that Cael had." He picks at his short beard. "I suppose both would be more likely, eh?" He stands up and creeps over to them. "I know what'll make you feel better!" he says in a sing-song tone. "Food!"

The door opens and in comes the sweet smell of cooked meats, breads, soups, everything. It's overwhelming and they float up out of their beds, stumbling through their light-headed fogs to collapse on the chairs around the table before devouring everything close to them.

"Who won the tournament?" Cael says through mouthfuls of turkey.

"The final match was between Olam and Kellin. I would have thought for sure that Olam would win, but Kellin won very easily, if not quickly. I mean, Olam does have a pretty small skillset, he just uses his weight. The heavy metals in the Wylaen people make them so solid they don't typically need anything else. I'm a little shocked they even let him compete. But Kellin won out with his swordsmanship, just chipped him away like you were doing," Landon says as he picks at the remaining food on the table.

"Did Selin recover?" Wynn asks.

"Oh yea, she's fine. Broke her leg, but Doctor Miamek set it and gave her some walking sticks. Even told her she'd be running in a few weeks, and I believe it. That girl is the toughest kid around. If you two hadn't beaten her she likely would've won the whole thing," Landon replies.

After they finish eating, they decide to get some much-needed fresh air. The stuffy halls are eerily silent and it's not until they open the doors to outside they realize why.

"It's the middle of the night!" Cael loudly whispers.

"Looks like it, doesn't it?" Landon says. "Well, let's head to the taverns. Always something going on there."

"Has the real tournament begun yet?" Wynn asks.

Landon shrugs. "It should have. The junior tourney was the first three days. The tournament itself begins right after the finalists on day three with a melee determining bracketing."

"Bracketing? What's that?" Cael asks.

Landon lets his head fall back and he sighs. "It determines who you're pitted against in the actual tournament. You guys know so little!"

Cael and Wynn both trip him and Landon stumbles forward, arms flying in circles trying to catch his balance. He steadies himself and as they're laughing at him their feet strike something solid mid step and they both fall flat on their faces. Landon then laughs at them and turns to continue on to the tavern.

"Cheater!" Cael calls out and Wynn adds, "Ass!"

The difference between the courtyard and inside the tavern was like being awake and dreaming. People were warm, loud, and alive in the tavern while in the castle the air was chilled and all were sleeping, or at least trying to. Landon squeezes out a few seats in a slightly less crowded table than the rest. They settle in listening and watching random folks tell short stories or play funny songs.

"Cael!" a voice calls through the noise. Olam slips through some large men and plops down next to them, his markings clearly shown in the dimmer light of the tavern cover his arms and upper chest. "Aye, fat man! C'mon here, it's the lad I roughed up!" He shouts to another table and a few folks negotiate a seat swap before sitting down. They appear a bit shorter than average but the boards creek as the lot of them set in.

"This here is me father!" He pats the older man's shoulder next to him. Much taller and wider than Olam, the same clean shaven face and long hair, but with no visible tattoos. "He's a bastard but a decent one. Named me after him he did, thought I turned out like him, lucky I didn't, eh!? Ya can call him Ollie, he don't mind it that much." He grabs the man to his left, thickly bearded with shaved head, thin and marked like he is. "Me brother and best friend, Cracker!" They chuckle at the name. "Ain't his real name, but ya can call him that. He's cracked a few skulls in his day and he's proud of it!" Finally he points to a younger man. "That bloke is Kellin. He won that tourney off me. I woulda had 'im if I weren't cursed with these slow arms! He's as good as they come, solid lad just like you Cael."

"Cael don't rightly need any introduction being as he and Wynn are blessed with fame round these parts, but this here is their friend, uh Lampen? Limpton?" Olam says attempting to make introductions to his companions.

"Landon, the name is Landon," Landon calls, visibly irritated, over the noise.

"What are you all doing up so late?" Cael asks as a serving girl drops a tankard of something on the table and hands mugs out to them.

"Ain't nothin worth doin' durin' the light o' day," Ollie mumbles, taking a swig of his mug. "It just be tradition at this point."

Cracker leans in. "We ain't like most folk round here. I guess Pa is, he ain't never found the stone worth his time, but we just come to let em know the House of Lahkrun is still well and good."

Olam pats his brothers back. "S'truth! We be more stone than man, eh!? Not like this here old coot!" He pats his father's back hard and Ollie inhales some of his drink and starts a coughing fit.

Olam is concerned for a moment but his father composes himself and shoots him a dirty look. "Ya twit! What're ya doin? Tryin' ta kill me?"

Olam snickers. "Aye, that's right, Pa, just like you to die in your ale." He looks across the table at the concerned faces and he shrugs. "We love the old man more'n we show, and he loves us more'n we know. It's all well 'n good lads."

"What about you, Kellin?" Landon asks, nudging into the tall, blonde, young man next to him. "What brings you out at such a time with this group of rabble rousers?"

"In truth, I appreciate their straightforward demeanor. It's such a welcome reprieve from the courts. They could do with a bit less rousing of the rabble." He smiles at his joke. "But the days are dull now that the tourney is over. The grand tournament taking place has yet to pique my interest and the jousting tournament is but a farce. Very few could ever hope to come close to Sir Feirtel; he'll win handily and without issue. It's already been seen in the first dozen challengers." He takes a sip of his wine glass. "Here at least, we have stories and music, and good company."

"Aye!" Ollie, Olam and Cracker raise their mugs and cheer.

"Well, count us in!" Cael says raising his mug and the group cheers again.

Landon takes their ales and pours them some water. *'You two need to take it easy still. I can feel you both struggling. That strain was more than you're letting on.'*

They spend the night eating at the tavern, all the while enjoying the music and company of their new friends. By the time they wearily stumble out of the tavern the sun is high in the sky and the grand tournament is in full swing. The clang of metal striking metal echoes through their heads the whole way back to their beds.

Chapter Fifty-Four

"Alright, come on now. It's getting *really* late, you two," Landon says shaking Cael awake. "It's already time for dinner. We've slept clear through the whole day. We can't keep on like this; it's not proper. Royal guests need to show their faces at least once a day!"

Cael sits up and rubs his head and mumbles, "You said something about dinner?"

Wynn rolls over and falls out of her bed. She pops her head over the side, "Didn't the guys say something about meat pies?" She tilts her head back. "I would fight Selin again for some meat pies right now!"

Landon sighs. "You two are insatiable, do you know that? I can't believe how much you think about food. It's actually impressive, in a disgusting sort of way."

They clean themselves up, still dirtied from their fighting a few days ago and leave their increasingly lived in room for the courtyard, waving to Thomas as they pass.

"You should come to the tavern later! It'll be loads of fun!" Wynn calls out to him without stopping.

"I don't know if I can, but I'll try!" His voice gets drowned out by the sound of fighting as soon as they open the large heavy doors entering the festival grounds.

"Let's watch a fight or two and then make our way down to the jousting, maybe watch a play and then we can end at the tavern. We'll likely be there all night and I'd rather not be sitting the entire time you two are awake," Landon suggests.

Wynn moans. "But the food!"

Cael smirks. "She's got a point."

"Fine, we'll grab something from one of the stands in the market but then we have to show our faces at the grand tournament at least a few times." He acquiesces.

Cael and Wynn hastily walk towards the square to buy some sweet breads and fresh smoked turkey before Landon catches up and drags them away to the tournament seats. As soon as they are close, Piers spots them and waves them over.

"My guests! Please you must sit with me." He shoos some of his entourage away to make room. "I'm absolutely thrilled that you've both made a full recovery. The court has simply been abuzz with talk of you both. It's been wonderous! You must make your presence seen more often so that continues, it would make my sisters die of embarrassment!"

"Our apologies, Your Highness." Landon bows his head slightly. "How goes the grand tournament? Any favorites yet?"

"Oarna's own Dame Elris shows great promise, but of course Sir Davin is the returning champion from North Liefland and is a favorite," Piers replies without hesitation.

The announcer calls out the next contenders, "Sir Bolin and Sir Beldor!"

Piers scarcely seems to notice the match beginning in front of him and continues, "So have you heard? You were the favorite after your victory over Selin, my dear Wynn?"

Wynn stares at him in shock. "Truly? I was expected to be the champion?"

Piers looks at her seriously. "Of course! Selin was trained by her father, a remarkable warrior. She was expected to achieve a swift victory but when you overcame her!?" He claps his hands. "It was simply stunning!" He turns to Cael. "Not at all to discount your achievements, you were of course wonderful as well. That Waylinn boy was a difficult competitor. Only through sheer force of will did Kellin win out. The match was very good."

"Sir Bolin!" the announcer cries and the crowd cheers as Bolin helps Beldor to his feet and they grasp arms showing friendship.

"Shouldn't we be watching the fights?" Cael asks.

Piers shakes his head. "Why? There is no reason to. They will bash each other until there is a victor as they do every year. It's dreadfully dull."

"You should come with us to the tavern and listen to music and stories!" Cael adds excitedly.

Piers laughs sharply. "Me?! In a tavern? Oh, I think not my dear friend, that would not do at all, would it? But if that's where your heart is, I cannot deny you. It would cause more intrigue about you both I imagine…. Yes, go to the tavern! Enjoy the nights, keep yourselves shrouded in mystery! At the ball everyone will be simply fascinated by you both; it is perfect!" He says in excitement and pats Cael on the shoulder lightly. "Good plan! My sisters will be furious, absolutely maddened! Quick now, go before too many eyes fall on you. Hide yourselves well!" He whispers, shooing them away.

Piers waves his shunned entourage back to his side and Cael skirts the edges of the royal viewing booth and the side of the ring with Wynn and Landon following closely.

The crowds are increasingly found at the tournament grounds, the jousting track and the stage in the gardens so staying out of sight is relatively easy. Once they enter the tavern they find the same group as the previous night already there and welcoming them as old friends. They plop down in their familiar seats with Olam and his family, joined quickly along with Kellin who has an attractive young woman on his arm.

"Who's this then?" Landon asks, patting Kellin on the shoulder as he sits.

"Esme, she's Duke Unther's daughter. Esme this is, Landon, Cael and Wynn," Kellin politely introduces his date for the evening and she allows all to kiss her hand.

"Royal knobs, eh?" Olam whispers with a sly grin to Cael and Wynn. "Oy, Cael, you fancy a drink? We've got the lot of it paid through till the end, ya just give a holler, right?"

"Well what about the rest of us?" Landon jokes.

Olam eyes him seriously. "Cael's me brother. Me and him shed blood together we did, makes us family."

Cracker knocks Olam on the head. "Ya daft nut, them's Cael's family so if ya be family with him ya be family with them. And if Cael's yer family, so's Kellin and his lady fer that matter."

Olam thinks a moment and shrugs. "He might be right on that. The nights are on us lads," he says and notices Wynn and Esme, "and ladies!"

They load up on meat pies and sweet juices, and after pleading with Landon who begrudgingly agrees, they enjoy less than fine wines, passing the night away with loud, if not always good, music. Laughing through the limericks and jokes at the royal family's expense. Olam starts a jig later in the night, dragging Cael then Wynn and soon the whole tavern into it.

By the time morning arrives, they're exhausted and ready to sleep through the day once more. They stumble to their rooms in the castle and pick at some fruit and drink left on their table before falling asleep.

When their eyes open late into the afternoon, they decide to make a few stops around the festival before heading to the tavern. Keeping Piers plan in mind they sneak their way over to the horse track where the jousting tournament is taking place, making certain they are seen by as few people as possible.

"Finally! I love jousting matches, the amount of skill it takes is..." Just as they arrive Sir Feirtel knocks his opponent off in the first pass, Mathys barely having time to announce them before it was over. Landon's mouth falls open with a blank stare.

"What were you saying about skill?" Cael laughs as he smacks Landon on the back. "Because it looked like that one knight got speared to the ground with the least effort I've ever seen."

Wynn chuckles along. "Kellin did say that Sir Feirtel was going to win easily. Maybe there'll be a few more rounds?"

Landon's head sags. "No... that was the final round." He sighs and looks over to a crowd forming in the center. "They're crowning him now. He's the champion again. Let's just get out of here before the crowd starts to disperse."

"We could go watch one of the plays?" Cael suggests.

Landon ignores him and pushes onward, "It'll probably be best if we stay out of sight. We've already used our public time for the afternoon. Let's head over to the tavern and relax." He sighs. "Besides, we've only got a few days left before the ball and then the final leg of our journey."

Landon leads them wide along the edges of the courtyard until they reach the market. The warmth of the tavern hits them as soon as the door opens, making them keenly aware of the chill in the air outside.

"Right, it's like that with all the royal families. There's always been someone else laying claim and causing uprisings." The tavern is relatively quiet this day so they sit and listen to the man standing by the fire.

"And it's no different with the royal family of Oarna. King Arlem has done decent by his people, but still there are those that don't think too highly of him. The king had many cousins all claiming to be the rightful heirs of the Oarnian throne. Rather than publicly denounce their claims, he simply ignored them until one day, they all just vanished." The man by the fire faces the crowd and waves his hands, "Now I'm not saying that he had them killed or exiled. Who can truly claim to know, other than His Royal Majesty? But! I do know that enemies of the royal family, those that get a little too much attention, make a little too much noise, they all simply disappear. Just like the claimants to the throne. Sure, he's done decent by his people, but any man that deals in the darkness can't truly be good, can he?"

As the man next to the fire swigs his mug and heads to the bar to order more, the tavern erupts in conversation which soon turn to arguments. Each table split between believing the tale and defending the king.

"King Arlem seemed nice enough. Why is everyone upset with him?" Wynn asks.

Olam huffs. "Just peasant talk, don't ya pay no mind to that nonsense. These folk always wantin' something ta put their anger in. Easier ta lay blame than ta try and fix your own damn problems."

Cracker and Ollie both smack him on the head at the same time.

"What's that then!?" Olam glares at them both. "Ya know it be true!"

"Lad, ya can't just move yer mouth and not use yer brain! These folk got all the right ta think what they will. Folk got problems, and it ain't hard to see they can't fix em on their own. Yer mum and I work hard ta make our money and ta keep our name clean. Ya best not sully it by spoutin' nonsense. And ya best not be feelin' like yer owed nuttin' neither, understood?" Ollie chastises him.

Olam blushes. "Sorry Pa, ya know I didn't mean nothin by it."

Cracker smiles at Cael and Wynn, "Don't mind him, right? We'll throw him ta the woods 'nd teach him proper when we get back home. He don't know what it's like not havin' things. Not knowin' 'nd thinkin ya know, now that's just plain dumb ain't it?"

Kellin sits heavily on the bench alongside Landon. "Enough of this, please. Let us enjoy the night as we have, be merry and help me forget my lost love."

"Ah, the love of youth." Landon grasps his arm. "You and...and." He pauses for a short while and Kellin turns up to him with tears in his eyes. Landon chuckles. "Lad, I can't even remember her name! I was trying to help, I swear it!" He curls over and the table laughs with him.

Kellin pounds the table. "Her name was Esme, you heartless toads! I loved her!"

Ollie raises his mug. "Ta love!"

The table raises their drinks and toasts, "To love!"

Kellin wipes his watery eyes. "To love and friends!"

The tavern continues their arguing until a young woman takes the stage with her guitar and begins playing beautiful music. Suddenly everyone forgets their arguments and sits silently listening, enjoying the company and warmth that the tavern offers.

As she stops playing and the trance is broken, an older man takes the stage with a harp and lulls everyone back into a comfortable waking sleep. The night continues with many musicians taking their turn on the stage, the sound of music creating an ideal background for the friendly conversations that are had.

The tavern empties earlier than usual, most patrons wanting to wake in time for the final tournament bout in the late morning. Landon is the first of the group to doze off and Cael helps him to his feet before saying their goodnights to all and leaving for their beds in the castle. Surprised it's still dark out, they walk freely to their room. Sleep is difficult to find with so much energy left, but they do find it after laying awake in their minds for a long while.

Chapter Fifty-Five

They awake and soon find themselves at the tournament grounds once again. Neither Sir Davin nor Dame Elris advance to the championship bout, surprising all of the festival guests. As the sun reaches over the castle walls lighting the field, the announcer finally calls the two warriors. "His Royal Highness Prince Harold, firstborn of King Hector of South Liefland!"

A knight clad in what looks like pure white leather armor walks confidently into the ring as cheers from a growing fan base nearly drown out the announcer.

Mathys waits for the cheering to die down before he introduces the second competitor. "Sir Zaitah, alchemist and envoy to King James of Kaldia!"

Cael and Wynn's mouths drop as they see truth to the words, Zaitah walking on to the field to cheers.

"Father made that armor..." Cael mumbles.

Wynn adds, "And that sword, remember?"

Cael nods. "He made it of steel and extenite. I still remember when we found that rock."

Landon stares at the field dumbfounded. "I did not expect this at all."

Cael and Wynn go to shout to Zaitah but Landon stops them, "If you call to him now he'll lose focus! Be patient."

The duelists grasp arms and offer a slight bow before moving back to their positions. The trumpets sound and Zaitah moves like the wind, taking a few steps forward and swinging his sword high. Harold blocks with his shield and whips his flail towards Zaitah who stretches his shield arm out slightly to help absorb the impact.

Cael whispers, "Incredible, it's really him."

Zaitah moves like a lightning streak across the field, landing slash after slash upon Harold but none with enough force to penetrate his armor. Harold matches Zaitah's movements but the swing from his flail leaves openings for Zaitah to expose. Moving easily out of the flails wide reaching blows Zaitah quickly closes the distance between him and Harold. He slams his shield into Harold's helmet causing him to take a step back. Harold in his frustration throws his shield down and grasps the flail grip with both hands. His swings come faster and his movement less obstructed and forecasted. Zaitah moves fast, but not fast enough and Harold strikes from all angles. He absorbs them with his shield but soon the toll begins to show as flakes of metal are blown off.

"Impressive, pay attention here," Landon says.

Zaitah moves closely as Harold swings his flail, throws his sword into the ground and grips the chain, stopping the flail. He slams his shield into Harold's chest and as Harold stumbles, Zaitah pulls the sword from the earth and swings with all his might, cutting so deeply into Harold's left shoulder armor that the sword gets stuck. Zaitah places his foot on Harold's chest, pushing hard to remove the blade. Harold grasps the blade and helps pull it free, showing it barely made it through leaving only a superficial cut beneath the armor.

Zaitah changes his tactics and relies on his speed rather than his shield to chip further away at the exposed area on Harold's shoulder until soon Harold can hardly raise his arm. Suddenly with a wild and unexpected blow, Harold swings with so much force that Zaitah's shield explodes and the flail continues to his chest. Zaitah falls back, but scrambles to his feet and the fight continues.

Zaitah, more hesitant without his shield, defends against the wild swings, waiting for an opening. Harold sees his hesitation and throws his flail at Zaitah who hits it down out of the air, but Harold, already on the move charging his opponent full force, lifts Zaitah off the ground and slams him down. The weight of both cause Zaitah to lose consciousness for but a moment. In that moment, Harold claims his victory and the announcer confirms, "Prince Harold of South Liefland!"

Zaitah stands and Harold embraces his opponent. They share words briefly before King Arlem beckons Harold forward to bestow the champion his sash and ceremonial sword.

Cael and Wynn hardly wait for the announcement before charging through the crowd and leaping on Zaitah who stumbles, still out of breath from his bout. As he steadies himself he sees his brother, "Cael?! What in Finra's name are you doing here?!" He squeezes tightly before dropping to his knees. They let tears flow freely, "Not in my wildest dreams…" Zaitah mumbles.

Cael manages to wipe his tears and calm his sobbing enough to speak. "What are you doing here of all places?" He says wiping his eyes.

"That's a long story. But I should ask you the same thing? What are you doing here?" Zaitah says standing them both up. He notices Wynn still attached to his side. "Who's your friend?" He smiles wide patting her on the head.

Wynn wipes her eyes laughing through tears. "It's just so good to finally meet you."

"What are *we* doing here?! What are *you* doing here?!" Cael demands. "Why are you so far away from home? Why are you fighting? Did Mathys say you were an alchemist for King James? What happened when you left?!"

Zaitah steps back. "Slow down there, baby brother! Let's get out of the middle of this crowd. Everyone is staring at us and it's a little unsettling."

"We can go to the tavern! It's a bit early, but it'll be warm, good food and we can stay out of sight. We're used to all the attention because we're kind of important. I wouldn't expect you to be used to it." Cael says smirking uncontrollably.

Zaitah laughs, "Oh sure, of course, I bet you're loads of important around here. Are you a lady in waiting? You have the figure for it."

Cael swats at him, "Even if I were, it'd still make me more important than you!"

Zaitah swats back, "Alright, you're all types of famous. Now lead us out of this crowd before they attack me for berating a lady of your station."

Zaitah removes his armor and examines the cuts and bruises on his chest and arm. "Take good care of these!" he says to the barkeep as he hands him his sword, armor, and remnants of his shield.

"Come on then, sit down! Tell us what in the good green grove you're doing here? How'd you get here anyway? It took us months!" Cael says unable to control his happiness.

"Months? Why would it take months? Unless you walked alongside a small wagon or something? It's only a month of hard riding from Kaldia to Oarna," Zaitah asks, confused.

"It's a long story, but we did end up having to walk from North Liefland after a few weeks at sea," Landon says.

Zaitah nods. "Ah, well if you take the scenic route then yes it'll take a lot longer. So tell me all about your travels!"

Cael shakes his head, "Wait, what about you?! Alchemist *and* envoy to the King of Kaldia?! How?! And what happened after that day in the city? I want to know everything!" Cael asks excitedly.

"After finishing my education at the university, it just sort of happened. Honestly I don't really remember!" Zaitah chuckles. "It's kind of weird; it's all a little blurry. Probably because you took off right around then, you little brat!"

"Well, I suppose, I mean I didn't really take off you know. I wouldn't have left if I had any choice," Cael mumbles.

Zaitah rubs his head. "I know little brother, I know. I'm glad you're doing well. Look how you've grown already!" He leans back and looks him up and down.

Cael puffs his chest. "Yup, I could pretty much thrash you like Harold did these days."

"Why were you fighting over here anyway?" Wynn asks, confused.

Zaitah stares, stunned. "Ah, well Wynn, I took to dueling at university and got pretty good. I imagine Cael's half decent too, Father taught us without ever really trying. Soon as I got into it, my muscles just took over; all that play fighting put to good use. Out of school I began working with the king's councilors. My talent was seen and they gave me tasks where having both a royal alchemist and swordsman would be useful. I was sent here along with a few others. Apparently, it's customary for each king to send a few champions to the Oarnian winter festival. Perhaps because it was the first of all the festivals."

"But what happened when you left Rensfort to go to Waylinn?" Wynn presses and Zaitah pats her head but quickly catches himself. "I'm sorry! You're so much like Cael, I forgot myself for a moment."

Wynn smiles. "We are a bit alike these days."

Cael and her laugh and Zaitah looks to both of them. "Am I missing something? What's happening?"

"It's a long story. But what of your trip to Waylinn? Didn't you say there was a way to fix the dreams?" Cael asks.

"What dreams?" Zaitah asks, confused.

Cael and Wynn stare for a moment. "Are you poking fun? The nightmares we had before we left? The whole reason we're here?"

Zaitah holds his head. "The nightmares, yes, I remember speaking with someone about them, but..." He says struggling to recall, "I don't think they could help me. When I got back, you were already gone. I never thought I'd see you again, but Father and Mother were certain you'd come back. They convinced me that we needed to imagine you were going to school somewhere and would be back in just a few years like I was."

Cael breathes a sigh of relief. "So they're doing well?"

Zaitah nods. "As well as could be expected; they miss you certainly. But I'd say for the most part the days pass just the same as they had before. I spend most of my free time with them, which isn't often, but it helps. There isn't as much warmth as when you were there, but I manage to get a chuckle out of them now and again."

Cael and Wynn squeeze Zaitah between them. "Thank you."

Zaitah laughs nervously. "What's this about?"

"Just so glad to see you..." Cael says.

"How's Clout?!" they nearly yell together.

"He's with me now. How do you think I got here so fast? He's lazy around you, but he's a working horse to be sure!" Zaitah smirks, "Wanna see him?"

They shoot out of their seats and push Zaitah down to the stables where Clout is waiting. Before they get there, he's already rearing up in excitement. The stable hand tries to calm him but Cael and Wynn run passed and open up his gate. He nuzzles them both and nips playfully at their hair as he bounces up and down unable to contain himself.

They squeeze tightly and let tears of joy fall from their faces.

"So, what's with these two?" Zaitah asks Landon.

Landon shrugs, "Who knows?"

After letting them brush and feed Clout as much as he can handle, Zaitah pulls a stool up. "So, tell me of your adventures. What brings you here?"

They take turns riding Clout in circles and excitedly telling Zaitah all about their journey so far, making sure to steer clear of anything that could worry him.

"And Wynn might have won the tournament, but my soul near left my body when Olam hit me!" Cael laughs but stops short and stares a moment. "Wait, how did you not hear of us? Piers spoke with everyone telling them our names and where we were from, you must have heard?"

Zaitah's smile fades as he thinks back. "I don't think I did. I mean I know I didn't. If I had, I would have obviously tried to find you. I did only just arrive a few days ago."

Wynn eyes him curiously. "Is something wrong?"

He turns to her. "No... well, yes. The group I came with, we have to leave tonight. I'm trying to think of why we need to leave and how I can find a way to stay. It's been bugging me. All I know is the king requested that we return as soon as possible and we agreed. I imagine they're waiting for me now, but I wasn't going to leave without spending time with this little goof!"

They rush to embrace him again. "You can't leave already!"

"Well, you said you both were leaving after the ball anyway, right?" he asks and they nod their heads. "So it would've only been another day at most, and we got to spend all this time together. More time than I usually can handle with you, you walnut."

Zaitah squeezes them both too tightly and Cael struggles, wheezing with the last of his breath, "You ass!" before they rip free and shove him off his stool.

"Can you at least stay to eat dinner?" Wynn asks.

Landon chuckles. "You two do realize that it's past midnight, right?" He points to the sky and the moons bright and high overhead.

Zaitah looks shocked. "Damn, I have to go! Come on, give us smooches!" He leans in and forces a kiss on their heads as they struggle free. "You work hard and come home soon, understood?!" They nod. "No time for tears, we've already done that, right? You'll be back smithing in no time."

They brush Clout all the way to the east entrance where Zaitah's companions stand anxiously. As they near, one shouts, "Finally! We were meant to leave as night fell!"

Another one snickers. "Not even a good excuse either, he's with kids! We thought one of those fair maidens caught your eye."

Zaitah waves them off. "This is my family you feckless twits. Besides we're only slightly behind schedule, so long as Jerin doesn't get sick again and Nichol doesn't stop at every alehouse from here to Kaldia." He sighs. "Let's move."

"Oh, now he wants to move," one of his group mumbles.

They all embrace again and Zaitah hops on Clout.

"You're going to have to let go of him for me to move," he says and they slowly untangle their fingers from his mane. "We'll see each other soon. I promise."

"We'll work really hard to get back! Send Mother and Father our love!" they call as he waves goodbye.

"What, no love for your brother?" he calls back.

Cael yells "Ass!" once more before he rides into the darkness.

Landon lets them stand at the gates, lost in their thoughts. He watches as their tears slowly fade while the moons wane in the night sky. After the streaks on their faces dry, he drapes his arms around their shoulders, "Come on, we should get to bed. If Piers has his way, tomorrow will be exhausting and we'll be glad for the rest."

They step lightly through the castle, following the now familiar hallways back to their room and sit on their beds thinking of family and friends and how their lives had changed. They are grateful to have Landon as their guide, saving them from a fate similar to Wynn's family. Their situation is a truly awful one, but

Landon and Jean have managed to make it more than just bearable, even enjoyable at times. They sleep easily as they count their many blessings and thank the king that sent Zaitah to them one last time before they leave for another world.

Chapter Fifty-Six

"What are you doing? Still asleep? Unacceptable! You must wake up, wake up now! Follow me! Up! Up!" They are shaken awake and rub their eyes as Nero peers down over them. "Quick like sparrows, come quick!" He pulls them out of their beds.

"What?" Cael mumbles. "Nero, it's so early.... Why are you here?"

"Why am I here? Why!? I have made beautiful masterpieces for you both! And the large one as well, but he is gone and you are here so I am taking you. I will take him later," Nero cries in exasperation.

"Alright, we're coming," Wynn grumbles. "Just, can we get something warm to eat first?"

"Eat? Eat!? You wish for something to eat?!" He laughs maniacally. "I have prepared spectacular dresses for you! I have found the gorgeous colors, I have sewn the perfect lines. I have worked the fingers until bleeding for days while you fight like a dirty man for no reason. You cause chaos while I have made perfection!" He moves quickly to Cael. "You as well, your figure was a muse, your build so very lithe, your complexion so very rough and tanned, highlighting your bright searching eyes! I have built wonders for you both! So let us go!"

Nero leads them to his work room and he shows them their formal attire. Wynn is presented a deep gold gown with a crinoline expanding the bottom fabric out into a bell shape. Blue sapphire pieces sewn in create a shimmering effect along the seam of the neckline. The dress has beautiful snowflake patterns with a whisper of blue cloth sewn as an outline, barely noticeable unless they inspect very carefully. The effect is remarkable. Magnificent golden and sapphire necklace, bracelets, rings and earrings are paired with the dinner gown.

He then presents her with her ballgown and Wynn gasps in delight. A pure silver gown, much more fitting to allow for easy dancing and without the crinoline. No excess designs take away from the gorgeous coloring. Nero presents her with stunning jewelry alongside the gown. He offers a silver and diamond necklace to accentuate her neckline and sapphire earrings.

"Yes, they are beautiful." He points to his assistant. "You, go fetch Arabella and find a man to take this one as well. I'm not sure what else can be done other than a good wash, but we will see it done!"

"Ah, your attire, young man, is right here." He holds out a green and gold shirt with dark green trousers. "Notice the patterns, they are mesmerizing, yes?" The gold inlay is an awe-inspiring pattern of squares and triangles wrapped in circles that somehow also manage to connect and repeat the pattern over and over while the green changes shade slightly creating a separate pattern alongside the shapes.

"And for the ball!" He holds out a maroon and silver silk shirt with black designs barely visible upon the deep maroon. He adds black trousers to the set. "Voila! You will all be beautiful!" He leans in. "I tell you a secret! The large man looks a peasant next to this! I had no time! Shameful yes, but it is to be. I had to ensure you both made a grand entrance. Many know of the larger one, he is not common but not rare. You two, you are brand new! You must be treated carefully as all will wish to see you, all eyes will pry. My work will be seen by all! They will say, 'Nero is truly genius!' They will all wish for me to make their gowns!"

Arabella walks in with Kit.

"We're here for—Oh my!" she cries out, seeing the dresses in Wynn's arms. "Come quickly! We have so much work to do!"

She pulls Wynn down the hallway and Kit stares at them. When he turns to Cael, he clears his throat, "Let's trod on then quickly! We've got all the work to do!" he mimics Arabella and pulls Cael down the hallway after them.

"Yes, prepare them well! They must be washed thoroughly!" Nero shouts as they are dragged away.

Arabella and Anastasia quickly rinse Wynn down before hastily working their way through the steps of grooming, saving the hair for last.

"Up or down?" Anastasia asks and Arabella smiles holding up the golden gown. They both squeal.

"Up! We can braid it and tie it around front and when you're preparing for the ball we can unbraid it and that will create a luscious and splendid wave. Everyone will adore you!" Anastasia shrieks, pulling Wynn's hair tightly and braiding one side while Arabella does the other.

Kit scoffs at the sound of the ladies giggling in the other room. "Them lady folk just chattin' away. I don't think it's right, that. They get all the fun stuff and us lads get none of it. Look at these grim clothes...." He holds up Cael's dress wear. "Dark colors, plain cloth really. Don't take my words wrong now; they're a right bit nicer than most of these men folk. It's just, well it ain't fair is what it is. Let me go get Thomas and Phillip." He rushes out the door.

Cael reaches out and cries, "No!"

But Kit's feet are already pounding down the hall.

"Not Phillip," Cael mutters under his breath.

Moments later, Thomas and Phillip open the door and immediately shriek in delight. "These are yours, yes?!" They hold up his clothes. "You demon wolf! How came you about Nero's favor? This is unacceptable! Thomas, I say to you that I have wanted for Nero's clothes for so long! This little man child gets them freely?! Life is cruel!"

Thomas nods sagely. "Indeed, sweet Phillip, indeed. But we must not show jealousy; it is petty! We must do our best with young Cael!"

And with that they begin their work. Not wanting to cut any corners, they fully wash him again and spray him down with perfume. They dress him in the dinner ware and lightly oil his hair. Once again, they try to color in his light mustache with charcoal, but this time Cael stops them.

"Please no!" He begs. "I'll look a fool!"

The shrug, reluctantly agreeing. "If you wish to be a man child then so be it."

Phillip and Arabella sneak the two back into their rooms fully dressed, shoving them in and hastily closing the door. Cael and Wynn stare at the door listening to the laughter and conversation growing quieter as the footsteps fade down the hall.

"Why am I not surprised," Landon says from the shadows.

Cael and Wynn turn around slightly startled.

"Why are you just sitting here in the dark!? You scared us damn near into the ground!" Cael complains.

"It wasn't dark! The door was opened letting enough light in for me to see, but then those two buffoons threw you two goofs in here and closed the door!" Landon chastises them with a smile on his face.

Landon lights the fire and they are struck by his appearance. His eyes and face are stunning, Nero would be justifiably elated to find that Landon's clothes, plain in comparison to Wynn or Cael's, compliment him perfectly. His ivory colored dinner clothes hug his tall and athletic build beautifully, and his long hair gracefully sits just passed his shoulders. The beautiful blue eyes are complimented by a turquoise ascot and cuffs.

"Hey, you don't look too bad," Cael says staring at him.

Wynn adds, "You are rather handsome when you're not talking or eating or traveling or being mean or—"

"Alright! I get it! Thank you!" Landon says, putting his hands over his face and sighing. "… so rude."

"When's the feast anyway?" Cael asks, feeding the fire.

"Should be any moment, I was worried when you two were gone but Nero told me you were being 'beautified' and prepared to wear his 'master collection.' I thought it was rabble, but those outfits are actually not awful on you both. I'm sure Piers and Nero will be ecstatic to see the reactions you'll get," Landon replies enviously.

"What's it going to be like? Do we sit next to Piers? What will they serve?" Wynn asks.

"Do we need to do anything special? How many people are going? How long is it?" Cael adds.

Landon shakes his head and sits down next to them. "What's got you both so anxious now? Nerves finally reaching you? I suppose that's decent. You didn't worry this whole week; that's a bit impressive actually."

"Answers, man!" Cael says, playfully shaking him

Landon waves Cael's hands away. "It's a formal dinner, it'll be very ... well, very formal. Everyone here, of note at least, will be there, so hundreds I imagine. Just have fun, but don't say anything unless someone approaches you. Stay close to me and Piers. He'll help you I'm sure."

"What about the ball?" Wynn asks.

"The ball is a little different. There are rules," he admits, nodding his head. "More so for Cael than you, but at the ball you're only meant to enjoy yourselves. I'll keep my eyes on you both, but I imagine the uptight folks will get more and more loose as the night moves along. The ball is where everyone will be making a play to get close to you two, hoping to leech some of the attention or simply to find out who you truly are. It'll be a very interesting game."

"Alright, so it's not a big to do," Cael says, calming himself down.

Landon pats him on the shoulder. "Don't be nervous, lad. It seems daunting, but they're just people like anyone else. A bit more gold in their pockets than most, but they rise and fall like the sun and moons so they feel they have more to prove. You're not the ones who need to worry because none of this matters at all. Tomorrow we're gone and everyone will forget about us. But tonight? Tonight you're both holding all the cards, so take advantage of it!"

Piers busts in the door and spreads his arms. "My royal guests! It is time! Let us walk to the great hall together, yes?" He opens his eyes and takes a step back. "Veera's eyes! You all look absolutely perfect! Stunning! Wonderous!" He tears up with emotion. "This is more than I could have ever asked for! I'm just so thrilled that my sisters will be feasting on envy and jealousy tonight!" He grabs Cael and Wynn by their hands. "Come quickly! We simply must go right away so all can see how spectacular you look! My royal guests are all the talk and now they look truly royal! Nero has worked a perfectly unexpected bit of magic and I am so happy!"

Piers leads them towards their seats. They pass by tables long enough to sit everyone here and more. He moves down the length of the room. They continue toward a section reserved for the royal family and their guests overlooking the entire great hall.

Dozens of people begin piling into the room and mulling around. As they finally make it to their seats, Piers holds up his hand and gestures to a corner. "We must wait until Father arrives to sit at the table." Piers scans the guests as they enter the hall and begins talking, surveying the crowd. "That there is the Duke of Benilay; his brother sold much of their estate to fuel his many vices. Oh, that over there is the Prince of North Liefland, Jasper. His father rarely mentions him, very embarrassed, but the public knows of him so what can you do, yes? There's Father's military commander, Vellen; he's always wearing his most favorite frown everywhere he goes. That is the Duchess of Leckinbury. She has such exquisite taste, but she's so very ugly so no one ever notices. There's the princesses of Kaldia, our winter festival always draws them out of hiding. So odd that they hide given they are quite pleasing to the eye, yes?"

Piers continues on, gossiping about nearly every person who enters the room. He stops whispering as members of the court wishing to gain favor approach him to pay compliments but continues as soon as they leave.

Piers grabs Cael and Wynn's hands and squeezes. "My sisters! Oh, this is perfect! Let us ignore them for now. They will surely come to us and then we can make them look pathetic and jealous!"

Just as Piers hoped, Princess Emilia and Princess Elise slowly make their way around the table. They stop frequently to speak quickly with guests just as Piers had before continuing on their very clear path towards Cael and Wynn. Despite walking towards them, they never look in their direction until they greet Piers.

"Hello dearest brother! It's so very rare for you to come home, I think Rosé rather suits you well. Don't you Emilia?" Elise says.

Emilia nods. "Yes, certainly. Rosé is filled with blithering idiots and commoners, fit for someone like you Piers." She turns her head towards Wynn but doesn't look at her. "I cannot begin to understand why either of you would have hitched your cart to our very simple-minded brother, but I can tell you now it will do you no good. Whatever your reasons, he has no influence and can do nothing for you. He will never be king and he will never rule." She turns her eyes on Wynn, they go wide for the smallest of moments before she composes herself. A blink and it would have been missed, even looking straight on it would be easy to mistake as imagination.

Elise smirks at Wynn. "I'm so glad that Nero took all the time he needed to design something to fit your color and frame, it must have been dreadfully difficult."

Emilia giggles. "I'd hasten to say near impossible if it hadn't been for the creativity of our dear Nero!"

"Thank you, it does fit rather well." Wynn smiles back.

Landon steps between them and bows, "Your Royal Highnesses, it's wonderful to see you again."

"Who are you?" Emilia says curtly. She doesn't wait for a response before pushing Landon and Piers out of the way, looking Cael up and down. "My, Nero has done a fine job," she says, playing with her necklace.

Elise blushes behind her sister, meeting Cael's eye.

Before Cael can say anything, the sound of trumpets fill the room and the king begins walking down the grand staircase. Everyone moves to their seats and waits for the king to speak.

King Arlem opens his arms welcoming the room with a smile. "Friends, family, honored guests, thank you for joining us on this holy day of renewal and purity. We once again come together to celebrate this festival and to give our thanks to Finra. As is tradition, Archbishop Eklan will lead our prayers."

The king steps back and presents the archbishop, suitably dressed in his amber colored robes and mitre adorned with emeralds and brown diamonds.

The archbishop bows to the king before addressing the crowd with an echoing voice, "We accept this winter as Finra himself created it so. Vashir's wrath had borne sin unto this peaceful place, and we must accept the winter as our time of purity and cleansing. To refresh and renew our bodies and souls. Only truly pure may we walk the garden of eternal life where Finra waits for each of us. In life, we may fall to the cold just as we see the plants and animals around us fall during winter. But those who endure will be cleansed. The *Book of Purity* teaches us that these mortal forms are but a garden for our souls to seed. Just as the mightiest tree's sprout from their humble beginnings, our souls will sprout from our mortal gardens. Our journey in the life after is one of many paths, but only one leads to Finra. If we are to reach Him, we must care for ourselves and those around us. We must accept our winter punishment and we must strive daily to live pure lives."

He places his hands ceremoniously in a bowl. "Today, on this solstice, the night will steal the day. Darkness holding longer in the endless war, the light fading faster. But tomorrow it will grow stronger. We accept this day of darkness and rejoice in its embrace knowing well that the light within us will grow stronger as the morning sun rises. We wash our hands in this sand as all things come from and return to it."

Servants pass around ceremonial bowls of fine sand ground to a powder for the guests to cleanse their hands in.

"We raise a glass, to honor the light." The hall all raise their glasses. "We drink of water to sate our souls thirst."

They drink.

"Now we take this food unto our bodies and celebrate life." The Archbishop sits in his seat and takes a bite of food. As soon as he swallows, the room fills with the sound of moving chairs and plates marking the end of the sermon and the start of the feast.

They look to Piers for guidance on how to act and what to eat, copying his actions. Once they've eaten a bit and relaxed, they start reaching for food and choosing what they wish. The whole room quickly devolves into hundreds of conversations and they feel comfortably invisible in the noise.

"I've heard many things about you two." King Arlem's voice startles them but he sets them at ease with a quick smile. "All good things, I assure you. But I was wondering how much of it was true. You are both quite young to be emissaries for King

Thokrin, and I find it nigh impossible for you to have fought in the Battle of Miral Plains. Some things I know to be true are that you've found yourself in the company of one of the finest trackers in the world, Cael here is the brother to the King of Kaldia's own alchemist and you are both acquainted with the King of North Liefland. If nothing else, those are quite impressive statements, but why? Why are you here and how came you to be connected with nearly every royal family in the Five Kingdoms?"

"It's an absolutely wonderful story, Father! They've been warring and defeating foes across the land and have gained a marvelous reputation—"Piers begins to answer for them.

Cael speaks ahead of him, "I beg forgiveness Prince Piers, but I think the truth can be shared with at least your father, don't you?"

Piers is taken aback and huffs, crossing his arms and slinking down in his chair. "Yes, well go on then." He mumbles in irritation.

"We met Landon by chance in Kaldia. He helped us when no one else could and he's still helping us now. We're to set sail in the morning for our final destination. It's been quite fun living this fireside tale with everyone here at your castle, but I'm afraid none of it is true," Cael says, disappointment in his voice.

The king laughs. "None of it true? Young man, what I said before I know to be true. And if this journey of yours brings no other accolades than the ones I've listed, you've already impressed me. For two so young, even younger than Piers here, to have traveled the Five Kingdoms, met with kings and competed in the winter festival tournament? I speak truthfully when I say that I am excited to see what you both accomplish next."

Landon stands up and grabs Cael and Wynn by the shoulders, winking at them. "Actually, Your Majesty, they've accomplished a fair bit more than that. Cael is a skilled blacksmith and hunter. Wynn survived with nothing, all alone, for near half a year. They endured one of the most difficult experiences known to us at the Isle and did so with no training. They sailed through a storm the likes I have never seen before. They were attacked on the road by more than two dozen thieves and riding with just three mercenaries, they fended them all off. All of this they've accomplished before their lives have even truly begun."

The king nods along looking more and more impressed and Piers eyes grow wider the longer Landon speaks.

"Well, why didn't we say those things!?" Piers cries out in exasperation.

The king places his hand on Piers's arm to calm him. "I cannot imagine having experienced what you both have at such a young age, I'll have to keep a close eye on you two. Once your training is done, perhaps we can find a place for you here?"

"Perhaps," Landon says, sipping his wine.

Wynn nudges him and whispers, "Why did you tell him all that?"

Landon turns away, greeting the guests around him and responds silently, *'It's difficult for us to appreciate the true scope of what we've accomplished because time separates everything. When your deeds are listed clearly like that, and especially listed to a king, you begin to recognize the strength you possess. Confidence in yourselves and in each other is what will allow you to grow stronger and reach further than you could dare to dream.'*

"I have high hopes for you both!" Landon says, reaching around Wynn and ruffling Cael's hair.

They continue the feast, unable to stop smiling. Their cheeks soon start to hurt, but it's a happy pain. After eating their fill, they lean back in their seats to find very few people still remaining in the great hall.

"Everyone's getting ready for the ball." Landon answers before they ask. "We should too."

"Thank you, Your Majesty, for the kind words." Wynn says with a curtsey.

Cael bows. "It was an experience that we will cherish as a gift."

"It was freely given, just as your presence was a gift to us," the king replies, shaking their hands.

As they turn to leave, they notice the remaining guests in the hall staring at them mouths agape.

"That was a tremendous sign of respect the king just bestowed upon you, shaking your hands like that. If I had to guess, I'd say he wants you both to continue enjoying the attention you've been getting," Landon whispers as he ushers them out of the dining hall and into the hallway.

They arrive back in their bedroom and begin preparing for the ball. Landon has a dark green outfit with not much flair other than a few rather odd brown designs creating a very tree or bush like appearance. Cael and Wynn hastily put their formal wear on. They take turns using a small bit of reflective metal to ensure their faces are clean and tidy.

"Should I ..." Cael starts to ask with the bit of charcoal out.

Wynn laughs. "No, those men are buffoons! We look amazing as we are."

"Yes, you both look beautiful," Landon mumbles. "Now let's go." He buckles up his straps. He turns around dumbly and as his eyes lay upon them for the first time his mouth drops. "I'm ... I don't know what to say. Wynn you look like true royalty, I feel like I should bow or do something."

Wynn blushes. "Oh shut it."

Cael brushes his clothes. "Well what about me?" he asks indignantly.

Landon eyes him closely, "You look amazing. But not as amazing as me!" Landon laughs. "Let's go quickly now. I'm excited to see what this night has in store for us all."

Chapter Fifty-Seven

Landon leads them to the courtyard doors where a line has formed around the corner. Two guards open the way for each group of guests separately. The crowd around them in line all whisper amongst themselves, but it's clear the topic of conversation is Cael and Wynn.

As they make it to the front of the line and turn the corner, the guards open the doors. Their eyes fall on the courtyard completely transformed. No stages or tracks remain. No tournament rings or dusty trails. An impossible feat, the entire courtyard has gone from a week's worth of being worn down by hundreds of guests to appearing as though none of it ever happened. The smell of flowers and perfumes hit them immediately upon stepping foot outside the castle walls and onto the soft, thick grass of the courtyard. They walk in awe, feeling the dark green leaves and bright white flower petals in their fingers. The path comes to an archway and opens up to the main grounds. A smooth polished stone floor replaces the grass and on the other side a slightly raised wooden platform where music is softly played adding to the dreamlike ambience.

They move towards the seating, pure white cloth covering the seats and tables. Carafe's of white wines waiting on each one. Every table having a plate of pastries covered in white creams. They are greeted by Mathys who leads them to their table at the front.

"This is all so pretty," Wynn says sitting down and clenching her fists in excitement. "What do we do now? When does the dancing begin?"

"Enjoy the pastries and have a drink!" Landon says, reaching over and pouring himself a glass. "Breathe in the night air." He takes a deep breath and smiles as he exhales.

They happily join him and set their nerves at ease. As each guest passes them, they are greeted with a small curtsey or bow. They wave to each person, feeling as though the ball was for them alone and fiercely enjoying the attention.

The royal family arrives, and the music stops as they walk to their larger table directly next to Cael, Wynn and Landon. The king grins at them seeing them dressed perfectly for the occasion. Piers, Emilia, Elise and the Queen Erelia sit at the table and the king ceremonially offers his hand out to his bride with a bow. She grasps his outstretched hand firmly and he raises her to her feet. A harp begins playing a smooth tune and they take to the floor dancing beautifully as they likely have for years.

A few moments pass and then Piers offers his hand to Wynn. She hesitates a moment nervously, but Landon nudges her into accepting.

"What do I do?" she whispers to Piers as he whisks her off to the dance floor.

He whispers back, "Just do as I do!"

Landon stands and pulls Cael up inconspicuously. Too nervous to be confused, he follows Landon to Emilia and Elise and Landon offers his hand down to Emilia who smiles and lets herself be guided to the floor. Cael does the same and Elise matches her sister's grace.

Cael's heart begins pounding as if he were on a hunt and he mumbles anxiously, "I don't really know how to dance."

If she is disappointed, she doesn't let it show.

"It's a very simple dance," she says quietly without looking at him. She grasps his hands and places them properly above her waist and the other gripped with hers outstretched near shoulder height. Cael watches her feet and matches her steps well, surprising them both.

Moments later, the floor is filled with pairs of guests. All dancing in small circles around one another but also in a larger circle around the four pairs of them in the center. It looks like the world is spinning around them. Wynn and Piers grin wildly as all eyes fall on them. Cael is too focused on his feet to notice anything, not even the eyes of Elise in front of him hoping to be seen.

After the first ceremonial dance, it becomes a free for all with men or women asking to dance with whomever they deem fit. Most of the guests deeming Cael and Wynn as the perfect partners. Landon continues his dance with Emilia while Cael and Wynn have a line of suitors seeking their hands.

Names escape both of them and they hardly have time to breathe as each partner fires questions at them in quick succession, hoping to gain any insight as to who they truly are and if anything could be gained by aligning with them. Older guests and younger guests all offer their hands to dance, and not knowing what else to do, they accept them all. The night draws on and the game becomes easier for both Cael and Wynn. The more questions they are asked, the easier they find it to respond with as little or as much detail as they want, whether true or false. It becomes a fun game as each person leaves happily with fresh information to take their companions or frustrated receiving nothing new.

The short time in between their dances is spotted with quick bites of deliciously soft, fluffy deserts and sips of surprisingly light sweet, fermented fruit drinks.

They sit for the rare moment of relaxation, enjoying their drinks and deserts. Cael feels a tap on his shoulder and lets himself sigh slightly before turning around to Elise.

"Hello!" he says, quickly swallowing the food in his mouth.

She extends her hand. "Would you care to dance? Again, I mean?"

He nervously accepts her hand. Wynn's eyes go wide and she covers her face, hiding her surprise. Cael shoots her a playful scowl and lets himself be led to the floor.

Prince Harold walks over to Wynn. "Will you join me?"

He bows and offers his hand. Wynn graciously accepts and joins Cael and Elise in their dance. Cael shoots her a surprised look and she sends his earlier scowl back to him.

"For whatever reason my dumb brother had to invite you, I'm glad he did," Elise says, smiling as they dance together.

Cael blushes. "I still don't understand why he invited us because we're just normal people."

She looks at him seriously. "You heard my father. What you were before your journey, you are no longer that person. You are more now with Landon and my father behind you. That alone makes you special."

Cael smiles back at her and they spin around, letting the world fall away.

"I saw you with Zaitah. How do you know him?" Harold asks Wynn politely as they circle the floor.

"He's our... I mean Cael's brother. How do you know him?" she replies curiously, having difficulty separating her shared emotions with Cael.

"I met Zaitah months ago. He was on a very interesting quest with his professor," he says, keeping his form perfectly still, leading them along their dance.

Her curiosity eats away the moments until it gets the better of her. "What was the intent of the quest?" she tries to ask as uninterestedly as possible.

"It was a quest for an answer, but the question I cannot say." He allows himself a smirk. "But I can say the answer."

She waits expectantly but his patience wins.

"Well, what was the answer?" she asks stubbornly.

He laughs coyly, "The answer was yes." He returns to his passive form as they spin. "But I have another question for you. How do you know Landon?"

"Well I have a question for you. How do you know everyone?" she asks, feeling chills as her irritation fights through Cael's excitement.

Harold maintains his even composure, "Ah, but I asked you first. Decency dictates that you shall answer my question before I answer yours."

Wynn huffs with her impatience. "Landon is a friend of Cael's. We're on a journey."

Harold's eyebrows raise. "Both of you, truly? You and Cael? To the Isle of Storms?"

Wynn stops moving in surprise but Harold forces her along. "We must continue." He allows Wynn to regain composure before answering. "While Zaitah and I were discussing his question, Landon arrived with a company of men from North Liefland. More than that I cannot say."

They finish their dance and Harold leads her back to her table and whispers in her ear, "Trust yourself."

She sits in silence trying to puzzle out the cryptic message. Cael plops down next to her with a wide grin painted on his face.

'Harold told me to trust myself,' she thinks.

Cael laughs. *'Well, what a vague thing to say!'*

'He also told me that Zaitah and Landon know each other, and Zaitah met him seeking an answer to a question.'

Cael sits up. "Do you think it means something? Why are you so worried about it?"

She shoots him a look.

'Fine, fine. But don't you think that this would be louder to people listening for it?' he thinks to her.

She shakes her head. "You're right." She leans in and whispers to him, "I think Zaitah left for Waylinn searching for an answer to your dreams, right?"

Cael nods. "Yes, but Harold is from South Liefland."

Wynn gets irritated. "Which is north of Waylinn. Maybe this professor decided to meet with Harold in South Liefland? Who cares? All we know is that Zaitah and Landon met, but Zaitah and Landon aren't admitting they met. Why? What happened?"

Cael shrugs off their irritation. "Maybe they don't remember? It's not like Zaitah would have been shouting that he's my brother, and they never met before so it's possible, right? Just a random person that you meet for a moment? Not everything has to mean something."

Wynn huffs trying to find an argument but sighs. "You're right. I suppose… But you have to admit, it's all just weird."

Cael nods his head. "I'll give you that; it's weird. But it's probably just weird and nothing else. Coincidences happen all the time."

Cael puts a few pastries on their plates and they pick at them while sipping their drinks.

"Hello, Wynn. Would you like to accompany me?"

Wynn turns as Kellin offers his hand.

She hesitates a moment before Cael pushes her. "She'd love to!"

Cael finishes his drink and squeezes through a crowd of suitors, catching Elise's eye and motions to the floor. She excuses herself and they giggle as they run to the floor, arm in arm.

Before long, Wynn is dancing happily with Kellin as they laugh about the tournaments and their friends. Talking about everything and nothing and forgetting everything else. The four of them spend the rest of the ball together. Eating, drinking, and dancing the night away.

As the night begins to fade, they say their goodnights and head back to their rooms. Too exhausted to change, they collapse on their beds without a care in the world and sleep deeply.

Chapter Fifty-Eight

"Pack your stuff, the ship's ready." Landon voice floats into their dreamless sleep. He shakes them softly at first but gives up and hits them with a pillow. "Wake up," he says sternly, trying to stay quiet.

"Hmm?" Cael manages to get out before sleep pulls him under again.

Landon shakes them both and Wynn kicks her leg at him. "What're you doing? We just fell asleep."

"The ship is ready; it's nearly dawn. There's a nice easterly wind coming down from the mountains that the captain wants to capitalize on," Landon says as he begins to pack their belongings in travel bags.

Cael sits up, eyes still closed and legs thrown out in front of him. "What's happening?" He yawns with a long stretch.

"You two! If I didn't like you both so much, I'd hate you." Landon sighs and his sigh becomes an order. "Look, I've already packed your stuff. Let's go!"

"Alright, we're going," Cael says, rolling off the bed, but his feet don't make it out in time and he falls to the floor with a thud. "Ow."

His voice is muffled from being smooshed into the floor and Wynn gets up and leaves to the adjoining washroom.

"Where are you going?" Landon's voice is sharp with irritation.

"To go pee," Wynn says, defiantly.

"All the other recruits are on the ship and waiting for us. The seekers are holding the captain in port but we need to leave right now, so hurry up," he replies, ignoring her tone.

Cael pulls himself to his feet and stumbles into the washroom as Wynn leaves.

"Did you pack all of our things?" Wynn asks, changing into her traveling clothes and folding her dress neatly.

"Yes." Landon huffs. "Can we go now?"

Wynn searches through the pack and scowls at him as she rummages through the drawers and pulls out Jean's dagger. "You missed this!"

"Well, you have it now, so let's get going," Landon replies curtly.

Cael bumps into the table as he wanders out of the other room and picks up his travel sack. "Alright, man, we're ready to go." He yawns again. "No need to get all twisted up about it."

Landon hurries them through the castle and lifts them into the carriage, calling to the driver, "Thank you again, Benjie. I'm sorry it's so early."

"Don't fret on it, friend. I've done earlier! We'll get you down to the docks in no time," Benjie says in a jolly voice.

As soon as the carriage starts to rumble along the road, Cael and Wynn are lulled back to sleep. Landon sighs but allows them to rest until the docks. He climbs around to sit with Benjie and they ride in silent companionship. The city comes alive with the small dancing light of lanterns reaching out and meeting the suns dawning rays.

Cael and Wynn begin to stir from the noise around them just before Benjie pulls their carriage up. The same harbormaster from Rosé, Ganlin, walks to the carriage and seeing the cargo helps them down and promptly directs them to their vessel. "Off to the Isles? Should be decent traveling, fair weather, good winds," he says.

"Thanks, Ganlin," Cael mutters, barely able to stand on his own feet but managing to board the ship with some effort.

Ganlin waves. "Safe journeys."

"Oh, look who finally decided to show up," a man about Landon's age calls from the bow of the ship, surrounded by a shockingly large group of children.

"Mikal, it's good to see you as well," Landon calls back. "This looks like more than we discussed. How many nihls are here?"

"Is our cargo not as precious as yours? Would you rather we left these children out to die?" Mikal replies, venom in his voice.

Landon makes a calming gesture. "I was just asking a question, Mikal. Let's try and get along for at least the next few days, alright?"

Mikal turns his back and leans against the handrail glaring out at the ocean. "Sure, we should all be blessed that Landon the Emir decided to sail with us lowly seekers."

A handful of other seekers stand quietly around their charges, avoiding any potential conflict. Landon waves away the confrontation and heads towards the captain's quarters.

"Remus, good to see you!" he calls, grasping the captain's arm.

"You as well, friend. Too bad you didn't make it earlier. Jacques had planned on seeing you a few weeks ago. Any trouble on the roads?" Remus asks.

Landon shakes his head quickly. "Trouble? Me? You must be thinking of someone else!" He laughs.

Remus smiles back. "Of course, how could I assume you would get in trouble of all people, eh?" He chuckles. "Alright, should be a nice smooth ride in through till the Isles." He turns to Cael and Wynn, "Relatively speaking, of course. We still need to navigate the storms." He leans in. "But lucky for you I'm the best captain around." He winks and pats their heads. "Go ahead and load in your cargo. Landon, we've got a cabin for you."

"Enough room for the three of us?" Landon asks.

Remus raises his eyebrow but doesn't miss a beat, "Should be, yeah."

Landon leads them down a set of solid stairs through the small vessel and into one of only a few separated sleeping rooms. Cael and Wynn hardly notice anything around them as their exhaustion begins taking over once again. They drop their packs, collapse on the bed and let their dreams steal them away.

They wake up feeling rested in a cabin on a ship sailing the seas. The end of their journey on their minds, but also thinking back to the beginning. How it all began on a ship much like the one they ride now. Though this vessel is slightly smaller and the wood has less character than on their last captain's ship. There was a warmth to that ship. Even with Derik and his group causing trouble, the passengers were in a generally good mood. But not here, there is only despair clinging to this vessel.

They walk out onto the deck and are welcomed by a chill air and the open water all around them. The mist off the waves makes it feel colder than the air itself. Landon spots them and signals them over to where he and Remus are sitting in the cabin and speaking. The group of adolescents largely keep to themselves, staying quiet. Cael and Wynn hear hushed whispers as they walk by them.

"Have a seat." Landon invites them to the table. "What's that look about?" he asks them as they sit.

"What's wrong with those kids?" Cael asks bluntly. "Why are they all huddled together like that? And why are they staring at us?"

Remus leans back in his chair and waits for Landon to respond. "I told you before, I'm not a seeker." Landon says.

Remus laughs. "You can say that again."

Landon puts a hand on Remus' shoulder silencing him.

"You two were lucky," he continues and waves for them to be quiet. "Before you say anything, I know you don't think you were. Some part of you still thinks I'm awful and likely some part of you always will. But if you wonder what it would have been like if another seeker found you, well wonder no further." He gestures beyond the door and to the children just outside, cowering on the deck.

"It's difficult to see them like this, but it's not hard to see *why* they are like this. You both know what happens to some families. One lazy seeker can cause a lot of unnecessary harm, almost as much as those Sephalim rebels. Most seekers will become complacent, they just find the dreamers and take them.

They're told not to explain too much, so most don't explain anything at all. I don't have what it takes to be a seeker, but they are invaluable. Think about this, after all you've seen, after the traveling and meeting all those people, do you really believe that the masses would accept us? Power is precious. If everyone realized what they thought to be power was not even the beginning? Well, that would frighten them. The only truth you need to accept is that we are a scary type of different, and that people just like you are fighting hard to protect our lives because that is what they believe to be precious. And whether you choose to believe it or not, those men and women out there, those seekers, those are our best hope at ensuring our lives and livelihood continue. They might be seen as evil, and the friends you make will all have stories helping to paint them in a bad light, but without them, most of us would be dead. We'd be burned or hanged as evil demons sent from Vashir or whatever anti-god their religion expresses."

Remus nods. "Sounds crazy, but I've seen something of it, and Landon has seen more than his fair share of it."

They absorb what Landon tells them and sit quietly thinking on it. Landon lets them have a moment before he ruffs their hair. "Come on then, go meet those other kids! They'll be your roommates for the next few years and you don't want them thinking you're privileged, trust me."

He shoos them out the door and closes it behind them. The group of children stand still, staring at them, watching to see what they'll do. As Cael and Wynn approach, they are assaulted with questions asked barely above a whisper.

"Who are you? Where are you from? Who is the man you're with? Why do you get a room? What's your name? Aren't you scared? Are we really magic? Do you know what's going on? Do you know the captain? What did he tell you? Do you know anything? Are you rich? Why are your clothes so clean? Did you travel far? What were you talking about in there? Is there really going to be a big storm? How old are you?" the group asks all at once.

Cael and Wynn become nervous as they are surrounded. All of the kids seem more and more aggressive and the group feels more like a mob as they close in around them. Wynn and Cael shut their eyes and take a deep breath easing their nerves. When they open them, they no longer see an angry mob forming, only a scared group of kids taken from their families and forced to march for who can say how long. Rather than fearing for themselves, they begin feeling pity for the group.

Cael sits and Wynn follows. Without saying anything, the entire group sits around them and huddles in close.

"My name is Cael and this is Wynn," Cael says in a soft soothing voice that's similar to if he had a mind to coax a rabbit out of its den.

"We're from Kaldia. Where are you all from?" Wynn asks and a chorus of answers echo around them.

"Waylinn."

"North Liefland."

"Kaldia."

"South Liefland."

"Oarna."

"Alundra."

Children from all of the Five Kingdoms and more are there.

"And what are your names?" She asks as the answers fade.

The chorus continues, "Skyla. Helden. Celeste. Gerry. Jurin. Keth. Marten. Eko. Vincent. Starr. Alvida. Rosa. Lane. Irida. Thlef. Fei. Jade. Renka. Uriel."

"I can't remember all the questions you asked," Cael begins and the cacophony of questions starts again, but he holds up his hands to still them. "But! I'll just tell you everything we know. After all we're in this together. Right, Wynn?" he asks.

She nods. "Right!"

"The way Landon told it...." Cael begins describing their new lives and the seekers role in protecting them.

As he finishes a young girl, Celeste, calls out, "These seekers don't protect us. They told us our families would never remember us!"

Keth adds, "Or they just kill them...."

"I know," Wynn says, "My family was killed but it wasn't a seeker."

"Some of these seekers are bad, they might do cruel things. Things they shouldn't be allowed to do. But worse, there's a whole other group that's out there killing families. Families like Wynn's.

And maybe even some of yours were hurt by these other people. I know it's confusing. This whole thing is wrong and unfair. We shouldn't be taken from our families. But what we've seen is that the world would care less for us than even those rebels do."

"That's stupid!" Eko cries. "These people hurt us. My neighbor wouldn't do that to me!"

The group of children agree adamantly, nodding their heads up and down forcefully.

"Your neighbor doesn't know you can do this." Cael says as he plucks a piece of his hair and lights it on fire. The group look on in amazement.

Wynn smiles. "Or this!" She visualizes Eko and as many others as she can in her mind and imagines a butterfly flittering above their heads. A few of them gaze in awe as the rest of the group stares at them dumbfounded.

"She's showing them a butterfly, but only they can see it." Cael winks

"How'd you learn all that?" Starr asks.

Cael and Wynn set about detailing their adventures, leaving out the royal encounters to avoid from causing too much envy. The group settles in and is enraptured by the tales, listening attentively to every detail.

As they reach their practicing on the road with Jean, Mikal overhears them and runs over.

He lifts them up forcefully and shouts, "You used your gifts openly?! You could have destroyed everything we've worked so hard to protect! You could have killed us all!" He raises his hand to strike and on instinct Cael moves quickly out of reach of his swing. He grabs Mikal's wrist and pulls him off balance while Wynn kicks his leg, knocking him hard to the ground.

Landon rushes over and picks Mikal up, turning around angrily towards Cael and Wynn. Before he can yell, Mikal pulls him back. "You taught them! How much? Just because you're an Emir, you think you are above our laws? What if they were caught? What if someone has seen them and they are spreading word as we stand here!?"

The other seekers, astonished at the accusations look at Landon with disgust.

Landon gestures for him to calm down, but Mikal dives into Landon's mind. Seeing their journey from start to finish, watching Landon teach them on the deck under the stars, seeing them join and Landon listening to Jean and them recount their journey and their progression.

Landon feels the intrusion, a disruption of his own thoughts and recollection of all that Mikal sees. Mikal shouts to the other seekers. "He taught these children so much that they've joined!"

In his anger, Landon solidifies the air around Mikal, holding him perfectly still. Slowly the air in his lungs is released. The seekers stare in disbelief, but one steps forward. "He meant no harm, Emir Landon! He was rash. We accept his actions and will present them to the council!"

Landon's face changes quickly from rage to shame and he releases Mikal. "I apologize Nola. There's no need to take this to the council. Mikal will never make an attempt like that on me again. Will you, Mikal?"

Landon scowls down on the ground where Mikal is on his knees catching his breath. Mikal glares at Landon with pure hatred in his eyes but nods his head in agreement.

Nola helps Mikal to his feet and hands him to the other seekers. "I think it's time for dinner and then bed. That's enough stories for today, children." She ushers them below deck.

The deck empties, leaving Cael and Wynn alone with Landon.

"We're sorry, we didn't think that you would get in trouble here." Cael apologizes.

Landon hangs his head. "It's not your fault. Mikal is right. I shouldn't have taught you." He looks at them seriously and places his hands on their shoulders. "But sometimes, you just have to make your own decisions. You must trust yourself to know what's right even if others think it's wrong. Come on, let's get some food before it's all gone," he says, resting his arms around them and leading them to the galley.

They eat with the group and notice the kids acting differently. They are less scared and more willing to talk. The seekers hurry the dinner along and send everyone to their bunks, hoping to speed the journey along with a lengthy night's sleep.

Chapter Fifty-Nine

They rise with the morning light, the rest of the passengers still sleeping off their journey. The two of them quietly go about their morning routine, not wanting to disturb Landon. They grab a few bits of salted meat to chew on before heading up to the deck.

As they step outside, they're greeted with one of their favorite sites. The gorgeous sky already a palette of colors from the sun's morning journey. The sea mirrors the sky even in the choppy water. Darkness and stars are still high above, but the dawn slowly pushes back the mystery of the night and shows the beauty of the day.

They gaze out at the water as it moves past them, staring into the depths.

"What are you two doing up so early?" Landon's voice calls from the stairs.

"Nothing," they reply together.

Landon greets them with a smile. "That never gets old, does it?"

The peaceful scene is shattered as the ship collides with something in the water and tilts sharply to its side. They grip the railing and steady themselves. The passengers panic below deck and all gather above searching for any damage.

"Dear, it wasn't that hard, they're fine. Yes, I know. Yes, dear. Eh hem, tiny humans! Can you hear me? What, dear? Yes, I know they're all tiny. Would you like to address them?"

Landon peers over the edge. "Hello?" He calls out confused.

The voice responds, "Yes, dear, you were right. They did respond. Very good."

"Where are you? We can't see you." Landon asks.

An enormous creature breaks the surface of the water just off the port side of the ship. All of the passengers back away quickly, even the seekers are shocked by what they're seeing. The captain stands still, mouth agape in awe.

"I didn't know whales could speak," Landon replies to the monstrous beast in the water as calmly as he can manage.

"Did you hear that, dear!? They didn't know we could speak! I'm quite unsure of why we're helping them. They are quite hideous above the water as well. Right, of course. Very small humans! There are other very small humans coming towards your floating wooden vessel. Say again, dear? Oh, yes. They are planning on capturing the tiniest of the humans and of course to exterminate the larger of the human breed. Yes, dear, children, I know the word. I already said that, dear. No, dear. Yes, dear," the whale says.

Landon calls to the seekers. "You all heard this?" They nod and Landon turns his attention back to the whale. "Kind whale, can you assist us? How far out are they?"

"No, we cannot. We are already very late for our trip to the southern seas and if we are not there shortly we will miss the season!" he calls back, irritated and spouts water from a hole in the center of his head. "Very well, dear. They are twenty or thirty strokes towards the claw star. But that is all I can say."

"How many are there?" Landon pushes.

The whale spouts water again. "My Love has said that she heard as many as she hears now."

"Including the children?!" Landon says anxiously.

"I do not know. That is all I will permit. Good day," the whale replies before submerging beneath the waves.

Landon turns around, trying to calm himself while the other seekers struggle to comprehend what they just saw.

"What should we do, Emir Landon?" One of the older seeker's pleads. "Do we turn around?"

Remus shakes his head. "We can't, we're sailing with the wind right now. If we turn around, we'll be fighting a losing battle. I don't know how far a stroke is or where a claw star is, but if they're trying to overtake us, they'll be in a lighter vessel."

"So what do we do?" Nola asks Landon.

"Give me a moment to think!" He replies angrily.

"Think with us! We cannot help if we do not know what you're planning," she shoots back.

"You're right, Nola. We can't run, and if there are more than twenty of them we're in real trouble. The whale said they're after the children, so we know who they are. If they have more trained than we do, even with the untrained alongside them, we'll be in real trouble. We have the four of you, Remus and myself." Landon counts them off.

"Where's Mikal?" He asks.

Nola looks around. "He was in front of me coming up from below deck?"

Alvida yells out, "He's rowing away! He took the little boat!"

Landon and the other seekers rush to the rear of the ship and watch as Mikal rows feverously away.

"Coward!" Landon yells before he goes still and the water begins to freeze out in a straight line towards the dingy.

Nola grabs his arm. "Let him go, Landon! That does us no good!"

Landon holds on for a moment longer before he releases and the ice breaks in the waves. "So now there are five of us. Have you all kept up with your training? Remus is well trained at stilling the ocean through the storm but you three, have you trained outside of your seeking?"

"Not in a combat situation!" One of them shouts nervously.

"Lerin, we need to focus. You're seekers! Seek them. We need to make a plan. If we can find out what their plan is, we can counter initiate, or avoid them all together. Marius, can you try and disrupt all of our thoughts so the patterns don't reach them? Nola, take the children below deck. We must protect them at all costs." Landon issues the orders.

"I don't know if I can disrupt all the waves," Marius says. "But if I can get somewhere quiet I might be able to."

"Use the captain's cabin," Remus says. "If you close the door it gets as quiet as you'll find out here."

Nola rounds up the children and brings them down the stairs. Cael and Wynn stay above.

"We can help!" Cael says.

Landon nods to them appreciatively. "Remus, how much longer till the storm wall?" He asks.

"We're not set to reach it until afternoon. Nothing we can do about getting there faster," he replies.

"Lerin, anything yet?" Landon asks.

"I just can't concentrate! My damn nerves are on edge," he says, shaking violently.

Landon places his hand on his shoulder. "It's alright, just do what you can."

Lerin calms down and focuses his mind fully on seeking. Landon sits with Cael, Wynn, and Remus planning the defense.

The sun rises higher and Lerin calls out, "I've found them!"

Landon walks over. "That was really fast! Unless they're very close?"

"They're not far out now, about eight leagues off our port. I'd guess we have until noon. Listening for them is so much easier out here with nothing in the way, no other..." He goes white. "There are... Twenty-three. I can feel twelve gifted. They're planning on coming in under the cover of fog."

"Fog on a clear day?" Cael asks but answers his own question. "They're going to create the fog."

Landon nods. "Yes, but this is good. We know what to expect."

He paces back and forth along the deck of the ship. "So, they'll cover their approach. Even if we had the energy, we couldn't freeze all the water or stop the air because we'd be stuck as well. With the amount of them, I'd imagine they'll be prepared to counter-attack right away." He thinks out loud while he paces. "We could clear the fog, but then they'd attack immediately. If Marius has blocked our thoughts, they would be having a difficult time tracking us already, so they might suspect. Even if they don't, they'll likely board the ship planning on a fight. But they might be overconfident and hope to sneak aboard in the fog cover. We could take out their forward party if they do that. The amount of heat it would take to light their ship ablaze is too much. They'd be able to douse it quickly regardless. I think our best bet is hoping they come aboard slowly and silently. Once they start their attack, we need to funnel them. I could do that."

Cael stares at him waiting. "So that's it? We just hope?!"

Landon nods slowly, "That's all we can do."

They prepare themselves for what's to come. Cael and Wynn connect and settle in calmly. Before any of them are prepared, the fog rolls in. Landon places himself looking off the starboard side and Remus moves to the wheel. Cael and Wynn sit patiently at the top steps of the deck, waiting for the signal.

The pitter patter of clothed footsteps surrounds them in the fog. Landon stands still as stone waiting for his moment and it comes. One of the attackers sneaks behind him, hoping to take him out silently with a dagger. The dagger hits solid air and Landon turns around quickly grabbing the blade from the surprised assassin and plunges it into his chest. Cael and Wynn watch as another rushes past them towards Landon. They grab his feet and he slams into the deck. Remus incapacitates him and rushes to help Landon who is now fighting a handful of attackers. More men begin funneling in to join the fray but are disoriented as Cael and Wynn focus on placing images of more defenders in their minds. They swing at empty air but soon realize the source and protect themselves from their mental attacks.

Landon and Remus are overrun so Cael and Wynn sprint out from the stairs. Wynn has Jean's dagger and Cael quickly grabs another weapon from one of the fallen and they begin swinging wildly. Wynn cuts a deep cut along the arm of an assailant. Cael kicks him over the railing. The fog disappears and the scene before them is cleared. The attackers aren't funneling as Landon had planned. Half of them are dragging children from below deck to their ship.

Landon and Remus had somehow been able to push back a half dozen before the fog cleared. Moments after the fog dissipates, a woman boards their ship and throws Cael and Wynn off with a powerful force. They splash into the water and begin to panic. They flail their arms struggling against the water but suddenly feel calmed and climb back up the rope ladder.

Strong hands reach down and lift them the rest of the way up before pushing them towards a group of attackers, "Get these two on the boat now!"

As they get to their feet heir eyes fall on Beckett.

"You!" Wynn yells as she begins slashing furiously with her dagger.

Cael grabs another blade off the deck and heats it up quickly joining Wynn in her attack, thrusting straight for Beckett's chest.

Beck freezes the blades in midair, grabbing the dagger from Wynn and knocking Cael's to the ground. "I'm impressed, you've both learned quickly. Care to test your skills?" He says smiling.

A force of hot air blasts three men away from Landon and off the side of the ship. Ice forms around their bodies, pulling them beneath the surface. Landon rushes toward Beckett, throwing thick needles out from his waist pocket. Beck grabs Cael and Wynn and throws them toward his ship before blocking the needles with his arm. They bounce off and he slams his fist down into the ship, cracking it and sending Landon up into the air.

Landon's fall slows as he rights himself, still above the ship he covers himself in a sheet of mist and pellets of ice begin shooting towards Beckett. Beck slams his foot on the board of the ship sending it straight up into Landon's chest. Blood trickles down the splintered wood as Landon pulls himself free. He collapses for a moment, a large spout of water reaching over the side of the ship and grabbing Beckett, pulling him overboard.

Beck grasps the rail, struggling to break free. A sickening pop as his leg is pulled from its socket. Landon sinks into the wood and Beck solidifies the boards again, trapping Landon beneath. He pulls himself up, slamming his leg back into place.

"We don't have time for any more games, we have to go before the storm-wall!" He calls, reaching out for Cael and Wynn.

They shove him aside and work to free Landon from the boards. They focus intently and manage to alter the solid state to just malleable enough to pull Landon above and rest him on the deck.

The attackers drag the last of the children onto their boat, leaving all of the seekers bloodied or dead. Two of the attackers run towards Cael and Wynn but Beckett puts his hand up, "No! Don't harm them!" He orders.

"Take them or leave them, Beck! We don't have time, the storms are upon us!" A man calls out as he works to untie their ships.

Beckett faces the storms, wind whipping already, pulling their vessels into the wall of rain and thunder. He grabs for them, but they cover Landon's body like a wolf protecting her cubs.

He hands Jean's dagger back to Cael. "For you to have met them both already…." He stands staring at the storms.

Their minds begin to swirl as memories are pulled from them.

"You think me evil?" He turns back to them, his face serious, "Your minds have been poisoned… You two are meant to be more than this! How can you be so easily deceived?" He looks to the storms, "I could just take you…"

Beck moves off the ship and kicks the plank away, "We're out of time. Arimel will make certain you survive this storm and when we meet again, I will make certain you know the truth."

He grips the railing and the sails on his ship fill with air, sending their vessel flying across the water and out of the storms. Cael and Wynn, confused and lost, turn back to Landon's bleeding form. They roll him over revealing too many cuts to count and a deep puncture wound to his chest that's bleeding heavily.

"What is going on?!" Wynn cries out, "I knew we shouldn't have trusted Landon or any of these people!"

Cael shakes his head, "There's no time! We have to make it through these storms! We can fight later!"

Landon coughs, regaining consciousness again. "You're alive." He moans.

"I don't know for how much longer," Wynn screams over the storms.

"How do we make it through these storms?!" Cael's voice, barely audible over the pounding of rain and waves.

Landon tries to sit up but falls back down. Cael and Wynn help him to a seated position. "You need to sail through this. I can't help…. If Remus were here he could…. You've done it before, right?" Landon tries to laugh but coughs up blood. He opens his eyes, "Beckett searched your memories… didn't he?" He coughs again, "... I'll... I'll explain everything once we're safe..." He coughs more blood. "I promise."

"Just shut up! We need to make it through this. We'll do it, you stay here," Cael says quickly.

"I'm not going anywhere." Landon mumbles before passing out.

Cael drops to his side and checks for a pulse. "He's alive! We need to get through these storms and get him some help."

"Or we could let him die." Wynn shrugs as a wave crashes over the ship.

They reach for Landon's body as it slides across the deck with the water.

"We'll figure this out later! We need to survive first, Wynn!" Cael calls back, throwing Landon back to the center of the ship.

"We can't sail through this!" Wynn points to the sky.

Cael agrees, "So we just hold on! Grab Landon's other arm and wrap your arm around the handrail! We'll just try and stick it out!"

"Why don't we drag him below deck!?" Wynn shouts.

"I just think we should stay up here!" Cael shouts back.

They tightly wrap themselves up in the railing and Landon's body as the boat nears the wall of storms. Lightning strikes in quick succession all through the grey wall of clouds as rain pours down in front of them. The waves pound into ship and they are thrown about. They grip tighter, holding on for their lives. Landon opens his eyes for a moment before he plunges back into unconsciousness.

The waves get more chaotic, throwing the boat clear of the water and it slams back down with such force it cracks the wood.

"We need to bring the sail down!" Cael shouts over the storm. Wynn nods her head and wraps her body around Landon's as Cael crawls over to the sail. He begins untying the knots and the sail and mast are torn from the ship leaving a jagged stump where it was moments before. Cael falls back to his knees and crawls over to Landon and Wynn.

"That works!" he yells.

They clench their hands around the rail and Landon, absorbing the impacts of the waves. Arms burning with each movement. Lightning strikes their ship and briefly catches the captain's quarters on fire before a wave puts it out. They stay clenched for so long the pain begins to numb and they have to keep checking to see if their arms are still locked around the railing.

A wave shoots them high into the air before they slam back down. The ship snaps like a twig and is swallowed by the sea. They go under and struggle to pull Landon's body above the waves. Landon wakes up again and is startled by how low he's set in the water. He sees Cael and Wynn and he grabs them both. With one last bit of strength, he propels them forward, toward a dim light in the sky. He drags them until his body no longer works, and when he stops moving, they drag him. The storm wall retreats, leaving the sea filled with energy. They drift along with the current, struggling to stay afloat, arms too tired to swim. They check on Landon's breathing, worried that it's becoming shallower. They pull him with the last of their strength to still waters. A lone dock in the distance catches their attention and they fight to reach it.

They make their way onto a small beach beside the dock and collapse.

The soft crunch of sand catches their ears. They roll onto their backs and look up, seeing an older man with a long beard, his dark green eyes staring down at them.

"I've been waiting for you two."

About The Author:

Born in a rural town in northern Tennessee, D.R. O'Shea had quite a nomadic existence prior to settling in New Hampshire. He credits his many early adventures for sparking a lifelong passion for exploration, creativity and an insatiable appetite for learning new things.

When not writing, O'Shea can be found hiking the wilds of his chosen home state, visiting his favorite places around the world, painting or strumming a few bars on his guitar.

Fans who would like to learn more about D.R. O'Shea and the magical world of Ryn Dvarek can visit www.DanielROShea.com or follow @RynDvarek on Facebook and Twitter.